Winworth
EST 1521

S E C R E T S of W I N W O R T H
B O O K   O N E

APATHY

L . K .   R E I D

Cover Design by Pretty in Ink Creations
Editing by Maggie Kern at Ms. K Edits
Formatting by Pretty in Ink Creations

PLAYLIST

As most of you already know, music is such a ginormous part of my writing process, and this playlist is one of my favorite ones.
You can find the full playlist on Spotify.

Let It Burn - Written by Wolves
Wilt - Holding Absence
Nobody - Faith Marie
ULTRAVIOLENT - Crywolf
Enemies with Benefits - Blind Channel
Satan, Hello - KAMAARA, 8oz
Redeemer - Palaye Royale
Erase - Imminence
Fuck ALL the Pain - KAMAARA
Bully - KAMAARA
Demons - Written by Wolves
Astronaut In The Ocean - Our Last Night
it's okay to be afraid - Saint Slumber
ULTRAnumb (Acoustic) - Blue Stahli
Amphetamine - MNQN
Rescue My Heart - Liz Longley
Dark Storms - Our Last Night
winter - Our Last Night
Help Me Through the Night - Written by Wolves, Kellin Quinn
High - Zella Day
Emerge Part II - Ruelle
Lost in Control - The Relentless
Live Wire - Meghan Kabir
Sara - We Three

Lose You To Love Me - Andromida, Halflives
*One Day The Only Butterflies Left Will Be In Your Chest As You
March Towards Your Death* - Bring Me The Horizon, Amy Lee
Fade to Blue - Roniit
Desire - Violet Orlandi
Demons - Omri
Cross - Echos
Pressure - Fifth Dawn
Heaven in Hiding – Imminence
Yelena Belova - Lorne Balfe
Cruel Summer - Malia J, Think Up Anger
Suffocate - Nathan Wagner
Warfare - Katie Garfield
White Flag (Reimagined) - Normandie

To a sixteen-year-old Leila.
You will be okay.

AUTHOR'S NOTE

These characters started whispering in my ear around January, and at the time, this story had a completely different plot.

But I let it cook for a bit.

And then Skylar started shouting, but she told me different things. Painful things. Things I, at first, didn't really want to write. Not because they weren't good, but because they were too real and were hitting too close to home.

While Ophelia represented my anger, Skylar showed all my broken pieces.

I always loved the occult, and when the idea about The Order started meshing with the messed-up life Skylar had, all the missing pieces clicked together, and I wrote it.

And for the first time since I started this journey, I really wrote for myself.

This book also has situations, scenes and conversations that happened to me when I was a teenager. And before you start worrying about my childhood and the way I grew up; I feel like I need to say that those parts of my life that sneaked into this story were not just the bad ones.

I do feel like I need to warn you about the contents

of this book. This is in no way sweet romance. Some of the situations are painful to read. You will read about drug use, about mental and physical abuse, about messed up kids and parents who should've cared more. You will also find scenes that might be too gruesome for some, and if any of the above-mentioned things are not okay with you, then this definitely isn't a book for you.

I also have a small favor to ask.

Please don't leave spoilers, and once you get to the end of the book, you will understand why.

And most of all, thank you for reading and for joining me on this crazy journey.

If you liked the book, please consider leaving a review. It would truly mean a lot to me.

"My heart is lost; the beasts have eaten it."

Charles Baudelaire, The Flowers of Evil

PROLOGUE

The sound of silence.

    I've heard that phrase so many times, but I never knew what it really meant. Not until now.

    Or maybe I still didn't know what it was. Maybe this silence was only inside my head while the rest of the world kept screaming.

    Crying.

    Asking for help.

    Actually, now that I thought about it, all of us were screaming. Just constantly fucking screaming—some silently, some loudly, some with a smile on their face. There was no age, no race or gender limit, but every single one of us had some kind of pain. We carried it somewhere deep inside of our chests, in our bones, in the smallest atoms of our bodies. We carried it and learned to live with it.

    But we shouldn't have to. Right?

    We shouldn't have to live with it. We shouldn't have to suffocate—day after day, month after month, and year after year, until the screaming became too much for us to bear. Until our vocal cords became too sore, and our bodies couldn't handle the pain overflowing us. Until we decided it was too much, too long, and we decided to stop it.

We shouldn't have any kind of pain to carry at all. It pissed me off, this unfairness life always threw at us. Didn't it piss you off?

I bet it did. I bet you wanted to change something so many times. I bet you wanted to scream and laugh, and love and hug. I bet you wanted to be happy before life decided to fuck you up and cast you aside as if you never meant anything. As if it was your fault, you were dealt this shitty hand in life. It wasn't your fault. It was never your fucking fault.

My whole life, I wanted to get to this point. To stop feeling, to stop thinking, to stop the shit suffocating me. And here I was, finally surrounded by the sound of silence, and I didn't know what to do. Monsters weren't here anymore. They couldn't hurt me any longer. It felt great.

Floating.
Silent.
Weightless.

I just wanted this feeling to last, but I knew it couldn't. I felt the reality lurking on the edges of my mind. I knew what was coming, what I found myself in, but I didn't want to admit it. I didn't want to think about it, even though I knew.

There were sicknesses in this world even holy water couldn't wash away.

ONE

SKYLAR

"Open up, pretty girl."

Laughter bubbled up from my chest, the taste of it like sin on my lips as his scent filtered into my nose, and his eyes flashed with danger, burning into mine. But I opened my mouth—I always do. The bitter taste of the happy little pill exploded on my tongue and my body trembled, preparing itself for what was about to come. It was futile, fighting the inevitable, and I learned the hard way how much it hurt when my obedience wasn't up to his tastes.

"Swallow it," he grunted. My throat worked as the pill slipped down, waiting to erupt inside my body, giving me a little bit of happiness to replace this numbness in my veins. "Good girl."

My eyes misted as I started focusing on the peeled wallpaper behind him. The faded golden swirls on what was once a teal background now looked like sinister vines spreading all over the wall. I waited as the clock on the nightstand ticked, as my heart started beating faster, and as everything I never wanted to happen started coming closer and closer. So fucking close I could already feel his hands on my body. I focused on the swirls as he pushed my body onto the bed, and the view of pretty little swirls was replaced by the bland ceiling.

filled with dark spots.

Tick-Tock.

Tick-Tock.

It continued ticking as he lifted my shirt over my stomach, keeping it underneath my breasts. My eyes fluttered as the dark spots on the ceiling started changing shapes, dancing above us, telling me everything was going to be okay.

He pressed his mouth above my belly button, licking his way over my heart, over my soul, chipping away the pieces of me. As he got greedier, as my eyes shut down, my shirt got lifted over my breasts, exposing me to his vile eyes. I never looked at him. I never wanted to look him in the eye, because I feared that the truth I would see there wouldn't be his downfall, but mine.

"Lift your arms up," he instructed, and as an obedient little girl, I obliged, slowly falling for the satisfied smile on his face. "You're gonna be the death of me." *I hoped so.* "Touch yourself. I want to see you touch these pretty tits."

My body wasn't my own anymore, and like watching a movie in slow motion, my hands pressed against the puckered nipples, and I arched my back, inviting him back in. Because I always did. I always welcomed him back.

The sound of the belt dropping to the ground sent my heart into a frenzy. I knew what was about to come. His breaths turned deeper as I spread my legs wider, showing him my covered pussy. He gripped my knees and started spreading me wider and wider, until he crawled on the bed, settling himself between my legs.

I hated the wetness coating me and the laughter, the frenzy… I hated being used to this, but words died on my lips, even though I wanted him to stop. My skin burned as he ripped my panties off, throwing them to the other side of the room.

Three thick fingers entered me in one turn, burning my insides, burning my soul away. He started pumping in and out, making me loathe myself as moans erupted from my chest.

I hate him.

I fucking hate him.

But I needed him because he had my happy little pill. He had all the pills, and I needed them. Today was a happy one. The other day I screamed and screamed and screamed, until his fist connected with my cheek, sending me to the floor. But I continued screaming. I continued crying. I continued begging to be free, even as he tore the clothes from my body and sliced me in half.

And then I stopped screaming and started grinding against him, just like now.

"You're my good little whore. Aren't you?" Yes! I needed to… Oh God. I needed it to take over. "Answer me!" he roared as he slapped my tit, making me scream.

"Yes!" *I need more, more, more.* "Please."

He slapped the other breast, then squeezed, never letting the pain subside. Not that it ever did, even when he wasn't the one touching me.

"More," I begged as he started slowing down. "Don't stop."

"Shhhh." He pressed a finger against my lips as he removed the other three from my pussy. "I'm gonna make you feel good, but I need you to keep quiet." He leaned down, igniting the fire within as his dick pressed against my opening. "Can you do that, pretty girl?"

I nodded, unable to speak. I was unable to move, afraid he would take away the pleasure that was so close.

"Good." I could see the wrinkles around his eyes, over his forehead, and I focused on the three lines between his eyebrows, avoiding his eyes. He pulled me up, holding my hands in front of me. "Open that pretty mouth."

He leaned back as I positioned myself on my knees and placed my hands on his hip bones. With one hand, he took a hold of his dick, with its angry red tip and pale skin, and with the other one, he pulled my head closer until the tip of his cock pressed against my closed mouth, seeking entrance.

"Open."

I pulled my lips over my teeth and opened up as he dragged the tip over my bottom lip.

"So beautiful," he groaned. With one thrust, he entered my mouth, cutting off my oxygen supply as he hit my throat. I wasn't ready—I wasn't ready at all. I started coughing around his dick, but I couldn't move away. He held the back of my head as he kept sliding in and out, lost in his own pleasure.

My eyes watered as I tried breathing through my nose, but the gagging didn't stop. It increased with each new push, with each new grunt, my mouth watering around him, but the fucking bastard didn't stop.

"Take it," he grunted. "Take it all, pretty girl."

Tears fell over my cheeks as he kept going, but my body didn't take a hint of what was happening. Not entirely.

Sickness spread over my body as I felt myself grinding against the mattress, looking for friction, chasing the high from earlier. I felt sick with myself, but there was nothing I could do.

My soul didn't belong to me anymore.

"Touch yourself." His grip on the back of my head increased, but his thrusts slowed down, allowing me to breathe. "I want us to come together."

Half-crazed and half-lost, I touched my navel before my fingers traveled between my lips, and touched my clit, sending jolts of pleasure through me. I moaned around him, smiling, almost laughing as I entered one finger into my opening, then the second one, and the third one, trying to make it feel how his fingers felt inside.

Sick.

I was a sick, twisted girl.

"That's it." He pushed inside my mouth. "Do you want to come?" His voice was a grunt, a promise, and I wanted it to come true. I wanted the fake little promises and the sweet nothings he could provide.

I pressed against the spot inside, but it didn't feel the same. It didn't feel the same as his fingers.

The foul taste of his precum slid down my throat, and I knew if we didn't come together, he would leave me dry. I pushed my fingers faster and as the familiar sensation appeared at the bottom of my stomach, I knew I was close.

"Suck it." I gripped his hip and started moving my head faster, not waiting for him to move me. My fingers worked in sync with my mouth, and when I pressed my thumb against my clit, wiggling on my knees, he erupted into my mouth, groaning, breathing hard, making me swallow each drop, when all I wanted to do was vomit. As I clenched around my fingers, letting the sensation take over me, I screamed against the limp dick that was still in my mouth.

He moved the hair from my face and started wiping the spilled tears, soothing me, praising me, loving me.

"You're my best girl, sweetheart. You will always belong here, with me, on your knees."

But I wouldn't. *I would rather die.*

7

If you saw the world burning, would you let it burn or would you try to extinguish the flames? Or would you be the one that set it on fire? Maybe you like to think that you would be the one to save it, but have you ever looked deep inside of yourself only to realize that you were the villain all along?

I was surrounded by people who thought themselves to be heroes, when, in reality, they were nothing but vicious villains, setting everything on fire.

I sat in the car, staring at the pale orange walls of Winworth High, willing myself to move so that I wouldn't miss the first class. It was a new school year, after all — my last one — and I just wanted to get it over with. Some people loved high school, some hated it, and I was indifferent. I guess when you live in a town filled with serpents hiding in the skin of angels, you learn how to be indifferent. You have to, if you want to survive.

I grew up in the town of Winworth, in Washington State, and while you might be enamored by its picturesque scenery, beautiful mountains, rich history, and winning football team, I knew better. This was a new hell, but you couldn't see the depravity until you started peeling off the layers from the walls and opening the doors where all its secrets lay still.

It was one of those places that could lure you in, make you fall in love with it, and by the time you've realized the sickness spreading throughout its streets, it was too late for you to get out. Some people had a choice whether they wanted to be here, but I didn't.

I was a Blackwood, a founding family, a legacy, and no matter what I wanted to do in my life, I knew that living here wouldn't be enough. No, Winworth demanded a lifelong, generations-long sacrifice, but I wasn't going to be another sacrificial lamb. The promises

I made to myself, the dreams I had to fulfill, it was all waiting for me after high school.

Trying to clear the fog from my mind, to push the last night to the back, my eyes caught on a group of people I knew very well. On my left side, five parking spots away, a couple of guys from the football team of Winworth High tossed a ball between each other, earning hoots and hollers from the people gathered around them, who were waiting to be noticed by the Golden Boys of Washington State. I used to be like them. I used to dream about high school and the experiences it would bring.

But then… It didn't matter anymore.

What did matter was a lean body I knew very well, seated on the hood of his Jeep Wrangler, with his eyes burning into mine. A self-proclaimed king, captain of the football team, and the shiniest star of our school, Kane St. Clare. We grew up together, running around the yard at his family home, chasing each other, loving the wind on our skin, and hating our nannies every time we had to go in.

But Kane wasn't the boy I grew up with, and I wasn't the girl he once knew.

Not that it really mattered, because I wasn't searching for that boy that used to chase away the bad dreams and put Band-Aids on my knees. He had what I needed, and I had what he wanted.

Escape.

The cool and calculating way he was looking at me should've been scary, but my system was still overloaded with the drugs I swallowed last night. I couldn't find it in myself to care. He's been trying to get in touch with me for the last three months. He called, he texted, he came to my house, but I never answered. What was the point? Kane loved imagining things that weren't really there, and somewhere between fucking me and giving me what I wanted, he made himself believe that he was in love with me.

Utter bullshit, if you ask me.

None of us knew what love really was. Could you taste it? Could you describe it? It was a universal feeling, yet everyone described it differently. What Kane felt for me was nothing more than chemical attraction and the need to lose himself in something else other than grief.

I looked away, ignoring the way my neck burned as he kept staring at me, and started fumbling with my bag, taking a bottle of Adderall into my hand. I probably shouldn't be taking these after last night and the euphoria I went into, but it couldn't hurt. I opened the lid and placed three pills in my palm. Lauren said to be careful with the number of pills, but screw being careful.

With one swift move, I placed all three of them in my mouth, then reached for the bottle of water, uncapping it and taking one big gulp. I wanted to close my eyes and forget about everything around me, but I knew if I did that, silence wouldn't be greeting me. Every time I closed my eyes, I could feel his filthy hands on my skin. Just like a whisper, his voice was always ringing in my ear, and no matter how much I tried, I could never escape.

Lifting my eyes toward the rearview mirror, I adjusted it so that I could check my makeup. The bruise on my cheek was almost gone, but I couldn't risk anybody asking about it or where I got it, so I managed to hide it with layers of foundation. My lifeless blue eyes stared back at me, and I realized how pale I was, even with the soft blush I applied this morning. I usually didn't bother with makeup, but when Lauren, my best friend, mentioned how frail and pale I started looking, I knew I had to do something. At least my pale blonde hair wasn't tied in a bun today. Some days, even breathing took too much energy from me, so taking a shower and washing my hair should be regarded as a grand feat.

While the tourists loved visiting our town during the summer, going into the mountains and renting the cabins there, soaking in the sun, I preferred the four walls of my room and books to be my company. It's been getting harder pushing my body to get out of the bed in the morning, feeling achy, uncomfortable, and just wanting to disappear.

But I had to survive this year and then I would be free.

I pushed open the door of my car, taking my bag with me and shivering from the early chill Winworth was famous for. It didn't matter which time of year it was; mornings were always fucking cold. I looked up toward the mountains surrounding us, seeing the fog still lingering on the top, hiding the forest in its cold embrace.

Voices traveled toward me, one in particular annoying the shit out of me. I didn't have the strength to deal with Kane this early in the morning, especially not after everything that has happened between us. My brother never really liked him, and maybe I should've listened to him.

God, I missed Dylan.

He was four years older than me, and on days like today, my whole being missed him, wishing for him to come home. He left Winworth three years ago to study in Seattle, and while he was less than four hours away, it still felt like an eternity between his visits. He came only once this summer, and that once wasn't nearly enough for me. He promised to visit during September, since our father kept him in Seattle during the summer, showing him the ropes in our company. I hated it.

I wanted my brother back. I know, I know, it wasn't healthy clinging to someone like this, but Dylan was the only one who could understand me, or, well, at least what I was willing to share with him. He was also the only one who could still make me laugh. The last two years without him constantly by my side felt like an eternity without the sun.

Even now, as I walked across the schoolyard, heading toward the door and avoiding the stares of seniors gathered on the staircase, the only thing I could see were the memories of the first day of high school and Dylan driving me. It was just too bad that he wasn't enough to keep the monsters at bay.

"Skylar!" I turned around and saw Lauren heading in my direction, looking happy. Way too happy for eight in the morning. Her auburn hair bounced around her shoulders as she caught up with me, her lips spreading into a smile. "What's up, Sugar Bum?"

I scowled. "You're way too happy today."

"You would be too if you listened to me when I told you to stop by my house before school." I looked at her eyes, seeing the dilated pupils and redness taking over the otherwise white sclera. I wanted to laugh because I couldn't remember a single school year that didn't start with her high and me scowling.

"What did you take, bish?" I pushed her shoulder, earning a cheeky smile.

"A little bit of this, a little bit of that," she started explaining as she hugged my shoulders and started pushing me toward the entrance. "I brought some for you as well."

"What if I don't want it?" I asked. "What if I'm turning over a new leaf this year?" We knew that was highly unlikely to happen.

"Bitch, please." She scoffed. "The day you turn over

a new leaf and say no to the goodies I manage to snatch from my brother, would be the day that the sun properly shines in Winworth."

She had a point there. I loved running away from reality, so much so that on some days, I couldn't tell the difference between what was real and what was fake. And I loved it. I loved those moments where I couldn't hear anything but my heartbeat thundering in my ears. Or when my mind didn't try to remind me of everything that was waiting for me outside of the sweet oblivion drugs were providing.

"What's your first class?" she asked as we reached the entrance to the school. "I have biology with Mrs. Raleigh," she groaned.

"You mean… Medusa?" I made a face. There was a story from the older generations that Mrs. Raleigh could literally turn you into stone with her cold and impassioned face. Her classes were the only ones I never tried to skip because I knew what the consequences were and if I could help it, I wouldn't be failing biology.

"Don't fucking remind me. She's probably gonna start talking about meiosis and mitosis, and I am not high enough to actually listen to that crap today."

"You never actually listen to her." I laughed. "I don't know how you do it, but she never calls you out for your half-assed presence and the other shit you tend to pull."

"It's just part of my charm." She snickered. "But for real," she lowered her voice, "I'm going to combust if I have to listen to them the whole day. Kane and the gang were talking about going to the crypt today."

That made me perk up. "When?"

"Fourth period? Are you free or —"

"I will be." I grinned as the bell started ringing. Students started rushing around us, heading toward their classrooms. "I'll see you later?" I looked at her. "I'll just head to the crypt after the third period. Okay?"

"Absolutely."

Maybe today wouldn't be a bad day, after all.

TWO

Skylar

I always hated the smell of this school. No matter how many times they renovated it, how many times they tried to make it look more modern, more approachable, the moldy smell always stayed. Generations have passed through these halls, and no matter how many times they try to cover that wall next to the classroom for biology that had a red circle painted by some vandals years ago, it always seemed to seep through the white color. I was still in elementary school when that incident happened, but the whole town talked about it the entire year. They never caught the culprits.

I loved the stories people tried to spin, going from bored teenagers to satanic cults hiding in our town. Not that I could blame them. Winworth was famous for its foggy days, that eerie feeling wrapping around your bones like a vine around a pillar, making you see things that weren't really there. If you typed 'creepy towns in the United States', Winworth would pop up as one of the first ones. With the population of a little bit over ten thousand, you most definitely knew your neighbors. And just like every other town, people here were wary of outsiders. Tourists still loved visiting us during the summer, investigating the caves up in the mountains, and trying to find a good story for their blogs.

I always wanted to laugh at them, because while they chased the ghosts of the past, they were missing the real monsters lurking around the corner—watching, stalking, waiting for their prey to fall into their hands. If I were them, I would have never set foot in this town. If I were them, I would avoid this whole area, because nothing good could come from a town with a history as violent as Winworth.

Lost in thought, I shivered as a hand landed on my shoulder, halting me in my steps. Long, strong fingers were the first thing I saw as I looked to the side. "Watch where you're going," a deep voice boomed, eliciting chills all over my body. The hair at the nape of my neck stood up as my heart thundered in my chest. Before I could lift my head to see the owner of the voice, he walked away, showing me his back. An oversized black hoodie covered his body, and I hated that I couldn't see more than his back.

It took me a moment to realize that he actually stopped me from walking into a sign for the wet floor, because my brain decided to focus on other things. Dylan hated my blatant dismissal for my surroundings, while I secretly loved the ability to disconnect from the rest of the world and just exist, even if it was only for a minute.

The tall stranger disappeared into the sea of other students, and instead of gawking after him, I started walking again, going around the puddle on the floor. The last thing I wanted today was to end up face-first on the floor. Knowing my track record, gravity and I were not best friends. I wrapped my hand around the strap of my bag, pushing through the freshman gathered around the classroom for English lit, looking excited about the new year, new possibilities, new friendships.

I was once like them. I was full of life, wanting to

experience everything high school had to offer, but somewhere along the way, I stopped caring about it. Somewhere along the way, I lost the will to care.

I filtered inside the classroom with two other girls from my grade, ignoring the stares and pitiful looks from both of them. People had questions about the end of the last school year, but I didn't have answers. I just wanted to forget that May twenty-fifth ever happened and move on. Unfortunately, that was easier said than done when everything in this town reminded me of that fucking night, and every single person apart from Lauren and Dylan kept reminding me about things I wanted to forget.

The inferno that blazed through that night was just a cherry on top of a very fucked-up year.

I lowered my head and scurried past them, heading toward the back of the classroom, where I knew that another reminder was going to wait for me. But instead of seeing Kane in his usual seat, right next to mine, it was a person I had never seen before. But wait…

It was the guy in the hoodie.

My breath caught in my throat as I stood in the middle of the classroom, gawking at the high cheekbones, and eyes the color of midnight blue as they connected with mine. Every living being had an energy they showed to the rest of the world, but this guy… If I had to describe it, it would be with one word—violence.

He wore violence like an expensive cologne, and I wanted to drown in it. I wanted to drag my hands through his thick, black hair, to get lost in the dark abyss of his eyes, and let the darkness take over. My hands trembled, and I gripped the strap of my bag as if it could center me. As if it could help me with these thoughts coursing through my mind.

He dragged his eyes over my body, going from my

head to my toes, and I could see a tattoo on his neck, peeking from the collar of his hoodie, a stark contrast on the pale skin. Somebody cleared their throat behind me, and I moved my eyes from him, refusing to see the reaction after his perusal. My cheeks were burning, and I knew they were already colored red, which probably made me look like a tomato.

I had never had this kind of reaction to another person. This visceral feeling in my gut was not something I was used to. A few years back, I accidentally touched an open wire in Lauren's house, earning a small electroshock, but this thing I felt when I looked at him, this overwhelming need to come closer, to touch, to feel — this was far worse than those electroshocks.

My ribs started closing around my heart, pressing, cutting off air, the closer I came to him. I dared to look again, to see if he was still looking at me, but his eyes were plastered on a window on the other side of the classroom, completely ignoring me.

Well, okay then.

I dropped my bag to the floor and pulled a chair, slowly settling next to him. Goddammit, I wasn't going to be able to focus if I had to sit next to him for the whole year.

How the fuck was I supposed to concentrate on Mr. Morales, when the guy next to me smelled like cedar pine, cigarettes, and danger?

Lauren was going to love this shit. Not that there was anything specific going on, considering that the tall, dark, and dangerous stranger ignored my entire existence. Annoyed at my entire reaction to him, I bent down to take out the books from my bag when a voice I knew all too well boomed around us.

"What the fuck are you doing in my seat?" I looked up, seeing Kane with his eyes narrowed at the new guy.

Truth be told, I was hoping that he wouldn't try to sit here this year.

I dropped one of the books on the table with a thud, trying to draw Kane's attention to me, but his gaze stayed firmly placed on my new desk buddy, who kept quiet the whole time. Mr. Broody — as I decided to call him — started checking out the desk, going so far as to bend down and check beneath it.

"Are you fucking deaf, or just plain stupid?" Kane roared again. This would've been amusing if it wasn't eight in the morning, and if I had managed to get that coffee before I got to school. But I was exhausted, pissed off, and my cheek still throbbed from that hit I got a couple of days ago.

"No," my new neighbor finally spoke as he straightened up. "I'm just trying to find your name written on the desk, but I can't see it anywhere."

I wanted to laugh at the nonchalant way he said that, but one look at Kane and I knew that my laughter would cause more harm than good. Kane's eyes held a promise of cruelty, and as I looked at the rest of the classroom, I noticed all eyes were directed at us. I fucking hated this kind of attention, and Kane knew it.

I also knew why he started this whole scene. He sat with me during those last couple of weeks of school after everything happened, and he got it in his head that I belonged to him somehow, now that the… now that things were different.

"Listen, buddy," Kane placed his hands on the desk, leaning toward Mr. Broody. "You're new, so let me explain a few things for you." *Here we go.* "This school, this fucking desk, they don't have to have my name written anywhere for them to belong to me. Trust me, every single person will tell you that what Kane St. Clare wants, Kane St. Clare gets."

The new guy leaned back and crossed his arms over his chest, smirking at Kane. "Is talking about yourself in third person a medical condition, or is that just your ugly persona?" he asked. "You might want to check that out."

I swallowed the snort threatening to erupt from me, and turned away, taking another notebook from my bag.

"You are a motherfucking—"

"Asshole? Idiot? Jackass? Cretin? Would you like me to go on? I'm not sure if your peanut-sized brain can come up with all the terms."

This time, I couldn't stop myself. As I opened a notebook and took a hold of a pen, the laughter I was trying to hold in erupted, echoing around the classroom.

Kane glared at me. Mr. Broody smirked. I couldn't stop myself as my shoulders shook and my eyes misted. "I'm sorry," I choked out. "It's just… Oh God. I can't." I had to text Lauren and tell her about this shit.

"Skylar!" Kane admonished, but I couldn't care less about his feelings or his pompous ego.

"Just go and sit somewhere else, Kane," I uttered, still snickering. "He's right. Your name isn't written on the table."

I begged him to stop this silly game he started playing a few months ago, but instead of pulling back, he kept pushing until I felt like I couldn't breathe. He used to be an amazing friend, but after the incident, it was as if the Kane I knew completely disappeared, replaced by this person that only took but never gave. He didn't listen to me because he didn't want to be alone.

I wanted to help him. I wanted to be there for him, but not like this.

For a fleeting moment, his chestnut-colored eyes filled with pain, piercing through my chest. The last thing I wanted to do was to hurt him even more. But what he was doing, *no*, what we were doing, wasn't healthy. This co-dependency he started developing was suffocating, and the only thing I wanted was to run away from him.

We weren't together — we would never be together — yet he behaved like he owned me.

"Yeah, listen to Skylar, Kane." Mr. Broody smirked. "You might as well find another place to sit because I'm most definitely not moving away from here."

"Skylar?" Kane still kept looking at me, silently pleading, begging me for things I wasn't willing to give. When he gets out of this weird place he found himself in, he would understand that it was better for all of us if we quit it now.

"Go and sit down, Kane," I croaked, my throat suddenly parched. I wanted to look away, to avoid seeing the anguish flickering over his handsome face, but I couldn't. I hated this person he'd become. I hated who I was. The last thing Kane needed was a girl with a fucked-up head, just because he thought he could fix whatever was wrong inside me.

The sound of a chair scraping over the floor pulled me back from my reverie, and when I looked to the side, Mr. Broody wasn't sitting anymore. He stood up, towering over Kane, who was already close to six-foot-two. The devil-may-care attitude was gone, replaced with that violent surge I felt when I first saw his face.

Dark eyes, shadowed by darker eyebrows, were fixed on Kane, and it felt as if time stood still as he spoke again. "You should really, really listen to her," he hissed. "If you don't like me now, you'll like me even less if I have to come around and show you to your seat."

"Hey." I stood up. "That's enough." I placed a hand on his shoulder. The last thing I would've expected was the zap of electricity that traveled through my arm, all the way to my chest, into my stomach, sending a frenzy through my whole body.

He jerked away as if my touch burned him, and his wild eyes zeroed in on me, caging me. For the second time in just a couple of minutes, the rest of the world ceased to exist as he held me imprisoned. What was probably just a minute felt like an eternity, until the voice of Mr. Morales broke through the fog in my mind.

"Good morning, class."

The sound of chairs moving, students chattering, and textbooks opening filled the tense air, but my whole body burned with a need I couldn't quite explain. Mr. Morales started talking about his summer and asked the students to share their stories. I dropped to my chair, plastering my eyes on the green board behind Mr. Morales.

I could feel the dark eyes on me. I could feel the energy buzzing between us. It felt like a living, breathing thing, and yet I couldn't look at him. I didn't want to look at him, because the last thing I needed this year was to get involved with somebody whose whole persona yelled danger.

Who the fuck was this guy?

Cold air slammed into me as soon as I stepped through the back entrance of the school, heading toward the garden area. They tried to keep most of the layout of the mansion once they turned it into Winworth High, hence the ridiculous garden area on the backside. It was absurd that they decided to turn this place into a school at all, considering its history and everything its original owner did here.

Some say that Balthazar Corvin was a wealthy merchant, but the darker stories are the ones I always paid more attention to. Some urban legends say he was part of a group that used human sacrifices to bring more wealth to themselves. Others say that he was a paid mercenary who used this place to torture those he was hunting. Over the years, some students swore that they could still see his ghost roaming the hallways of the school, hiding behind the pillars on the first floor, seeking revenge over those that betrayed him.

While I didn't exactly believe in any of those stories, I loved listening to them. There was something interesting in dark occults that always pulled my attention, and this town was filled with stories just like that one.

Other students started filling the garden, taking their break after the third period, but I wasn't going to stay and try to socialize with any of them. Knowing Lauren and the rest of our friends, I probably wouldn't be coming back at all.

The fog was slowly lifting from the ground, but as I looked up, I still couldn't see the tops of the mountains surrounding the town. I had a feeling that today wouldn't be one of those rare sunny days. The gravel scrunched beneath my feet as I marched next to the group of cheerleaders settling on one of the tables. Hailey, one of our friends, wasn't with them, and I hoped Lauren told her about the crypt and where we went.

It must sound weird, us hanging out at an old crypt when the rest of the population tried to avoid cemeteries as much as possible. But when you lived in a town that had more cemeteries than diners, you didn't have much choice. Besides, at least no one would bother us there, and it wasn't like we were disturbing the dead. Lauren found the place three years ago, while she was hooking up with one of the seniors.

That guy was as creepy as they came, loved having

sex in the cemetery and Lauren, of course, went with it. I wasn't sure who was crazier—her or him. But it did land her in the crypt when they tried to hide from the groundskeeper, and the idea was born.

I rushed toward the gate separating the garden from the football field and went left toward the broken part of the fence. Whoever cut through it was a genius, because if I had to go through the main entrance, either a security guard or one of the teachers would have caught me. We weren't allowed to leave the school grounds while classes were still on. At least not while we were still minors.

Kane and Lauren didn't have to worry about that shit, since both of them turned eighteen over the summer. Rowan and Danny, the twins that hung out with us, were turning eighteen in three weeks, and were no doubt planning a party. Which only left Hailey, Beatrice, and I that would have to use this way to sneak out of the school. But I guess that there was something about the adrenaline coursing through my veins when I did this. You never knew who could catch you.

It made me feel alive, no matter how fucked up it sounded. I knew that my parents wouldn't give a shit if the school called them to report on me missing classes, so I didn't give a fuck about missing them, either. Dylan was the only one who threw a tantrum when he found out about me skipping school, and me getting fucked up at the cemetery that was just a few minutes away from the school wasn't his idea of fun. But Dylan wasn't here anymore, and knowing his schedule, he won't be here for at least three more months. I know it was ridiculous, but as soon as he left for Seattle to start university, it felt as if a part of me left with him, and I was suddenly lonely. It felt as if he abandoned me—at least the irrational part of my brain thought so—even though I knew that he didn't have a choice.

I shook my head, shutting off thoughts about Dylan and the fact that I missed him like crazy. As soon as I exited on the other side of the fence, I felt like I could finally breathe. These first three periods were hell to get through. The first one was spent with me trying to ignore the burning need to look at my new desk partner, and during the other two, I kept thinking about dark eyes and these weird feelings he seemed to draw out of me. I honestly couldn't wait for that bell to ring. While Mrs. Montgomery, our history teacher, kept going on and on about the current situation in the world, I felt as if the walls were closing in on me.

One year, Skylar. You have to survive one year and then you'll be gone for good.

I couldn't wait to leave this town behind. This depravity, this sickness, these deranged people that liked to wear their pretty little masks. I wanted to leave it all behind and start anew. I just had to be smart and survive. I just had to shut my mouth when he called and try to get through this without losing the remaining pieces of my mind.

The air smelled like rain, and as I ran across the street, heading toward the entrance to the cemetery that was located right next to Clayton Bakery, I prayed that it would rain. I hated this in-between period where it started getting humid but it wouldn't rain. At least with rain, I could pretend that it was washing away the sins and tragedies surrounding our little town.

I stopped in front of the gate leading into the cemetery, looking for the groundskeeper. He almost caught us once as we sneaked in at two in the morning. I knew that we had to be more careful if we wanted to keep coming back here. While my parents didn't give a shit about my whereabouts and what I'd been doing, it wouldn't look good if the senator's daughter was caught getting high at the local cemetery.

All of us had something to lose, and only Hailey and Beatrice weren't part of one of the founding families. Kane was a St. Clare, Lauren a Maddox, Rowan and Danny a Lacroix, and me a Blackwood. All of our parents would shit a brick if any of this came out, especially after that party back in May.

I ran between the tombstones, heading toward the other side of the cemetery where all the crypts were located. All our families had their own crypts, and one day my body would probably rot here, forever bound to Winworth. Thankfully, our families preferred the Hylan cemetery, right next to the old church in the center of the town, and they wouldn't be caught dead here. I almost snickered at myself and my thoughts, but in reality, I was disgusted by our families. Even a cemetery was unworthy of their perfect bodies, as if the dead cared where they were buried.

Unfortunately, not even the dead rested easy in Winworth.

This cemetery was used by the people living on the East Side of Winworth, or as my lovely parents loved to call them, lowlifes. We all heard the stories about gangs running free on that side of Winworth, people missing, drugs flowing through the streets as if they were water, but we were forbidden from crossing the bridge connecting the two parts of this town to investigate for ourselves. And I was curious. I wanted to see if the stories were true.

As I came closer to the area that housed the crypts of various families, most of them abandoned and no longer used, I thought about the kids we had in our school that came from the East Side of Winworth. We all looked the same, but I could see the bullying some of the seniors from the West Side kept inflicting upon the lower classman that didn't belong to their social circles.

If you asked me, it was complete bullshit. Our mayor behaved as if the East Side of Winworth didn't even exist, always mentioning only the West Side. I know how I sounded, like a whiny girl that kept talking about the unfairness of the situation but still wasn't doing anything to change it. But how could I change the way people viewed the East Side of Winworth and their inhabitants, when I couldn't even fix my own problems?

The only solution I had, not only for that problem but for all my problems, was to get away from here. Nothing good could ever come from this godforsaken place. Even nature here knew that the sinister things ran the show, and I couldn't even remember the last time I saw the flowers in full bloom, unless they were dahlias or roses. Our gardener once tried to grow daisies, after I begged him to buy seeds, but nothing ever came out. I could still remember the disappointment on his face, and him explaining that the weather here wouldn't let them grow. But I knew better. People weren't the only poisonous thing around here. Air, soil, water—it all carried its own poison, and the longer you stayed here, the sicker you got.

Before I could reach the crypt where we usually hung out, a branch broke somewhere behind me, and I froze in place, trying to hear anything else. I heard footsteps on the wet ground, a crow screeching from above me, and I turned right, hiding behind one of the crypts. I tried to calm my breathing as the footsteps came closer, and closer, and closer, until I couldn't hear them anymore. Was it the groundskeeper? Goddammit, I didn't see him before and I was so careful.

Fuck, if he found me here, I would have to come up with a story about an old ancestor that was buried here.

Shit, shit, shit.

I pulled my phone out, checking if Lauren had texted me, but the screen remained blank. I just hoped that they weren't already here. We could spin the story if one of us was found here, but five teenagers at the cemetery, in the middle of the school day... Yeah, he wasn't going to believe us. I looked up, struggling to drown out the screeching of the crow, but there was no use. I couldn't hear anything but the wind that started increasing and the annoying bird. I took a step forward, attempting to see if anyone was around, but before I could fully see the area in front of me, a hand landed on my mouth, and somebody started pulling me backward.

I started thrashing against them, hitting their sides, trying to pull away their hand, while a scream lodged inside my throat, and my eyes started watering from the lack of oxygen. Whoever the person was, they wore gloves, and they were much taller than my five-foot-six. Panic gripped my insides, and my stomach started turning, but my captor was relentless. Tears fell over my cheeks, but instead of increasing the pressure, my captor slowly released me. It took me a moment to realize that instead of silence, laughter was what welcomed me.

I turned around, only to see Kane standing next to the crypt where we usually hung out, with Danny right in front of me, and Rowan laughing his ass off, standing behind his brother. Lauren was nowhere to be seen, and neither was Beatrice, nor Hailey. I didn't have to be a genius to know what just happened.

"You motherfucking—"

I ran toward Danny who was obviously the one that dragged me, scaring the shit out of me.

"I am going to kill you!" I screeched as I launched myself at him, hitting his chest with my fists, while he continued laughing. Kane, Danny, and Rowan were all

28

part of Winworth High's football team. I knew that my hits did nothing to him since the guy was built like a brick wall, but I was going to try. "What the fuck, Danny?" I yelled as I kept pummeling at his unmoving form. "Goddammit, I thought I was going to die."

"You should've seen the look on your face." The motherfucker laughed as he took a hold of my hands, stopping my unsuccessful attack. "Are you crying?"

"No!" I ripped my hands away from his grip and wiped my cheeks, just as Kane approached us, looking concerned.

"Are you okay?"

"No, I'm not fucking okay, you idiot." Rowan was still laughing, clutching his stomach, and mumbling incoherently. I narrowed my eyes at him, ignoring Kane altogether. "I'm glad this is amusing for you, Rowan. I wonder if you'll laugh when I switch the cocaine you love snorting so much with baking soda?"

He immediately sobered, a horrified look taking over his face. "You wouldn't."

"Fucking try me," I spat out. "And you!" I looked at Danny and took a step closer to him. "I'll make sure that Lauren knows what a fucking shithead you are."

Alarmed, he reached for me, but I took a step backward and started walking toward the crypt, turning my back to all three of them.

"Skylar!" Danny yelled, but I didn't want to talk to any of them. I lifted my hand, showing him my middle finger, and ducked down, since the entrance to the crypt was smaller than the rest of the space. "Come on!" His voice followed me all the way in, but I continued to the bench on the far side of the crypt and dropped my bag on it.

Their footsteps followed me in, and I kept my back turned to all of them, going through my bag and pulling out a pack of cigarettes and a lighter, just before Kane spoke again.

"Sky—"

"Fuck off, Kane." I lifted the cigarette, placing it in my mouth, and lit the lighter, illuminating the space. I dragged the first smoke in, loving the burning going through my throat, all the way to my lungs.

"I thought you stopped smoking?" His voice was nearer now, but if he came any closer, he was going to get punched in the face. My hands still shook from the adrenaline surge and the prank they pulled on me, so the cold shoulder it was.

"And I thought you stopped being an idiot." I finally turned around, taking another drag of the cigarette. "But I guess not."

I sat on the bench, still looking at Kane. He didn't say anything else, but I could see the twitching in his left eye, and when I looked at Danny and Rowan, neither one of them could look me in the eye.

Good. Fucking amazing. I should've listened to Dylan when he asked me to carry that pocketknife he bought for me, but I always thought that nothing bad could happen to me here. Not that anything happened, but somebody else could've ambushed me like they just did, and instead of sitting here, smoking my cigarette, I could've been in some creepy van, on the way to God knows where. As soon as I got home today, I was going to put that fucking knife in my bag.

Winworth was full of creeps, and with my track record and the number of times I sneaked outside during the night, it was better to be safe than sorry.

"We're sorry, Skylar," Danny mumbled as Lauren strolled in, followed by Beatrice.

"What are you sorry for?" Lauren asked, looking from me to them. Kane turned on one of the lamps in the corner, while Rowan fumbled with the other one, illuminating the room. "Danny?" she looked at him again, waiting for an answer.

"Yeah, Danny." I smirked. "Tell her what you did." I leaned down, placing my elbows on my knees, dropping the ashes from the cigarette on the floor.

"Sky," he groaned, avoiding Lauren's eyes. "Come on."

It wasn't a secret that Danny liked Lauren, who liked playing the game of hot and cold with him. I felt sorry for him, but I knew why she didn't want to get involved with him. Lauren had a worse track record with guys than I did, and that was saying a lot, considering that my first boyfriend ended up cheating on me. I dumped the second one because I started liking his friend, and the third one... Let's not get into what happened to the third one.

"Skylar?" She looked at me now as she moved the hair from her face. Danny's eyes pleaded with me, and for some reason I didn't want to destroy whatever he was trying to build with her. I knew that they hooked up a couple of times, but Lauren kept avoiding the whole talk he wanted to have. We both knew that if she knew about what took place today, she wouldn't give him the time of day.

"Nothing, babe." I smiled, still looking at Danny. "I'll tell you later."

She narrowed her eyes at me, but I shook my head, not wanting to get into it again. My hands finally stopped shaking, and I threw the cigarette on the floor, extinguishing it with my booted foot. She approached me and sat on my right side, while Beatrice went to Kane, who sat down on one of the fallen pillars.

"Where's Hailey?" I asked as Rowan started playing "High" by Zella Day on his phone, keeping the volume low. The acoustics here were strong enough to keep it at that volume, and I wanted to laugh at the meaning behind that song.

"She's coming," Beatrice responded instead. "She's apparently bringing somebody with her."

Fuck, Hailey. "Another stray?"

"I don't know." Beatrice shrugged. "You know how she loves including people."

Yeah, I did know. She loved bringing new people to our parties, but this was the first time that she wanted to bring somebody here. We were extremely careful about this place, and bringing a stranger was a one-way ticket to a disaster.

"Do we know—" Kane started, but before he could finish the sentence, a smiling Hailey appeared at the door, looking at all of us.

"Well, aren't you guys poster children for gloom and doom?" Her singsong voice echoed around the crypt, and Lauren snorted next to me, shuffling through her bag.

"It could be worse," Rowan started. "You're lucky we're still coherent."

"Yeah, yeah." She brushed him off and came to his side, taking his phone from him.

I looked at the door, expecting the person she was bringing to appear, but there was nobody. "I thought you were bringing someone?"

"Oh, he's coming."

He? Who the fuck did she get involved with now?

I didn't have to wait too long to see who was coming, because as soon as she said that, a familiar body filled the entrance, and the dark abyss I was getting lost in this morning captured me again. Dark, disheveled hair, chiseled cheekbones, but the hoodie he wore wasn't on him anymore. It was tied around his waist, while a black t-shirt hugged his upper body. Without the hoodie covering his arms, I could see all the tattoos climbing from his hands toward his shoulders. His eyes traveled over the crypt, meeting everyone's eyes, even Kane's, until they landed on mine.

"Hi." One word. One simple, fucking word, and my insides felt like they were burning all over again.

Did it have to be him, for fuck's sake?

THREE

SKYLAR

Feelings were tricky little things, and some people never mastered the art of hiding them from others. That wasn't the case with Mr. Broody who kept looking at me with an impassionate look on his face, perusing me as if I were an object he had a right to stare at. I felt naked under his dark, observant eyes, completely open to the world. I hated every single minute he kept looking at me.

Was this how others felt when I looked at them? It wasn't a secret that I loved studying people more than I loved talking to them. You could learn a lot when you stopped talking and started observing how others around you behaved. You learn from those stolen little glances—their nervous ticks, the way they chew their bottom lip when they feel uncomfortable talking about something, or how they behave in the presence of those they respect or even love. I knew that it was wrong in a way, but once I started, I couldn't stop.

The way he was looking at me right now was the same way I looked at other people. Almost bored, like me sitting here was as irrelevant as the *No Trespassing* sign in front of that old house at the end of the street where I lived. Unfortunately, I couldn't look away, even as I felt Kane's burning stare on the side of my face. I couldn't stop looking at him, because even though he didn't show anything on his face, his aura spoke for itself.

Some people carried darkness like children carrying their favorite blankets or toys until they were ready to part with them and embrace new things. But the thing with darkness, the thing with pain, was that once you got used to it, you didn't want to let go. My therapist loved talking about all these steps, all these things I should be doing to break through the clouds in my mind, but what he failed to realize was that I didn't want to break through. Every time I thought about living without that dark embrace, without the familiar burning in my chest, I would panic because I didn't know better.

I wasn't familiar with carefree living, where the wicked whispers coming from my mind didn't exist. And I knew I carried it around like a blanket. I knew that the way I carried myself threw people off, and I liked it — loved it, even. But I knew why I was the way I was. I also knew things about every single person in this room, except for him, and that unnerved me.

He took a step forward, studying the walls of the crypt, his energy filling the space, but I still couldn't get a good read on him. Normal people show at least some emotions, yet the only ones I saw from him so far were the ones from this morning, and I wouldn't call those emotions. He was mocking Kane, and then he got pissed off. I thought since he came with Hailey, she would be a lot more interested in him, but she kept looking at Rowan, giggling at something he said.

"What's your name?" Lauren was the first one to ask. Yes, what the fuck was his name? I was torturing myself the whole morning, trying to forget about the entire encounter before class, and I didn't even know his name.

"Ash," Beatrice answered instead. "His name is Ash, and he's kinda new in town."

Ash. His name tasted like a forbidden fruit as I played with it in my mind, rolling it over my tongue, nibbling on the three letters, but I was too afraid to say it out loud.

"Kinda?" I cocked an eyebrow at him instead, waiting for him to talk. Was this cold exterior just a projection or was he really so indifferent to the world around him? As he came closer to me, I suddenly craved another cigarette, just so I could occupy myself with anything but this mindless obsession. I loved and hated his attention, and I hated that I wanted to hear his voice. The few fleeting moments from this morning were not enough to satisfy my morbid curiosity, or to feed the monster he awoke when he stopped me from walking into the wet sign.

"I was born here," he answered in that gravelly voice I decided to hate. "We moved away when I was six years old."

"Really?" Kane scoffed. I was surprised he still didn't protest over him being here, considering their conversation this morning. "What's your last name?" I knew why he asked, we all did. Our last names held power we couldn't even comprehend, and knowing his, Kane would know more than Ash maybe wanted him to know. I suddenly didn't want him to tell him his last name.

I didn't want Kane to go in that direction, because if he started behaving like our parents, our cousins, aunts, and uncles, I wasn't sure that I would want him around anymore. And for some fucked-up reason, I still wanted him around, even if it was to just keep an eye on him.

"Why?" Ash turned to the side and looked at Kane. "Are you planning on marrying me, or is that part of the initiation to your little club?"

Lauren guffawed, scaring the ever-loving shit out of me. "Oh. My. God," she wheezed. "Did you just ask the mighty Kane if he's planning to marry you?"

"Was I not supposed to?" One side of his mouth lifted in what could only be described as a small smile. "No offense," he looked at Kane, "but you're not my type."

"Not. His. Type." I looked to my right side, scowling at the tears running freely down Lauren's cheeks as she kept laughing at the idiocy coming from his mouth. "You have to sit with us, come on."

She moved toward the edge of the bench and pulled me with her. He closed the remaining distance between us, an annoying smirk I wanted to wipe away playing on his face. I sneaked a look at Kane who was throwing daggers at Ash's back. I had a feeling whatever game Ash was playing, wasn't going to end well. Kane loved being called the King of Winworth High. A quarterback, a captain of the football team, coming from one of the richest families in town, he seemed to have it all. Or at least, that's what he wanted people to think, because the truth was too hard to accept.

The same scent I was trying to forget, filtered through my nose as he sat on my left side, intoxicating me, captivating me once again—cedar pine, cigarettes, even rain. I tried making myself smaller, almost invisible, but it was almost impossible to do with Lauren all but pushing me into him, and his shoulder touching mine. I thought I imagined that zap that happened when I touched him, but as his arm brushed against mine, the same miniature shock traveled through my body, eliciting shivers in its wake.

I looked at Beatrice who was dragging her hand over Kane's chest, trying to draw his attention, but his eyes were on the three of us, or, well, on the two of us. When the first chords of "Amphetamine" by MNQN filled the crypt, it felt as if the tension started slowly dissipating, and as Lauren pulled out a see-through bottle filled with pills, the grip of anxiety finally started leaving my body.

"What do you have there, Sugar Tits?" I smirked at her, ignoring the broody energy next to me.

"Wouldn't you like to know?" She grinned, but we both knew she was going to tell me as well as share.

"Yo," Rowan yelled. "How many should I roll?" He held a small bag of weed, while Hailey pulled out a little box from her backpack, which I knew had all the things needed to roll that weed into a joint.

"Skylar, no," Kane started, and I cut a look at him.

"Seriously, Kane?" The audacity. "Count me in, Ro," I said while I kept looking at Kane.

"Sweet. Ash?"

"I'm in too," Ash retorted as I turned to him, breaking the silent battle I was waging against a pissed-off Kane.

Instead of feeling cold with the freezing temperature inside the crypt, I was burning inside, and it was all Ash's fault. The moment my eyes landed on a tiny scar on his chin, I wanted to know how he got it. My eyes roamed over the rest of his face, from the high cheekbones to his full lower lip with a piercing looped on the left side. It's been such a long time since I felt like this. Like one small touch from him would send a blazing inferno through my body, and I wouldn't mind.

My mind was waging a war with the rest of me. I was curious by nature, and the fact that he wasn't showing any emotions was drawing me in more than anything I had ever felt. There was something inside of me, pushing me to find out everything about him, but there was also a part warning me that poison always comes wrapped in a shiny package.

And this guy, the way he looked at me, the way he dismissed Kane, he kept luring me in and he didn't even know it. It didn't take a genius to know that I was completely and utterly bored with most of the things in my life. Nothing piqued my attention anymore. People, parties, studying, love, hate, none of it mattered to me. Copious amounts of drugs, of alcohol, of trying to forget who I was and what was happening around me — none of it worked in shutting out the voices in my head.

Yet, one look at him this morning, one touch, and that's all it took to drown out the whispers in the dark, and the heavy Winworth's air that kept suffocating me for years. Mischief and promise of danger, that's what laid hidden in the depths of his cobalt eyes, and like a sailor succumbing to a siren's song at the sea, I was drowning in the hurricane disguised as a high school boy.

"Is there something on my face?" he murmured, and I noticed how close our faces were. If I lifted my head a little bit higher, I could press my lips to his. Maybe I would be able to draw out some kind of reaction with that? My fingers trembled from the need to touch him. My teeth tingled because I wanted to sink them into his bottom lip, to pull that piercing, and to cover him with everything forbidden I carried with me.

But I couldn't.

"No." I shrugged, putting some space between us. "I always wanted to get my lip pierced but didn't have a chance. It's fascinating."

"Really?" He smirked at me, knowing full well that I was lying. But instead of calling me out on it, something flashed in his eyes, and he turned away from me, looking at the rest of the room.

The moment his eyes weren't on my face, I felt like I could breathe again. What was it with him that piqued my attention so much? It couldn't only be the whole devil-may-care attitude because there were other people in our school, in our town, that behaved in a very similar way.

Was it the fact that he didn't really care about what Kane thought, or what anybody else had to say? I'd known him for a couple of hours, but I could already see that he wasn't somebody who would bend for social norms, and I respected that.

"So, Ash," Danny started, as the smell of weed trickled through my nostrils, and I looked at Rowan who held the blunt between his lips, looking at us. "Where did you guys move from? Oh, wait. Shit. I just realized that we didn't really introduce ourselves."

Leave it to Danny to behave like a welcoming party. Beatrice snorted, and Hailey rolled her eyes, because this is what Danny did. Every single party of his, he had to behave like the fairy godmother, involving the strangers in a conversation. Hailey collected strays, but Danny... Danny kept them.

"I'm Danny." He pointed at himself. "That's Rowan, my twin brother." He looked at Rowan, whose hands were now on Hailey's shoulders. "You already know Skylar." The bastard smirked. "Lauren, our favorite troublemaker." She lifted her right hand, showing him her middle finger, and I started laughing because he wasn't exactly wrong.

Where Lauren went, trouble followed. She was a magnet for mini disasters, and trust me, I should know because I was usually the one accompanying her when all of them happened.

"I love you too, babe." Danny smiled at her. "Hailey, our favorite cheerleader, who supports the

Winworth Crows with passion—both on and off the field."

"Well, I'm not the only one on my knees, Danny," Hailey retorted, as Rowan placed a blunt between her lips.

"At least I know what I'm doing when I'm on my knees, Hales," Danny mocked, earning a glare from Rowan.

"Cut it out, dude."

God, we were a mess. Every single one of us. I had no idea how we ever ended up hanging out together, considering that conversations like this one took place between us, most of the time.

"There's nothing wrong with being on your knees," Ash suddenly interjected. "Besides," he spread his legs, his knee touching mine, and placed his hands on his knees looking at Danny, "it's none of our business if she wants to be on her knees or on her back, or on her feet."

"Why, thank you." Hailey smiled at him, but Rowan... instead of glaring at his brother, he directed his gaze at Ash, whose face I could no longer see from this position.

Danny cleared his throat, finally realizing what an idiot he was. "Right." His eyes landed on Kane who didn't say another word after asking Ash for his last name. But he kept his eyes plastered on the two of us until I noticed what he was looking at. Half of my body was plastered to Ash since Lauren kept pushing me into him. Not that the bench had enough room for us to move around, but the darkening of Kane's eyes started worrying me.

I would have to talk to him about all this nonsense he's been spewing around, and this caveman-like behavior, as if we were together.

"You know Kane, our Golden Boy," Danny

continued with the introductions, despite the chilling energy in the room.

"We've met," Ash responded. They sure fucking did.

"And Beatrice, Kane's girl."

I wanted to fucking laugh, because while Beatrice would give her left kidney for Kane to even look at her, he didn't want her. At least, not anymore. Not after what she did.

"Sky," Lauren nudged me, pulling my attention to her. "Do you have water or you wanna take these dry?" I looked down, seeing five green and yellow capsules laid in her hand.

"Where did you get those?" You remember when I said that Lauren attracted danger like a magnet? This was what I was talking about. Out of all of us, she was the only one that dared to go to the East Side to score drugs, weed, and other things I didn't want to know about right now.

My parents weren't the only ones that didn't give a shit about their kids, but unlike me, Lauren wanted hers to care. She wanted them to see her, to talk to her, to acknowledge her, not just give her money so that she would keep her mouth shut. You danced on the fine line of safety and danger, and going to the East Side was a sure way to make them notice her—if she was ever caught there, of course.

But over time, I had a feeling it developed into something else, and while she didn't want to talk about the person that managed to get her drugs, I knew there was more to the story than she was willing to share.

"My grandma came the other day." She laughed. "The doctor prescribed her Tramadol for the back pain, but you know her. She doesn't want to take anything that isn't plant-based, so she asked me to get rid of these."

She wiggled her eyebrows, looking all comical, and I would've laughed if my attention didn't revert back to those five pills and the feeling they were going to give me.

She brought Tramadol once before, and the feeling of nothingness that came with it was exactly what I needed then. It was what I needed now.

"So, like a good granddaughter, I'm about to get rid of them."

"How many?" I looked at her. "Is it only one pack?"

"Nah, babe, I have three." She pulled the three boxes from her bag, wiggling them in front of me.

Perfect.

I turned to Ash, only to realize that he was looking at me already. "Do you have any water with you?"

"You can take them without water. They're capsules, you won't taste anything."

"I know that, smartass. But if I'm swallowing five pills at once, I would rather have some water with me."

"Skylar!" Kane's voice boomed through the crypt. I looked at him, annoyed, since I knew the lecture that was about to come. "Do not take those pills."

Hypocrite. Motherfucking hypocrite.

When he kept drowning in sorrow and despair, chugging two, three, and four bottles of Jack Daniels, all the while snorting cocaine up his nose, I never said anything. Maybe I should've. Maybe I should stop this madness we had going on here. He was no one to tell me what to do.

"Fuck off, Kane."

"I have vodka," Hailey chirped. "Here." She pulled the see-through bottle from her backpack and walked toward me, extending it to my waiting arm.

"Thank you." It was even better than water.

"Are you trying to kill yourself?" Kane asked. He

was really starting to get on my fucking nerves.

"If I am, you'll be the first one to know, babe."

I turned to Lauren and grabbed the five capsules from her hand. I placed them in my mouth, keeping my eyes plastered on the idiot who kept trying to destroy the entire mood, uncapped the lid on the bottle and placed it to my lips, chugging a hefty amount.

I could feel the capsules sliding down my throat, followed by the burning sensation caused by the clear liquid.

"Atta girl!" Lauren shouted, as the rest of the group started laughing. All but two, but I only cared about one of them at the moment.

Ash's eyes were plastered on the side of my face, calling me, urging me to look at him, and I did. I turned toward him and smiled as I wiped my mouth on the sleeve of my shirt. "You want some?" I pushed the bottle of vodka toward him, expecting him to refuse.

But he didn't.

He took the bottle, his long fingers grazing mine, and guzzled a hefty amount. His throat worked as he swallowed, and as he removed the bottle from his lips, I wanted to replace it. I wanted to climb into his lap and learn all of his secrets.

Self-destruction came in many forms. Mine was in the form of guys who would no doubt break my heart, and the drugs that could numb my whole body.

He put the lid back on and placed the bottle on the floor, not once moving his eyes from mine.

"Fuck this shit." Kane suddenly stood up and started walking toward the exit. "I'm out of here."

"Kane!" Beatrice screeched and ran after him, while the rest of us stared at the empty doorway.

Hailey started laughing, moving toward the pillar where Kane and Beatrice had been sitting. "That escalated quickly."

"Don't start, Hailey," Rowan warned.

"What?" She crossed her legs, smiling at him. "He's been behaving like an idiot. What the fuck is that shit?"

They kept arguing, going back and forth over Kane's behavior, but I zoned them out, picking up the bottle Ash placed on the floor, ready to take another sip.

"Is he your boyfriend?" The voice on my left halted me. "Kane," Ash clarified when I started gawking at him.

"Oh, hell no." I laughed.

"Are you sure he knows that?"

God, his voice felt like silk over my skin, caressing every inch. As the capsules I swallowed started working, when the drowsiness and numbness started settling in, I knew I was close to succumbing to what I wanted to do.

"Not my problem if he doesn't. I was very clear about the things I wanted and things I didn't want."

"And what do you want, Skylar?" He leaned closer just as Lauren stood up, leaving me alone with him. I could feel his breath on my cheek. I could feel the energy zapping between us, but I didn't want to relent that easily.

I leaned into him, reaching his ear. "Everything," I answered and slowly pulled away, putting some distance between us. "And nothing."

While his face remained free of emotions, his eyes told the story I wanted to read. There was a torment there, a promise of sweet, wicked things he could do to me, but my body wasn't my own, and I didn't want to pull him into my mess.

I was fascinated by this tug but was also terrified of it. If I let this happen, *he* would find out, and I couldn't have that. Kane was safe because Kane didn't have this effect on me.

I didn't want to fight for Kane, because in reality, he

was never anything more than a friend I fucked when both of us were bored. Yeah, Kane obviously developed something, or at least he thought he felt something for me, but whatever he felt wasn't enough to keep me close to him.

Because I didn't want him.

I knew Kane for most of my life, and yet in one day, Ash managed to do what neither Kane nor any of the other guys I fucked ever did. He fascinated me.

But it couldn't happen.

Before he could say another word, Lauren's voice pierced through the air. I turned around, seeing her standing next to Danny, smoking a joint, looking happy.

"Did you guys hear what happened yesterday?"

The blood in my veins froze because my yesterday was the stuff of nightmares. My mind understood that she wasn't talking about that. How could she when she didn't know about it? But my body still remembered his hands on me, branding my skin, leaving invisible marks that could be felt even when he wasn't around.

"No, but I'm sure you're going to tell us." Rowan chuckled.

"Yeah, yeah, go and suck a dick, Ro."

Danny wrapped his hand around the back of her neck, smiling at the interaction she had with his brother. I wondered if Lauren saw how much Danny wanted her. Was she blind or was she trying not to see?

"They found a body next to that road leading to Emercroft Lake."

"No fucking way." Hailey's surprised voice filled the space. "Seriously?"

"Yep." Lauren nodded as she leaned onto Danny. "Apparently, it was some chick. Just started university."

"Do they know who it is?" Danny asked.

"I have no idea. I overheard two of our maids

47

talking about it. It's just so sad, you know?"

Yeah, it was sad. Dying was not something people could comprehend as positive, but I knew that there were worse things than death.

There were worse fates, and I just hoped that none of my friends ever found out about them.

I moved further away from Ash, putting more distance between us, until I was close to the edge of the bench. His midnight blue eyes narrowed at me, realizing what I've been doing.

"I don't bite, much."

Maybe he didn't, but I knew someone that did more than that. And those marks... Those marks are not the kind I would like to see on Ash's skin.

FOUR

SKYLAR

The moment we came back to the school, I knew something was wrong. Lauren walked along my side as we went through the garden area filled with students. Some were crying, some looked terrified, while others simply looked… lost.

"What the fuck happened?" Lauren asked, taking in the scene in front of us.

Three girls from our grade stood together next to the fountain in the middle of the garden, huddled together, crying. I couldn't see Kane or Beatrice among the other students, but I had a feeling that neither one of them went back to school after leaving the crypt. Kane was too pissed off to deal with the school for the rest of the day, and Beatrice being Beatrice probably followed him.

Under different circumstances, I would've followed him as well, but it was better to cut him off now than to lead him on when nothing real could ever happen. I mistakenly thought that he would be able to handle the arrangement we had during the summer, but I was wrong. Hurting him pained me, but I could never tell him why I started it in the first place.

If I did, he would end up dead, and that was the last

"Look." Lauren pointed toward the back entrance, where several teachers stood, their pale faces telling a story of their own. Whatever happened, it wasn't good. "They look scared."

No, not only scared. They looked fucking terrified.

Our history teacher, Ms. Brown, was consoling two female students whose faces I couldn't see since their backs were turned to us. The whole place looked like something out of a movie. Grief and despair coated the air with their filthy little hands, and as the two policemen stepped through the door with our principal, Mr. Donaghue, it was clear to me that whatever had happened, wasn't a small feat.

Crows sang their wicked song of death, flying above our heads, like messengers announcing the impending doom. As I looked to the sky, the first droplet of rain fell on my face, rolling over my cheek, toward my chin. The dark sky above our school suddenly filled with a flock of birds flying in the direction only known to them. Omens of evil were everywhere, and I needed to know what happened.

"Lauren." I looked down, following her line of sight toward where the two officers spoke with the two girls from our grade. Casey and Anna seemed to be shaking, only held up by their boyfriends as they stood behind them. "Can you ask around? See what happened."

Out of the two of us, Lauren was much better at socializing with other people. I preferred to keep to myself and to keep my mouth shut, unless I knew the person I was talking to. Lauren was a social butterfly, and she would be able to gather what had happened much easier than me.

"Do I have to?" she moaned. "I kinda don't want to talk to people today."

"You're talking to me."

"Yeah, but you're not people. You're more like an alien." Her irises were still shot wide, and I could only assume that mine were the same, but I didn't have it in me to care. I smiled at her before I nudged her toward two freshmen watching the same scene with the officers as we did.

As soon as she started walking toward them, I felt him behind me, his energy electrifying my body. I wasn't sure if it was the number of capsules I swallowed, the vodka I drank, or maybe the weed we smoked, but I could feel him everywhere. Around me, inside me, in my head, in my veins… He was everywhere.

Even when I stood up from that bench back in the crypt, distancing myself from him and walking to Lauren who stood with Danny, I could still feel him as if he was standing next to me. He didn't touch me, yet I knew that if he did, my whole body would burn with desire. Ash was dangerous, too dangerous for me, for my mind. I wished I didn't have such a visceral reaction to him, but I did, and I knew I would have to do something about it.

My issues had issues, dammit, and tangling myself with someone whose essence screamed danger wasn't the smartest thing to do. So, distance. Yeah, I had to put some distance between us.

It's only the first day at school and it already wasn't going how I planned. I was supposed to lie low, avoid temptation, and he… he was the biggest fucking temptation of all. Whatever he carried inside of his soul called to mine.

Strong fingers sneaked underneath my hair, reaching the back of my neck, leaving a blazing trail in their path. I couldn't understand my body's reaction to him. It wasn't like this was the first time I was attracted to somebody, but it was never like this.

51

This felt raw, unhinged, animalistic, and dangerous.

I was alive, but I wasn't living. I was touched, but never understood. I was loved, but never really seen. Adults labeled me as problematic, while most of the kids my age described me as weird.

My skin tingled from where he touched me, and instead of moving away, I leaned back, seeking more, asking him to take a hold of more, without speaking the words. Understanding what I wanted, he came closer until his chest almost pressed against my back.

I could see Lauren not too far away from us. I could see worried faces, sadness taking over, but I couldn't hear anything from the whooshing sound in my ears, as my heart thundered inside my chest. I was still drowsy, but with every soft caress, with every little touch on the back of my head, he was bringing me back to life.

Just as I started succumbing to his touch, to this crazy feeling, I remembered what was at stake, and his touch stopped feeling like a caress, and more like a punishment. I couldn't enjoy this feeling. I couldn't let myself fall for him, no matter how much I wanted to.

I took a step forward, moving away from him as if he burned me. I was playing with fire here. If *he* found out what was going on today, I wouldn't be the one paying. Oh no. That sadistic piece of shit knew that he couldn't hurt me physically, so he always chose those closest to me.

"You're avoiding me." It wasn't a question, but a statement, and I didn't want to lie to him. I wanted to get to know him. I wanted to know all the tiny secrets— where he got that scar, why he looked like a thunderstorm and smelled like everything forbidden to me. "Why?"

Why?

Why?

Why?

There were a million reasons why, but I couldn't tell him any of them. I wouldn't tell him any of them because this burden of mine was only mine to carry.

"I'm not avoiding you," I responded, still looking forward, trying to focus on Lauren.

"Yes, you are." He was suddenly closer, too close. I couldn't see him, but I could feel every inch of him. "I thought we were getting to know each other back in the crypt."

I swirled around and crossed my arms across my chest. "You thought wrong." Dammit, being this close to him I could see all the colors playing around his irises — cobalt blue with yellow spots. But what fascinated me more, what kept me enthralled in his icy stare was the anger threatening to swallow me whole.

He kept a cool façade, a pretty mask for the rest of the world to see, but what I was seeing now was far from the cold and indifferent Ash I met today. I never knew true fear until I looked in his eyes. I never knew that one person could hold so much power in their eyes, but he did.

While my brain told me to run from him, to hide and save myself, my body started betraying me, wanting to be closer. Just like a moth to a flame, I was drawn to him, and I couldn't understand why.

I broke the connection before I could do something stupid and turned around to look for Lauren again. I didn't know how much time passed, but as I started ignoring the blazing inferno standing behind me, I could see her walking toward us, seemingly concerned.

"What happened?" I asked as soon as she reached us. The whole atmosphere was creeping me out, and the fog that was slowly descending from the mountain, definitely wasn't helping.

53

"You know Megan?" Her voice trembled as she asked. Gone was the carefree attitude and happiness she carried around.

"Uh—"

"Tall, blonde, annoyingly chirpy." She started describing her. "Always sitting in the first row during physics class?"

"Barely," I murmured. Megan was just one of those girls you knew but didn't necessarily talk to. Or at least, I didn't talk to her. Truth be told, I didn't talk to most of the people outside of our circle. Being a Blackwood in this town meant that almost everybody wanted something from you, and I was tired of fake smiles and polite answers because they were too afraid to anger me.

I wasn't my parents, yet nobody wanted to see that—except for Dylan.

I shook my head, clearing my thoughts and trying to focus on what was happening around me. "Why are we talking about her again?" I asked Lauren. I didn't like the terrified look on her face, or the pale color of her skin.

"Because she's missing."

Missing.

Just like the others over the course of the last couple of months. Girls and guys our age were disappearing in the middle of the night, only for their bodies to be found days later. Just like…

"Since when?" Ash asked, while I kept staring at Lauren.

Missing.

Oh my God.

"Do they…" I cleared my throat. "Do they know anything?"

Lauren shook her head, her wild red hair bouncing around her shoulders, the only splatter of color in the otherwise dark day. Ash stepped in front of me, talking

54

to Lauren, but I couldn't hear a word. I could see his profile, his lips moving, his throat working with every word said, but my mind was as far away from here as possible.

I used to love memories. I used to look at pictures from my childhood, from school, and think about the happier times. But now… Now all of my memories always go back to one I would rather forget. They always go to the place, to the person that wasn't here anymore.

They always go to the smell of burning flesh, that first disappearance and fear like no other.

They always go back to May and that godforsaken night.

"Skylar!" I jumped at the sound of Lauren's voice, waking me from the trap my mind was laying out for me.

"What?"

I could see the worry in her eyes because we both knew what this situation reminded me of. And not only me.

"They're sending us home for the day. Most of the students are frightened and they want to talk to some of the students that were there last night with Megan."

There? Where were they?

"They went out last night?"

My limbs were heavy, and I knew I was having a hard time understanding everything she said.

"I just explained what happened," she huffed. "Not even a minute ago."

She did?

"I-I'm… I'm sorry, L. I guess I wasn't listening."

She came closer, taking my hands into hers. "It's fine. This might not be the same situation, you know? So, get that out of your head. I can already see those wheels turning, connecting this with what happened to…" She stopped herself before saying his name. "You know what? Let's just get out of here. My parents aren't home right now, and the pool is heated."

She started pulling me toward the school, and I tried ignoring the stares and whispers around us. I focused on the brightness of her hair and the presence behind me. Ash trailed behind us without saying a word, and I could only assume that Rowan, Danny, and Hailey followed.

Lauren said everything was going to be okay, and I wasn't sure if she was trying to assure me or herself. Four months ago, all our lives were turned upside down when the first disappearance occurred and to this day, none of us could understand what exactly happened. None of us could explain the body they found that night, after the fire swallowed the entire cabin.

We only knew what they told us.

The body belonged to Zane St. Clare—Kane's brother and my boyfriend.

FIVE

ASH

When I was about nine or ten years old, I fell off my bicycle and managed to cut open my knee. There was only one other time when that kind of pain took a hold of my body, and as the blood kept dripping down my leg, the onslaught of memories attacked me, making me remember what I was trying to forget. Or, well, what my mind was trying to shield me from.

That day was the first time I saw my uncle cry, and the first time I learned the full truth. That was the same day my uncle told me not to wallow in pain, but to use it to focus and change things. And I did.

I lived for the moment when we would come back to Winworth, to right what went wrong, but I didn't expect her. I didn't expect to feel anything but the burning anger, and yet I did.

Skylar Blackwood used to be just a name on paper. She used to be the face in the dark I would think about when the pressure of what we needed to do would become too much to bear. The first time I saw her picture was the first time I knew what hatred felt like.

Brilliant, white smile and silver eyes filled with promises of paradise. She had everything, while my brother and I had nothing.

So, she became my obsession. My little secret, and even though she didn't know who I was, I knew more about her than she wanted me to. I knew how she looked with a smile on her face, and how she looked with tears streaming down her cheeks. I knew everything because she became my job. She became the golden ticket, and to get to them, I had to get to her first.

But I didn't expect to see this version of her. No, I expected the same smiling girl my uncle showed me when I was eleven. I expected the brightness in her eyes, not the apathy flickering around her body like a protective shield. She was just a pawn in this game we were playing, but I couldn't allow myself to feel sorry for a Blackwood.

No. The poison running through her veins was enough to remind me why we were doing this and what was at stake. She was just another privileged brat who couldn't know how fucked up life could really get.

Lauren swam toward the edge of the pool, pulling me back from my thoughts as she started speaking.

"You're a quiet one, aren't you?" she asked, looking right at me. If only she knew.

You'd be surprised at the amount of information you could get just by being quiet. People tend to overlook the quiet ones, thinking that we either aren't paying attention, or we aren't interested. But those assumptions were the ones that helped me gather necessary information when they least expected it. Take for example this situation right now.

I was here for less than a day and I could already see that Danny wanted to have something with Lauren, while she avoided being alone with him. I could also see that this group of theirs was as unhealthy as it could get. I wasn't sure if it was co-dependency or if it was because they were just thrown together and decided to run with it, but whatever it was, none of them wanted to be here.

With the exception of Lauren and Skylar, who seemed to get along much better with each other than with the rest of them. Talking about Skylar, she seemed shaken by whatever took place back at the school.

I didn't think that the girl they were talking about was part of their group, considering that all of them here, except for Hailey, belonged to one of the original families, and Megan definitely didn't. No, there was something else eating at her insides, and as she kept staring at the darkening sky above our heads, I wanted to know what was happening in her mind.

What happened to the smiley girl I remembered from those pictures?

"You can't take your eyes off her," Lauren started, pulling my attention back from Skylar to her. I tilted my head, taking in her wet, auburn hair and dark twinkling eyes. She looked like a regular girl, but every single one of them here was unknowingly bred for the depravity waiting for them. Whether they knew or not wasn't my concern, but I wondered what pushed people to turn vile.

"You should go and talk to her." Lauren smiled.

"And why is that?" I leaned down, holding a bottle of beer in my right hand. "Why should I talk to her?"

Another interesting thing about Lauren was that she never knew when to keep her mouth shut. I was certain that she wanted only the best for her friend, but right now, she didn't know that the information she was feeding me with wouldn't help Skylar.

"There are... things about Skylar no one knows." She looked at her. "Hell, I'm her best friend and I don't know everything. Truth be told, I don't think any of us know her at all. I'm not sure if she knows herself." Interesting. "This past year has been hell on her. What happened three months ago…" She took a deep breath and looked back at me. "Look, I think she just needs someone, and seeing you two together today makes more sense to me than her and Kane."

"Is he her boyfriend?" This conversation was getting interesting.

"Who? Kane?" She started laughing. "He wishes, but he could never replace…" She trailed off, losing the smile from her face. "Anyway…" Lauren cleared her throat. "He's not, and between you and me, he never will be. But not for lack of trying. I just don't think that he and Skylar are compatible enough for all that to happen."

"And you think she would be compatible with me?"

"No, not really." She shrugged. "But it would do her good to have some fun at least. Besides, she doesn't talk too much, you don't talk too much, see, perfect."

Perfect, indeed. Little Lauren was a true matchmaker.

I just wondered if she would feel the same about putting me together with Skylar if she knew the whole story.

"Just think about it. And you could always use a friend."

A friend. I would have laughed if the situation wasn't sad at its core. Skylar Blackwood and I could never be friends. What they did to us… No, friendship would be the last thing between us.

"And what if I'm an asshole? What if I hurt her?"

I wasn't sure if my words rendered her speechless or if she just didn't expect me to say anything at all, but the carefree attitude she was showcasing was immediately replaced with something sinister.

"Then I guess I would have to kill you." She smirked as she swam away, once again leaving me alone.

I sat there, unmoving, looking at the spot Lauren

vacated, thinking about what she said. Her words rang in my head, and if this was any other town, any other families, I would think about those words as silly, empty threats, fabricated by a teenage girl who wanted to appear tough. But I knew about these people.

I spent my life learning everything I could, so that I would be prepared once the time came. And now that I was here, I just hoped I was strong enough to withstand the storm that was about to happen.

But before I could dwell more about the past and what the future was about to bring, a commotion on the other side of the pool drew me in. My eyes zeroed in on two figures, arguing, but not loud enough for me to hear anything they were saying.

When the fuck did he get here?

Skylar and Kane stood on the grass, facing each other. He seemed angry, and I would be too if I were in his place. It was obvious from everything I saw and from what Lauren told me, that Kane liked Skylar a lot more than she liked him. He behaved like a jealous boyfriend, while she obviously didn't give a fuck.

Which worked in my favor, I guess.

The only thing that didn't work in my favor was the burning rage in my gut as he took a hold of her arm, pulling her closer to him. The other thing that definitely didn't work was the way my body reacted to her. When she touched me in the classroom, I felt as if a thousand tiny electric shocks traveled over my body from the place she laid her hand on.

When she looked at me in the crypt, I forgot about the plan, about the past, future, consequences and all the other things that were important to me. I forgot that Skylar Blackwood was nothing but an enemy. Nothing but a means to an end and someone I had to use to get to what I wanted.

Something inside of my soul screamed at me to get over there and pull her away from him. Something in the way she stood in front of him, quiet, submissive, didn't sit well with me.

Before I could talk myself out of it, I started walking around the pool, heading toward them.

"Oh shit," Rowan exclaimed as I passed next to him and Hailey, who were making out on one of the loungers. I didn't stop even after he called my name.

A whooshing sound filtered through my ears, and nothing else mattered but getting to Skylar. I wasn't a saint, and I wasn't here to save her. But if anyone was going to hurt her, it would be me.

She didn't know that I held her life in my hands. Skylar Blackwood was mine to break, and no one would touch her but me. No, Kane wasn't a part of my plan and he had to be removed.

"Ash!"

I could hear them behind me, trying to catch up to me, but I was already almost reaching Kane and Skylar. I hated how she seemed smaller than she actually was, standing in front of him.

"Ash! Stop, goddammit!" I didn't know if it was Rowan or Danny, but they were too late. I was already next to Skylar, pulling her behind me.

Kane's blazing, dark eyes focused on me instead of her, and I knew. I could see it there. This guy wanted to destroy me. When I saw him this morning, standing there, behaving like he owned the whole world, I couldn't pass the opportunity to fuck with the Golden Boy of Winworth.

I could smell the alcohol emanating from him. I could see the bloodshot eyes, dilated irises, and the cruelty shining from them. Just like his parents. I guess that the apple didn't fall far from the tree.

"Why is it," he stepped closer to me, until his face was mere inches from mine, "that everywhere I look today, everywhere I go today, you're there?"

"Aww," I mocked. "But I thought you loved seeing my face."

I mocked him, because if I didn't rein in my emotions, everything we planned for would burn in flames, and we would be done before we could even start.

I winced as Skylar dug her nails into my arm, but I couldn't look at her now. Violent people were unpredictable, and whatever had him upset obviously had something to do with her. Not to mention, the amount of drugs he must have taken already mixed with alcohol and a foul temper, it could all lead to a disaster. I kept my eyes on him, shielding her from his sight.

I counted on him hating me at first sight. I counted on him feeling threatened by me, but I didn't count on him getting violent.

Was this the first time he was getting violent with her? My heart squeezed thinking about it, because no matter what, no one should lay their hands on those weaker than them. I loathed men who couldn't handle real life and whatever was bothering them — the men that would take their frustrations out on their families or their friends.

"Fuck you!" Kane bellowed as Skylar started pulling my arm, trying to take me with her.

"Ash," she pleaded. "Let's go. Leave it be."

I took a step back, grinding my teeth, because while a part of me knew that I couldn't start waging wars without a proper strategy, the other part of me wanted to rip Kane's throat out.

You can't be reckless, my uncle said. *Patience is a powerful tool. We waited this long; we can wait a little bit longer.*

Patience.

I was many things, but I wasn't a patient person. Dozens of schools and a record with more stains than blank places could attest to that, but I would have to rein in my temper until the time was right. I couldn't do anything until all the pawns on the chess board were placed properly. Our time was coming, and this little town wouldn't know what hit them.

Turning toward Skylar, I failed to see the fist flying to my face, and before I could react, I was on the ground, with Kane straddling me. I could hear the screaming all around us, but I focused on the fists coming closer to my face.

"Kane!" Skylar screamed. "Stop it!"

But this motherfucker wasn't stopping. If anything, he increased his pace, and just when I thought he was going to stop, he wrapped his hands around my throat, cutting off the oxygen supply. The promise of obliteration was written all over his face as I started fighting back, trying to push him away. My hands connected with his face, forcing his head backward, but the adrenaline coursing through his veins was propelling him further.

Patience. I had to be patient because this was what I wanted. To see Kane crazed, jealous, livid. To see him fall apart in front of everyone he cared about. I just had to survive this, tonight.

"I'm going to kill you, fucker," he sneered. The position he was in gave him an advantage over me, and as black spots started dancing around the periphery of my vision, I knew I wouldn't be able to last much longer.

Out of nowhere, a mass of blonde hair and a tiny body knocked him off of me, going to the ground in a heap of limbs and screams.

64

"Skylar!" a feminine voice shouted. I wasn't sure if it was Hailey or Lauren. I started pulling myself off the ground, coughing, inhaling more air than necessary.

"Are you okay?" A voice filtered through my mind and as I looked up, I realized it was Hailey. I focused on the loose strands of her chocolate-brown hair, controlling my breathing and clearing out my mind.

"Here." She pushed a bottle of Jack Daniels in front of me, shaking it slightly and waiting for me to take it.

I lifted one eyebrow, slanting my head to the side, and looked at her. "Really?"

"What? It's either this or pool water. I'm pretty sure you would rather have this."

She did have a point, but I would rather have a glass of water than this. The ghostly feeling of Kane's hands around my throat was still ever-present in the forefront of my mind, and as I took the already uncapped bottle and took one large sip, I could feel the burn stronger than it usually was. I pressed a hand against my raw throat, trying to swallow past the pain, trying to shake the dizzy feeling from my head. I wanted to get up, wanted to check up on Skylar, but I didn't have enough strength in me to get up now. Faraway voices trickled through the air, and I turned my head to the side, seeing Skylar's back going inside the house.

The amber liquid sloshed in the bottle as I threw it to the ground. As I wiped my mouth, I noticed that Kane was nowhere to be seen.

"She went home," Hailey answered as I started looking around, hoping to see Skylar coming back. "Lauren took her."

I leaned back, seeing Danny and Rowan talking animatedly. "And Kane?" I asked her as I looked back at her. "Did he go back with her?"

Hailey took a deep breath and sat down next to me,

taking the bottle from the ground and draining the rest of its contents in one sip.

"I honestly have no idea where he went, and I don't really care."

"I thought he is your friend?"

She scoffed at my remark and threw the now empty bottle away from us.

"That's like saying that cats and dogs are friends. Kane isn't my friend. He never really was and I don't want him to be."

"Why's that?"

"Seriously?" She laughed. "He just attacked you, told God knows what to Skylar, and was so high that he didn't even realize what he was doing until Skylar jumped him. Do I look like I want him to be my friend?"

"I don't know." I shrugged and straightened myself up. I flexed my hand reflexively against my throat, wincing from pain.

"That's gonna bruise," she mumbled. "If you were a girl, I would tell you to cover it with some concealer, but since you're not a girl—"

"Yeah, yeah, I get it."

The day was already getting darker and as the lights around Lauren's house started turning on, I knew I should be going as well. But I wanted to know more.

"Does this happen often?"

"What? Kane?"

I nodded. "It just seems that none of you were as fazed about this as I was."

Hailey crossed her legs and turned fully to me before she started talking again. "Kane and Skylar are… complicated, to say the least. You've been here for one day and you've already managed to piss him off, and I gotta tell you—you need to be careful. Kane might seem like a spoiled brat, he might act like one, but people in this town are never what they seem." Don't I know that. "He was never my favorite person, but it's like a switch was flipped and he became this…" she trailed off. "I don't even know how to describe him now. He has an unhealthy obsession with Skylar who doesn't really give a shit about him. It would be funny if it wasn't sad. But what happened with his brother…" She suddenly stopped, her eyes widening, looking around us. "I shouldn't be talking about this with you."

"Well, the guy did try to kill me, so I'm pretty sure that I would love to know everything there is to know."

She looked behind me, then to the side, as if she was checking if anybody was listening.

"Okay, look, I like you. You seem okay, and you didn't grow up here, which in my book, is a major plus right now. But you didn't hear any of these things from me, because if they find out that I told you—"

"Don't worry." I placed my hand on top of hers. "I won't say a word."

Her face showed the battle she was waging inside her head, but when she spoke again, I knew I had her.

"Okay. Three months ago, Kane's brother went missing…"

Pieces of the puzzle slowly fell into their rightful place once Hailey explained what happened three months ago in Winworth, and Kane's idiotic behavior. I was told stories about this town, about these people, these kids my age, but seeing them interact with each other was a completely different thing from everything my uncle ever told me. Listening to Hailey talk about the nightmare that fell over their town was another thing entirely.

I heard what happened. The entire world heard what happened here, but I wanted to hear it from someone who was close to them. Someone who could give me more insight into their fucked-up relationships and depraved shit they were throwing themselves into. Information was power, and how you used it could make or break whatever you had planned.

I feigned shock as she described the gruesome details, the heartbreak and panic; the soul-shattering event that changed their lives forever. It took everything in me not to react as she talked about it as if it was the first time for something like that to happen in this town. Though, I had to admit, I was surprised that somebody from the St. Clare family was taken, which also told me that this time it was different.

This time, the game had changed and none of them were ready for what was about to come. I left as soon as she finished telling the story, explaining that I had to catch dinner with my family. Danny and Rowan offered to drive me home, but I preferred walking. If I could help it, I would like to keep them all as far away as possible from my brother and my uncle.

I stopped on the bridge connecting the West and East Side of Winworth, staring down at the river coursing underneath, darkened by the night that has already fallen on the town. Winworth was founded on blood and tears, and secrets so deep that even a thousand years of trying to dig them up would result only in uncovering more secrets and more depravity that has wrapped its filthy hands around the roots of this place. I was told the story of Winworth more times than I could remember. My uncle made sure that my brother and I knew where we came from, and why we had to leave.

Once I remembered the night that changed our lives, he told me everything, leaving Sebastian, my brother, out of it.

Five founding families fled here in the fifteen-hundreds when they couldn't handle the church that was hunting them and burning all their sanctuaries to the ground, anymore. Blackwood, St. Clare, Maddox, Lacroix, and my own, Crowell, settled in between the two mountains, in the valley of the river coursing below me now. The elders here loved spouting lies to the young ones while talking about the history of Winworth, excluding all the gruesome details.

But we knew better.

Those five founding families created the disease here, letting it spread all over the town, its people and all the surrounding areas. I wasn't sure if Emercroft Lake, the town separated from Winworth just by the mountain, had the same history, but I wouldn't be surprised if they managed to dig their claws in there as well.

My family was almost completely destroyed twelve years ago — only my brother and I survived. I was six years old when the unholy inferno came barging into our house, swallowing everything in its path. I was six when I came face-to-face with true evil, hiding behind the mask of a kind businessman.

They destroyed our lives and now we were going to destroy their sick world. The plan was already set in motion, and their kingdom was going to fall.

I stepped away from the rail and started walking toward the darkened street. There wasn't a person in sight, and I knew why. The East Side of Winworth was not a place where you wanted to find yourself in the middle of the night. Doors were shut, windows enforced with the metal bars and even the local police force didn't dare to come here if they didn't have to.

Local authorities abandoned the people here, and I knew that my family was one of those at fault for that.

The story goes that shortly after Winworth was established, the wealthy families started occupying the parts of the land near the forest and the river, taking their friends with them and giving them land that was good for crops. In the process, they pushed those that weren't considered a "blue blood" to the other side of the river, letting them fend for themselves.

Well, letting them fend for themselves and at the same time using them for their wicked games.

I wanted to laugh at the fake picture they were trying to present as I looked at the buildings closest to the bridge. If you were a tourist just walking on the bridge or on the other side, the East Side of Winworth would look exactly the same as the West Side, with their beautiful architecture and welcoming energy. But if you walked down the street and took the left turn, you would see the true picture of this side.

Closed shops with wooden panels over their windows lined the streets, because people here didn't have enough money to enjoy the treats from local bakeries or to go to the coffee shops during their break. If you drove further down the road, following the signs toward the factory for aluminum, you could see the true face of misery. You could see the children running all over the street, missing pieces of clothing, with their dirty little faces and starved eyes.

You could also see the vicious men and their calculating gazes as they watched those same kids, counting the years until they could use them for their business — until they could condemn their lives to eternal agony. But people always saw only what they wanted to see, and even when the truth was right in front of their eyes, they almost always chose to keep their eyes closed, so that they could preserve their own peace of mind.

And I didn't mind that, I understood. But I couldn't understand how humanity could fail this much. How could all those politicians close their eyes when it was obvious that this part of Winworth was completely neglected and almost forgotten? Laws didn't exist on this side, and the only rules you had to follow were those imposed by local gangs who came into power when people that were supposed to take care of the entire Winworth stopped caring for those that didn't wear branded clothes and golden smiles.

I could feel eyes on me as I took the right turn at the end of the street, heading toward the alley I used as a shortcut to get to our house. The East Side of Winworth reminded me of one of those medieval cities in Europe, resembling a labyrinth more than a town people lived in. The only street that was wide enough for two cars was the one connecting the bridge with the rest of Winworth. The other ones were barely enough to have one car, let alone two.

Uncle Neal hated that I didn't want to use the car to go to school, but I preferred walking. It would surprise you how much thinking you could do while on foot.

My eyes traveled over the faded, peeling paint on the buildings. Most of the tenants here either worked in the factory or in West Winworth, trying to survive until the end of the month. From paycheck to paycheck, wallowing in misery, and instead of leaving this godforsaken place, they stayed.

As I passed the only open store on this side of the town, with its flickering light right above the door, I could already see the gate leading to our house. It was a sad reality these people had to suffer through, but until the remaining founding families agreed to change something, we could do nothing but talk about wanting

71

something better here.

The shrill sound of my phone ringing broke through the silence of the night, and as I started opening the gate in front of our house, I pulled it out, smiling at the name on the screen.

"I'm in front of the house," I spoke, pressing the phone between my shoulder and my ear.

"Is it done?" My uncle's voice reverberated in my ear. "Are you in?"

"What do you think?" I laughed. "They welcomed me as if I was always part of their group."

"Good, good. And they don't know who you are?"

"Nope," I answered and walked to the front door. The light illuminated the pathway as the front door opened, revealing my uncle standing there with a serious look on his face. "They don't suspect a thing," I started, ending the call on my phone. "And they won't suspect anything until it's time."

They wouldn't suspect a thing because none of them knew that we existed. Twelve years ago, I stood in front of a man with a knife and a sinister smile, pleading for my life, trembling from the fear coursing through my veins. And when he plunged that knife into my stomach, when the scream tore from my throat, swallowed by the fire spreading through our house, I promised if I survived it, that I was going to come back.

I was going to come back and hunt them how they hunted us.

SIX

Skylar

Zane St. Clare was eighteen years old when he died. Only a year older than me, and as bright as a supernova, I couldn't help but fall for his charm and pretty face that always seemed to be adorned by a smile. He shone so bright that every single person that had ever met him, wanted to be in his presence, to soak that brightness, that positivity.

And now he was gone.

Maybe if we weren't just a bunch of spoiled brats who thought that they could play with dangerous things, he would still be alive. Maybe if we reported everything we knew about his disappearance, he would still be alive.

A thousand "maybes", a thousand missed opportunities, regrets, and anger, but none of those could fix what we did. I went over what happened a million times, thinking it through, trying to figure out the missing pieces of the story and who had kidnapped him, but it was futile chasing after something that was lost. I guess that's what hurt the most, what annoyed me the most was the fact that they never caught the person that killed him.

Or perhaps what annoyed me the most was the fact

that I blamed myself for what happened. If it wasn't for that stupid idea we agreed to, Zane would still be here.

"You're fucking slow today," Lauren started, stopping a few feet in front of me.

Since we were in elementary school, we used to go to the cabin on the riverbank owned by my parents. Kane's family used to own the one on the other side of the river, until... No, never mind. I had to stop thinking about that night and everything that happened prior to it.

If I continued thinking about Zane and what could've been done to avoid that fatal night, I would end up in an asylum. The drugs we were taking stopped working three days ago, when the images haunting me day in and out, continued flashing in front of my eyes.

It's been seven days since Megan went missing, and people were already losing hope of finding her. She either ran away or worse — she was dead.

It was Lauren's idea to come here today and spend the night. Winworth wasn't exactly the place that had events going on during the weekend, and since all of us seemed to be shaken by what happened with Megan, she wanted to cheer us up. Truth be told, cheering us up was just an excuse to organize a party. Most of us had simply closed ourselves off, hiding away from the world, dancing with our demons, drowning in the numbness overtaking our bodies. But Lauren, being Lauren, was undoubtedly already bored sitting in her house for the entire weekend.

And who could blame us? The memories of May twenty-fifth kept crawling back into my mind, reminding me of the mess we made. And we couldn't tell anybody. No one knew about the plan Zane made, or who was involved.

Zane was a wild card, always wanting more than he

already had. He was the brightest one of all of us, but he was also the reckless one. When he came up with that idea... I still couldn't understand why none of us said no. And we should've said no.

One of us should have been mature enough to dismiss the crazy shit he was coming up with.

Zane wanted to escape, to run away, but in order to do all that, he needed money. A lot of money. The kind of money none of us had, regardless of who our parents were. When he spoke about a life outside of Winworth, free from the clutches of our parents, free from all this darkness surrounding us, this suffocation we were all going through, we all said yes.

He wanted to fake his own kidnapping, and like reckless fools, we all agreed to help. Little did we know that the little prank we were pulling would turn out to be real. He was supposed to be kidnapped on May fifteenth, and his parents were supposed to be contacted on May nineteenth for the ransom. He wanted to fake his own death and get a new identity, but he never got to do that.

He never got to do that, because on May seventeenth, we lost all contact with him. He was supposed to be in Seattle, hiding out, waiting for the ransom to be delivered to the old amusement park on the East Side of Winworth. One of us would have to take it after they all cleared out.

But when he didn't answer his phone, when all communication was lost, we knew that something was wrong. Kane even went to Seattle to see him in person, but Zane was nowhere to be found. We tried everything—his friends from Seattle, places in Emercroft Lake where he could've gone, but he wasn't there. We thought he was pulling a prank on us, trying to scare us, but when the night of the party rolled over, when we were all gathered at the cabin owned by the St. Clare family, that's when all hell let loose.

When the blazing inferno started illuminating the night, when we almost burned down with the house, we knew that somebody else was fucking with all of us. When the firefighters arrived at the scene, when the fire started reaching new heights, they pulled out the body.

A body that didn't belong to any of us because we managed to escape.

A body that belonged to a boy I liked, to our bright star. We realized that playing with fire and trying to escape from this godforsaken place might be harder than we ever thought. In one night, our innocence burned away. Our dreams shattered as windows on the second floor exploded. The place we all loved burned with our friend, and the life we knew disappeared in front of our eyes, eaten by the angry red flames in the middle of the night. We never found out what really happened.

No one ever came out as a culprit, and all five of us kept our mouths shut about the plan we previously concocted. Police questioned us. Kane and Zane's parents pretended to be devastated, but the truth was — they never even realized that he was missing.

We swore to take that secret to our graves, but not a day passed where I didn't think about the future Zane could have had. If it wasn't for six silly teenagers who thought that the world danced how they played, he would've been alive.

Maybe if I said something or did something. Maybe if we told them what we knew about his whereabouts when we realized that he was really missing, he wouldn't be dead.

I had too many regrets about things we did and secrets we kept. But the problem with the skeletons we were keeping in our closets was that they never really stayed hidden. And even if they did, they ate you alive. They pulled your soul, they damaged your heart, and they made you paranoid to the point where you didn't want to exist anymore.

I didn't want to exist.

I just wanted to forget about everything. I wanted to forget about our plans, our dreams, and silly little promises, because they were all gone. They all burned away with that fire. Even though they said that he was dead before the fire, it didn't help knowing that while we drank and partied inside the house, his body was in one of the rooms.

We hadn't been there since that happened, and while we wouldn't be going to the same cabin, it didn't help that if you looked toward the other side of the river, you could still see the remnants of the cabin where our lives changed.

I didn't think that any of us were ready for death to knock on our door, regardless of if it was for us or someone we cared about. I wasn't ready to face the reality—I would never be ready. Zane was more than just my boyfriend. He was my friend. Him, Kane, Lauren, Danny, Rowan, Beatrice, and I, we all grew up together, and when he died, it felt as if a part of us died with him.

I wasn't the only one feeling that way. I could see how Danny and Rowan watched his locker in the school. Or how all our eyes traveled toward the place where he used to sit in the cafeteria and in the crypt. We all missed him, but it was more than that.

We all blamed ourselves for what happened.

Unfortunately, none of us knew how to move on without destroying our own lives. At least, I didn't know.

Self-destruction always came easily to me, and it

always came in different shapes and forms. People often thought that self-destruction came in the form of drugs or alcohol, but that wasn't the truth. When your mind was telling you that you shouldn't exist, when everything you ever loved started feeling insignificant, you found ways to destroy little pieces of yourself so that nobody else would notice.

I was a coward who didn't want to leave my brother. I was a coward who didn't want to slit my wrists, because I always thought about the people that would have to clean up the mess. I was a goddamn coward because I did nothing when someone I used to care about was in trouble.

I was still a fucking coward because I didn't want to help Kane, who was still struggling with the death of his brother. So, I destroyed myself.

Pills, alcohol, faceless strangers in the middle of the night, sleepless nights, and toxic thoughts, I used them all, because feeling nothing was better than feeling everything. When the drugs hit my system, when alcohol burned my tongue, I couldn't remember the smell of burning flesh, or the screams echoing in the night. I couldn't remember the tears on Kane's face, or the fear on Lauren's.

I couldn't feel the searing pain in my soul, the guilt, because they numbed it all. They made me forget, and I didn't want to stop.

Even when *he* touched me, when *he* made me do things, I couldn't feel anything else but the pure disgust, because I allowed it to happen.

I played the game of a perfect little smile when Dylan asked me if I was okay, because I couldn't let him see the depraved thoughts in my head. I craved violence because the pain of the body always quieted down the pain in my head.

"Skylar!" Lauren yelled, and I realized why.

I was standing on the edge of the cliff, where we could see a part of the river as it went toward the town. If I took one more step, this could all end—my life, my pain, their pain, memories, everything. This suffocation could cease to exist.

But what about those I would be leaving behind?

I couldn't leave Lauren, not now. I couldn't leave Kane, even though he scared me more than he excited me now. They lost one friend, and I couldn't be the next one to die.

"I-I'm sorry." I took a step back. "I was just thinking."

"Dude." She grabbed my arm, pulling me further backward. I could hear the panic in her voice. I could see the fear in her eyes, because we both knew I wasn't all right. None of us were. "You looked like you were about to jump."

"Don't be ridiculous." I laughed, but it sounded fake. It always sounded fake, but none of my friends called me out on it. None of them commented, because all of their smiles looked the same as mine—fake. "I would never jump."

My words seemed to do the opposite, and instead of reassuring her and removing this fearful look from her face, her lips tightened into a thin line and the grasp she had on me became harder, as if she could hold me, save me, from what I was about to do.

I couldn't explain it to her without hurting her, but this deadly waltz of life was killing me slowly. Day by day, hour by hour, I was always doing something that was bad for me. I was killing my body, and I was killing my mind, because being a walking dead felt better than feeling everything I felt in May.

"Just… Be careful. Okay?"

I nodded, since I couldn't taste any more lies on my tongue and agreeing that I was going to be careful would be the biggest lie of them all. Lies, secrets, dark whispers, they were slowly wrapping around my soul, choking me, cutting off everything good and light.

"Any news on Megan?" I asked as I stepped away from her. Lauren finally let my arm go, but the weary look on her face was ever so present, and I wanted it gone. I wanted her to think about something else, instead of worrying about me.

She shook her head, pulling the bottle of water from her backpack. "No," she answered as she uncapped the bottle. "They have no new leads, nothing. She literally disappeared from the face of the earth."

"Do they think it's —"

"Connected with Zane," she interrupted me. "No. Dad thinks she ran away, but her parents are dismissing that theory."

Lauren's father was a sheriff in town, and she managed to get all the information firsthand, before it even came out to the public.

"Did she have a boyfriend?" I asked, and took a bottle from her, taking a mouthful of water.

"We're talking about Megan, Sky. She didn't go anywhere but to school and church. Hell, she was practically a saint. Church was the only place where she spent time, if we exclude school, so that whole theory of her running away with a boy makes no sense. If one of us disappeared, then yeah, maybe you could suggest that we ran away with some guy, but not her."

"Then where the fuck is she?"

Don't get me wrong. I felt bad for her and her family, but I didn't exactly give a damn if I never saw her again. This whole situation was hitting too close to what happened with Zane, and with all those other girls missing and then appearing after a couple of days close to the town. It sent chills over my skin, and I couldn't shake this feeling.

"I have no idea," she shrugged. "I just hope she turns up soon. Dad's been spending more time at the station than at home, and I hate this sinister feeling floating through the city." That makes two of us.

Sometimes living in Winworth felt more like a nightmare than real life. I wasn't sure if it was the environment or everything that had happened in the last year, but I had a feeling that the streets of Winworth carried more secrets and more darkness than any other place in the country. Maybe it was the constant foggy weather and rainy days, but the atmosphere was almost never cheery.

The one thing I did love about this area was the nature. If you were lucky enough, you could hear the wolves howling deep into the night, or you would see squirrels preparing for the winter while you walked through the forest.

Winworth was surrounded by mountains on all sides, with the thick evergreen forest climbing up, covering the stones of the mountain. Hikers loved this area, and they usually went to Emercroft Lake after finishing here. On those rare sunny days, you could see the mountain tops playing with the clouds, and instead of the macabre song of crows, you could hear the soft chirping of the birds.

I turned around, taking in the horizon in front of me as the sky started darkening, and the night slowly started cloaking Winworth. I could see a couple of lights being turned on in the distance, but we couldn't see the entire town from here. Only a couple of houses on the northern part were visible from here. I loved this feeling of being able to escape it all at least for a little while.

The ping from my phone pulled my attention back from the sight in front of me, and to the unknown number showing on my screen.

Huh?

I took a step forward, moving away from Lauren who was too busy taking a picture of the sight in front of us, and started unlocking my phone. A deafening roar tore through the silent afternoon and the ground beneath my feet crumbled down. As I started losing my balance, I could barely hear Lauren screaming my name.

I slid down between the trees, shielding my head as I went deeper into the forest. The colors of the forest blurred together, and I closed my eyes, fighting the force of gravity pulling me lower and lower. I gasped for air, feeling the pain in my ribs, on my back, on my legs, my body turning from one side to the other as I rolled down the hill until I hit something solid, knocking my breath out.

"Fuck!" I yelled, trying to straighten myself up. The smell of wet soil and pine trees surrounded me as the ringing sounded in my ears. My back hurt, my head ached, and I couldn't hear Lauren anymore.

Opening my eyes slowly and seeing the darkness surrounding me, I realized I went down further into the forest than I initially realized. The trees blocked the light down here, and I started feeling my pockets for my phone. I must have dropped it while rolling down here.

Goddammit.

With my hands, I started touching the ground, trying to understand my surroundings. Branches and wet ground played beneath my fingers until I touched something cold, something foreign and sinister.

"Oh my God," I gasped.

My heart thundered inside my chest, and as my fingers explored further, I knew. I just knew.

I was touching fingers.

Cold, wet fingers.

As my eyes adjusted to the darkness, the scream tore from my throat, followed by the onslaught of tears and fear like no other.

"Skylar!" I could hear Lauren now, but knowing she was near did nothing to soothe my nerves.

There was a body in front of me. A *dead* body.

Her blonde hair was caked in blood, and the lifeless blue eyes stared at me, the terror etched on her haunted face. I followed the line down her neck with my eyes and shrieked when I realized that only half of her body lay in front of me. Her torso was ripped away from her legs that were disposed of next to the tree above her head. The clothes on her body were ripped open, exposing her midriff and the slope of her breasts. Her bloodied intestines mixed with dirt and leaves were scattered all over the place, creating a connection between her legs and her upper body.

"Holy shit. Holy fucking shit." I started scrambling backward, trying to get as far away as I could.

My hands caught on something sharp as I tried moving away from the girl, from her stare, but the pain never really registered in my mind from the shock I was going through.

I could see the light shining through the dark forest, and as it caught on her soulless face, I drew a shaky breath, fighting the tears that were freely falling down my cheeks.

"Sky… What the fuck?" Lauren's voice echoed around us. "Oh my God!" she screamed. "Oh my fucking God!"

Her hand landed on my shoulder, and she started pulling me further backward, the light from her phone still illuminating the girl.

"I-It's Megan," I cried out. "Lauren, that's Megan!"

I knew that face. I saw her smiling more times than I could count. I saw those eyes twinkle when she talked to her friends and when she was happy. There was no happiness on her face right now. There was only terror, a nightmare, and I didn't want to think what she went through.

"Sky, what is that?" Lauren pointed to Megan's stomach, illuminating the area.

The foreign-looking inscriptions and sigils were carved into her stomach, creating dried, bloody marks. The scream that was building up inside of me escaped, thundering around the forest. There was so much pain on her face. So much fear, that even in death she looked like she wanted to scream. Her face was pale, bruises on her cheeks, with blue lips open at half-mast.

"This is—"

"We need to call the police, Lauren," I interrupted. "We need to go up and call the fucking police."

I felt dirty and violated. When I looked down, I could see the blood over my hands, and I wasn't sure if it was mine or hers.

"Fuck," I mumbled, rubbing my hands over my pants. But the more I rubbed, the more it started spreading. "Fuck, fuck, fuck, fuck…"

"Hey, hey." Lauren took my hands into hers, dropping the phone to the ground. "Stop it."

"She's just… She—"

"I know, Sky, but you need to get up and we need to get the hell out of here."

I tried. I really did try getting up, but as if the weight of the world rested on my shoulders, my legs wouldn't work. They remained plastered to the ground.

"I can't."

"Yes, you fucking can," she argued. "Come on." She

gripped my arms and started pulling me up. My knees shook as I finally stood up, leaning against the tree.

Her presence was overwhelming. The stench of death was everywhere, and I wanted to bathe myself in bleach to remove this depravity from my skin. But I knew that this was going to be just another demon to haunt me.

"Skylar?" Lauren started, her voice strained.

I turned around, following her line of sight. "What?"

She was staring at Megan, at her torso, and as she turned her phone up, I could see exactly what. I didn't see it before, didn't notice it, but I couldn't move my eyes from the spot now.

My name was carved into her chest.

SEVEN

Skylar

The police sirens echoed around us, as I sat shivering in the paramedics' ambulance, trying to grasp what I saw. Lauren was next to me. We huddled together underneath the blanket one of the paramedics placed on us, but it did nothing for the shivers both of us had coursing through our bodies. I couldn't look at my hands, keeping them under my legs, because I knew I would see the blood.

My blood, from the cut, mixed with hers.

Her cold eyes kept flashing in front of me. My name carved on her skin, her hair, the same color as mine... Jesus fucking Christ, who did this?

Neither one of us said a word after the police arrived. After we saw my name on Megan's skin, the adrenaline kicked in, and we went up the hill almost running, trying to get away from the gruesome scene we witnessed. She's been missing for seven days, but according to the policemen I overheard talking, she was dead for less than twenty-four hours.

Apparently, that explained the amount of blood on her and the lack of bugs eating at her flesh.

Who fucking did this?

That one question kept coursing through my head.

Winworth was many things, but it wasn't a home to

killers, especially not serial killers. And who would carve my name? Why?

"The second victim," one paramedic whispered to the other when they thought we weren't listening.

The second victim. I couldn't comprehend how someone could do something like this to another person. I saw enough documentaries, enough horror movies, enough pain and sorrow, not to be fazed by these things, and yet when my hands touched her cold ones, I recoiled.

I wanted to scream.

I wanted to run away. The fear that I felt in that moment was greater than anything else I had ever felt in my life. It was slithering, like a snake in the grass. It crawled up my spine and took residence in my head, refusing to leave. Its cold fingers touched every part of my body — they touched my soul, spreading the festering darkness throughout.

Fear was a familiar thing for me. I grew up surrounded by evil, but seeing it like this… Unhinged, left loose, it woke something primal in me — the need to run and never look back. Whoever did this was not in their right mind.

And my name… My name was there. Somebody hurt her. No, somebody killed her and carved my name on her pale skin.

My stomach lurched again as her face flashed before my eyes, the utter terror obvious on her. The violence that wrecked her, that took away her life, it couldn't have been inflicted by anything else but a monster.

I'd always believed that there was always something good left in people. That there were parts of them you could love, parts you could cherish. But whoever had done this, they were the worst kind of monster.

Even animals wouldn't attack unless they were in danger. Even the biggest predators roaming our planet wouldn't attack for the fun of it.

But people… Us, human beings, we were the worst monsters.

We fed on the weaknesses of others. We took and took and took until there was nothing else left to take; until we sated the dark desires coating our insides, turning us into something vicious.

Something evil.

The monster that caused this malevolence—I couldn't call them a person anymore—they terrified me. It scared the living shit out of me, knowing that there were people out there who could do such a thing. This brought back what happened to Zane, and I couldn't help but think that all of this was connected. That somehow what happened to him, whoever happened to him, was now killing other people.

"Are you girls okay?" A masculine voice tore through the thoughts occupying my mind, and as I looked up, I noticed that it was one of the first officers who came to the scene.

"We just found a corpse with my name on her body, Officer. You tell me. Are we supposed to be feeling okay?"

I was bitter, cold, chilled to the bones from what I encountered, and he asked us if we were okay.

No, I wasn't okay. I was angry. I was devastated by this whole ordeal and the only thing I wanted to do was to get home and sleep for a year. But I had a feeling that every time I closed my eyes, her face would flash before them, and the peace I yearned for would never come.

"I'm sorry, Ms. Blackwood. I can't even imagine how hard this must be for you."

"No, you can't…" I paused. "Or maybe you can, I

don't know."

"Still…" he paused. "I am sorry. I have a daughter that's a few years younger than you, and I hope that she never has to encounter such a thing."

"I hope so too," I replied, staring at the badge on his chest.

"I do need to ask you a few questions." He crouched in front of me until his face was leveled with my knees. Lauren kept staring at the spot on the ground, quiet, in shock. Shortly after we called the police, the sky opened up, washing away the sins on the ground. It felt as if the sky cried for the young life that would never walk this earth again, and the rain that felt soft in the beginning, gradually increased, hitting my face with a punishing strength.

Was I to be punished for a crime I had no part of?

"Did you know her?"

I gripped the blanket tighter, as the shivers wrecked me. My teeth chattered, causing additional turmoil in my head. I couldn't escape the noise—the sirens of the ambulance, police cars, radios, and the white noise buzzing in my ear.

I couldn't escape the pitiful stares from the officers and paramedics that came to the scene.

"I did," I answered. "Well, we were in some of the same classes, but we weren't friends, if that's what you're asking."

Another sob lodged itself in my throat, but I wasn't going to cry. I wasn't the one whose soul was now restlessly looking for absolution, traveling far away from her family and friends. I wasn't the one that was violated so badly, that even the officers who have seen terrible things in their lives had to turn away before continuing to mark the crime scene.

They ripped her body in half, leaving her disposed

as if she never meant anything. They left her there so that the wolves roaming these woods would find her and finish the job. I wasn't sure if they expected anyone to find her, but they must have known that leaving her body so close to the trail meant that somebody would.

"Have you seen anything suspicious?" he questioned, and I almost laughed at the absurdity of it.

"You mean, apart from the whole corpse in the woods?" I asked, blinking slowly. "What else would there be?"

"I mean," he cleared his throat, "did you see anybody else there?"

"No, Officer. It was only Lauren and me. Well, it was only me at first, but you get what I'm trying to say."

"How did you end up down there?"

"I fell. We were going down to the cabin next to the river. Once we reached that clearing before heading down the path, I fell."

"And you're sure you don't know anything about this?"

"I knew she went missing. I was at school that day, but that's all I know."

"It's just weird." He started scratching his beard. "You two went to the same school, and now we find her here with your name carved into her chest."

"Officer, are you accusing me of something?" I narrowed my eyes at him, disbelief passing over my face.

"No, not at all." He smirked. "We just have to remove all the possibilities."

"Listen. I don't socialize with a lot of people at school. You can ask anyone, and they'll tell you the same thing. I don't go out unless it's with our group of friends. That's all. My life is extremely boring, Officer," I squinted at his badge, "Parsons. Do you really think that I would carve my own name on a person I killed?"

"So, you did think about killing somebody before?"

"I'm seventeen!" I roared. "Why in the ever-loving fuck would I want to kill somebody? Who does that kind of thing?"

He seemed like he wanted to ask something else, but when a shadow fell over us, the relief washed over me and the officer stood up, coming face-to-face with my brother.

"I believe you're done here."

The cold expression he reserved only for those he didn't like was now directed at Officer Dick, and if his annoyed scowl was anything to go by, he didn't expect to see him here.

Dylan and I looked so much alike that some people believed we were twins. In reality, he was four years older than me, and the only person I could turn to when I needed help.

He kissed my boo-boos and wrapped my hand when I cut myself. He was the one that explained to me how my body was going to work once I entered puberty, because our mother was too busy ignoring me.

When I managed to find my phone, while climbing up the hill, and once we reached the area where we had some reception, he was the first person I called. I knew he was in Seattle, busy with school, but I didn't know who else to call.

Dad was in New York, attending a funeral of an old friend, and Mom… I wasn't gonna go there.

I all but jumped from the ambulance, throwing myself at him. Without missing a beat, he caught me, turning us away from the officer that still stood there, gaping at Dylan.

The familiar scent of cinnamon and apples wafted through my nose, calming all of my senses. Dylan felt like home and everything good in this world.

92

"You're here," I mumbled against his chest, my voice muffled. I clung to him, and I couldn't care less. I wanted him to hold me forever and take away the monsters trying to crawl into my mind. I wanted to forget Megan's face, those lifeless eyes, the questions the police had asked me and the cold that clung to my bones.

My brother always kept the darkness at bay, shielding me from everything and everyone that wanted to hurt me.

"Are you okay, Little One?" he asked against my hair, cradling my head to his chest.

"Ms. Blackwood," the officer started again.

When my brother turned around, his icy tone slithered through the air. "I said, you're done here."

"But—"

"She's a minor. Do I have to report you for questioning her without a guardian present with her?"

"No, not at—"

"Good." He dismissed him before he could utter another word. "We're going home."

"But—"

"I said no," he gritted. "It is a very simple word. No. My sister is freezing, in case you haven't noticed. After what she saw, she needs to rest. How would you feel if you were in her skin right now?"

"I-I didn't," he stammered. "I didn't mean to—"

"You didn't mean to be caught." Dylan pulled a card out of his pocket and handed it to the officer. "If you have any other questions, you can reach me or our lawyer. Whatever suits you best."

He stroked my hair, again ignoring the officer, and as soon as his hand landed on my head, my breathing calmed down, and the thundering of my heart silenced, leaving behind just the soft thud against my chest.

"Let's go home, Little One. You need to get out of

those clothes, and you need to eat."

"I'm not hungry." I buried my face deeper into his chest, hiding my face from him. "I just want to sleep."

"Okay." He chuckled. "Then we'll just sleep. Come on." He moved away from me and took my hand. "My car is close by."

"What about Lauren?"

"I'm taking both of you home."

A smile spread over my face, momentarily pushing the horror I had experienced to the back of my mind. There was a certain kind of comfort in knowing that someone out there cared about you, and that they came when you called.

"I think she's in shock," I murmured, looking at Lauren. "I tried calling her parents, but they didn't answer."

"It's okay." Dylan put me down and walked toward Lauren, who kept staring at the spot on the ground. "Lauren?" he carefully asked. "Let's go home."

"I can still see it… her and her eyes." Her voice trembled as she spoke. "She looked so scared, terrified."

"I know," Dylan answered.

Officer Dick walked away as Dylan took a hold of Lauren's arm and started pulling her up.

"You're gonna be okay," he started, reassuring her as tears cascaded over her cheeks.

I have never seen Lauren this shaken. She seemed stronger and braver than I was when we first found Megan, but as soon as the police arrived, she shut down, refusing to talk.

She finally looked at Dylan and then at me, her lower lip trembling.

"I'm scared, Sky," she whispered. "I'm really, really scared. And I don't—"

"Lauren!" a voice boomed through the clearing.

When I looked to the left, her father, Sheriff Benjamin, was rushing toward us, his eyes on Lauren. I had no idea why he wasn't the first person to arrive at the crime scene, but I didn't want to ask.

"Dad?" She moved away from Dylan. "Oh God!"

She ran, meeting him halfway, clinging to him as I clung to Dylan. I couldn't hear their voices, but as Sheriff Benjamin started stroking her back, I knew she would be better off with her family than with me and Dylan.

"Hey," Dylan spoke, his hand on my shoulder. "You're shivering."

"I-I'm just so cold." *Cold like Megan.*

"Hey, hey." He pulled me into his embrace. "No one's gonna hurt you, okay? I won't let them."

"But you weren't here," I sobbed. "You're not here anymore. She had my name carved into her skin, Dylan. She—" I choked. "She looked like me. The same hair color, the same color of her eyes…" I trailed off.

"But she isn't you."

I wanted to believe him. I wanted to believe that everything was going to be okay, but how could it ever be when there was a killer in town, targeting girls. Girls that apparently looked like me, carving my name in their skin, and butchering them.

"I know, but—"

"No, I don't wanna hear it, Little One." He placed his lips on top of my head and squeezed me tighter. "Nothing is gonna happen to you, and that's a promise."

I lifted my head, meeting his eyes, soaking in his strength, in his confidence.

"Okay." I nodded.

"Okay?" He smiled at me. God, I missed seeing that smile.

"Yeah, okay. I believe you, but can we please go home now?" I pleaded.

He wrapped his much bigger hand around mine and started pulling me away from the paramedics, and through the throng of officers gathered around, toward his car.

Walking next to him, I felt like the world couldn't hurt me. Like what I saw would just disappear because he said so. I couldn't even count the number of times he defended me against our mother. The number of times he held me throughout the night when the nightmares I was trying to escape from decided to take a hold of my mind, holding me captive until the very next morning.

And even when I couldn't tell him what my dreams were about, he still held me, no questions asked.

But the most important thing, I realized as he opened the passenger door of his car, ushering me inside, was that he came.

He always came for me.

EIGHT

Skylar

Swollen blue eyes stared back at me from the mirror, as I stood in front of the sink in the bathroom, trying to wash the blood from my hands. But just like in the forest, no matter how hard I scrubbed, or how many times I used the soap, I still felt dirty, violated, and scared. The smell of the pine trees and wet soil was so deeply ingrained in my brain, that even after lighting all the candles in my room, they couldn't erase the smell.

The smell of death.

I kept thinking about Megan's last moments and how she must have felt knowing that there was no way out. What were her last thoughts? Did she blame us for being too late to save her?

Was she conscious when that monster carved my name on her skin?

God, seeing my name there, so violently engraved, made me sick. Just thinking about it made me want to hide, get away from this place. I kept coming back to the last time I saw her in front of the Kraftmart this summer, standing with her mom, laughing at something she said.

Wasn't it weird that only when a person died, we thought about all the things we could've done for them? Maybe if I had talked to her, maybe I would've liked her and we could've been friends. Maybe if she had been with us, she wouldn't have been walking alone at night that Sunday before school started and she wouldn't have been kidnapped.

But one question that kept popping up much more than the other ones was, maybe it was supposed to be me? I didn't know any other Skylar, and the eerie resemblance the two of us shared couldn't be missed. Whoever the killer was, they were after me. I knew they were after me.

"Sky." The door of the bathroom rattled as Dylan knocked. "Are you okay?"

Was I okay? No, I wasn't fucking okay.

I wasn't seeing myself in the mirror. My eyes weren't mine. My lips didn't belong to my body. My hair looked exactly like hers. Blonde strands colored with red, and a lifeless face stared back at me. I was seeing her, her pleading eyes and lips forever frozen as she screamed.

But no one heard her.

"Skylar!" Dylan bellowed.

"I'm fine," I lied. "I'll be out in a minute."

I didn't want him to come in. If Dylan saw this lost look on my face, he would get more concerned than he already was, and I didn't want him to worry about me.

Yes, I went through something traumatic, but I would be okay. Right? People do this all the time, and they survive those traumatic experiences. I was alive, I was well, and I was going to forget about her haunting blue eyes and the violence spreading through that forest.

But I was lying to myself, and I knew it.

I was a good liar, good at pretending that everything was okay when nothing was. Nothing was ever going to be okay, because seeing her like that—her young life extinguished before it could even start—reminded me of Zane, and it felt as if my insides started burning again with the pain I was trying to forget.

No, no, I couldn't deal with this shit. I talked the good talk, but when it came to facing reality, I was a chickenshit who couldn't comprehend what was happening. I knew what monsters looked like—they're pretty faces, pretty smiles, charming fucking bastards, living in the perfect skin.

But when you knew what the monster looked like, you could survive. This time... This time I didn't know who the monster was. And worst of all, what if the monster isn't on the street? What if the monster is in the mirror?

What if I was to blame for her death? After all, whoever killed her might have been after me.

Fuck, fuck, fuck... What if somebody knew about Zane and our involvement in it? What if somebody was playing a game with all of us? But who?

My phone kept buzzing on the sink, the incoming messages and calls all going unanswered and unopened. I couldn't deal with people right now. I should check on Lauren, but I didn't have it in me to be social anymore today. The rest of the guys probably found out what had happened by now, and I was sure they were the ones trying to reach me.

But I was tired—tired of people, tired of tragedies, tired of living the life I hated. I just wanted to disappear, to get away from here, to forget about Winworth and everything that has happened here.

I looked at the small stand with drawers next to the sink, knowing what was inside. Knowing that it could help me forget, at least for a little while. I was getting too dependent on these pills, but I didn't know how to deal with reality and everything that was going on around me. I didn't know how to be present and save my mind at the same time.

So, I pulled the first drawer open and took out a small burgundy box holding all my hair ties and clips I used to use as a kid. No one would ever look in here, and it was the perfect place to hide the small bag Lauren gave me three months ago.

I hadn't needed to use it before, because we always hung out together, and either she or Kane always brought what I needed. And if it wasn't them, then *he* always had what I needed to get through the night.

My hands shook as I opened the lid and threw the colorful hair ties on the top of the stand, followed by the pins I never really used anymore. The colors were a stark contrast to what was going on through my head, through my body and my heart. They were the reminder of a time when I was just a little girl, wearing rose-colored glasses and believing that the world was a happy place. I wished someone had told me earlier that the world wanted nothing more than to destroy us.

I wished I knew what was going to happen to me, to my friends, because then I would've been prepared. Then my mind wouldn't be such a fucked-up mess like it was now. I could feel my heart beating rapidly, echoing in my ears. Sweat gathered above my upper lip as anticipation started building inside my veins.

The rush of calm was what I needed. A quiet place for my mind and nothingness that followed, that was the high I always chased. Drugs that made my heart race, that made me feel happy, those weren't the drugs I needed right now. I wanted to quiet the demons whispering in my ear.

I wanted to stop eyeing the razor on the bathtub, calling me, whispering that everything was going to be okay if I picked it up and sliced it through my skin. I didn't need any more scars, and I didn't want any more blood.

Not today.

Removing the paper hiding the bag, I stared at it, the ten white pills calling my name. Everything was going to be okay now. I was going to be okay now.

I took the bag out and threw the box on the floor, the sound of the impact echoing in the silent bathroom. My phone kept buzzing, my heart kept thundering, but my attention was on the plastic bag in my hand and the oblivion that was about to come.

Oxy.

A sweet temptation, sweet oblivion, and devastation. I was warned that Oxy often led to heroin use, but I didn't give a fuck at this point. I just wanted to forget, and if swallowing two or three or four of these could help me today, so be it.

I filled the glass standing on the sink with water, and sat down, leaning against the door. My entire body shook, anticipating what was about to come, knowing the effects, craving the release in this form. I untied the knot on the bag, and took out three of them, placing them on my palm.

Last time Lauren and I did Oxy together, we took two each, but this time I didn't have alcohol to amplify the effects.

The bitterness exploded in my mouth as I placed them on my tongue. Taking the glass filled with water, I pressed it to my lips and gulped down, feeling the three pills traveling down my throat to my stomach.

Now I just had to wait.

"Skylar!" The door rattled against my back as Dylan started knocking, sounding angry. "I swear to fucking God, Sky. If you don't get out of there, I'm gonna break down the door and come get you myself."

Perfect Dylan. Always the savior, always the favorite one.

Our mother never failed to remind me what a fuckup I was, and how I could never be as perfect as Dylan. But it wasn't his fault our mother hated her younger child.

"Sky," he started again when I didn't answer. His voice was barely a whisper, a plea, begging me. "Please, Little One. I'm getting worried about you."

I wanted to get up and get out of the bathroom. I couldn't be here when the drugs started working, but I was too tired. My body felt sore, and I could barely move my legs now that I was sitting.

I tried. God, I tried.

Pushing the glass further away from me, I put the bag with the remaining pills inside my pocket and started pushing myself off the ground. The headache that was threatening to explode in my head finally reared its ugly face, and as my temples throbbed, and my eyes started misting, I knew I was going to be extremely fucked when the drugs started working.

At least I wouldn't feel any pain. I wouldn't feel anything.

"Goddammit, Skylar." I could hear the frustration in his voice. "What are you doing in there?"

I finally managed to push myself up, and as I opened the door, I came face-to-face with him.

"Dying." I laughed. "I had to use the toilet, Dy." I pushed past him, keeping the smile on my face.

"You were using the toilet for an hour and a half?" he asked just as I dropped on the bed.

God, my muscles throbbed both from that goddamn hike and from the fall. I couldn't have Dylan here when the Oxy finally hit. I could already feel it spreading through my body as I started getting drowsier. Just a little bit longer and the memories of her pale face and that fucking stench would finally be gone.

At least for a couple of hours.

"I didn't know we were now counting how many hours we need to be using toilets for." I smirked, but he didn't look amused. If anything, Dylan looked pissed, and I hated it.

His hands went to his hips as he kept staring at me. The usually styled blond hair was now disheveled, the strands falling over his forehead. His icy blue eyes narrowed, and jaw clenched, but he didn't say a word. He still hadn't changed from the black pants he wore earlier and the white button-down shirt. The only difference was the rolled-up sleeves resting at his elbows.

I knew he could see right through me, through these fake smiles and the cheery personality, but I was tired of him worrying about me. First with Zane, now with this, it was too much. I wasn't his responsibility even though he acted more like a parent than our mother did.

Our father, Judah Blackwood, was mostly gone, spending the majority of his time in Seattle. As a senator and a CEO of the company my great-great-grandfather founded, he had to be there. I was just pissed that we had to stay here, while both he and Dylan lived over there. I hated spending time with our mother when they were around, not to mention when they weren't.

I never really understood what made her resent me, and I didn't ask. Sometimes lies were better than the truth because we could believe in whatever we wanted. Sometimes pretending that everything was all right was a better way to live than to think about every single wrong thing that was waiting for us.

Dylan took one step forward, then two and then three, until he was standing in front of my bed, hovering over me.

"Are you mad at me?" I asked, feigning innocence

he could easily see through. Focusing on him and his eyes, his smell and his clothes helped to remove the images of the gruesome scene I witnessed today. As my body started relaxing, my muscles losing the strain, I felt happier than before.

I knew it was a temporary happiness. A temporary fix to a million problems I had, but it was better than having to live through the nightmare tonight. My room was mostly shrouded in darkness, softly illuminated only by the lone lamp in the corner of my room.

"Dylan?" I asked again, breaking the silence. "Come on." I straightened up, holding myself up on my hands. "You can't really —"

But I didn't manage to finish the sentence, because in the next moment, Dylan was on the bed with me, pulling me onto his lap, and hugging me to his body. His arms wrapped around me, holding tight, and his head disappeared into my hair, hiding him away from me.

"Hey." I pulled one arm out and started rubbing his back. "What's wrong with you?"

Instead of an answer, I received an even stronger hug, until one of his hands sneaked into my hair at the nape of my neck, pressing my face into his shoulder.

"Dy," I mumbled, my voice muffled by the soft fabric of his shirt. It smelled like him, like home.

That's what Dylan always was for me. *Home*. The only one that cared enough to understand my mind and everything I was going through.

"As much as I missed you and as much as I like this after the shit that has happened today, you're scaring me."

Soft lips pressed against my cheek, then my temple, until he reached my forehead, holding them there for a moment. He started dragging his hands through the strands of my hair and slowly untangling it. I moved my own hand to his hair and started playing with the short strands at the back of his head, moving to the top of his head, where he kept his hair longer.

"I would never forgive myself if something happened to you," he started in a strained voice. "Never."

"Dylan," I whispered. "You had nothing to do with this. Whoever did it... I don't know, they must be sick."

His eyes flashed with something unfamiliar, but as fast as it appeared, it also disappeared, replaced by the soft look he always had for me.

"I know, Little One. I know I had nothing to do with this, but I wasn't here. I wasn't here to protect you."

"You're here now, and that's all that matters."

Still dragging his hand through my hair, he simply nodded and kept quiet while he continued looking at me. The hand I had on his hair dropped down as my body started experiencing all the effects I was waiting for. This happiness that was coursing through me was a lie, but it was a lie I wouldn't mind living.

The anxiety I felt before started dissipating, and as my head fell onto his shoulder, he started moving us toward the headboard of my bed, still holding me close to him. A smile played on my lips, but as the vertigo started dancing around my head, I let my eyes close, placing my hands against his chest.

"You need to change, Little One," he murmured against my hair. "And you need to take a shower."

I did. I knew I needed to do both of those things, but the pain in my shoulders started spreading over my back, connecting with my bruised ribs. The hammering in my head quieted down as the pills took over, but I didn't want to move.

"Later," I murmured. "I'll do everything later."

But he didn't listen to me.

Softly pushing me away, he laid me down on the bed, and stood up. I could hear him walking through the room, the opening of the wardrobe as its doors squealed, and the rustling of fabric. I wanted to open my eyes. I wanted to get up, but instead of fighting the sleep slowly creeping up on me, I gave up.

Warm hands touched my stomach, slowly, slowly, pulling the shirt I wore up, reaching my chest. A giggle escaped from me, vibrating through my chest, as Dylan pressed his palms on either side of my waist, finding that hidden spot that always made me squirm and laugh.

"Dy," I laughed. "What are you doing?"

He tickled me again, laughing with me. "Changing you of course." Still keeping my eyes closed, I felt it when the fabric came to my chin, and I lifted my arms above my head. "Can you lift yourself up?" he asked in a hoarse voice. This entire day was no doubt stressful for him as well, and I obeyed, inching my upper body higher. The shirt slid over my head, my arms, and with a soft thud, hit the floor as Dylan threw it somewhere in the room.

"You are my sunshine," I started singing as he moved down to my pants, unbuttoning them. "My only sunshine…" The sound of the zipper being lowered mixed with my voice. "You make me happy…" I lifted my butt and Dylan started pulling my pants down, goosebumps following his movements as my skin became exposed to the chilly air in the room. "When skies are gray," I choked out when he finally removed the pants from my legs.

"Shhh," he soothed me, his hands roaming over my legs, landing on my knees. "Everything is going to be okay."

I nodded — at least I think I did, when his hands disappeared, and the sudden drumming of my heart I didn't expect made me open my eyes, looking for him.

"Dylan?" He stood in front of the wardrobe, his back turned to me, the strong set of his shoulders hunched down as he held something in his hands. "Come back to bed," I slurred, my words echoing in the room. "Please."

He turned around, his face contorted with fear, with worry, with all the unspoken things he didn't want to burden me with. I patted the spot next to me, inviting him back.

In two long strides, he was next to the bed, holding a shirt I haven't seen in ages in his hands.

"Is that…?"

"Your SpongeBob shirt." A small smile played on his lips. "Remember when I brought this?"

"How could I ever forget?" How could I forget that he bought it for me, while traveling through the country with his friends?

"Arms up," he instructed, holding the shirt up. I complied, lifting my arms above my head, and he slid the shirt over, letting it fall over my body. I pushed the shirt on my back, up, and unclasped the bra biting into my skin, pulling away the straps through the sleeves of the shirt and throwing it to the side.

I could feel his eyes on me as I moved back toward the headboard. When the mattress dropped under his weight, I closed my eyes, and turned to my left, inch by inch, climbing over him.

The soft fabric of the comforter came around my shoulders as he pulled it over us, and I nuzzled my face against him, letting the smell of fabric softener, cinnamon, and apples comfort me. To let me believe that everything was going to be okay.

"Don't leave me, Dylan. Please don't leave me."

His hands tightened around my shoulders as he

settled down, keeping my body draped over his.

"I'm not going anywhere," he croaked. "I'll always be here."

Good, I wanted to say, but it was as if my mind and my mouth weren't in sync anymore, and instead of trying to talk more, I let myself fall into the sweet oblivion, knowing that he was going to be here to keep the demons at bay.

If I had my brother, I didn't need anything else.

○

I had no idea how long I was asleep for, but when the loud voices woke me up from my peaceful slumber, I knew it was longer than I initially planned for it to be.

The morning sun was illuminating my room, and as I turned around looking for my phone, I realized I was alone. Dylan must have gotten up before me. The clock on the phone showed eight in the morning, and my eyes widened, remembering the time we came back yesterday and how long I had been asleep for.

I slept for almost fourteen hours, when usually I wasn't able to get more than four hours during the night.

Doors slammed in the distance, and I pulled myself up, slowly stretching my body and wincing as the pain ricocheted from my lower back, through my entire body.

"Fuck," I moaned as I threw the comforter off of me, and slowly stood up and walked toward the mirror in the corner of the room. The jeans I wore yesterday were haphazardly thrown on the floor next to my wardrobe, and the white SpongeBob shirt I had on definitely wasn't the one I wore yesterday.

"Of course." I slapped myself on the forehead. Dylan changed me last night, just before we went to sleep.

I turned around and started lifting the shirt, only to be welcomed with an angry-looking bruise, slowly turning purple at my lower back.

"Shit."

I thought that the soreness I felt last night was only a temporary issue, but as I walked to the bathroom, I knew that wasn't the case. My head still throbbed, probably both from that slip yesterday and the amount of sleep I got.

"You can't fucking go there!" Dylan's voice traveled through the house, and I rushed to the bathroom, locking the door behind me. My heart thundered inside my chest, and Megan's lifeless eyes flashed in front of me.

"No, no, no," I moaned and gripped the sides of the sink. The glass I left yesterday was still on the floor, and the hair ties were still scattered over the stand next to the sink. "This can't be fucking happening."

But as I looked up, taking in my disheveled appearance, the gruesome pictures kept filtering through my mind, reminding me of the sickening scene in the forest.

No, I couldn't let this happen.

I turned to the bathtub and turned the water on, letting it fall freely, as I stood there, transfixed, watching it disappear into the drain. I didn't have time to take a bath, and if I wanted to make it to school today, I had to be quick.

I pressed the switch to direct the water flow into the shower head and took off my panties and t-shirt. The steam started filling the bathroom, playing around me. When the first stream of water hit my body as I stepped into the bathtub, I started feeling more like a human than the corpse we found yesterday.

Knocking sounded on the door, but I didn't answer as I kept the shower head above me, letting the water wash over my hair, my entire body, ridding me momentarily of the filthy feeling I was enveloped in. I washed my face, my body, and after soaping myself and washing it all again, I turned the water off and slowly took a step outside the bathtub, careful not to slip on the tiles.

My lower back ached, and I would have to ask Dylan to put some cooling gel on it. I just hoped it wasn't anything serious because I wasn't up to another visit to the doctor this year. Those two days after the fire in May were enough to last me a lifetime.

I wrapped a towel around my body after dragging it through my hair, and unlocked the door, stepping inside my room.

Only the room wasn't empty, and a boy—*a man*—I least expected to see today was sitting on my bed, staring at the bookshelf on the opposite wall.

"What the fuck are you doing here?" I bellowed, anger taking over my body. He had no fucking right to be here.

Ash turned around, his eyes lazily going from my naked legs, over the towel hiding the important parts of my body, to my face.

"Good morning to you too." He smirked.

After the crypt and the mess at Lauren's house, I avoided Ash like the plague. If he was in the room, I would walk out. If he was in the cafeteria with the rest of the guys, I would eat in the garden. The only place where I couldn't avoid him were classes, but I was trying.

It also didn't help that every single person kept bringing him up during our conversations. And then there was Kane, who went from being obsessive to straight out deranged, starting that night at Lauren's place.

He was high, angry, hurt, reminded of his brother

and what happened in May, and instead of talking like a normal human being, he wanted to drag me with him. He started asking about Ash—if I liked him, if I wanted to fuck him, and I knew that there was no use arguing with him when he was like that. And I would've handled it if Ash didn't interfere, angering him even more.

And when Kane attacked him, I didn't think. I jumped on him, knocking him to the ground. Needless to say, I was embarrassed over the entire situation and Ash getting involved. No matter how much my body wanted to feel that electricity whenever we touched, he was wrong for me, and I was wrong for him.

I hated that my own body was betraying me in his presence, while he seemed cool and collected, without a care in the world.

"I asked you a question, Ash." My body trembled, both from the remnants of the drugs and his presence.

"Your brother is an asshole," he said as he stood up, again perusing me from head to toe. "I came here to see if you're okay, since you obviously forgot how to use your phone."

"I didn't forget. I just didn't want to answer."

He came closer and closer until the tips of his boots started touching my toes.

"Hmm," he grunted and took one wet strand of my hair, pulling it to his face. His eyes closed as he inhaled and exhaled. "Vanilla."

"Ash." I took a step backward. "What are you doing here? I'm not gonna ask again." I looked at the closed door of my room, wondering where Dylan was.

"He let me in, Skylar. Don't try to run away."

His fingers started dancing over my skin, right above the line where the towel stopped. With feathery touches, he dragged his hand from the column of my throat, to the breastbone, teasing me, drawing me closer

111

into his embrace.

I could almost taste the danger he brought with him. I knew his type, all too well. I knew it because his type was what I always went for.

Dark, dangerous, and toxic.

The way he watched me, the way he touched me, it all held the promise of the sweet violence my body craved. I wanted pain because I wanted oblivion. I wanted drugs because I wanted to forget.

I wanted to stop feeling, because the turmoil in my gut was too much to deal with. I was drawn to him.

I didn't know why or how, but it was as if the light switch was turned on inside, and I craved the fire he carried in his eyes. But I had to remember the things I needed to do, the things I promised to deliver. I could already feel the pain I would be in if I didn't or if I misbehaved.

"You've been ignoring me, darling." He leaned down until his lips were a whisper away from mine. "And I hate being ignored."

"Ash," I protested, but it sounded more like a moan, and it was all it took for him to press his lips to mine and to push me to the wall.

My lower back protested as he pressed his body to mine. As his hands sneaked around my neck, holding me tight, his teeth clamped on my lower lip, pulling a moan from my chest. His other hand went underneath the towel, traveling over my thigh, until he reached my hip and pulled my leg up, wrapping it around him.

He pulled back and started rubbing his thumb over my lower lip as my breathing became erratic. I couldn't speak. I couldn't think, and just when I thought he was going to pull away, he leaned down again, his sleek tongue seeking entrance. Our teeth knocked against each other as I finally opened my mouth, letting him in. I wrapped my arm around his neck, pressing our chests together.

A familiar fire burned at the pit of my stomach, and as he held my leg around his hip, I started rotating my hips, seeking friction, trying to feed the need spreading throughout my body.

"Ash," I moaned in his mouth. "We can't—"

He cut me off with another kiss, pulling, biting, kissing, soothing, driving me wild. His other hand disappeared underneath the towel, and when his fingers finally touched the skin of my lower stomach, I was ready to combust.

"God—"

"God has nothing to do with this, Skylar." He smirked. He pressed his thumb against my clit, sending shock waves of pleasure throughout my body. "There's only me."

He bit down on my collarbone as he dragged his other finger from my opening to my clit, teasing me.

"Please," I cried out.

"Please what?" His teeth clamped on my neck, followed by his lips as he soothed the spot.

"Please fuck me with your fingers."

I didn't have to ask twice. As his lips landed on mine, his two fingers entered me, pressing on the sweet spot inside my pussy.

"Holy fucking shit." I started moving my hips, crazy with need and desire.

"That's it. Use my fingers."

And I did. I swiveled my hips while he held his fingers there, at the same time kissing me, biting me, leaving his marks over my body. He suddenly started moving, quickening the pace of his fingers, and as the familiar burn started, I started moving more, seeking more, asking for the release.

"Do you want to come, Skylar?" His eyes flashed with unspoken desire as he asked. The midnight blue was barely visible from his enlarged irises.

"Yes!" I screamed.

He slowed down, grinning the entire time. "Yes, what?"

"Yes, please."

"Good girl." His words registered in my brain, but I was too far gone to care about anything else but the friction of his fingers over my clit and inside my body. I needed more, more, more, and as if reading my mind, he pressed harder on my clit, and entered me with a third finger.

He stretched me wide, pain swirling in my brain with pleasure, and I was—

"Oh. My. God. Ash!"

"Shhh." He pressed his forehead to mine. "We don't want your brother to know what a dirty girl you are."

"Please. I'm begging you." My entire body was trembling, preparing for the eruption.

He brushed against the same spot again, and the moan erupted from my chest, caught by his lips. He devoured me, ate me alive, and I allowed it because this was better than what I did to myself last night. This high was better than what drugs could ever give me.

In and out, his fingers kept pummeling. When my eyes started rolling to the back of my head, he increased the pressure, until the sweet eruption I was chasing tore through my body, shaking me from head to toe. He kissed me, catching the moans threatening to spill over my lips, muffling them as I shook in his hands.

"Skylar?" Dylan's voice suddenly echoed around the room, as he started knocking on the door. "Why is the door locked?" he asked, and I threw an accusatory look at Ash.

He smiled as he removed his hand from me and licked his fingers.

"He doesn't know you're here?" I whispered, afraid that Dylan would hear us.

"Skylar?" Dylan knocked again. "Is everything okay in there?"

"Y-Yeah," I croaked. "I just had a shower. Give me a second."

Silence and then, "Breakfast is ready. Just hurry up."

"Will do!" I answered, trying to calm my racing heart.

I turned to Ash who took a step back and sat on my bed.

"What the fuck, Ash?" I tightened the towel around my body, suddenly feeling shy in his presence. "How did you get up here?"

"Balcony." He pointed to the open door, leading to my balcony. "I must say, I like this whole hide-and-seek."

"There's no hide-and-seek, you asshole." I walked to the sliding door leading to the balcony, remembering that it had definitely been closed before I went to the bathroom. He was suddenly behind me, leaving a blazing inferno on my skin as his fingers traced the path from my shoulder to my hand.

"No? Then why don't we go downstairs, and I could have breakfast with you and your brother."

"Ash." My voice shook. "You need to go."

"And what if I don't want to?" he asked, turning me around. "What if I want to play?"

"Ash—"

He lowered his head, pressing his lips against my pulse. "What." *Kiss*. "If." *Bite*. "I want to." *Suck*. "Stay here with you?"

My body tingled everywhere he touched, and I fought against this attraction I felt toward him.

"No." I pushed him away. "We can't do this."

The playful smirk he wore earlier disappeared, replaced by a wicked smile and the promise of retribution in his eyes.

"We'll see about that." He came closer and placed a kiss on my cheek. "I'll see you later. Have fun with your brother."

He exited through the sliding door, taking away all the warmth I'd been feeling with him.

What in the ever-loving fuck was that?

NINE

ASH

My lips still vibrated, remembering the feeling of her lips on mine. Her taste, her touch, her moans and cries, they were already etched in my mind. I expected to feel disgusted, revolted, but my body wasn't listening to my mind, and I wanted more.

I wanted to bite, lick, and suck every inch of her body, and I couldn't, because succumbing to my desires would mean betraying my family. Skylar Blackwood was my enemy. Her entire family was an enemy we vowed to eradicate. It didn't matter that my body wanted to feel her hands on me, my mind had to win this war. It didn't matter that she tasted like the sweetest sin, and I wouldn't mind being the sinner, or that her eyes flashed with desire that could consume me, because she was who she was and I was on the opposite side.

We weren't a match made in heaven, but she didn't know it yet. I could see it there, the fight she was trying to start, how she tried to push me away, but she felt this just as much as I did. She just didn't know that what we felt meant nothing, because there were forces stronger than our desire.

I made a promise when I was just a child and I planned to fulfill it. Nothing, and nobody, least of all a

Blackwood, would stand in my way. I waited my whole life for the moment when I would be able to avenge my parents for what the other founding families did to us. The scars on my back were the constant reminder of that vicious night, when they betrayed us, throwing us aside.

Now was the time to get it all back. To get the Crowell name back into town.

They thought they destroyed us all, but they forgot the first rule — never leave any survivors. And me and my brother, Sebastian, we were the survivors. We were going to be their worst nightmare. They just didn't know it yet.

As I drove down the street toward the bridge connecting the two sides of Winworth, I couldn't stop thinking about the sick history this place had. Winworth had so much beauty and so much depravity, that no matter what we did in the upcoming years, nothing would cleanse it from its sins. My uncle used to say that there were places on earth whose soil was filled with so much blood, that nothing good ever came out of them.

Winworth was one of them.

I always wanted to laugh when people talked about the history of this place, and the alleged witches that had escaped the trials and settled here. They weren't completely wrong, but it wasn't the witches that built this town from the ground up. No, there were darker forces that played their wicked games here, building the town on skeletons of those they sacrificed.

When our ancestors came from Europe, they didn't just bring their families, food, and clothes, they brought something much darker, wicked in its nature.

The Black Dahlia.

The worshippers of Satan. Sons and daughters of Central and Eastern European pagans, who hid under the cloak of night, worshipping the dark forces rummaging through earth. They hid until the church found out about their wicked deeds and then they had to run.

And they ran, until they came here, loving the nature and seclusion this area offered. Loving it so much that they decided to shower its soil with the blood of their sacrifices. And my family was one of them. My ancestors were one of those who came here, and who destroyed the land and everything surrounding it. They poisoned young minds, turning brothers against each other, taking children in the middle of the night, and controlling the entire town.

They were still doing it.

The Order was created by five families, who tried to gain more power, more money, more territory, because what they had wasn't enough for them. Others followed, seeing the growing riches of those families, thinking it was all due to the satanic worshipping they were doing.

I liked to think that they managed to get more money and more power because they were shrewd, ruthless, and without remorse. Because they knew how to play people, how to get what they wanted using their silver tongues and the money they already had. They sold their souls for power, tricking others to join them, making them believe in the dark forces.

But there was never Satan or a demon who came to claim their souls. People loved blaming the underworld for their depraved deeds, because they didn't want to accept that their souls craved it and Heaven or Hell had nothing to do with it.

Unfortunately, I didn't know enough about the Black Dahlia to strike immediately, which was why I needed to be here. I needed to learn their secrets, to get to their meetings, because you couldn't take down the empire from the outside. No, you had to get in, make them trust you, make them see you as one of their own.

Our uncle was never a part of The Order since he wasn't related to us by blood. He and our father were best friends, who met at university, sharing the same love for history and the written word. Before he died, our father shared some things with our uncle, but not enough for us to understand how everything worked.

Besides, I couldn't go against the four most powerful families in the United States with only memories of a traumatized kid and a couple of documents that only mentioned meetings and those involved, but nothing else.

Our father wanted to leave The Order and Winworth. When I was six years old, he and our mom were getting ready to leave all of this behind and disappear when the Blackwood, St. Clare, Lacroix, and Maddox families decided that the only way to leave this place was in a body bag. So they hunted us, burned our house down, and killed my parents in front of my eyes.

I still couldn't remember how Sebastian and I got away. Maybe we were lucky or maybe somebody saved us, but it took me years to remember everything about that night. Years to understand that my parents dying wasn't just a freak accident, but an act of monstrous human beings who didn't want to risk their secrets.

I could still remember cloaked figures surrounding us, chanting the song of death, and my mother's tear-stained face as she pleaded with them to let us go. Sebastian was four at the time, and I was glad that he didn't remember any of it. I, on the other hand, remembered everything.

I remembered Judah Blackwood as he held the dagger against my father's throat. I remembered Harlow St. Clare as she laughed at my mother, while she held me against her body, squeezing my arm until I screamed.

The people that lived here didn't know that they were surrounded by snakes. They didn't know that they were being fed with poison since the day they were born. They were the prisoners of the town that never wanted to let them go. The missing girls, the whispers in the dark, they were doing it again.

They were preparing for Samhain.

My phone rang, breaking through my thoughts. I picked it up from the passenger seat and looked at the screen.

"Aren't you supposed to be in school?" I asked as soon as I placed the phone to my ear, hearing the chuckle from the other side.

"Well, we're both supposed to be in school, but that apparently isn't happening today," Sebastian answered. "Where did you go?"

"I had something to do." I didn't want to talk about her with him. Unlike our uncle and me, he was still convinced that nobody had to get hurt. That we could just go to the police and report everything we knew about the Black Dahlia.

If only it was that simple.

Judah Blackwood controlled this area in more ways than one, and Harlow St. Clare held the reins in his pharmaceutical company as a CEO, while he shook hands with other politicians, plastering a fake smile on his face. The Maddox family controlled the police here and the Lacroix family owned Lacroix Corp., an investment company in Chicago.

Wherever you turned, they would have their hands on it. Not to mention that most of them had connections deeper in the underground with the Russian Syndicate and the Outfit. No, these weren't the people that you could just report to the police.

Besides, who would believe us? The reports for our

parents' deaths showed that it was a freak fire caused by faulty electrical wires. It was even signed by the chief of police, and by the time firefighters arrived at the scene, the house we used to live in was already burned to the ground, leaving nothing but ashes and pain behind.

"You had something or someone to do?" he asked, snickering at the same time. I told him about my plan for Skylar, but Sebastian being Sebastian was adamant to change my mind. After seeing her picture on *Snapgram*, he started nudging me to go after her for all the wrong reasons.

"None of your business, baby brother."

"Argh," he groaned. "Can we please lose that nickname? Please?"

"No can do, baby bro," I teased. "You are younger than me."

"Only two years younger. I'm sixteen not six, and if you saw how some of the girls were eyeing me, you wouldn't be using that name on me."

"Hmm, do they know about the blanket—"

"No, Ash," he threatened. "Don't you dare."

The story about the blanket he used to carry around as a child always worked.

"As much as I love hearing your lovely voice…" I started speaking as I parked in front of the pub a few feet from the bridge. "I would like to know why you're calling me."

"I need to ask you for a favor."

I turned the ignition off and unfastened my seatbelt. "I'm listening."

He hesitated for a moment, the line going silent.

"Seb—"

"I want you to teach me how to drive," he blurted out, piercing my heart.

Our dad or mom was supposed to teach him how to

do that, not me. I loved our uncle, but he knew more about cars than kids, and most of the time it was up to me to make sure that Sebastian wasn't walking with his shirt inside out, or that he actually did his homework. After he found out about our parents' death and after we came to him, it was as if the only thing he could think of was revenge against the people in this town.

I never really asked why or how, but I had a feeling that it went further than just not liking what they were doing to innocent people, or what they did to his friends.

"Ash?" Sebastian's voice tore through my thoughts. "Will you do it? I understand if you can't, but—"

"Of course I'll do it, Seb." I dragged a hand over my face, hating that he had to ask me. If our parents were alive and he asked me the same thing, I wouldn't hesitate to say yes, but that hole in my chest where they used to be seemed to expand even more with this request. "When do you want to start?"

"Really?" His voice, laced with excitement, drew the first real smile today from me. "You'll do it?"

"I'll do it. I don't know why you sound so surprised."

"Well…" he cleared his throat. "You've been quite busy with… things."

Things being the plan to avenge our parents and use the kids from the other four founding families to get in.

"Seb—"

"It's okay, Ash. I understand, trust me I do. Or at least, I try to understand. I just wish that there was another way."

I wasn't sure if I wanted to do this any other way.

They deserved to pay for what they did. They deserved to have their perfect little worlds shattered just how they shattered ours. They deserved to feel pain and despair, just like we did.

The only problem was that Sebastian couldn't understand that. I was both glad and displeased with that. Glad, because that meant that my brother was a much better person than I was, and displeased, because he mostly didn't want to have anything to do with our plans. But he was still my brother, and even if he refused to accept the truth, that these people wouldn't hesitate to kill both of us, I would still protect him.

"Seb," I took a deep breath before continuing, "how about this weekend? We can start then, and we'll see how it goes."

"Really?" The excitement in his voice pulled at my heartstrings. I couldn't remember when the last time he sounded like this was.

He protested when Uncle Neal and I announced that we would be returning to Winworth this year. We grew up in New York and Sebastian didn't want to leave the life he had there. Maybe if I had something worthy of staying for, I wouldn't have wanted to leave either, but my entire life has been dedicated to this. I didn't know anything better.

When I was eleven years old, Uncle Neal bought me my first knife and taught me how to use it. When I was thirteen, he bought me a handgun and brought me to a clear field, showing me how to shoot at the target. At the age of fifteen, when all my friends celebrated the end of the school year, I was spending my nights reading about Winworth and its most prominent families.

Sebastian tried to fight us on this decision. He begged us to stay in New York, to stay with his friends, to not be a part of this battle, this war, yet he still couldn't understand that we weren't merely following this battle. No, it came to us because of who we were, because of our last name. And as long as these people lived freely, we wouldn't be safe.

When we left Winworth after our parents' deaths, Uncle Neal lived in Texas, but we had to be constantly on the move. I couldn't even remember how many schools we had to change because one of Judah's spies was closing in on us.

Sebastian couldn't understand because he was too young when it all happened. I couldn't force him to understand, but I could protect him even when he thought that he didn't need protection. Leaving him behind simply wasn't an option, and even though he sulked and pouted for the last two months since we came to Winworth, he had to stay.

There was no other way.

And this sign of happiness, of excitement, was the first since we came here. I just hoped that he would be able to find more things to be excited about while we were in Winworth.

"Yeah, really." I laughed. A lone figure entering the pub drew my attention, and I knew it was time to let Sebastian go. "Hey, listen. I gotta go, but I'll see you later. Okay?"

I opened the door, welcoming the fresh morning air coursing through Winworth. For all its depravity, it did have nature like no other place. The cities we used to live in were usually crowded, much bigger, and a lot more polluted. Here, the people actually cared about the river and the surrounding area.

"Okay," Sebastian answered. "Are you gonna be home for dinner?"

I stepped outside of the car and slammed the door behind me. "I don't know," I said as I started walking toward the pub. "I'll let you know. I'm not sure what my plans are for the day." I did know, I just didn't want him to even think of snooping and trying to befriend those serpents.

"All righty. I'll see you later then."

"Bye," I mumbled and cut the call off. I wasn't sure if he was in school or at home, but wherever he was, I just hoped he wasn't going to get into trouble. Sebastian was too trusting, too naïve for this world we lived in. If we weren't careful, he would become just another casualty of this war, and I couldn't allow that.

I pulled my other phone, checking the screen for any missed calls. As expected, there was a message waiting for me.

Cerberus is in place.

Good.

With hurried steps, I crossed over the sidewalk and headed straight for the pub. A dark Harley-Davidson stood a couple of feet away from the entrance, closer to the bridge than this side. I hadn't seen it before, and it had an insignia that I have never seen.

Could it be?

An elderly couple exited the pub, holding hands and smiling at each other. I couldn't help but think if our parents would be the same if they managed to live long enough to reach this age. Unfortunately, I didn't have time to dwell on what-ifs and the things that could never happen. I pushed past them and entered the pub.

I hadn't been here before, but I visited enough pubs when we traveled to Germany to know that they definitely got the idea from there. The interior was mainly decorated with wood, from the walls to the floors, giving the medieval feeling to it all. Two crossed swords were the first thing you could see, standing proud just behind the bar, manned by one bartender. I looked around, noticing that it wasn't as busy as I expected it to be.

The entire side of the pub was covered with windows, and I could see the river surrounded by trees.

The balcony on that side was mainly empty, sans the one lone figure I saw entering the pub earlier. The cigarette he had between his lips lit up as he flicked the lighter in his hand, and he started looking over the edge of the balcony, toward the river.

I had never seen him before, but something told me that this was my guy.

I nodded at the bartender as I crossed past the bar and between the tables, heading directly to the balcony. The stranger pushed the hoodie off his head, revealing the dark hair—longer on the top and cut short on the sides—and the array of tattoos peeking through his collar. He looked around until his eyes landed on me, and his lips pulled at the side, in what he probably thought was a smile.

I've seen scary people in my life, angry people, but I had never met anybody like him.

As I exited through the glass door, leading to the balcony, my face was hit by the wind that was colder than on the other side. I pulled the collar of my coat higher, trying to shield myself from the cold, while he stared at me. I wasn't fazed by a lot of things, and people often told me that I looked like I didn't give a shit about anything—and I mostly didn't—but this guy looked like he could eat me for breakfast, and just continue with his day as if nothing happened.

"Are you Lars?" I asked as soon as I stepped closer to him. The cigarette he lit earlier dangled from his fingers as he leaned back, staring at me.

"Maybe," he answered with a cold expression on his face, pulling another drag of the cigarette. "Are you the Crow?"

I pulled the chair opposite of him and sat down. "Maybe. You don't look like somebody called Lars." I smirked and took the packet of cigarettes in front of him, opened it, and pulled one out.

"I don't?" He grinned as I lit up the lighter and placed the tip of the cigarette on fire, letting the smoke coat my insides with one inhale.

"No," I answered through the cloud of smoke I exhaled. "You definitely don't."

He kept looking at me, unmoving, studying me. I always hated when people did that. Skylar did that as well. She kept staring at people, trying to read them, to gauge their reactions. I bet it pissed her off when she couldn't see past the mask I chose to wear.

"I like you, kid." He laughed and extinguished the cigarette, only halfway done. "I'm Indigo."

He removed the zipped hoodie he had on, revealing a cut with an emblem I saw once before, when we were moving from San Francisco to Orlando.

Sons of Hades.

We all heard the stories about them. The gruesome tales used to scare the kids at night. They were a walking nightmare, and he was here, meeting with me. I didn't like this. I didn't like this at all.

"Relax, kid." He chuckled. "You look like you've seen a ghost."

I cleared my throat and leaned back, still looking at the emblem. "I've heard of you guys."

"Oh, really?" His eyebrows shot up. "Then I can assure you that whatever you've heard," he leaned toward me, "the truth is ten times worse."

For the first time since we came here, I was scared.

Six months ago, a guy named Lars contacted us, offering to help us execute our plan. We never met him, never learned his last name or where he came from, but he had information on The Order that no one else did. After careful consideration, we decided to go with it, and to let him feed us the information we were missing.

For example, every twenty or so years, The Order had to choose a new leader, a new high priest, and for that to happen, the sacrifices had to be made. It bothered me that we didn't know his real identity, but everything he told us was true.

"Right," I mumbled. "I'm sure you have better things to do. I was told you would have information for us. Well, Lars said—"

"Yeah, I know what Lars said, but I'm not exactly sure if you would want to know this."

"What do you mean?"

"I mean," he looked around us as if he expected someone to be listening, "some things should be left alone. Some things should be handled by adults, kid. And some—"

"First of all," I interrupted. "I was never a kid. They didn't give me a chance to be a kid. Do you know what it feels like to lose everything you loved?"

"As a matter of fact, I do. I also know that look in your eyes, because I've seen it before on someone very close to me. And do you know where he is now?" His eyes narrowed at me. "In the fucking hospital, fighting for his life, because he was too reckless, too blinded by revenge, that he didn't plan shit properly. So, I'm gonna ask you only once. Did you think this through with a cool head, or are you going to end up getting killed in the process?"

He took a mouthful of water, all the while looking at me. He wanted to know if I was reckless, if this plan wasn't going to end up with me six feet under. Truth be told, I didn't know.

I had no idea if getting close to them wouldn't end up with me in a body bag, failing to fulfill what I had promised. But I did know that I wouldn't be able to sleep at night if I didn't see this through. I knew that if it wasn't for these people, for this town, I would have had a happy childhood, or at least, a childhood with both of my parents alive.

I wouldn't have this constant burden on my shoulders, this constant pain in my gut, and the scars on my back if it wasn't for them. Maybe I was too reckless.

I was recklessly getting involved with Skylar Blackwood, but I liked to think that I was just doing my part to secure that spot in The Order. Taunting her brother this morning wasn't the best idea, but I couldn't resist.

When he looked at me like I was a mere peasant, I couldn't stop taunting him with everything Skylar and myself allegedly did. I could see it then, the same darkness swirling in his eyes, like it did in his father's. I just knew that he was a part of it, that he knew everything there was to know about the Black Dahlia, and I had to push him.

Maybe it wasn't the smartest idea, considering that he would be one of those voting for me to be a part of The Order. Maybe getting myself tangled with Skylar wasn't the smartest idea either, but I couldn't resist. I had to know the girl I only ever saw through pictures and stories. I had to know if she was worthy of saving or if she was just like everybody else.

"We have a plan, Indigo. A proper plan, not that it's any of your business. I wouldn't be sitting here with you if I didn't have one. Lars trusts us enough to share the information we need in order to take them down. So, are you going to continue sitting there, acting like a concerned parent, or are you going to tell me everything you know?"

Brutality was second nature for these guys, and I knew that if I pissed him off, I wouldn't be getting what I needed. But dammit, he was pissing me off. He was feigning concern when he didn't know anything about us. Just because his friend fucked up, that didn't mean that I would too.

Uncle Neal taught me well, and with him being an ex-military, I knew more about weapons than an eighteen-year-old should know, but it was necessary. If we were to get out of here alive, we had to know how to defend ourselves, if it came to that.

"Okay," he finally answered.

"Okay?"

"Yeah, kid. Okay. But you will need allies. These people." He scoffed. "If we can even call them that, they have connections everywhere. The things they've been doing over the years..." He trailed off. "I'm not gonna bother you with that, but you need to know what you're getting into."

"Are you talking about the Syndicate?" I asked.

"You know about that, huh?" He smiled. "Maybe you do have a proper plan."

"Yeah, maybe I do." I had to know.

"The leader of the Syndicate, Nikolai Aster, is dead." That was news. "With him being dead, they will be extremely careful with the outsiders and the new members. You already know about their freaky Samhain rituals, and the new high priest, right?"

"Yeah, Lars told us about that."

"Well, the thing that Lars didn't tell you is that their meetings aren't held in some house here."

"What do you mean?" I placed my elbows on the table, leaning closer to him.

"Winworth has catacombs underneath the ground. Catacombs that are spread all around the town, built by the first settlers, the first families."

Catacombs?

"They're keeping their ceremonies there, in the

main chamber, located underneath City Hall," he continued. "Only the members have those keys. While Lars knows where the entrance is, he can't tell you how to get in. That area is under surveillance twenty-four-seven, and The Order has guards keeping it away from curious eyes."

"Where is it?" I asked, anticipation building up in me. This would be the first step to getting to them. If I couldn't infiltrate The Order, then I could send the authorities to their hiding places. Even Judah Blackwood wouldn't be able to get out of that. But I also needed documents, to prove their involvement with recent deaths and disappearances. I had to find something that could connect them with my parents' deaths.

"Are you sure you want to know?"

"What do you think?" I huffed.

"Then what's your plan?" He looked unconvinced, and I understood why. Here I was, basically a child in his eyes, trying to take down an entire dark empire. "You said you have one."

"I do." I grinned. "I'm going to become a part of The Order. The best way to take them down and find out everything I need to know is if I am there, with them."

"And you don't think that's idiotic and reckless? Wait, fuck idiotic and reckless, how are you going to pull that off?"

"Because I'm a legacy." I smiled wider. "I'm a Crowell."

TEN

SKYLAR

"Why are you all dressed up?" Dylan asked as soon as I came down for breakfast.

It was weird seeing him at the table after so many months, but it felt good having him here. Even if his nagging was going to drive me crazy if he continued like this.

"Um, I'm going to school?" It sounded more like a question than an answer, and the narrowing of his eyes told me everything I needed to know.

"No, you're not."

"Excuse me?" I came closer to the table, vexed with his entire demeanor. "You can't tell me what to do, Dy."

Seated at the head of the table, he kept looking at me, all the while holding a croissant in his hand. I loved my brother, adored him, but he could irritate me like no other person could. When we were kids, he would fuss if I fell, hovering over me like a mother hen. If he noticed I was sad, he wouldn't let it go until I told him what bothered me. When Zane died, he wanted to stop his studies, so that he could stay at home and take care of me.

As if he needed to take care of me.

The moment Ash left, and after overthinking the entire thing, my body still tingling from his touches, I knew that Dylan was going to pull something like this. It wasn't in his nature to let things go, and the mere possibility of me being in danger was going to turn him into an overbearing and overprotective brother. That was the side of him I didn't love all too much.

As soon as I started dating Zane, he started hating him. If he called, Dylan would get annoyed. If he came over, Dylan would rather choose not to be around, than stay and watch a movie with us. The number of times I had to beg him to behave was exorbitant, and I never wanted to deal with that version of him again.

If I didn't know any better, I would go as far as to say that he was jealous.

"Sky." He took a deep breath, as if preparing himself to talk to a small child. "You went through a lot yesterday."

"And yet, I am fine!" I thundered. "You can't expect me to stay here the whole day. Life goes on. What I saw and what happened yesterday... Well, I can't do anything about it."

"Somebody carved your name into that girl's chest!" he bellowed, slamming his fist on the table.

"H-how," I stammered. "How do you know about that?"

He fisted his hand, glaring at the table, refusing to look at me. I hoped that he wouldn't find out about that. It was bad enough that the entire police force of Winworth knew, but I wanted to spare him the details. Or maybe I just didn't want to think about that. And maybe, just maybe, I wanted to pretend that the name on Megan's body wasn't the same as mine.

"That officer from yesterday called. He wants you to come down to the station to give your statement."

"But I don't know anything," I argued. "If I hadn't slipped, I wouldn't have found her and —"

"No, Sky." He finally looked at me. "If you hadn't gone into the fucking forest, and I told you a million times that you guys shouldn't be wandering through there, you wouldn't be in this situation."

I sat there, gawking at him as his words registered in my head.

"Well, I am extremely sorry that you didn't get a sister that would sit at home and do nothing but go to school," I sneered. "But you're stuck with me. I refuse to play the part of the perfect little daughter and the perfect little sister, while you guys do whatever the fuck you want to. I'm not a child—"

"Then stop acting like one!" he roared, catching me by surprise.

Dylan never yelled at me. Hell, he never ever raised his voice around me. This side of him was something I hadn't seen before. After yesterday and Ash this morning, the last thing I wanted was to have to deal with whatever crawled up his ass.

Stupefied, I studied him and the sharp intakes of breath he was taking, but I couldn't say a word. I didn't ask for special treatment because we found a body in the forest. I never asked for anything. Yet he loved pretending that I was still a little girl who didn't know how the world worked. If only he knew... If only he knew about the things that were hiding inside my head.

If only he knew that I wasn't a little girl anymore, because I wasn't allowed to be. I refused to sit here while he unleashed all his fury at me.

"Where are you going?" he asked as I stood up and started heading toward the exit from the kitchen. We usually had breakfast here, rather than in the dining room, but the idiot managed to make me lose my appetite in a matter of minutes. "Skylar?" he bellowed when I continued walking without answering.

135

"Goddammit," sounded behind me, but he could go and fuck himself if this was how he imagined this day to go. His footsteps echoed around the hallway, and as I rounded the corner heading toward the large staircase, leading to the first floor, his hand wrapped around my arm, turning me to him.

Only lit by the wall lamp, his face looked more dangerous than ever before, but I was too tired of men throwing me to this and that side and expecting me to do only what they wanted me to do. My father wanted me to attend the university in Seattle, Ash... Well, I still wasn't sure what exactly he wanted from me, but I was sure that he wanted something, and now Dylan was trying to control what I did and where I went.

I didn't like it.

He was supposed to be the one person in my life that would ask me what I wanted to do before making any decisions. And yes, I was a child. I was a goddamn teenager who had to deal with things that no other teenager could even comprehend.

"Where are you going?" he asked again, pulling me closer to him.

His body heat enveloped around me, and in the tiny hallway, he seemed to be everywhere. I always wanted to know how he managed to be both scary and caring at the same time. Even though he held me to him, he wasn't hurting me.

But men never hurt us intentionally, at least not at first.

It always starts small, with punishing touches, poisonous words and restrictions that only make sense to them. And if Dylan was going to be that kind of a man, I didn't want to be with him today.

"Where do you think I'm going?" I reverted back, pulling my arm free from him, but he didn't budge. "Let go of me, Dylan."

"Sky," he whispered, placing his other hand around my neck. "Don't be mad at me. I can't stand it when you're mad at me."

"Dylan—"

"Look at me," he requested, but I kept staring at his neck instead of his eyes. "Please." His lips pressed against my forehead as his thumb played against the pulse on my neck. "Gimme those pretty eyes, Little One."

"I'm really pissed off at you," I mumbled, refusing to look at him. "Like, really, really pissed."

"I know, I know." He hugged me to him, cradling my head against his chest. "I shouldn't have said that. I'm sorry."

He started making circles on my back with one of his hands, while still holding me to him. I was pissed at him, but I was also glad he was here. I could torment myself and him, and hold a grudge, but I had no idea how long he was going to stay, and who knew when I would be seeing him next.

"Forgive me?" he asked, taking a step back, holding my cheeks in his hands. "I'm just worried about you. There's a maniac out there, and we don't know if he or she is targeting you or if the name was randomly placed, but I don't want to see you hurt."

"I won't be hurt." I placed my hands on his wrists, squeezing him, trying to reassure him. "But if you lock me inside, I will go crazy. I need to feel normal. I need to put this behind me and continue living."

A moment of silence, a moment too long, and when his eyes softened, when the Dylan I always knew came back to me, I knew I had him.

"All right," he said. "Get your things. I'll drive you to school."

"Really?" I smiled. "You're not gonna go all caveman on me and demand I stay at home, get married, and have ten million kids."

He pinched my side, finally smiling. "Smartass. Who said I would ever let you get married? No one would ever be good enough for you."

"Oh, I don't know. I have a couple of candidates," I joked, taking a step back, slowly exiting the hallway.

"Is that right?"

"I mean, you'll have to let me go one day."

Something passed over his face, something foreign, just like last night, but before I could even think about it, it vanished, replaced by an easy-going smile.

"I will never be able to let you go, Sky. You're the best thing that life has ever given me."

My throat closed, emotions flooding through my body. He always knew what to say and when to say it, to make me feel better about myself.

"And you are the best thing life has given me as well, Dylan. You'll always be my favorite." I sniffed as I started heading toward the stairs. "Oh hey," I stopped, remembering the voices, knowing that Ash talked to him. "I thought I heard you talking with somebody before and doors closing. Who was it?"

With his hands on his hips, he stood there, watching me. "Just some guy trying to sell something. I told them we weren't interested."

"Huh." Really? Why didn't he want to tell me about Ash?

"Hurry up," his voice boomed around the foyer. "I need to finish something in town after I drop you off."

He started walking toward the living room, and all the while I kept thinking—why did he lie to me?

The parking in front of the school was completely empty of people when we pulled in. When I looked at the clock, I figured that second period had already started and most of the students were already inside. Since you could see the parking area from the teachers' lounge, most of us avoided hanging out here if we were skipping classes. There were a few blind spots in the building, like that area beneath the stairs in the East Wing, or we simply left the school grounds completely.

Winworth High always seemed spooky to me, but without the students milling around, the darkening sky above felt almost sinister, and I suddenly wished that I had stayed at home. But if I started avoiding school because of what happened yesterday, knowing me, I wouldn't be back for the next three months. I was pretty sure that most of the student body already knew what happened. I just didn't know if they found out all the gritty details.

"Text me once you're done," Dylan spoke, breaking the silence in the car. "I'll pick you up."

I turned to the side, meeting his eyes. "I can catch a ride with one of the guys." I smiled. "But, if I decide to leave earlier, I'll let you know. We might go and hang out somewhere after school, so—"

"Skylar," he groaned.

"What? Oh, don't give me that look," I chastised.

"It's not safe."

"It never is safe in Winworth. Look around you, dear brother. This is the freakiest place in the northern part of the United States. Finding a dead body here is like buying street food in Thailand."

"I don't like this," he argued. "I don't want you hanging out at those creepy places."

"How do you know about our creepy places?" I

lifted an eyebrow. "Those are supposed to be secret."

"Come on." He started laughing. "The crypt, the old amusement park? I was your age once, and we didn't exactly hang out at the coffee shop down the street."

He did have a point. There were only so many places in Winworth where a bunch of teenagers could hide. We preferred the old amusement park on the clearing that was overlooking the East Side, but it was too far away from the school, and the crypt was easier to go to when school was on.

"Well," I opened the door, "I'll be careful. I'll see you later, okay?"

"All right." He huffed, obviously unhappy with me, but I didn't want to live my life in fear. I was scared, of course I was, but whoever killed Megan most probably already left town.

"I love you, Dylan," I yelled as I exited the car.

"I love you, too," he answered. "Be careful!"

"Always, Dy. Always." I smiled and closed the door, turning to the school.

God, I fucking hated this period between the summer and the winter. Winworth had only two seasons — extremely warm summer, and freezing winter. We loved taking trips to Emercroft Lake during the summer, escaping for a day or two, and it wasn't too far away. But winters here... Don't get me fucking started.

If it wasn't raining during October and November, it would be freezing cold. And December was just one big nope for me, with its foggy days and excessive amounts of snow. I had a friend in California who always moaned about wanting to live in a place with a proper winter, but he didn't know that those pretty commercials for Christmas were nothing like reality. Snow looked pretty at first, but then it usually became mixed with mud and water, and the next thing you knew, it was just shitty.

With hurried steps, I crossed over the parking lot, hearing the rumble of Dylan's car fade, leaving me all alone. Fucking crows were visible in the sky, flying low above the school. No wonder they chose them to be the official mascot of the school and the entire town. I had a feeling that they were always here, always croaking, always bringing this sinister feeling with them.

I pulled my phone out, checking the time, only to see an unopened message from an unknown number.

Huh?

The sliding door opened in front of me while I unlocked the phone, seeing the number on the screen for the first time in my life. I clicked the icon for my messages, going directly for the newest one.

Unknown: Did you like my little gift?

I passed by the lockers, heading directly toward mine at the other end of the hallway.

Me: Who is this?

I wrote as I stopped in front of my locker, near the biology classroom. I dropped my bag on the floor and turned to the locker, entering the combination on the lock. My phone vibrated again.

Unknown: Your beginning.

What the fuck?

Unknown: And your end.

Me: No, seriously. Who is this? If this is some weird prank, just stop wasting my time.

I placed my phone back into my pocket.

The lock opened with a click, and I picked my bag up, taking the notebook I would need for trigonometry. The bell started ringing, indicating the end of the period, as my phone started vibrating in my pocket again. I pulled it out, not expecting more messages from the unknown number.

Unknown: You still didn't tell me if you liked my gift.

The message was followed by a picture. A picture I never wanted to see again. A picture of a face that kept haunting me over and over again since yesterday.

Megan's tear-stained face was displayed on my screen. She had a gag in her mouth. She looked petrified, pleading with whoever was behind the camera.

Unknown: Did you like it?

Me: Who the fuck is this?

I typed with shaky hands, not believing what I was seeing.

Unknown: You'll find out soon.

Me: I'm going to the police with this, you sick fuck.

I clicked *Send* and started walking toward the classroom on the other end of the hallway. I could feel the erratic beat of my heart, threatening to jump out of my chest.

I had to show this to somebody. That officer from yesterday, maybe?

Unknown: Do that and you will never see your friend Hailey again.

Another picture popped up, only this time it wasn't Megan. I knew the backpack in the picture, and that chocolate-brown hair. I also knew the street she was walking on, heading to the school. He was right behind Hailey, and she didn't even realize it.

Me: No, don't hurt her.

I pleaded, typing as fast as I could.

Unknown: Then you will have to keep quiet.

Me: Yes, yes, I promise.

I could feel tears threatening to spill over my lids, but I couldn't lose my cool now. I took a deep breath and started typing again.

Me: Why are you doing this?

Unknown: I'm doing it for us, for our future. You'll see. We're going to be perfect together because you were made for me.

A sob caught in my throat as the students started filling the hallway, heading to their next class. I stood frozen in place, staring at my phone and his words.

Me: What do you mean?

Unknown: You were always meant to be mine. Sempiternum meam.

The words on the screen were getting blurry, my breathing erratic, and when a hand landed on my shoulder, I screamed loud enough for everyone in the school to hear.

"Whoa," Beatrice spoke. "What the fuck, dude?"

I lifted my head, clutching my phone to my chest. Students around us stared, confused by my reaction, and I couldn't stop shaking.

"Sky, you look as pale as a ghost," she murmured, stepping closer to me. "Are you okay?" She pressed her hand on my forehead. "You're cold. Should you even be at school today?"

No. Yes. I didn't know anymore.

My stomach lurched, thinking about Megan, thinking about the killer that was messaging me. This definitely wasn't a prank. Somebody was out to get me. Somebody was hurting people in my name, and I had no idea who.

"Skylar?" Beatrice's face turned even more serious, and I knew I was scaring her.

"I'm fine." I smiled. "Just… I saw one of those jumpy videos, you know, and got scared." *Liar.*

How was I supposed to get out of this? What was I supposed to do?

"Are you sure?" She still didn't look convinced. "Because you don't look so good."

And I didn't feel so good, but I needed a moment to think about my options. Who the fuck was targeting me and who would go after my friends?

"Yeah, totally fine." I took a step backward, heading toward the trigonometry classroom. "I'll just get going, but I'll see you later. Okay?"

My cheeks hurt from smiling, but I couldn't let her see me upset. If she figured I was upset over something, she would definitely pass it to Kane, and then I would have to answer questions I didn't wanna hear.

Without waiting for her answer, I left her with confusion lacing her face, and pushed through the sea of students gathering in the middle of the hallway.

Just breathe, Skylar. Just fucking breathe and think. Who would do such a thing?

But no matter how hard I tried to think about the person behind this, I came up with nothing. My phone felt like fire in my hand, but I didn't dare put it in my pocket, still cradling it against my chest.

Somebody was killing people in my name, and I had no fucking idea why.

ELEVEN

ASH

I pulled onto the gravelly road, following the GPS to the address Danny sent me. I didn't go back to school after meeting Indigo, deciding to hang around the town for a bit and explore the area around City Hall.

I wasn't able to go inside, but the amount of surveillance cameras on the building told me that it would be harder to get in than I initially thought. The Order controlled the entire town, and I guess that it was smart of them to have the area covered, especially if the entrance to the catacombs was there. But I was also sure that there was another way, and I was going to find it.

If I managed to get my hands on the old maps of the town, I'm sure I would be able to find another entrance to the catacombs. If there was an entrance, there must be an exit as well, especially if they were built during the time when people were smuggling things underneath the cities, hiding from the watchful eyes of law enforcement.

It was almost three in the afternoon when Danny called me, telling me to meet them at the old amusement park. They didn't want to go to the crypt today; too close to school and too dangerous after what happened yesterday. I knew that Skylar found a body in the forest but I only found out whose body it was after the bartender mentioned it when I was paying for mine and Indigo's bill.

Megan, the girl that went missing last week, was found by Skylar and Lauren. No one knew who dropped her body there. I didn't have time to question Skylar about it this morning, and I wasn't lying—I came because she was avoiding me throughout the week, and that simply wouldn't work for what we had planned. On the other hand, I wanted to touch her again, to see her, inhale that sweet vanilla scent she carried around.

Some primal part of me wanted her close, even if she was an enemy. I don't know if she was going to be here today. After what she went through yesterday, I doubted that she would go to school, but maybe I was wrong. Danny didn't mention who was coming, and I just hoped Kane wouldn't be there.

After that scene at Lauren's house, I haven't seen him around school, but I knew he was there. He was feeling territorial over Skylar, that much was obvious, but what caught my attention was the fact that she wasn't exactly thrilled to be with him. I didn't know much about her, apart from the little snippets we were fed over the last couple of years, but she didn't seem like a sweet and quiet type who would just roll on her back and wait for a guy to tell her what to do.

Something in her pulled at the strings in me and knowing what she went through yesterday didn't sit well with the little monster sitting in my soul. No, the entire day I had the insane urge to go to her and make sure that she was okay. My entire body hummed with the need to be next to her, and after everything I found out today, after fighting with myself, I felt tired.

But I couldn't pass up the opportunity to hang out with them. They were the next generation, the ones that were going to be initiated — if they already weren't — and I wanted in. Uncle Neal didn't exactly agree with my plan, but he let it pass. We both knew that even if he didn't approve, I'd still do it.

I pulled up next to the black Mercedes G-Wagon and turned off my radio just as "Avalanches" by IAMX started blasting through the car. Two other cars were parked on my left side — a red Audi A7 and a silver-colored BMW. They were definitely here.

Turning the ignition off, I opened my door and took the packet of cigarettes I bought on the way. If the other day in the crypt was anything to go by, I assumed that they already had everything else we needed. Rich kids who had more money than brains usually went hand in hand with drugs, alcohol, and bad decisions.

I was probably a hypocrite for describing them like that because I wasn't known for the smartest decisions. But unlike them, I liked to think that I knew what was wrong and what was right.

The metal gates in front of me were wide open, and I could see the decaying Ferris wheel on the other side. I had no idea how long this amusement park was here, but I could see the appeal. Once you turned down the gravel road leading to this place, there were no houses and no people who could see them here.

Birds cawed in the distance as I walked down the path, following the voices coming from the park. I recognized Danny's and his brother Rowan's, followed by feminine laughter that definitely didn't belong to Skylar. Was she here?

And why was I feeling disappointed if she wasn't?

I lifted my head and looked toward the mountain covered in fog. Since we moved to Winworth, I could count the number of times it didn't look like this on the fingers of my left hand. Fog was the constant companion of Winworth, regardless of the season.

Gravelly pathway scrunched underneath my boots and rounding the corner where the old ticket counter sat, I found them hanging at the old merry-go-round, laughing at something.

"Ash!" Beatrice screeched and started running to me. "Oh, you're just in time."

She held a bottle of Grey Goose vodka in her right hand, and with the other one, she hugged me and started pushing me toward the others. Rowan nodded at me, while Danny jumped up from the ground and came over.

"I'm glad you made it," he said as Beatrice ran toward Skylar who was sitting on one of the plastic horses, looking at her phone. So, we were back at that?

"Yeah, me too," I mumbled. "What is this place?" I looked around, noticing that the place must have been older than I initially thought.

"This, my friend, is Infernum."

"Infernum?" Disbelief laced my voice.

"Yeah!" Beatrice laughed. "Well, what's left of it."

"This place was fully functional back in the '90s, but they shut it down and left it here to rot," Danny explained as we walked together. "Which kinda works for us, since it's a perfect place to hang out."

I nodded at him, and instead of taking a seat next to Beatrice, who kept petting the spot on the wooden floor of the merry-go-round, I approached the dark horse Skylar was sitting on, annoyed by the lack of attention from her side. My fingers had been literally inside of her this morning, and she didn't even bat an eye at my presence.

"Sky." I touched her shoulder, only for her to jump in the spot, almost falling off the horse. "Whoa, there." I steadied her before she could hit the ground.

Round, silver eyes connected with mine, fear

evident in them, completely different from the girl I saw this morning. Her blonde hair was tied in a ponytail, but even the makeup she had on her face couldn't hide the paleness of her skin, or the dark circles around her eyes.

How did I not notice them this morning?

Because you were too busy fucking with her head. My consciousness reared its ugly head.

I pushed those thoughts aside, and placed my hand on top of hers, feeling the soft skin and remembering how she looked this morning.

"Are you okay?" I asked when she said nothing, feeling the eyes of the other three on us.

"Yeah." She grinned, but it was as fake as it came, and I hated it. I didn't know why. I shouldn't care, but I wanted to see the smile I saw years ago in that picture. This cold and distant girl in front of me wasn't who I was expecting to meet. "Just a little jumpy."

"You can say that again," Beatrice chirped. "You've been acting weird the entire day."

"Bea," Rowan warned, but Skylar was already getting off the horse.

"Oh, excuse me, your highness, but I kinda found a dead body yesterday. I would like to see you acting completely normal after something like that."

"I didn't—" Beatrice started but Skylar cut her off.

"Save it."

All four of us stood there, transfixed as Skylar marched away from us, disappearing into one of the tents.

"What did I say?" Beatrice looked at Danny, then at Rowan, and lastly at me. "She was acting weird."

"Ah, Bea," Danny groaned. "Skylar is a bit traumatized."

"Yeah, I get that, but—"

"It's okay. She's gonna come back and you guys can

continue playing nice," Rowan said as he got up. "I'll go talk to her."

"No." I stepped down. "I'll do it."

I picked up the bottle of Grey Goose Beatrice had left on the ground and walked in the same direction Skylar disappeared to. It was already getting darker out here, thanks to the cloudy weather and the surrounding mountains. I missed having an extended summer, like we had while living in California, but I didn't miss the humidity that came with it.

I did love the fact that I could already wear boots, even though it was only September, and they definitely helped as I went through the puddles leading to the tent. I uncapped the bottle and took a hefty sip before entering the darkened area, looking for Skylar.

A lone figure sat in the middle of the circle that used to be used by the performers, her blonde hair creating a curtain hiding her face. She seemed so small, vulnerable, sitting there all alone, and as soon as those thoughts entered my mind, I tried shaking them off just as fast.

I could pretend to care, but I couldn't really start believing that. That was simply not an option.

"Skylar?" I started once I entered the circle, coming closer to her. "Are you okay?"

"Yes," she replied, but she never looked up.

"Really?" I dropped down on the floor right next to her, placing the bottle between us. "Because to me—"

"I really can't deal with you right now, Ash," she cut me off, drawing circles in the sand. "The last two days were a pure clusterfuck, and you being here, trying to interrogate me, isn't helping."

Her raspy voice felt like a caress over my skin, and I wanted to record it and play it wherever I went. My heart clenched at the pain it was laced with, at the despair emanating from her body, and I wanted to remove it from her. I wanted to take it and throw it away, just so I could finally have those eyes on me, without that fear I saw earlier.

"Skylar." I leaned closer to her, moving her hair behind her ear, revealing her face to me. "We don't have to talk." I pushed the bottle toward her. "We can just sit here and do nothing."

She glared at the bottle for a second before she finally took it in her hand, opening the lid and taking a mouthful.

"Or we can drink." I chuckled, as she moved the bottle away, wiping her mouth. "Whatever you want to do."

She finally looked at me, her eyes blazing with fire that could burn us both. A fire I wouldn't mind dying for because I wanted what she had to offer.

"I don't wanna talk." She licked her lips, drawing my attention to them. "I want to forget."

I looked up, meeting her eyes again, seeing the meaning behind her words. I took the bottle from her, taking a sip, never taking my eyes from hers. As I dropped it to the ground, I wrapped my hand around her throat and pulled her to me.

With our lips mere inches from each other, our breaths mingling, our eyes blazing, I knew we wouldn't be leaving here tonight with our souls unscathed.

"Are you sure about this?"

"Just shut up and kiss me."

She didn't have to ask twice.

I wrapped my other hand around her ponytail, and pushed her head down, before I pressed my lips to hers, devouring her, drinking her alive. She moaned beneath me, pressing her hands to my chest before they traveled to my neck, gripping the short strands of hair at the back of my head.

151

"I'm gonna eat you alive," I croaked, my voice sounding foreign to me. "Is that what you want?"

"Yes," she cried out. "Just don't stop."

And I didn't stop.

Her plea was music to my ears. This was wrong, so fucking wrong, but I couldn't stop now. I've spent my life obsessing over her and her family, creating this picture of her, and none of it was true. I thought I would find a spoiled, bratty girl, but instead I found a broken young woman who was on a path of self-destruction.

I hated her, loathed her entire existence because of who she was, and yet, one look, one touch from her, could undo me and shatter everything I'd been working for. I was dancing on a thin line between passion and hate, and if I wasn't careful, I could burn myself and my family. I couldn't let a pair of silver eyes and the shadows dancing in them be my undoing.

No, I had to go ahead with the plan, even if a part of my brain screamed at me to stop while I had a chance. To stop before there was no going back.

But that part of me was already too late. The plan was already in full motion and these feelings could go to fucking hell, because I wasn't stopping. Not now, not ever.

"Do you want this?" I asked her as I pushed her to the ground, still keeping my hand tightly wrapped around her throat. Arousal flashed in her eyes, calling out to mine. Blood roared in my ears, and I could hear my heartbeat, thundering in my head, my blood boiling in my veins, because no matter what her last name was, my body wanted her.

I'd wanted her for a long fucking time, and now I would have her.

"Ash," she whispered, but she didn't answer my question.

"Answer me!" I roared, pressing on her pulse, and placing my other hand on her pelvis. Her entire body trembled under my touch, eager for what was about to come just like mine was. Burning desire and a touch of poison, and tonight, I wouldn't mind burning with her.

"Yes!" she shouted, her voice echoing around us, disappearing into the descending night. "I want this. I want you to fuck me."

I thought I would feel disgusted being here with her, doing this, but the feelings roaring through my body, dancing on my skin, were nowhere near close to disgust. My pants were a size too small as my dick woke up, willing to play, begging to be lost inside her heat. All thoughts of the hatred I felt for her family were gone, replaced by the carnal need to possess her, to have her all to myself.

All mine.

"Please," she pleaded while I took a second too long to think about all this. "I want to forget. I want to—"

I moved my hand from her pelvis and pressed a finger to her lips, cutting her off. "Shhh, don't talk." If she talked, I would have to separate her from the monsters crowding this town, and I couldn't lose sight of the things that were important.

My body wanted her, but my mind… My mind was on a different wavelength, and I couldn't wait to hear her screams, even if they were from pleasure.

I dragged my thumb over her bottom lip, then toward her cheek and went lower, until my entire palm was pressed against her chest. With her eyes fixed on me, I could see all the emotions unfolding on her face—need, desire, and fear. I wasn't sure if she was afraid of me or if that was the remnant of what happened to her, but whatever it was, I would take it.

I wanted to bottle it and carry it with me, because

one emotion stronger than desire was always fear. It could drive us mad, but it could also drive us to things we didn't know we wanted. And she wanted me.

She wanted a stranger, somebody unknown, to take her mind off of the things she was afraid of. Maybe she and I weren't so different, after all. Maybe we both just wanted to forget.

I didn't know what haunted her, but I knew what haunted me.

Their screams.

Their tears.

The smell of burning flesh.

My mother's terrified face and the stoic look on my father as they dragged the blade over his throat, letting the blood flow over the white t-shirt he always wore to bed.

I gripped the hem of the thin blue shirt she wore and started lifting it up, revealing the smooth, pale skin of her stomach. Her chest rose and fell with rapid breaths, but she couldn't move her head with my other hand still on her throat. I felt her throat working beneath my hand as she swallowed, but she didn't say a word as I started caressing her stomach.

"Your skin is so smooth," I murmured, almost to myself. So smooth, so unlike mine, which was marred with scars too ugly for people to see. I wondered if she would be satisfied with the lies I would have to spew at her about the slashes on my back and the burn marks on my upper arm.

She kept her hands to the side, waiting to see what I was going to do, and all of a sudden, I wanted to feel her touch on me. I wanted to feel that same energy that zapped through me every time she touched me. Back in the school hallway, when I stopped her from walking into that sign, I almost did nothing, but something inside of me didn't want to see her on the floor.

The only person she would be kneeling for would be me.

"Ash," she moaned when I brushed the underside of her breast, awakening the chills all over her skin. "I don't want to wait. Please."

"Hmm." I turned her around, pulling her legs around my waist and lifted her up. We were suddenly face-to-face, and I could almost taste the sweet venom she carried on her lips.

Like poison ivy, she could be the end of me with just one kiss. But no matter what, I wanted to taste her, to drink the poison from her cherry lips, to bite every inch of her, to hear her screams and my name on her lips as we both plunged into sweet oblivion.

Rational thoughts weren't with me anymore, and like a starved man, I dove, capturing her lips with mine, seeking entrance. I didn't have to fight her for too long because she already gave up this battle. She wanted this as much as I did, if not even more, and I wondered if she would feel the same if she knew the truth.

Would she look at me with the same fire, with the same need if she knew that she was just another pawn in this game of life, and I was the main player? Would she feel the same if she knew that she wasn't the queen on my chessboard and she never would be? She couldn't, because I would never forgive myself if I betrayed my parents like that.

I wrapped my arms around her, pressing her to me, letting her grind on my aching dick threatening to burst from my pants. God, this was both painful and exciting. With her hands around my neck, she started dipping them underneath my shirt, and I could feel her nails as she scraped them over my skin, no doubt leaving marks.

Marks over the other scars I had from the ones that

had the same blood rushing through their veins like she did. Scars that would always be a reminder of who I was and what I needed to do.

But for tonight... Tonight, she wasn't a Blackwood, and I wasn't a Crowell. Tonight, I would lock down the sinister thoughts I learned to live with, and I would surrender myself to the minx in my arms, letting her pull my shirt over my head, leaving me exposed to her.

She locked her ankles around my waist and did something I never would've expected her to do.

Skylar started caressing my hair, then my face, her feathery touches igniting the sleeping volcano in my soul. She was setting fire to my skin, and she didn't even know. I let her.

Lifting the bottle from the ground, she uncapped it and pressed it to my lips, slowly lifting it up. As soon as my lips closed around the rim, a soft smile touched her lips, but the wicked gleam in her eyes told me that there was nothing soft in her.

As soon as I gulped down the hefty amount of vodka, letting it burn through my throat, all the way to my stomach, she did the same, lifting it to her own lips, all the while looking at me.

"Sky—"

"My turn." She grinned and placed the bottle on the ground.

She tasted like vodka and sin when she placed her lips on mine. I let her have control for a minute or two, but I wasn't a patient guy, and I couldn't wait any longer. I gripped the back of her neck and with my other hand, I started unbuttoning her pants. My fingers grazed her stomach before diving in deeper until I brushed the edge of her panties.

I swallowed her moans, her pleas, her cries, and pushed her to the ground, depriving her of my lips. She started protesting, but she didn't get too far. I gripped her pants and started dragging them over her hips, feeling her shivering body, both from nerves and anticipation.

Her panties followed, and I could see her arousal glistening on her bare pussy, calling out to me. Like a man possessed, I didn't wait before I spread her legs further and dove, lapping at her clitoris. She moaned and arched from the ground, and when I entered her with two fingers, she screamed, creating the perfect symphony in my ears.

"Ash!"

My tongue ran circles from her clit to her opening, lapping at her juices, loving the smell of her. I pressed my other hand to her stomach, keeping her down as she started thrashing on the ground, moaning my name, begging, and screaming for a release.

I pressed against the sweet spot inside her, feeling her clench around my fingers. I almost came in my pants, knowing that my dick would soon be replacing my hand.

"Do you want to come, Moonshine?" I lifted my head and looked at her. Rosy cheeks and hair all over the place, with half of it still tied in a ponytail and half falling around her face, she looked like a goddess. I wished I could keep her because she made me feel.

She made me fucking feel, and I both loved and hated it.

"Answer the question." I pinched her clit and smirked at the look on her face.

"Yes. I want to come, dammit."

"Are you sure?" I started removing my fingers when she clamped her legs closed, keeping me inside her.

"Please." Her eyes connected with mine. "Just… Please."

I watched her, reading her face, memorizing every inch, every curve and gripped her knee, spreading her open again. Protests reappeared on her sinful lips when I stood up, but as I pulled the wallet out of my back pocket and took the condom out, she quieted down, watching my every step.

Unbuttoning my pants and pulling them down with my boxers, I almost moaned as my dick sprung up, finally free from the restraints. Her eyes widened at the sight of me, licking her lips as she held herself on her forearms.

I ripped the foil of the condom with my teeth, and with eager moves, I dropped down on my knees, pulling her to me. I wrapped my hand around my dick, gritting my teeth, wanting to get lost in her, but I didn't want to end this so soon. With her eyes on me, I pressed the head of my dick against her clit and started dragging it through her slit, teasing her opening, reveling in the sharpening of her breath.

I moved back and started stroking my dick while she ate me with her eyes, waiting for my next move. Time stood still as the electricity buzzed between us, as she laid in front of me, spread open, with her pussy glistening, waiting for me. The fire burned higher and higher as I stroked myself, making us both wait for what we wanted.

"Shit," I grunted as my hand went up and down, and I closed my eyes, seeing her still as the darkness shrouded my sight. I almost jumped from my spot as a pair of softer, smaller hands pressed against my chest, and when I opened my eyes, I saw her kneeling in front of me. She removed her shirt and gazed up at me, holding herself still.

She dragged her hands over my chest, all the way to my abdomen, coming close to my aching dick begging for release. But not yet, not like this. She moved my hands away, and wrapped hers around my length, pressing a soft kiss over my heart, then over both of my pecs, going toward my nipples.

Her tongue danced against the puckered buds, sending shock waves through my body, while she stroked my shaft, gripping me tight.

I couldn't wait anymore. I didn't want to wait, and as she started going lower, I pushed her to her back and leaned over her, guiding my dick toward her opening, sliding in and holding myself still.

"Holy—" I started.

"Fuck," she finished for me.

The walls of her pussy clenched around me, holding me hostage in her warmth, driving me insane. Inch by painful inch, I slowly slid in further, going all the way in, spreading her wide. I gripped her hip with one hand, while I held myself on my other hand placed next to her head. My lips tingled from the previous kisses, and I wanted to taste her again, to drown in her moans, in her intoxicating scent crowding us.

"Ash," she moaned as I started lowering myself down. "I need you to move. Please." With hooded eyes, and golden hair spread around her head, she looked like a fucking angel beneath me. I dropped down, taking her lips again, biting her lower lip and soothing it with my tongue.

I started moving my hips, slowly at first, loving the vise-like grip she had on me. With every new move, every new hit to that sweet spot inside her, she moaned, she gasped, and when she wrapped her arms around me, dragging her nails over my back, over my damaged skin, I started losing control.

An animalistic growl tore from my chest, and I increased the pace, the sounds of our skin slamming against each other the only other sound around us. My grip on her hip increased, and I knew she was going to have bruises tomorrow. And the animal inside of me, the little monster that suddenly woke up wanting to devour her, loved it more than anything else in this world.

My mark on her skin, my dick inside her, and her eyes only for me, fixated as if she couldn't get enough just like I couldn't.

"Fuck," she yelled, breaking the kiss, and closing her eyes. "Faster, Ash," she begged. "Please go faster."

And I did. I braced myself and started slamming into her with punishing thrusts. Her hand sneaked between us, and she started rubbing her clit, chasing her own orgasm. I was close, so fucking close, I could feel my orgasm coiling at the bottom of my spine, waiting to erupt.

"Moonshine," I growled and bit her neck. "Please tell me you're close."

Because if she wasn't, this would be very embarrassing.

"Oh God," she screeched. "That's it," she said as I changed the angle. "That's the spot."

I focused on that, lifting my upper body from her, and gripping her hips with both my hands. Beads of sweat gathered on my forehead and on my upper lip, and I could see the same on her. One lone bead glistened between her breasts as they bounced with every new thrust, and her hand gripped the sand beneath her, holding herself, while the other one ferociously worked on her clit.

"Oh, shit!" she screamed. "Ash, Ash, Ash—"

"I know," I whispered, unable to talk any louder. "I know, baby."

Her mouth opened as her legs started shaking around me, and with a guttural scream, I watched as she came undone in front of me, rubbing herself frantically, prolonging her orgasm. Her pussy held my dick in a tight grip and when black spots started dancing around the periphery of my vision, I let go and slammed into her, feeling the orgasm tear through my body, almost knocking me out.

I collapsed on top of her, unable to stay upright anymore. Sand and our sweat mixed together, but instead of pushing me away from her, she started stroking my hair and humming an unknown song, filling the empty space around us.

My mind was completely blank, spent, and I was unable to move my body.

But I had to, even if I wanted nothing more than to stay here for a little bit longer and forget about the things I needed to do. Everything I tried to lock down started pouring back into my mind, and I stiffened as her hands glided over my scars.

Why was it that the things we shouldn't want were the ones that always felt right? Being here with her felt both right and wrong, and yet I knew that wasn't my mind talking. That was my heart. My tired heart wanted nothing more but to forget about the horrors of the past and live life like a normal person, without grudges accompanying us every single day.

However, I couldn't forget who I was and who she was. Instead of allowing her to continue her little exploration of my skin, I pulled myself up and removed the condom, tying it up and throwing it to the side.

I refused to look at her, to see the hurt in her eyes, because I knew what I was doing now.

I was rejecting her.

TWELVE

Skylar

There are those fleeting moments in life where your mind goes completely blank, and all those worries, all those dark thoughts seem to evaporate into thin air, leaving you breathless, free, happy. I didn't have many of those anymore. I think I could count on one hand the number of times I didn't have to worry about something, and after so long, I forgot how it felt.

Not to think, but to feel.

I've spent years chasing the high that would make me forget about my life and the people around me, but I never succeeded. At least not fully. Yet, Ash managed to do that. He made me forget, made the wheels inside my head stop, and during that time inside that tent, everything was perfect. There were no thoughts, no darkness shrouding my mind, just the feeling of his hands on my body, his lips on mine, and his dick moving inside me.

It felt better than that Oxy I swallowed the other day. It felt better than the whole bottle of vodka I drank at that party in July. And I wanted more.

God, I craved more.

A week has passed since Ash and I had sex, and I felt like I was going to burst if I didn't get that feeling again. This felt worse than coming down from a high. My skin was itchy, my hands shook, and I knew it wasn't from any of the drugs, because I took a Tramadol this morning, thinking it was shitty withdrawals that sometimes happened.

But no, this was from him.

He didn't want to look at me after he disposed the condom, but I didn't give a shit about that. He didn't have to look at me as long as he fucked me, as long as he made me forget. Dylan was behaving like a mother hen around me, and even my father came home, constantly asking if I was okay and if I needed anything. My mother was still on her trip in Costa Rica, spending the money she didn't earn, and I was glad her poisonous mouth wasn't anywhere near me right now. There was only so much I could take at the moment.

And the messages... Fuck, the fucking messages. I thought it was a prank, that somebody was just messing with me after what happened in the forest, but that was just my wishful thinking. The first one terrified me, but it wasn't until the second one came that I realized I was dealing with a psychopath. They always came from a different phone number and three days ago I received a third one, explaining in detail everything he was going to do to the next girl, because he couldn't have me.

Yet.

That *yet* haunted my days and nights. I couldn't sleep. I couldn't eat. I couldn't think. I couldn't do anything about it, because whoever it was knew everything about me. The only thing I did know is that it was a male because he told me. The sick bastard told me to call him Iblis and to find out what it means. When I googled the name, I found it was what they called Satan in the Quran.

After that interaction, I decided to stay inside at all

times. School and then home, because if he found out anything else about me, he could harm my friends, my family, hell, anyone I had any contact with. But I was itching to go out now.

No, I was itching to forget and there was only one person who could make that happen, and he was completely ignoring me. If I thought that first week was bad, it was nothing compared to this one. From Tuesday to Wednesday, he didn't come to school, and when I saw him on Thursday, he looked at me like I'd killed his entire family. Every time I tried talking to Ash, he either all but ran away from me, or we would be interrupted by Kane. I had nothing to say to Kane, and no matter how much I hurt for him and the memories that were haunting him with all these disappearances, I couldn't help him.

God, maybe I should go to the police?

But if you go to the police, who knows what would happen. My subconsciousness reared its ugly head.

Fuck.

What was I going to do? I was okay dealing with one monster—at least I knew his face. But this one, this Iblis or whatever his name was, he was an enigma. Was somebody trying to hurt me to get back at my father? But this person never mentioned anything about my father, and if that was the plan, wouldn't they just kidnap me and get it over with? Wouldn't he—

"Skylar?"

I jumped from the bed at the sound of Dylan's voice as he entered the room, and the water I had in the glass I was holding splashed all over my hands.

"Jesus, Sky," he started and walked toward me. His strong hands enveloped mine, taking the glass from me and placing it on the dresser opposite of my bed. "Are you okay?" He touched my forehead. "You're extremely pale."

I lifted my head, fighting the tears and the knot in my throat, because I wanted to tell him. God, I wanted to tell him everything, but I couldn't. His life was more important than mine, and the psychopaths I had in my life would attack him first if I ever said a word. No matter how much I wanted him to be here with me, I wanted him gone right now. I wanted him to go back to his life in Seattle, to be as far away as possible from here. He was the one person I wouldn't survive losing.

Dylan was the most important person in my life, and as I stood there inhaling the sweet scent of his cologne, I only wanted a hug. Nothing more. He couldn't solve my problems, but he could make me feel safe, even if it was only for a little while.

That's all I needed. Five minutes of peace, five minutes where my mind wasn't trying to come up with all these absurd scenarios. Five minutes where my body wasn't shaking like a leaf, from fear, anxiety, from the need to run and run and run, and never look back. But there was always a "but", if I ran — who could guarantee that the demons wouldn't follow me?

"Sky," Dylan murmured again and removed the hair that fell over my face. I didn't wait for him to ask more questions, because I knew we would only end up fighting. I hated how much he worried, and he hated how reckless I was. So instead, I pressed my face into his chest, letting the smell of violets from the detergent we were using calm me down.

He always felt like home, and as he wrapped his arms around me, holding me tight, I let myself relax. I pushed myself to think about happy things, our childhood, and the smell of the freshly cut grass — me running around the yard and Dylan chasing me. I pushed myself to think about the day I would leave this godforsaken town, finally leaving everything in the past.

And it helped.

For those five minutes while he held me, I didn't think about the darkness lurking around every corner. I didn't think about Megan's dead eyes, or the messages popping on my phone. I didn't think about this insane craving I had for Ash, or the pills sitting in the first drawer of my dresser, calling my name. I didn't think about any of that.

I allowed myself to be happy, or, well, I lied to myself to calm my racing heart.

"You're really starting to scare me, Little One," Dylan whispered, stroking my hair. "This isn't like you. I've been here for two weeks, and you've barely left your room."

I shrugged, not wanting to elaborate on the reasons why I decided to lock myself inside and ignore the rest of the world. Lauren thought I wasn't in the mood, but it was so much more than that.

"You usually want to do things when I'm here. We didn't even go for dinner outside of the house, not to mention anything else. Now that I think about it, I can't remember the last time I saw you eat properly." He placed his hands on my upper arms and took a step back, searing me with his eyes. "You are eating, right?"

Goddammit, Dylan. Just don't ask me that. Please, please, please…

Masks were wonderful things, but they had expiration dates just like everything else, and mine… mine was cracking. I don't know how long I would be able to pretend that everything was okay, when each day was becoming darker and darker, and it felt as if it would never stop.

This endless despair, endless need to disappear, it was suffocating me.

"Skylar." His tone wasn't as soft as it was a minute ago. "You are eating, right?"

"If I tell you that I am, will you let it go?"

"Goddammit, Sky!" He started pacing the room, and I started bracing myself for a lecture I didn't want to hear from him. "Are you out of your mind?" Here we go. "I can literally see the veins beneath your skin! That's how pale you are." Yeah, as if I didn't know. He suddenly stopped a few inches away from me and I didn't like the serious look on his face. His left eye started twitching, and he ground his teeth before he asked the next question. "Do you have a new boyfriend? Is he making you do this?"

"What?" I laughed. "No! I don't have a boyfriend."

"Then why aren't you eating?"

"I just." I shrugged. "I'm not exactly hungry."

"Tough luck, Little One, because if you don't get your ass downstairs for lunch, I'm gonna carry you."

"You wouldn't."

"Try me," he threatened as he started walking out of my room. "Dad is here today, and he wants to see you before he leaves in two hours. You have five minutes."

Five minutes?

As bile rose to my throat, a well-known taste of anxiety, the drumming in my ears only increased as Dylan started retreating toward the hallway, leaving me alone with my thoughts. I loved my father, but I didn't want to talk to him today. Judah Blackwood, our father, was just like Winworth. Only two moods existed for him, and if today wasn't one of the good days, the only thing I would hear during this lunch was him criticizing every little thing about me.

"Dylan!" I protested. "That's not—"

"Five fucking minutes, Skylar!" His voice echoed through the hallway, and from my past experiences, my brother wasn't the type of person that would give out empty threats.

I wasn't lying to him — I didn't feel hungry — but I couldn't let him worry about me.

○

The smell of roasted chicken seeped into my nostrils as soon as I walked down the staircase, stopping just outside the kitchen. My father was laughing at something, and Dylan's gruff voice penetrated through the air, warming me from the inside out.

I missed having Dylan here. I knew he was only one text away, but it was different from actually having him here.

My stomach growled as I passed through the kitchen, noticing that none of the staff were here today. Did Dylan send them home? The counters were spotless, dirty dishes were nowhere to be seen, and I wondered if Dylan washed it all. Who prepared the food?

Step by step, I entered the bright dining room, seeing my father at the head of the table, with Dylan on his right side.

"Skylar!" my father boomed with a smile and stood up, walked around the table, and stopped in front of me. "I missed you."

His arms came around me, pulling me into his embrace. I tried to relax, tried to remember all the good things, but as he dragged one of his hands over my back, I stiffened further, fighting the shivers racking my body. He had been away from the West Coast for a couple of days, attending a funeral for his best friend, Nikolai Aster. I would've thought that he would be in a sour mood, but he seemed genuinely happy to see me, even though he saw me just yesterday and lectured me about the importance of my safety and not to wander into the forest on my own.

"You saw me yesterday, Dad." I fought against the shivers and plastered a smile on my face, finally hugging him back.

"So what?" he asked as he pulled back. "Can't I miss my favorite daughter?"

"You mean your only daughter?"

He waved his hand and walked back toward the table. "Semantics." The chair scraped over the floor as he pulled it back and sat down, eliciting shivers all over my body. I fucking hated that sound.

Dylan kept looking at me as if I was going to start crying at any moment, reminding me again how annoyed I was with his behavior. I could understand him being worried, but this whole hovering, worrying, asking me where I was going constantly, messaging and calling me, it just had to stop. I already felt like I was losing my mind with everything that was going on around me, and his suffocating behavior wasn't helping.

"Sit down, Little One," Dylan started, indicating a chair next to him. I wanted to ignore him and sit somewhere else, but deep down I knew he was coming from a good place, and if everything else went to shit, at least I would always have my brother.

"So," my father boomed as he started cutting through his steak. "How are things?"

Really, Dad?

I walked toward the chair Dylan chose for me and sat down, removing the napkin from the plate, and placed it on my lap. I had to bite my tongue and swallow the retort threatening to erupt from me. Mentioning dead girls and my name on Megan's body, as well as cryptic and psychotic messages were not the themes I wanted to have today. My overthinking was already becoming too much to deal with, and I wanted to enjoy the quiet evening.

"Good," I murmured. "I'm probably going out in an hour or so." I refused to look at Dylan, keeping my eyes on the roasted potatoes in the middle of the table. But ignoring him was never truly an option and I could feel his eyes burning into the left side of my face.

"Skylar," Dylan all but growled, his tone full of unspoken warnings and words I didn't want to hear.

"Lauren is having a party tonight, just a small gathering," I continued, ignoring my brother. I picked up a few potatoes from the bowl right next to the roasted chicken and placed it on my plate. I wasn't hungry, but I'd be damned if I didn't try.

"Skylar!" Dylan's voice thundered around us and the fork he was holding went flying over the table, landing on the other side. "I thought we talked about this?"

"No, Dylan." I turned toward him. "You tried to order me around. You talked, I listened, and I decided not to follow your advice."

If looks could kill, I would be a dead person right now.

His face darkened, the menacing look replacing the otherwise loving, brotherly look he always had for me. He gripped the napkin he had on his lap and threw it on his plate over the half-eaten chicken breast and potatoes, then stood up.

"I can't believe we're having this conversation again."

"And I can't believe you're again trying to boss me around, when I am not a small child anymore," I threw back. Our father kept quiet, his eyes traveling from Dylan to me, and the other way around. He continued eating, ignoring the blazing inferno spreading through

171

the house.

I never thought I would say this, but I wished that Dylan had gone back to Seattle. At least then he wouldn't be growly all the time, bossing me around and trying to make decisions for me.

"It's not safe!" I flinched at the tone of his voice, trying to keep my emotions at bay. Now wasn't the time to lose it. "There's someone out there, killing people —"

"And what do you expect me to do, Dylan? Huh?" I was beyond angry. "Should I stop living my life because somebody carved my name on her body? Would that appease you?"

"It fucking would!"

The veins on his neck popped out from the force of his thunderous roar, and his face reddened, making him look as sinister as… No, no, no, I was not going to think about that. Not now, not today.

"You know what?" I stood up, placing the napkin next to my plate. "Fuck you."

I couldn't deal with him and his sudden mood swings anymore. He went from protective to overbearing in a matter of two weeks, and that was the last thing I wanted.

"Excuse me?" he croaked out, disbelief lacing his tone.

But I didn't stop as I walked out of the dining room, heading upstairs.

"Skylar!" His hand wrapped around my upper arm, halting me in my steps. "What the fuck?"

"You heard me," I answered and shook him off me. "You can fuck off for all I care. I'm tired of the constant hovering, constant yelling, and it needs to stop. I can't fucking breathe, Dylan!" My chest heaved as I fought for breath. "You are suffocating me. You and your overprotectiveness."

"Sky—"

His face shattered at my words, but it had to be said. I loved him, God... I loved him more than anything else in this world, but he had to stop with this nonsense.

"I-I didn't," he stammered and cleared his throat. "I'm just worried about you."

I crossed my arms across my chest, letting the anger fuel me. "Well, don't be. I'm fine, and no one is coming to get me." The crushed look on his face pulled at my heartstrings and no matter how much he annoyed me lately, I couldn't be angry at him for caring about me.

He was the only one that truly cared.

I took a step toward him and lifted my hand to his face. He didn't shave today, and my fingers tingled as I ran my hand over his cheek.

"Dy," I whispered. "I love you, you know?" He nodded, gulping at the same time. "But I can't live like this. I can't be locked inside the house anymore. I need to go out, see other people. I don't wanna let that monster control my life."

He placed his hand over mine, holding me hostage for a minute, or two, or three, but it felt nicer than our other conversations since he came back. His eyes sparkled with something unknown, something I couldn't quite understand, but I wasn't going to rack my brain over it now.

"You need to let go, Dylan." I placed my other hand over his other cheek, bringing us closer.

"I can't," he croaked. "You're the most important person in my life. If something happened to you—"

"But nothing is going to happen, silly." I smiled. "I'm fine, you're fine... We are all going to be fine."

I was a motherfucking liar, because I knew, some part of me always knew... I was never going to be fine. Some things in life were survivable, but others... Others ate you alive until the only things left were a hollow soul and a skeleton carrying the body you didn't want to own anymore.

But I had to make him believe that I was okay. I couldn't let him see what was really happening behind closed doors, when the monsters we both trusted came out to play. I couldn't utter a word, because the monster feeding me poison was closer than Dylan thought, which was why I wasn't as afraid as I should be of the killer out there.

"But you're my little sister," he started again. "You will always be mine to protect, no matter what."

"I know."

"And this situation... I don't know what to do, Sky." He shuddered underneath my touch. "I just don't know what to do."

I came closer, plastering our bodies together, and hugged him like our lives depended on it. He would never know how close the darkness lurked. He would never know how poisonous the streets of Winworth were.

Winworth was founded on blood and secrets, and the darkness still clung to it like a newborn to its mother.

His strong arms embraced me, cocooning me, creating a safety net around me. He thought he was protecting me, but I was protecting him. I would always protect him until my last breath.

"I really do need to go, Dy." He gripped me tighter. "Dylan," I warned. "Please."

I could feel his muscles flexing underneath his shirt, but after a few seconds he released me, stepping away from me.

"Okay." He nodded. "I'll try to be better." Oh, Dylan. He didn't have to be better, he just had to let me go. "But you need to be safe. Okay?"

"Yes," I agreed. "I will be. Trust me."

My phone vibrated in my pocket, and I reached for it without thinking, my mind a million miles away from here. I thought it was going to be Lauren, or even the psychopath stalking me, but it wasn't them.

It was *him*, and he wanted me to come to our place. He wanted to take one more piece of my soul.

THIRTEEN

Skylar

My scalp burned as he continued pulling my hair, keeping me on my knees.

It was his favorite position. Me defenseless, crying out, begging for release, begging for something I couldn't even voice. And tonight… Tonight he was more vicious than ever before.

"You are such a good slut," he groaned as he kept dragging his dick through my folds, teasing me, taunting me, poisoning me over and over and over again. Tonight, he refused to give me what I needed.

Tonight, he wanted me to feel everything, to scream, to cry, to remember the viciousness he bestowed upon me. Tonight, my happy little pill was nowhere to be seen, and my skin kept shattering under his touch.

The dark mahogany headboard in front of me became blurry as my eyes filled with tears again when he slapped my ass. The pain, the shame, there was no escape tonight. My cheek still throbbed from where he slapped me as soon as I walked through the door. My throat felt raw, and I kept swallowing the sobs threatening to erupt from my chest.

He wouldn't get the satisfaction of hearing my pleas for mercy, because this monster behind me, he didn't know what mercy was. He only knew pain, suffering, and the eternal damnation he was condemning me to.

He pinched my clit, drawing out another scream from me, another painful reminder that all of this wasn't a dream, but a nightmare, and I was never going to wake up. His labored breathing mixed with the sound of the pounding rain on the outside was like a symphony of terror.

Piano, mezzo forte, fortissimo, he went through the stages of quiet, louder, and extremely loud breathing. I remembered all those piano lessons Ms. Andrievich tried to drill into my brain, and Beethoven's symphonies I could never remember.

I focused on my fingers gripping the white sheets on the bed. I focused on the memories from the time when life wasn't so tragic, and when I thought that the future held something beautiful. I never thought I would end up here. Battered, bruised, broken, only looking for salvation in the form of oblivion, because I couldn't live with myself. I couldn't live with what he did to me. What I did to myself.

So, I ran.

I ran from my mind. I hid from my friends. I lied to my brother, and I kept searching for something that would take away this despair coating my insides.

"You're dripping wet for me," he murmured as he kneeled lower, placing his face in front of my pussy. "I'm gonna lick you, but you don't get to come."

No, no, no.

"You don't get to come, because you couldn't do one simple thing." Another slap against my ass. "You couldn't get the information I needed." *Slap.* "And for that, you will be punished."

"Please," I moaned as he slapped my pussy. I almost jumped, but I knew that would only anger him more. I gripped the sheets and braced myself. I accepted the punishment, even though it wasn't necessary.

"You had one job!" Another slap. "One fucking job!"

He massaged my ass where he slapped me earlier, and I couldn't help myself, moaning when he dipped one finger inside me. No matter how much I hated him, my body always betrayed me. My mind was screaming, my heart breaking, but my body wanted the release he could give me.

And I needed it now.

If I couldn't forget, if I couldn't pretend that this depravity didn't exist, I wanted to at least bask in the glow of an orgasm.

He wrapped his hand around my throat, pulling me backward, nestling his dick between my ass cheeks. "What are the St. Clares planning?" he asked again, as if I knew the answer to that question.

He wanted me to get closer to Kane, to use him and extract the information, but Kane was more fucked up than I was. He couldn't remember his own name most days, and extracting any additional information about his family was useless.

"I don't know," I cried out, choking on my tears, on my despair. "I swear, he didn't mention anything."

"Then maybe I should kill you both and get the information myself." He snickered in my ear and licked my neck, still holding me captive. "Maybe I should fuck you in front of him and break his heart."

No.

"That boy is in love with you."

Wrong. Kane thought he was in love with me, but he didn't know what love was. Love wasn't supposed to hurt. It wasn't supposed to suffocate you, chain you, trap you… It was supposed to be pure, freeing, not toxic and caging. We didn't know how to love.

What we thought we had, that wasn't love. That was lust. A need to have somebody else drown with you, so that you wouldn't be alone. And we were drowning.

All of us were drowning, we just didn't want to admit that. All of us had demons to fight, we just didn't know how.

I stopped fighting mine when Zane's body was found that night. I stopped wishing for salvation, for redemption, because those would never come.

"Did you like his dick, pretty girl?" he asked as the tip of his dick pressed against my opening. "Did his dick leave you hanging, or did you manage to come?"

He impaled me in one thrust, painfully stretching me, cutting through my soul. Every time he did this, he managed to tear pieces of me, and he loved it. He knew what he was doing. He knew I would never be able to go back from this.

Not because I didn't want to, but because I couldn't.

He branded me with violence. He branded me with sick desires, and I couldn't shake them anymore. I just wanted more and more and more until I couldn't take anything anymore. I didn't care who it was, as long as I got what I needed.

"You don't deserve anything better than this," he breathed in my ear, while searing pain rocked my body. "You are just a little whore, aren't you?" He slapped my ass again, and as he started dragging his hand closer to my opening, I stiffened.

"What?" He slowed down and pulled me up, his hand tightly wrapped around my throat. "You think you won't like that?" The headboard in front of me blurred, my breathing choppy as he kept squeezing my larynx. "You will love everything I do to you, and you'll beg for more. Because you're my little whore, pretty girl. You are only mine."

He pinched my nipple with his other hand, earning another desperate cry. I thought he would stop. I thought he wouldn't go that far, but I should've known that he wouldn't mind destroying me if it meant getting what he wanted.

Still with his dick inside me, he dipped one finger in my backside, making me moan and cry, plead and beg. I didn't know if I was begging for him to stop or to keep going. My skin burned, but as he kept pounding in me with sharp, heavy thrusts, the second finger joined, and in sync with his dick, he kept going in and out, stretching me until the only thing I could think about was coming and coming.

But that never happened.

He removed his fingers, stopping completely, my pleading only a whisper on my lips as he let me fall to the bed, with my hands next to my head.

I used to dream. I used to love, but it was all now erased, cloaked in darkness, forever lost to the monsters of this world. They didn't have to have red eyes or horns. They didn't have to kick you, but their words cut like knives, and this monster behind me, his words hurt the most, because he was supposed to be different.

Thunder roared through the skies, and I shivered as the demon behind me started moving, holding my throat, and flicking my clit. I moaned. I thrashed. I cried from pain and pleasure, but I couldn't stop him. Unlike the other times, I was going to remember this, and no amount of drugs or alcohol was going to erase this from my memory.

I wanted to say no. I wanted to deny him a million times, but the beatings were too much to bear. I learned how to keep my mouth shut. But I would rather die than let him think that he won. No, I was going to get away from here. I was going to disappear, and they would never be able to find me.

This town, these people, these monsters, they were going to be just a memory.

But I didn't know how long I would be able to do this. My body could take a lot, but my mind, my heart, my soul, they were shattering with each day. I feared that there would be nothing left by the end of the school year. I already forgot how it felt to be happy, faking smiles, faking contempt, because I didn't want them to ask me questions.

No, I didn't want Dylan to ask me questions. Pure, good Dylan.

I was good at hiding, locking myself inside my mind so that I wouldn't have to actively participate in what was happening around me. I did it now, because if I couldn't run away with the help of drugs, I could do it myself.

His grunts were far away from me, just an echo waiting outside the closed door of my mind. I let my body go, giving it fully to him, nodding when he asked me if I loved it, if he was the only person on my mind. I nodded when he told me not to come, but I wasn't here.

I was back in that tent with Ash. Instead of these two filthy hands holding me, I imagined it was Ash choking me, caressing me, punishing me, making me wait for him and his release. I imagined it was his dick pistoning, his lips tasting me, his scent enveloping me. I let myself get lost in pleasure, because it wasn't my father fucking me.

It wasn't a monster who was supposed to protect me, tarnishing my soul. I imagined it was Ash.

It was all Ash.

"You're so tight, pretty girl," my father whispered, but it wasn't his voice.

I lost myself in the land of dreams, where the person owning my body was someone I wanted, not someone I feared.

My father, Judah Blackwood, was a devil, a demon, a nightmare. He was the monster in those stories Dylan told me when I was a kid, and I realized way too late that he wasn't the caring and loving father I wanted him to be.

"Oh God," he moaned, placing sloppy kisses over my shoulder. I couldn't fight the chills spreading over my body, and the sick bastard thought it was for him. "Skylar, you're perfect."

"Yes, Daddy," I whispered because that's what he always wanted to hear.

"You're the perfect daughter." Bile rose in my throat every time he reminded me who I was to him. It was easier pretending that he was just a stranger than my father.

I gulped down the acid rising in my stomach and tightened the muscles in my pussy, urging him to come. I couldn't prolong this without the pills he always gave me. It was so easy avoiding his eyes, avoiding his face, pretending that his voice wasn't the same voice that read those stories to me before I went to sleep.

"You'll always be my favorite girl." He chuckled. "Always mine."

If I could, I would stab him in the heart for everything he did to me — for every threat, for every slap, for every piece of me he took with him. He shattered me, made me think I wasn't worthy, made me think that no one would ever believe me if I told them what he did to me.

"*My dad touched me like this as well,*" he told me the first time he brought me here.

How many times did I scream? How many times did I cry? How many times did I beg to disappear? But no one ever heard me, because Senator Blackwood held more power than anyone could ever imagine. I didn't have to know what was going on behind the closed doors of his study to know that the men he used to bring over to our house were not the kind of men you wanted to hang out with.

Nikolai Aster, Logan Nightingale, Agostino Romano, Frederick De Wolfe, they were frequent visitors, and I knew every single one of their faces from the television and from newspapers. They were supposed to be good men, but the first time Nikolai Aster hugged me, I knew that there was nothing good about them.

The first time Logan Nightingale undressed me with his eyes, my skin crawled, my stomach clenched, and I wanted to hide from them and their leering eyes. The masks they wore for the public to see were left at home, and the true monsters came out to play. I saw them for what they truly were — monsters.

And my father, the person that used to put Band-Aids on my knees, he was one of them. It shouldn't have come as a surprise when a year after I first met them, that my father told me to undress in front of him and start touching myself.

I was fifteen years old.

I couldn't tell Dylan. I couldn't tell my friends. I couldn't tell anyone because he threatened every person I loved. He made me feel like I was filthy, unworthy. He made me do things I never dreamed of doing. He fed me poison. He pushed me into the dark abyss, and I fell so hard, all the way to the ground and I couldn't climb out.

"Are you going to come for me?" He bit my earlobe, punishing me with each thrust. "I want to feel you squeeze my dick."

His other hand gripped my breast, flicking my nipple, pinching me, making me scream all over again.

And I let it go.

I let it all go because he knew I couldn't come for him without pain. He made me into this. He made me beg, plead, cry, because my body needed to be punished to get to the soaring heights only an orgasm could bring.

"That's it," he breathed into my neck. "Oh yes, yes, yes. You love my dick. Admit it."

"I love your dick, Daddy," I answered with a robotic voice, sounding nothing like myself. But that was the point, wasn't it? Not to be myself, because if I tried to be myself, I wouldn't get out of here alive.

I stopped fighting him long ago, because every time I ended up with a new cut, a new bruise, new damage to my soul. My thighs had scars he inflicted upon me. My heart had marks no one would ever be able to remove.

My soul bled and bled and bled, and I wasn't sure if there was going to be anything left of me once this was done. He was too powerful. He was everywhere, and I had to be careful with the plan I concocted. I had to. If he knew what I had planned, he would kill me before I managed to escape this town.

My hair fell over my face, over my eyes, and I welcomed the darkness as I closed my eyes, pushing my ass against him. The sound of his balls slapping against my skin, the sounds of our moans, my cries, the pouring rain, and thunder crying in the night, it was the song of depravity. The song of loss.

He increased his pace, letting me fall on all fours, and held my hips with bruising strength, letting himself go.

Ash, Ash, Ash, I chanted in my head as my body clenched around his dick.

My stomach tightened as my father kept pounding into me, drawing out the orgasm I didn't want to give him.

No, it's for Ash. It's all for Ash, not for him.

He flicked my clit, and I erupted around him, my entire body shaking, but it wasn't his name on my lips. It wasn't his poison killing me slowly. It was thunderous eyes and a violent touch. It was a guy I didn't only want, but needed. I needed him to chase away all the bad things surrounding me.

And I was going to find a way to get what I wanted, again.

O

"D ylan told me there's a new kid at school," my father started as I pulled on my sweater, careful not to touch the spots where he bit me. He was usually more careful, worried that people would ask questions if they saw me like this.

He could punish me, he could fuck me into oblivion, he could take everything away from me, but I still had to behave like a good daughter of a senator. He cared more about his picture and how people saw him than about his family.

"Yeah," I murmured and picked up my bag from the floor. "His family moved to town recently."

"What is his last name?" he asked and pressed the tip of his cigar to his lips, inhaling slowly.

"I'm not sure." I shrugged. "I can find out." *Liar.* I already knew his last name.

Ash Weber.

He wasn't mine to protect, but knowing my father, he would find out about this weird attraction I felt toward him, and he would hold it over my head.

No, Ash had to stay out of this.

"Good." He nodded, enveloped in the cloud of smoke. "Do that."

I crossed the room, heading toward the door, counting when I would be able to break down without him seeing it. Counting down the minutes until I would be able to breathe without his foul stench surrounding me.

"And, Skylar," he called out, stopping me in my tracks. I turned around, looking at him for the first time tonight. His hair was more gray than blond now, and his silver eyes just like Dylan's were not soft anymore. No, he was the worst thing that had ever happened to me. "Not a word to anyone."

"Yes, Dad." I surprised myself with how strong my voice sounded, but I guess that after two years of this, I learned how to hide my emotions. I was thankful that the voices inside my head kept quiet while I stood in the middle of the room, the stench of sex, cigars, and his expensive cologne tickling my nose.

I didn't wait for another word from him. I slowly opened the door, storming through the hallway of the darkened house, all the way to the front door. I didn't stop to take a shower, even though I wanted to get his filthy scent off my body. I didn't stop to look at myself in the mirror, because I didn't want to see myself. I couldn't face myself. All the other times he would leave me alone to gather my thoughts, but this time, he was the one staying behind.

Our family used to live in this house years ago, before I was born, before our parents got married, but they decided that living on the edge of Winworth was not suitable for one of the founding families.

So they moved, taking the land on Ashword Street, and building the house that now held some of the best and worst memories for me. Too bad it was the bad ones that started prevailing, and the good ones got lost.

I yanked the door open, letting it slam against the

wall. The smell of fresh rain and clean air welcomed me, slamming into me like a freight train. People often said that rain always came to wash away all the bad things on earth, and I wondered if I would ever be able to wash away the sins clinging to my skin.

Sins and tragedies, the only two things I had to offer.

I started running, jumping from the porch into the darkness, rounding the fountain perched in front. Rain poured over me, mixing with the tears streaming down my face. My chest hurt, my breaths rushed, but I just wanted to get away from this place. I wanted to forget, to erase these memories from my head.

I hiccupped, fighting the sobs shaking my entire body, but I still ran. There were no other sounds apart from the pouring rain and my feet thundering against the ground, not even caring about the shoes that would no doubt be ruined after tonight.

I didn't want to go home. I didn't want to look at Dylan and lie to him. I didn't want to look at Lauren and smile until my cheeks hurt. I couldn't lie to them.

But there was one person I could lie to. One person that didn't give a fuck about me, and as long as he didn't, he was going to be safe. One person whose name was like a melody repeating in my head, and I needed him tonight.

I slowed down as I exited through the open gates of the former Blackwood Manor, seeing my car parked just a few feet away from it. No one ever came to this side of Winworth, and my father knew he would be safe. His secret, my downfall—they would be safe from the people of Winworth.

Little did he know that these people wouldn't give a fuck even if he stripped me naked and tied me to the pole in front of City Hall. The only thing they cared about were their own lives, and if it didn't affect them, they looked the other way.

Lightning illuminated the night, distorted tips of the mountain visible from this side of the town. I pulled my keys from my pocket, unlocked the car and opened the door, welcomed by the silence. The forest on both sides of the road should've looked sinister, but there was nothing more sinister than what was sitting inside the house I just left.

Humid air somehow seeped inside the car, and turning the ignition on, I switched on the air conditioning, letting the cold air onto my face. I knew what I was going to do tonight. The screen of my phone lit up as I turned it on, and an array of messages both from Dylan and Lauren welcomed me, but I didn't want to look through them.

Instead, I rushed through my contacts until I found what I was looking for. I contemplated calling him throughout the week. I wanted to feel him again, but I was a coward, afraid he would deny me. Yet tonight... Tonight I had nothing else to lose.

The phone rang for what felt like forever, but when his gruff voice answered, the cold that started seeping into my bones suddenly evaporated.

"Hello?" He sounded confused, almost sleepy, but I didn't care if I woke him up.

"Meet me at Infernum. I need you."

And I dropped the call. I just hoped he would come.

FOURTEEN

ASH

What the fuck was I doing here?

I kept asking myself the same question over and over again, but the answers I had were too disturbing to think about. I tried to forget about her—the way she tasted, her smell, that wicked smile when I entered her for the first time. I tried to erase it all from my memories, but I couldn't.

As soon as I threw away that condom, I wanted more. I wanted to chain her to me, to take her everywhere, to take her away from here. I wanted her eyes on me at all times, and I almost forgot what it was that we came here to do. I almost forgot about my purpose, my revenge, all thanks to the pair of blue eyes and a cheeky smile. All because something in her called to me.

I was on edge the entire week, because even though my mind knew what we needed to do, my body rebelled, craving her more and more and more. Countless times I almost gave in. I almost took her to the janitor's room at school when she arrived in nothing but tight jeans and a shirt showcasing her stomach. And I wanted to punch Kane St. Clare when he talked to her.

I wanted to punch anything, actually, when she

smiled for everybody else but me. Sebastian avoided me, because I was like a tiger waiting to attack, and it fucking pissed me off. I wasn't this person. Girls came and went, but I never stuck around long enough to see where it could go. And one time, one fucking time that my blood hums from the nearness of her, it was the enemy I could never have.

If my uncle knew where I went tonight, he would be disappointed. I promised myself it would be only once. Only one fucking time, but when she called earlier tonight, I couldn't resist. At the sound of her voice, my dick jumped to attention, basking in that raspiness, remembering how she felt around me.

So here I was, cursing the fucking rain for falling. Cursing this life for sending Skylar Blackwood to me, for making me want her. I wasn't supposed to want her. I was supposed to use her, break her, throw her away, but instead I was rushing to meet her, to touch her, feel her, like a man starved. Jesus fucking Christ, this shit couldn't be happening.

Not now, not fucking ever.

I could barely breathe, anticipation building higher and higher, and it was only a matter of minutes until I would be able to touch her again. God, my fingers tingled at the mere thought of her skin. My lips ached, craving hers. I craved her sweetness. I craved her darkness. I wanted to know who destroyed the light in her eyes.

I took the same path as the other day, expecting her to be at the merry-go-round, but she wasn't there.

"Skylar!" I called out, but the only answer I got was the sound of the wind and rain around me.

Goddammit! Where the fuck was she?

I started heading toward the tent we fucked in, when a lone figure standing in front of the Ferris wheel, or, well, what was left of it, caught my attention. Her back was turned to me, her head upturned, staring at the sky, letting the rain wash over her.

What the fuck was she doing?

A lone lamp that still worked in the park illuminated her, showing the soaked hair and soaked clothes. I was already freezing from the wind howling through the night, but she was as still as a statue. I knew something was wrong.

Her pants clung to her like a second skin, showcasing her curvy backside and lean legs. The sweater she wore rode up, her lower back exposed to my eyes, and I wanted to drag my tongue over that creamy skin, chasing away the rivulets of water collected there.

With a lead weight in my gut, I closed the distance between us, stopping just behind her. She must have heard me when I called for her, so why didn't she respond? I looked up, trying to see what she was looking at, but the only thing I could see were the dark skies and the tops of the buildings belonging to the park.

"Sky," I whispered and placed my hand on her shoulder. She didn't flinch, didn't gasp, she didn't do anything.

Her arms were in front of her, and when I looked down, I saw a see-through bag she was holding. I didn't have to be a genius to know what it was. I was around enough people who chased nothingness day in and day out, to know that she was doing the same. She was running from something, but whatever it was, tonight it brought her to me.

Or, well, it brought me to her.

"Isn't she perfect?" she started, her velvety voice like a caress over my skin. "She is perfectly imperfect."

I moved to the side and looked at her face, seeing the smile touching her lips, but tears welling in her eyes.

"Who is?"

"Her." She looked up. "Abandoned, destroyed, but still so beautiful."

I looked up again, finally seeing what she was looking at.

A lone ballerina perched on top of one of the buildings. Half of her face was missing, the edges rotting, showing only the metal wires holding her together. The other half was still smiling, stuck in time, stuck in the moment.

"She could be an angel, or she could be a demon, but she's still standing."

Something in her voice pulled at my heart, blurring the lines I drew a week ago. Sadness laced her every word. Grief and despair were visible on her face, and I fought with myself. I fought against the pull she had on me, because I wanted to erase all those things.

Funny, less than a month ago, I wanted to see her suffer. I wanted to see her on her knees, begging for salvation, and now I couldn't bring myself to push the knife deeper, to hurt her more.

"Sky." I took a hold of her hand, the sound of the bag scrunching beneath our fingers echoing around us. "You're soaking wet."

"I wanted to get clean." She smiled and looked at me. "I wanted to wash it all away. My sins, my memories, my past, present, and future. I wanted to wash it all." Suddenly her smile disappeared, replaced by a frown marring her beautiful face. "But I couldn't. I couldn't wash them away. They're too deep, Ash. Their claws are too deep inside."

Her hair was plastered around her face, the dark rivers from ruined makeup a stark contrast against her pale skin, yet she never looked more beautiful than she did now. Broken.

She was broken and I hated it. I was supposed to break her. I was supposed to make her beg and cry and plead for her life, and somebody else beat me to it.

Or do you maybe hate it because you don't want to see her broken? My subconscious argued with me, grinning at me, taunting me, because we both knew I was lying to myself.

I didn't want to see her like this because I didn't want to break her. I didn't want to see her tears, her wounds and bruises, her despair. Fucking hell, I didn't know what I wanted anymore. But I couldn't let my heart, or my body, decide for me. This was only lust, only a temporary fix, a temporary escape from the fucked-up world.

I couldn't choose her even if every nerve ending in my body screamed at me to do so. She wasn't mine; she would never be mine. A year from now, I would be her biggest regret, because by then she was going to learn all of my secrets. I couldn't let her in. I couldn't give her my heart when there was nothing to give.

I could give her my body and my lips. I could give her nights but never days. And I could never think of her as mine, I just couldn't. I made a promise, a vow, and I was planning to fulfill it. A pair of eyes as blue as California skies could not mess this up for me.

She looked at me as if I could give her the world, when in reality, I was going to be the one that would shatter it. I could feed her lies to prolong what we had, but that was it. That was all I would be capable of.

She thought that sins coated her skin, but it was me. I was the sinner. I was the damned man, and once everything was said and done, she wouldn't want to have anything to do with me.

"Let's get you inside, okay?" For all my wrongs, I still didn't want her to catch a cold. "You're going to freeze out here."

"But I'm still not clean, Ash." Her lower lip trembled. "I'm filthy, just how he likes me."

He? My eyebrows furrowed, confusion running through my mind.

Did Kane do something?

"Moonshine, who?"

"I can't tell you, but, Ash—" she suddenly stopped.

"Yes?"

"Don't fall in love with me."

If she had slapped me, it would've been less surprising than this.

"What?"

"Promise me." She gripped my arm with her other hand. "Promise me you won't fall in love with me."

"I-I… Skylar, what are you talking about?" Where the fuck was this coming from? "We just met."

A sad smile appeared, her lashes fluttering against her cheeks. "That's what they all say in the beginning, before—"

"Before what, Moonshine?"

"Before they die."

FIFTEEN

Skylar

My head pounded as I walked to my locker. I ignored the curious stares of students in the hallway. I couldn't remember how I came home on Saturday, but I could remember Ash.

I could remember his worried eyes, his moving lips, and the way he held me as he took me out of that place. But I couldn't remember his words. I tried and tried to remember, but nothing ever came to me. I still didn't see him, and I just hoped that whatever I told him the other night wasn't something that would send him to an early grave.

Those two Oxys I swallowed as soon as I came to the Infernum obviously did a magnificent job, but the scenes I wanted to forget still clung to my skin. Even after scrubbing myself to the point of pain, I could still feel his hands on me. And he wanted me to remember. He wanted me to suffer like this, because every single other time, he would let me slip into the sweet oblivion, while he continued shattering my body, my mind, and my soul.

There was nothing left of my heart already. As Charles Baudelaire said, "*The beasts have eaten it,*" so he attacked me where he knew I was the most vulnerable.

My mind.

When all of this started, I didn't realize what he was doing. I didn't realize that he was trying to tarnish me, because what girl would ever believe that her father would destroy her like that? I sure didn't.

At first, it was the trips only the two of us took, then soft touches. Then his lips on my skin, and then the punishments when I wouldn't do what he wanted me to do. He wanted me to spy for him.

Ever since he became a senator, he couldn't observe everything that was going on in our little town, and like a madman that he was, my father craved control above everything. He didn't look at us like people; he looked at us as subjects placed here to do his bidding. You would think that becoming a senator would satisfy his desire for power, but no. I couldn't talk about the time before he revealed his true face to me, but I could talk about now, and if I knew one thing, it was that my father wouldn't stop until he held everything in his hands.

Fucking control freak.

God, it felt as if my skull was pressing on my brain, sending small jolts of pain every few seconds. I could blame it on the drugs, on the rain from last night, on the things that have happened in the old Blackwood Manor, but I knew it was the lack of sleep causing this kind of pain.

Our house on Ashword Street was new, but sometimes it felt as if the walls talked, groaning, screaming, whispering at night, and last night, restlessness took over, blocking my attempts to sleep. The rain and thunder roaring through Winworth kept me up, and my mind kept coming up with scenarios of what could happen.

I tried to forget, tried to push it to the back of my mind, but those cryptic messages I started receiving a week ago haunted me. I couldn't help but go through them again, trying to understand who was behind them. I was a nobody. This person, whoever they were, wasn't after me because my father was a senator, or because my family had money. No, they wanted me, and they wanted me to know it.

I felt trapped in my own life, and I knew it came long before that first message appeared on my phone. I lived in a prison, but I refused to accept the harsh reality and what was going on around me. It was so much easier pretending, so much easier slipping into the dark oblivion drugs and alcohol could provide, forgetting the pain and terror shivering through my veins.

When I thought about my future, there was never a place for freedom. I knew that the moment I ran away from this place, I would have to keep running, because my father wouldn't want me to talk. I was useful to him now, but what would happen to me when I became a liability instead of an asset? I would become a walking target with a bullseye right across my chest. Thinking about it sent shivers all over my body.

Would I ever be free?

Even the walls of this school, this place that once served as an escape for me, seemed to close in on me, with their eyes watching me, their poisonous lips whispering about me, about the state I was in. Thinking that the once happy girl must have lost her mind, slipping into the darkness because I was nothing more than a spoiled brat. People loved labels. They labeled me on that first day when I stepped in this school because of my last name.

And I wasn't my brother. I wasn't charming. I wasn't smiling all the time. I wasn't good with people. Interactions with others my age always felt strenuous, and I knew that the only reason I had more people in my close-knit circle was because we were all messed up in one way or another. Every single one of us had our demons, and we understood each other.

We understood that it was easier hiding from what really bothered us, than facing reality.

I often wondered what life was like for other people our age that didn't have demons whispering in their ears. I wondered if they smiled because they were truly happy, and what it must have felt to feel free. Did they wake up without the heaviness sitting on their chest, ready to embrace the day, looking forward to everything that life had to give them?

Or maybe I just complained a lot. Almost all our teachers repeated on a daily basis that we were just teenagers who didn't know how real life could really hurt. But what were we living through if this wasn't real life? How could it get worse? I knew that maybe one day there would be sun shining in my life, but right now… right now, it felt as if everything that could go wrong, went wrong.

One day, my life was a perfect picture of happiness, and the next, it all shattered down like a house of cards. I cursed that first touch, that first caress that sent my stomach roiling, something clawing at my insides, but I still stood there, stupefied, unable to move to say anything, because the person that was supposed to protect me was the one that hurt me the most.

That searing pain between my legs when he entered me for the first time… I would never be able to forget that. All the bruises, whispers, entrapment, it haunted me daily. Even when I didn't want to think about this nightmare, it still had a tendency to sneak in when I least expected it. It would hide in the corners of this building, on the wings of the crows soaring through the sky, in the cold cocoon of the wind blasting through Winworth. It would always find me.

I wished I had a metal heart. I wished that there was a way to lobotomize these terrors from my head, so that I wouldn't have to live with memories I didn't want to have. Maybe without memories, I would be able to live my life fully once I ran away from here.

Shaking ominous and impossible thoughts from my head, I unlocked my locker, holding my bag in my left hand, as something fell to the floor. A white envelope laid at my feet, daring me to pick it up. I dropped my bag to the floor and crouched down to pick the envelope up. I noticed my name scribbled in neat handwriting. No last name, no address, and no clues as to what it could be, but my name still stood there, the black ink a stark contrast on white paper.

Just like my name on Megan's body. The involuntary thought raced through my mind, momentarily freezing me. My hands shook, unable to take the envelope from the floor, terrified of what could be inside.

Was it him? Was it the deranged stalker I had? Or was it a plain, harmless letter somebody left for me?

When did I become so jaded that everywhere I went, everything I did, I could only see sinister intentions? When did my mind go so much off the rails that I couldn't see normal things?

Well, fuck that shit.

I picked up the envelope and straightened up, staring at the six letters of my name, caressing the paper. Just like everything else, my name tarnished even the purest things in this world. This paper, Zane, my friends… Was that why I was so attracted to Ash? Why my body hummed even when I only thought about him? Because he felt like danger. Because he tasted like violence, like the pouring rain in the middle of the summer, ruining those sunny days. Because I knew I couldn't tarnish him.

Whoever wrote my name almost danced with the pen, letting the ink flow over the paper like blood flew in our veins. It would've looked tender if it wasn't for an indent on the paper from where the ink touched it. I knew that whoever wrote it, didn't write it out of love.

This wasn't a love letter, and I didn't need my fucked-up head telling me that. No, this was something else, and I dreaded opening it. I both wanted to know what was inside and throw it away. But my curiosity won over, and instead of overthinking it like I usually would, I turned it over, ripping the delicate envelope, and pulled out the green-colored, folded paper hidden inside. I placed the envelope in my locker, my eyes locked on the viridian paper in my hands with trepidation coursing through my body.

I was a visual person. I connected memories with smells, sounds, words and places. I memorized people in colors, and I hid them in the lyrics of songs I listened to. I had a song for every person I've lost. I had a color for every person that stayed. There were those people like Lauren who reminded me of sunshine and perfect summer days on the lake, like when we were kids, and her parents would take us to Emercroft Lake. She reminded me of chocolate chip ice-cream, of lemonade, and of fresh breeze.

But others… Others like Kane, like Beatrice, Rowan, they reminded me of other things, other colors, and unknowingly, I started assigning songs to them, as if they already weren't here anymore.

But one person I never expected reminded me of more than just colors. He sneaked in somehow and hid under the surface of my skin. I cloaked him in viridian because he reminded me of Winworth. Dark and moody, quiet and observing, he was now in every song I had on my phone. And I loved that only we knew what happened that night. I loved that no one else saw how he looked when he came undone, when he held me, when his hands bruised my hips, when he looked at me with something more than indifference.

I loved that he tasted like sin and moved with punishing strokes. I loved that his eyes held a promise of violence, because that meant he wouldn't be destroyed by what I carried in me. I even fucking loved the way he looked at me when nobody else was looking at him — his imposing presence, his domineering words, and the devil-may-care attitude. But most of all, I loved that he made me forget.

He was better than drugs, better than alcohol, better than running away.

My demons were calling his name. They were whispering, urging me to go to him, to take him, recognizing him as ours. Ours to hold, ours to hide, because hiding was the only way for me to have him. He was the forest green, and I was the thunderous skies. We both carried secrets in our pockets, locked from the rest of the world. People like him, people like me, you could see it in our eyes. There was a promise of destruction there, of rebellion, of oblivion, and I loved that somebody else carried it just like I did.

Maybe the war he was brewing was different from mine, but it was still the same hell.

Kids that were never affected by sinister things lurking in the middle of the night had different energy zapping around them. They didn't know how it felt to be ripped from the inside out, only to be stitched back with all the vital parts missing. And I was glad for that. I was glad that not a lot of us had to carry these sins.

But Ash… Ash had everything I wanted.

His sins danced all over his skin. The perfect, vehement, desolating tango, and I wanted to learn the steps.

I jerked at the sound of a locker nearby snapping closed, pulling myself from the daydream and focusing back on the paper in my hands. Carefully, almost fearfully, I unfolded it, seeing the unfamiliar crest placed as the header. All our families had their own crests, but I had never seen this one.

An upside-down triangle, ending in upturned ends, with two lines crossing from each of the corners and a V at the bottom. The golden lines almost looked pretty, but when my eyes filtered over the page, stopping on the white ink on the dark green paper, my heart started beating, my palms sweating, and I gripped the paper tighter as the words blurred in front of my eyes.

In the beginning there were five, before the first light arrived.

But in between all the lies, only four survived.

Can you hear their screams, they echo in the night?

The damned have gathered, for the Union is about to start.

Do you want to know the secrets of Winworth, Skylar? Do you want to know where it all started?

I took a step back, my knees shaking uncontrollably, while I kept rereading the contents of the letter.

What the fuck?

On the bottom part, attached to the paper, was a black-and-white picture. A picture I had never seen and one I would never forget. Five hooded figures, with their faces hidden behind white masks, stood huddled together, their hands in front of their bodies and what looked like an altar with the same symbol etched into its front side, situated ahead of them.

Terror, fear, damnation, it all oozed from the photo,

204

and as if burned, I dropped it to the floor, my mind racing a thousand miles per hour. The urge to run rocked my body, and I took a step back, then another one, putting some distance between me and the terrifying picture lying on the floor. But even if I ran to the other side of the world, their soulless eyes would still haunt me.

Pitch-black, sinister, evil, so fucking evil, but I couldn't leave it on the floor.

No matter how much I wanted to disappear, to pretend that some things didn't happen, I had to face reality. I had questions.

So many fucking questions I felt like my head was about to explode. But most of all, I was getting angry. Furious at the psychopath stalking me and my friends, furious at this letter, furious at this sick picture lying at my feet. Furious at life and this place I called home. Lauren told me I was too apathetic for my own good, but what I felt right now was on a completely opposite side of apathy.

Anger.

Red, hot, simmering anger whispered through my veins, writing poems of darkness and fury on my skin. It hugged me, welcoming me into its embrace, and for the first time since this endless powerlessness, I felt strong. I felt formidable, ready to end this vicious circle in my life.

Screw them for fucking my life up.

Screw them for not loving me enough.

Screw them for looking at me with their judging eyes.

Screw them for the unspoken words whispered only behind my back.

Screw them for everything because I wasn't having it anymore.

I crouched down and picked up the picture, staring

at it as if it would help me to figure out who these people were. And maybe I couldn't, not by looking at it, but this letter, this was the key. This emblem, these words... whoever wrote this wanted me to know more. Winworth had more secrets than any other place in the United States and I planned on unraveling at least one of them.

I pretended to be blind when things went wrong, because it was easier feigning disinterest than dealing with monstrosities surrounding us. First Zane, then Megan, and who was next? Who would die because I didn't want to deal? Which girl was going to be found on the side of the road, or in the forest, or underneath that bridge separating the two sides of Winworth with my name carved on her skin?

One part of me wanted to slam my locker shut, turn around, and leave the school just so I could get high. Just so I could forget. But there was another part of me, an angry part, that wanted to make them suffer. I didn't just want to disappear anymore, no.

I wanted to make them pay.

My father.

My mother.

Their friends who stood by while they tortured my body and my mind.

They were guilty, all of them. While I destroyed myself, day by day, piece by piece, they stood idly on the side, allowing them to do this to me. And whoever this person was, messaging me, doing this shit to other girls, they had to pay as well.

I just didn't know how, at least not yet.

Slamming my locker shut, I put the picture in the front pocket of my pants and turned the green paper to the other side, my eyes widening at the text scribbled there.

Winworth Public Library – start there. Answers will

come to you.

Un-fucking-believable.

"Look who it is, guys," an annoying voice echoed behind me, and I gripped the paper tighter in my hand, closing my eyes. I didn't want to deal with her today. Actually, I didn't want to see her this year, but fucking karma, destiny, and all the other things I couldn't control had a different plan.

I turned around, coming face-to-face with Lilly Balland, the resident bitch of Winworth High. A self-proclaimed queen bee, social media influencer even though I didn't think that she actually knew what that was, and the biggest pain in my ass. Her dark brown hair was pulled in a high ponytail, and the nails I felt on my face once before, were colored red, tapping against her upper arm.

A year ago, when things looked a little bit brighter, while Zane was still alive and our lives didn't seem like a clusterfuck, Lilly hung out with us, pretending to be Kane's girlfriend. Unfortunately for her, Kane didn't have girlfriends. He had fuck buddies, girls that would throw themselves at him just because he was the captain of our football team and a St. Clare. For a moment, I felt bad for her.

It sucked liking somebody so much that you would stoop so low to do anything they wanted, while they never gave a fuck. I was there when Kane made her suck his dick in the living room of his home while all of us watched. I was there when she got so drunk that she didn't know it was Zane she started clinging to, while Kane had his tongue down another girl's throat. I was there when he told her to get lost, after the rumors of the two of them being a couple started surfacing and he found out she was the one spreading them.

And I was there when she posted that nasty video

of all of us drunk and high, snorting coke from the glass table in Danny's bedroom.

The favorite sons and daughters of Winworth, she named it. That night, my father busted my lip for snorting coke he didn't provide. That night, he made me swallow ibuprofen like it was chocolate, allowing only a bottle of vodka with it.

The video was taken down, but my scars lasted longer than one day. And when Zane died, she connected the dots and realized that Kane would never be hers because he started fixating on me. That was when her claws quite literally came out to play, when she attacked me in front of the school, rewarding me with three slashes across my cheek because I couldn't be bothered to defend myself.

But today... Today wasn't the same day. Today, I was too angry to give a fuck about her broken heart and whatever fantasy she concocted in her head. Today, I wanted to see blood, and if it was hers, I wouldn't mind.

"What do you want, Lilly?" I asked and picked up my bag, putting it on my shoulder.

The three girls always following her around like lost puppies looked like they wanted to be anywhere but here, but we all knew what rumors could do to people. Even if they wanted nothing to do with whatever this was, they had no choice. Lilly probably knew more about them than they wanted her to, and that fucking sucked.

Your friends weren't supposed to be the ones you should be careful around. Your friends were your people, your tribe, and if you couldn't trust them... Well, that wasn't friendship then.

"I heard a rumor." She chuckled, and I immediately wanted to drown out the annoying sound. People started gathering around, because we all knew that whenever she and I ended up in the same place, it couldn't end well.

I lifted an eyebrow and smiled at her. "Are you sure you weren't the one that started spreading it?"

Her face paled and she dropped her hands, taking a step closer to me. Looks were everything to her but looks could be deceiving. I knew that underneath this mask she wore, laid a scared little girl who wanted to fit in with the founding families. I knew her parents worked at City Hall, and that no matter how much she tried, she could never turn people to love her. She thought the video would ruin us, that it would show people who we really were, but even fucked up, high, and drunk, we were still more loved than she ever was.

"Megan." She said her name as a threat, and I knew. I just fucking knew. Her lips pulled into a smile, and without warning, my heart started beating faster. We managed to keep the fact that Megan had my name on her body a secret. No one knew, not even our friends.

Only the police officers, Lauren, Dylan, and whoever else usually gets involved with murder investigations knew about that shit. And now she did too.

"I know, Skylar," she taunted, her eyes sparkling with viciousness. "I know what they found in the woods."

"You mean what I found?" I spat out, taking a step closer to her. Bright, defiant, brown eyes stared up at me, and she took a step backward, her resolution visibly wavering on her face. "Don't fuck with me today, Lilly."

"Or what?"

"Or I'm going to break that pretty little nose of yours." I grinned. "And I know that Mommy and Daddy don't exactly have money for another plastic surgery."

The crowd around us gasped, shocked, because I never did this. I never fought back because what was the use? I realized a long time ago that no matter how hard you fought, or how much what people threw your way wasn't correct, masses would still believe lies over the truth, because they loved reveling in someone else's misery, rather than thinking about their own.

"You are such a —"

"Bitch?" I finished for her, enjoying the red spreading over her face. "You're not very creative today, are you? Usually you call me a whore because I fucked Kane." Another gasp, and the murmurs became louder. "You couldn't get more than a couple of minutes on your knees, because even your mouth wasn't appealing to him."

The three girls standing behind her took a step back and looked at each other, and I knew that whatever story she told them didn't have the information I had. And while I usually hated confrontation, hated raised voices and unnecessary drama, I was done with people walking all over me. Maybe it was because of the letter I still held in my hand, or maybe things just kept piling up, and I couldn't take it anymore.

I folded the letter in half and pushed it into the pocket of my jeans. "Just leave me alone, Lilly. This thing you've been doing is completely pointless."

I turned around and started walking toward the crowd, thinking she had enough, but I was wrong. Oh, I was so fucking wrong.

"At least my name wasn't carved in Megan's body, Skylar." She laughed, freezing me in place. "Maybe she got high with you guys, and you decided to cut her up and leave one final mark of the great Blackwood legacy."

Megan's lifeless eyes flashed in front of mine. The memory of her from last year was next — her smiling face, her blue eyes, hair the same color as mine. The memory of the tear-stained faces of students when I came to school the next day. The whispers in the wind, and the sight of my name on her skin. Her blood on my hands, underneath my nails, and I started rubbing my hands against my pants as if it was still there.

Red, red, red, dark crimson, and it was everywhere—in the periphery of my vision, in my dreams, on my body, on every surface I touched. I couldn't wash it away. I couldn't get rid of it. I couldn't do anything about it. Everything started rushing to the surface.

The fists slamming into me from side to side as my father released his anger on me.

The dismissive tone my mother used every time I talked to her.

Zane dying.

Finding Megan.

A psychopath messaging me.

It all came together like an avalanche, and I let it go. I released it with a roar as I turned around and rushed after her. Lilly's shocked face was the last thing I saw before I slammed her into the lockers on the other side, holding her by the throat.

"You are a piece of shit, Lilly!" I yelled. "An empty, useless, piece of shit, and if you disappeared, no one would care."

"L-Let me go," she choked out, but I tightened my grip.

"Yes, my name was on her body, and yes, I found her. If I could, I would swap our places in a blink of an eye, but I can't. And then you…" I laughed. "You come in here, running your fucking mouth, just like you usually do, wearing that chip on your shoulder. Look around you, Lilly." I stopped. "Is anybody coming to help you, huh? Where are your so-called friends? Where are your people?" It was my time to laugh. "You're

211

completely alone because you're a shitty human being. I'm not perfect, never claimed to be, but at least I'm not trying to ruin other people's lives because I'm not happy with my own."

"Skylar!" That fucking voice. It felt like fire over my skin, igniting the blood in me, and I pressed against her again. "Fuck!"

In the next moment, instead of the flowery perfume Lilly wore, the scent of pine and cigarettes enveloped me. He lightly gripped the back of my neck, sending rivulets of pleasure through my body.

"Moonshine," he whispered close to my ear. "Let go of her."

But I didn't want to let go. Didn't he get it? So many people did bad things, and they never faced any consequences. Lilly was just another bully who always got away with everything she did, and somebody had to stop her.

"But that somebody doesn't have to be you," he murmured, and I realized that I spoke those words aloud. "This isn't you, Moonshine."

"Maybe it is," I gritted out. "You don't know me well enough to know what kind of a person I am."

"Maybe," he agreed and pressed his lips to my temple. "But I know what I saw, and this isn't you."

But wasn't it? Wasn't I a creation of my parents? Neither one of them were good people. Maybe the same sickness in them was going to catch up with me as well, and one day I would be unrecognizable to people. I would be somebody they used to know. Somebody who could've been good but chose not to be.

"Oh God." I inhaled sharply, seeing the blue on Lilly's lips. I didn't know what terrified me more—the fact that she could pass out if I didn't let go, or the fact that my body hummed with satisfaction at the mere thought of her being hurt.

With heavy steps, I moved away from her, held by Ash who didn't move an inch away from me. My hands shook as adrenaline slowly dissipated from my body. As Lilly's friends crowded around her on the floor while she coughed, tears streaming down her face, I realized what I could've done if it wasn't for Ash.

I wouldn't have stopped and none of these people gathered around us would've intervened. And no matter what, I would've hated myself if I hurt her, because that wasn't me. I didn't go around fighting with people, but today was a fucked-up day. No, this entire year was fucked up, but today took the cake.

"Let's get out of here," Ash muttered, leading me through the throng of students blocking the hallway. "You're going to be okay."

Was I? Was I really going to be okay?

SIXTEEN

Skylar

Where are we going?" I asked Ash as we drove over the old bridge leading into the East Side of Winworth, where I've been to only once as a kid. Regardless of the way he behaved and the vibes I kept getting from him, for the first time in a very long time, I felt safe. For some unknown reason, I felt like I could trust him.

I wanted to laugh because I sounded like every single one of those girls in the books where they trusted the wrong guy. But weren't we all wrong in one way or another? It was so easy plastering labels to people, calling them villains, when we didn't know the whole story. Besides, there was one sentence that haunted me to this day, and the older I got, the more I could see myself in it.

"We are all villains in someone else's story."

And we were. Even the best of us could end up with that label, just because they somehow hurt somebody, even if they didn't want to. I guess that in a way, Ash was my villain and maybe I was his, but neither one of us were just black or white.

People in general weren't black and white. If we labeled ourselves in only those two colors, none of us would be able to stay within the confinements and our role in society would automatically be changed. People, for me, were always more gray than simply black or white.

You know the type of gray, like the sky during the summer, just before the lighting cracks through the clouds, illuminating the entire dome. The kind of gray you could see early in the morning in Winworth, only slightly broken by the rare sight of white clouds or pale blue skies. Heroes and villains, it was such a silly concept, because neither one of these sides was always good or always bad.

Heroes made mistakes. Terrible mistakes that got people killed, that pushed their loved ones away from them. Mistakes that kept them awake at night, choking them, rendering them speechless.

And villains… Villains were people who couldn't fit into the hero's suit. The people who made too many mistakes that those good deeds get forgotten. And how were the villains made? I always asked myself that question. Maybe some people were born evil, and the first time they tasted the sweet scent of fear, destruction, and blood, they became addicted, revealing who they were meant to be. Or maybe their life made them the way they are right now. Maybe they were good people who didn't have any other choice but to become something darker, something vile, because our society didn't want them how they were before.

If I was being honest, our society could fuck itself. We praised fake, white men, sitting in their pretty little chairs, issuing laws that only benefited themselves, while small people suffered. There were people all around the world whose skin wasn't porcelain white, and instead of putting all of us in the same basket, regardless of the color of our skin, our nationality, or our religion, our society somehow decided that they weren't worthy.

And who the fuck had the right to make those kind of decisions? How could we say that a mother and a father running from the war zone, trying to save their children, seeking shelter, were villains? Why? Because they were different? Because their youngest daughter didn't bear a Western name, or didn't have blonde hair? They were villains because they wanted a job, a new place, a better life, while men like my father sat in their comfy office chairs, getting richer and richer, stealing from the people that needed help.

True evil often hid behind the clothes made for heroes, and our society blindly followed them, believing in lies rolling off their tongues. So, no, I didn't believe in black and white, because I've met people who were supposed to be villains, and they were anything but. I've also met people who were supposed to be heroes, and they were the diseases destroying our world.

I sneaked a glance at Ash, wondering what he was thinking about. He hadn't uttered another word after he ushered me from the school, and I knew he was pissed. Don't ask me how I knew, I just did. Since that first day, I realized I studied him more often than not, and the tick that kept reappearing in his cheek told me everything I needed to know.

"Are you not going to talk to me?" I tried again. I had no idea what had him so worked up, and when he remained silent even after we passed all the houses, driving up into the mountain, I knew all my efforts would be futile. He didn't want to talk? Fine. He could keep with the whole broody bullshit because today wasn't the day where I would even attempt to figure him out.

His dark hair fell over his forehead, and my hands

itched from needing to touch him, to drag my finger over his cheekbones, to make him look at me. He called me Moonshine in school and it wasn't the first time he uttered that word. So what was happening now? I knew I didn't do anything to piss him off. In the grand scheme of things, Ash and I were nothing to each other. He was just a guy I fucked once and apparently a guy I couldn't stop thinking about.

I wanted to dive inside his mind just to try and get something from him. Usually, I was the quiet one. The one that observed everybody else. Lauren called it my "creepy people watching", but I found out that you could learn a lot about people by just observing them. By keeping quiet. By watching their body language, their smiles, the way they lifted their eyebrows, how the set of their mouths tightened when someone came to them, when someone they didn't like talked to them, and I didn't do it because I wanted to gather information I could use at a later stage.

I loved doing it because in a way, it was easier thinking about whatever was bothering other people than what was bothering me. In reality, it was just another form of me running away. But I didn't want to run anymore.

Yes, I still wanted to get the fuck away from this cursed town, but I didn't want to run from things keeping me up at night. I knew that there was going to be a point in my life when I couldn't run anymore.

For one flickering moment, I wanted to run away from Ash as well. When he stepped away from me, when he pulled on his pants in that tent, I wanted to run away because for some inexplicable reason, I felt as if he could see me. Not Skylar Blackwood, a daughter that could have everything just because my parents had money. No. I thought he could see the real me.

The terrified me.

The me that only one other person saw when I allowed him to.

But he obviously didn't want me to see him, and it felt as if somebody sucker-punched me, leaving a gaping hole inside my chest. He came when I called. He saved me from myself today, but all the other days, he pretended as if I didn't exist. Or, well, he tried.

I still caught him glancing my way when he thought nobody else was looking, and I couldn't decipher the emotions dancing on his face. Sometimes, I felt like he hated me, like he wanted to rip me apart, and other times, it felt as if he wanted to take me away, save me, hide me and cherish me until the end of the world.

He was a walking contradiction.

The silence in the car was suffocating, only broken by the buzzing of the motor and our breathing, as if both of us were just waiting to explode. I leaned down and turned the radio on, ignoring the sharp intake of breath from him when I came closer. What would he do if I just placed my hand on his knee? Would he push me away or would he let me soothe whatever was troubling him?

But I didn't do it. Not because I didn't want to, but I couldn't handle a rejection from him today. On any other day, I would have a better grip on my emotions, on my mind, but turbulence after turbulence and his rejection would be the thing snapping me in half.

A song came on, one I didn't know, filling the car, caressing my skin as the singer sang. Finally focusing on the lyrics, I almost laughed out loud at how suitable this song was for this entire situation.

I pulled my phone from my pocket and turned on *Shazam*, because the song was too good to pass.

"You've got to be kidding me." I laughed, staring at my screen. The car came to a screeching halt, and before

I could stop my body from flying through the fucking windshield, a strong hand pressed against my chest, keeping me plastered to my seat.

My hair fell around my face, my heart beating a thousand miles per hour, while the sorrowful voice of the singer filled the car, singing about enemies with benefits. I gripped my phone tightly before turning to him, anger coiling all over my skin.

"What the fuck, Ash?" I yelled, unable to stop myself. "You couldn't have, I don't know, stopped slowly?"

"Are you okay?" he asked instead, completely ignoring my question.

Un-fucking-believable.

Unbelievable.

I searched his eyes for a moment—a moment too long—but I couldn't get a read on him. I couldn't see anything on his face. No emotions, no panic, nothing. Absolute emptiness.

"You know what?" I threw my phone in my bag and started opening the door. "Fuck this shit!"

"Skylar!" he yelled after me, but his voice got muffled as I slammed the door of his car and started walking down the gravelly road, taking in the surroundings around me. He drove us all the way up to the mountain where caves were located, infuriating me even more.

Did he really think that I wanted to be in the forest after what happened to Megan?

Motherfucking, stupid, idiotic—

"Skylar!" His voice echoed around us, but I just increased my pace, trying to avoid muddy puddles. "Where the fuck are you going?" He finally caught up with me, taking a hold of my arm and spinning me around.

"Oh, so now you're ready to talk?" I seethed and pulled my arm from his grip. "I'm going home where I won't have to deal with you."

I turned around and managed to take one step, before his arms came around my waist, lifting me up from the ground. I screamed and started thrashing but the idiot wouldn't budge. He started carrying me back, passing the car and heading into the deep forest.

"Let go of me!" I pinched his arm, earning just a painful grunt, but he didn't let go. "Ash!"

"No!" he bellowed.

"Excuse me?" Who did he think he was?

"I'm so fucking angry at you. So, so angry, Moonshine." Oh no, he didn't.

"Well, the feeling is entirely mutual, buddy, but the difference is that I have a reason to be angry at you, while you abso-fucking-lutely don't."

Mr. Broody, as I named him on that first day, just kept walking through the trees, carrying me as if I weighed nothing. My thrashing went unnoticed, so I stopped trying. No matter what I tried, I knew he would be able to catch up with me. Besides, I didn't want to get lost in these woods. I knew the area down at the riverbank, but this side... This side was completely unfamiliar to me, and seeing the dark skies enveloping Winworth, I was pretty sure we were going to get some rain today.

And trust me, there were worse ways of dying than getting slashed by some deranged maniac.

"Ash," I tried again after a couple of minutes. "This is getting ridiculous." Nothing. Not one single word.

He started slowing down, stopping right in front of a large tree stump situated between the tall pine trees casting shadows on the area. The air smelled like rain, both humid and cold, while wind danced across my skin, bringing the scent of pine and mud, intertwining it in what I called the scent of Winworth.

My feet hit the ground when Ash finally let go of me and took a couple of steps away. The adrenaline fueled with the anger I felt earlier started dissipating, leaving behind the sore muscles and disbelief at what I almost did in school. I could've harmed her. I could've done something I wouldn't have been able to come back from, and if it wasn't for Ash, I would've. I could feel his eyes on my neck. I could almost feel his hands on my body, and I knew that once with him would never be enough.

Whatever this pull was, I wanted to feel it, to bask and bathe in it, to feel it on my lips, to taste it on my tongue. I wanted to go crazy with him, to scream his name, to cry out, to forget. Just to fucking forget.

"What is this place?" I mumbled as I placed my hand on top of the tree stump, feeling the rough surface beneath my fingers. I traced my finger along one of the circles on the stump, and I felt him standing right behind me. I didn't hear when he approached, moving like a cat, without a sound, but I felt him.

Just how I felt his hands as they circled around my waist, pulling me up into his chest. My entire body trembled from anticipation, waiting to see his next step. Waiting to see if that night in the tent was only a one-time thing or if he actually felt what I felt—crazy desire, need, molten lava in my veins when he was around.

He was in my bloodstream, in my head, and at that moment, I didn't care if he was just another distraction or something that was meant to be mine.

He inhaled sharply, burying his nose in the crook of my neck. I should've felt scared, unsafe, standing here with a person I met just a few weeks ago, but I didn't. I felt safe, protected, and no matter how much his body radiated with anger, his eyes betrayed him. His dark,

dark eyes, following my every move, reading me like an open book. They told me everything I needed to know.

He wanted this as much as I did.

"What are you doing to me?" he murmured almost painfully, as if speaking those words cost him more than he cared to admit. "It wasn't supposed to be like this."

"Like what?" I asked, afraid my voice was going to sound shaky and weak. And it did. It trembled just like the rest of me, but I couldn't give a fuck about pretenses right now. I wanted him to see me, the real me.

"All-consuming," he answered. "Crazy." He paused and took another inhale. "You make me feel fucking crazy and I don't know why."

"Ash—"

"I think about you all the time, Moonshine. You consume my days. You consume my dreams, and I don't know if I'm strong enough to exorcise you from my veins."

Holy shit.

"It wasn't supposed to be like this," he whispered, like he didn't want me to hear him. "You weren't supposed to be like this."

What? "Ash, what are you—"

But I couldn't finish my question because in the next second, he turned me around, and like a man starved, pressed his lips against mine, inhaling me, savoring me, licking against the seam of my bottom lip, urging me to open up for him.

I opened my eyes, coming face-to-face with the storm brewing in his. I wondered if sailors felt like I did when faced with the storm on the sea. Terrified but calm. Accepting the fate rolled out for them. I knew that he was going to be my ruin. And for better or for worse, I didn't give a fuck if he destroyed the last sane piece of my mind, as long as he kept all the other monsters at bay.

He calmed the demons in my head. This stranger, this storm threatening to destroy me, and I wanted more, so much more.

His hand snaked to the nape of my neck, threading his fingers through my hair, pulling my head back for easier access. Warm lips descended on my neck, trailing kisses toward my collarbone, then back to my waiting lips. A moan escaped from me, involuntarily, ripped from my chest, and the second one followed when he lifted me up, placing me on the tree stump.

I opened my legs, welcoming him in, and wrapped them around his hips, locking him in with me.

"You're going to be the end of me," he growled as he looked into my eyes. "And I won't be able to stop you."

"I-I," I stuttered. "Please," I begged. I didn't know for what. Release, salvation, oblivion, I begged for everything because I knew he could do it. He could give me everything I wanted, everything I needed.

He made me feel alive when I thought I was already dead. He made me feel like I could survive this year if I had him by my side. There was a war brewing in him, and whether it was selfish or not, I didn't want to know. Not now, because I feared that whatever it was would push him further away from me.

And I needed him.

I needed him to help me get through this mess. I just hoped I would be strong enough to let him go when the time came, because even though I was allowing myself this, I knew I couldn't keep him. I couldn't drag him into my world, and he could never know about the monstrosities hiding in the darkest corners of Winworth.

"You're driving me crazy, Moonshine." He bit on my collarbone. "And I'm so fucking angry at you right now. God." He dropped his forehead to my shoulder. "I want to spank you and hug you at the same time."

I voted for the second option, but…

"Why are you angry at me?" I asked before I pressed a kiss to his ear. "I mean, people are angry at me for one reason or another, but I can't remember doing anything to piss you off."

"She would have hurt you," he mumbled before lifting his head. He squeezed my neck, and I could feel the battle in every part of his body. "That girl in the hallway," he continued. "You were alone there, and she would have hurt you."

"I'm pretty sure that I was hurting her, and not the other way around." I grinned, loving that he was actually worried about me. I couldn't remember what happened the night before in the amusement park, and I feared I did something that would push him further away.

"Still, I didn't like it." He brushed his thumb across my cheek, burning the trail on my skin. "I don't like you being in danger."

"I wasn't in danger," I murmured. "She already attacked me once before, and this time I knew what to expect."

"She attacked you before?" Was his eye twitching? "When?"

"Relax." I smiled. "It was at the end of the last school year. There were certain… things, and well, she didn't handle it as well as she should've."

It felt like an eternity before he spoke again, and I couldn't read his face. He just kept staring at me. When the dam broke, he was suddenly everywhere. His hands were lifting my shirt, leaving me only in the black bra I put on this morning.

I wanted to touch him everywhere, burn my claim on his skin like he was burning his on mine. All the other ones before him faded away. My sick father, Kane, Zane, he pushed them all away from me.

"You're mine, Skylar," he growled after he claimed my lips again. "Do you understand that?" He held me in an ironclad grip, blocking my movements.

"Y-Yes," I croaked out. "I'm all yours."

Something flashed across his face — something feral, vicious, dangerous, something like sin — before he dove and bit on my lower lip. His other hand snaked beneath my pants, playing with the edge of my panties. I spread my legs further, urging him to come closer, to show me how much he wanted me.

To show me that I wasn't alone in this insanity. That the need coursing through me wasn't one-sided.

"I'm gonna make you scream, Sky." He grinned. "So fucking loud that the entire town is gonna hear you when you call out my name."

"Please," I moaned.

I placed my hands beneath his shirt, feeling the hard muscles on his stomach and the happy trail leading to his pants. He pulled his hand out of my pants and started fumbling with the button, his breathing labored, the dark hair falling over his forehead. I never wanted anyone as much as I wanted him at this moment.

The sound of the zipper being pulled down seemed louder than it usually was. I wasn't sure if it was the adrenaline or the fact that he was about to fuck me in the middle of the forest where anyone could stumble, but my heart thumped against my ribs like crazy, sending me into a high I have never felt before.

He was my new favorite drug. My new favorite tool to forget.

I lifted my butt to help him take my pants down, and I could see the evidence of his own arousal, straining against his pants. With every brush of his hands against my skin, I was getting higher and higher, and I knew I was going to tumble down like Icarus when he was falling to the ground.

"What's this?" Ash's voice tore me back to reality, and when I opened my eyes, I saw him holding a piece of green paper.

A piece of green paper that was completely unfolded, with his eyes going over the words written on it.

Shit.

"Give it back, Ash." I jumped from the stump and started pulling my pants up, hating the way his eyebrows scrunched together at the words written on it. I took a step closer to him, as he took another one backward, finally giving me his eyes.

All the warmth from before was replaced by what could only be fear.

"Where did you get this?"

"None of your business." I stepped forward and snatched the paper away from him. The lust I felt just a minute ago started dissipating at the mere sight of his face now. He wasn't here anymore. No, he was a thousand miles away, and whatever it was, I had a feeling he wouldn't want to share it with me.

"Do you know what it is?" I asked carefully, folding the paper again and placing it in the pocket of my pants. "Ash?" I urged again when he didn't answer.

As if waking up, he shook his head before he looked back at me. "No. I've no idea." His lips were pulled into a thin line, and a teeny-tiny voice inside my head told me that he knew more than he was sharing.

"Ash, if you—"

A familiar ringtone started blaring, echoing around the forest, and I almost jumped at the suddenness of it. I turned around and walked to my bag when it wouldn't

227

stop even though I wanted to ignore it.

I wanted him to talk to me, to tell me more than just the surface-level bullshit he was willing to share so far.

Lauren's name glared at me from my phone, and with a huff I clicked the green button, and pressed the phone to my ear.

"Lauren, now's not the—"

"Oh my God, Sky," she sobbed, and the alarm went off in my head.

"Lauren?" I sat down on the tree stump and buttoned my pants. "Are you okay? What's going on?"

"Oh God," she sobbed again, freezing the blood in my veins. "I thought it was you."

"What was me, Lauren?"

Ash slowly approached me and picked up the shirt that was haphazardly laying on the ground, extending it to me. He was observing me, just how I was observing him before, but I couldn't think about him right now.

"They found another body, Sky," she whispered. "They found another girl at the riverbank."

And just like that, I knew. I knew she was going to have the same markings as Megan.

"I just spoke with my dad, and he asked about you. She, uh…" Lauren cleared her throat. "She has your name carved into her skin as well."

All the warm and fuzzy feelings from earlier disappeared, replaced by sheer terror and knowledge that this girl was connected to the psychopath stalking me and messaging me. My blood ran cold and my hands started shaking. Disconnecting the call, I turned to Ash and uttered the words I didn't really mean.

"We need to go back."

SEVENTEEN

Skylar

When I stepped out of my house this morning, I never would've imagined that this day would end in this way.

Seventeen-year-old Heather Nessai was found at the riverbank, with acidic burns on her chest and my name carved in her stomach. To say that it made me sick to my stomach would be the understatement of the year.

What made me even more sick was the fact that I lied—again—keeping those messages cryptic, because I feared for my friends. I feared that they would end up dead because of me. Knowing now that killing Megan was not just a one-time thing, I had a feeling we were dealing with an extremely deranged individual.

It didn't help that Ash kept looking at me as if I was going to explode every minute. He kept quiet during the ride back to the town, and all the way to the police station, but he still kept looking at me. The difference was, I was too tired to look back at him. He knew something. The way he looked at that fucking letter, his reaction, I was so sure that he knew something I didn't, and I was going to find out what.

Wasn't it strange that the moment he came to town, these murders started happening?

And even though I wanted to erase these thoughts from my head, I started suspecting every single person in my close vicinity. Kane, Ash, ten other people, they all seemed fishy in my eyes, but I wouldn't be able to prove anything unless I went directly to the police with the messages the murderer was sending me.

Would they be able to find who sent them? Would they be able to track the person threatening me?

Or would they decide that I was somehow at fault for these murders in town?

Then there was my name carved into their corpses, like a beacon leading to me as a prime suspect. God, I wanted to run away from here. Just pack a bag and get out of this forsaken town.

But I couldn't, at least not yet.

Besides, even if I ran, I had a feeling it would do me no good. My father would find me no matter where I went. Dylan would blow a gasket if I just ran away without ever talking to him about all this.

And, I couldn't bear the thought of leaving Ash. He riled me up like no one ever did, but my blood sang when he was around.

So, here I was, sitting in his car at six in the evening, because the same police officer interrogating me that first day decided that he needed to keep me at the station for way longer than necessary. I wanted to throw the mug on the table at him, but I couldn't do that either.

I could count the number of things I could do on one hand, and none of those could help me find out what the fuck was happening in this town — the missing girls, then their bodies, then cryptic messages, and my name on their bodies. And that fucking letter from this morning, telling me to go to our local library to find out more about Winworth.

Did I even want to know more? I had a feeling that

the more I knew, the more danger I would be in. But I couldn't exactly just sit idly by and pretend that nothing was happening around me.

I could drown myself in drugs and alcohol, but that wouldn't help either. All those were temporary solutions to a lasting problem.

"Are you going to be okay?" Ash asked, while parked in front of my house. The light was on, on the porch, but I knew that nobody else was at home right now. Dylan went back to Seattle to finish some things, my father was finally out of town, and my mom was still on that fucking trip.

Our housekeeper, Vera, probably already went home, which meant I would be all alone in the enormous house. Tremors rocked through my body, mostly visible on my hands, but I shoved them underneath my legs, hiding my fear from him.

"Yeah." I nodded. "I'll be fine. Thanks for the ride." I picked up my bag and turned to the door, but he took a hold of my arm, stopping me from going any further.

"Just," he started. "Be safe, okay?"

Whatever it was that he wanted to say wasn't that, but I was too tired to push him for more. I had a feeling that it was only one tragedy after another, and I couldn't deal with grumpy Ash tonight. For some reason, I wanted him for more than just meaningless sex, and it was painfully obvious that he wasn't willing to open up enough for us to talk about it.

One second, he was telling me things like in that forest, and in the next one, he was completely closed off. I had enough shit in my life without adding his to the pile. So no, tonight I was going to take a shower, go to sleep, and forget that this day ever happened.

"I always am," I replied and pushed the door open, welcoming the cold air. As much as I hated the weather in Winworth, tonight it was a welcoming distraction from the disaster surrounding my life. We were in the middle of September, and the way the weather was behaving, you would think we were already in the middle of October.

The door slammed behind me, and I pulled the sweater Lauren brought to the station tighter around me, and started walking toward the front door. I opened my bag and pulled out the keys dangling from the string Dylan had given me a few years ago. I used to lose keys every second week, and after making me wear this stupid string around my neck, I stopped losing them. And when I didn't need to wear it around my neck anymore, I kept it, unable to throw it away. Dylan gave it to me, and parting with it felt like somehow pushing him away, and I couldn't do it.

The wind howled around me while an owl cried out close by. At least it wasn't crows today. I had a feeling they were everywhere these days, and while I absolutely loved them, they reminded me of death and all the sinister things coating the history of Winworth.

As soon as I started unlocking the doors, the tires of Ash's car screeched on the gravelly road, and I knew he was going to leave me alone for the night. I wasn't sure if I felt disappointed or relieved that I wouldn't have to deal with him and his mood swings tonight.

Maybe I wanted him to stay, to hold me during the night, but I also knew that would be too much to ask. I was tired of asking for things I could never have. I wanted him to do it himself, without me asking, but it was obvious that the two of us weren't on the same wavelength when it came to this thing between us.

The lights were on in the house, Vera most probably leaving them on for me. It was both terrifying and soothing, knowing that I was completely alone. I didn't want to call Dylan after they summoned me to the station, even though I knew he would've come. I didn't want to call my father, because with him being away, I knew I could breathe a little bit.

But the truth was, I was completely and utterly alone.

Yeah, I had Lauren and my other friends, but they all had to go home to be with their families. They were all terrified of this person killing people, and I had a feeling that this was only the start of the nightmare.

Locking the door behind me, I all but ran upstairs, ready to just forget about the day. It was too early to go to sleep, but I wanted nothing more than to curl up in my bed and forget that another young girl died because a psychopath was obsessed with me.

He called these murders his gifts, and it was only a matter of time before he was going to message me again. Truth be told, I half-expected it to happen during the day, but there were still no messages on my phone.

I glared at the device as if it could give me the answers I so desperately needed, but the only thing glaring back at me was a bright screen and the picture of a wolf I placed as my background. Throwing my bag to the floor as soon as I got to my room, I started removing my clothes, ready to just take a shower and remove the remnants of the day from my skin.

I thought about Lilly and her vicious words. I thought about Ash and the hot-and-cold game we were playing. I thought about Heather and her last moments, comparing her to the visions of Megan I could never forget.

The police hadn't shared with me if she was found in the same state Megan was but knowing that her chest was burned with acid left a sour taste in my mouth. As I stepped into the shower, letting the warm water cascade over my body, I started thinking about her family.

She was young. Too young to know that kind of violence. Too young for her life to be taken away from her. Too young to experience terror, and to go through these things. I often thought about the souls of those that died in a violent way.

Were they scared? Did they pray to God, saints, or the universe to take their pain away? What were their last thoughts before the monster took away their last breath?

Maybe it was morbid thinking about all those things. No, I knew it was morbid thinking about those things, but sometimes I liked to think that I maybe kept them in my memory, even if it was in a morbid way.

Or maybe focusing on all these things was taking away my guilt and the fact that I was probably withholding the key to bring the murderer to justice. I knew I was selfish. I was choosing the lives of my friends over the lives of the rest of the people. The fact that I didn't receive a single message from that same number in days scared the hell out of me. I should've been relieved, but I had a feeling that this only meant that something worse was coming.

I could hear my phone buzzing, vibrating against the surface of the sink where I dropped it, but I didn't want to see the number on the screen. If it wasn't one of my friends or Dylan, it was most definitely the killer, and thinking about some deranged person roaming freely on the streets of our town was the last thing I wanted to do.

I closed my eyes instead, letting the water wash over me. Letting it clear me of the sins coating my skin, even though I knew that no amount of water would be enough to wash away all of them. But I could try to get myself rid of them.

The first thing I needed to do was to get out of here.

Only then would I be free of the sicknesses marring my skin.

○

I woke up with a start, blinking through the darkness of the room, immediately looking for my phone. After the shower, I just collapsed onto my bed, planning to take a quick nap and then wake up to finish my homework. But looking at my phone now, I could see that my nap ended up being a full-blown sleep. Instead of waking up at nine as I planned to, I managed to sleep through all six alarms I set for myself.

It was already past midnight, and I decided to just continue sleeping instead of getting up now, but a loud crash echoed through the house, freezing me in place.

What the fuck was that?

I looked toward the door, my vision getting clearer in the dark, my heartbeat gradually speeding up. Did I imagine that sound?

I threw the blanket off of me and moved to get up, picking my phone up at the same time. Maybe I was just being paranoid? Maybe the crash came from outside of the house? Maybe it was just floors creaking and my overactive imagination turned it into something else?

But when the second crash came, this time closer to my room, I knew I wasn't imagining things. Somebody was in the house with me. Someone uninvited, and I had a feeling I knew who it was. My throat closed as I took a hold of the door handle, trying to open it without too much sound, hoping that this wasn't what I thought it was.

Maybe it was Ash coming to surprise me? Or maybe... Maybe Dylan or my parents came back home, and they didn't let me know beforehand? Yeah, it could

235

be one of these options, and as I swung the door open, my phone tightly clutched in my hand, I peeked a glance to the hallway, contemplating my options.

But even if my brain was trying to calm me down by creating these possibilities in my head, my body knew that I was in danger. The skin on the nape of my neck stood up as footsteps creaked from the staircase, and my flight-or-fight instincts kicked in without thinking.

I pressed one hand against my mouth, muffling down any sounds of my breathing, and tiptoed toward the study opposite of my room, thankful for the already open doors. I swallowed the cry of despair threatening to erupt from my throat, and tried to calm myself down, tried to think.

I had to do something, for fuck's sake. Something, anything.

I plastered myself against the wall next to the door inside the study, listening to the sounds blanketing the silent night, but I couldn't hear anything but the thundering beat of my heart. It was as if my ribs were closing in, tighter, painfully tighter, around my heart, squeezing me to death, cutting off my ability to think, ability to breathe, to move, to…

No, no, no, no, this can't be happening right now. This can't be fucking happening.

There was a potential serial killer in my house, and my body and mind were betraying me in the moments where I needed to be sane. Where I needed to think with a cool head.

I couldn't move because moving could uncover my position. I couldn't shake the dreary feeling wrapping itself around my bones, and fear I never felt before started seeping into my pores, sneaking in like smoke from the fire that permeated clothes.

My vision started getting blurry and not even a

second after, I felt the wetness on my left hand still pressed against my mouth.

I was crying. I was fucking crying, and I didn't even realize.

An involuntary sob clogged itself in my throat, choking me, killing me from the inside, but I couldn't let it out. Or maybe, maybe, maybe, maybe all of this was inside my head.

Yeah, there was no killer in the house. It was only me and my fucked-up head.

And I almost believed myself, until the creaking sound echoed around the hallway, just outside the study.

Oh my God.

I should've called the police while I was in my room. I should've been smarter, because now I couldn't turn my phone on without it illuminating the entire room.

Another creak, another step so much louder than before, and another tear rolled down my cheek, hitting my hand. The rustling of clothes as the intruder entered my room was almost enough to push me to run, but I had to wait. Just wait and listen.

One step, and then the second one, and then I dared to sneak a peek from around the corner. Maybe if my adrenaline wasn't at an all-time high, I would've passed out from the sight in front of me. But when my eyes zeroed in on the wide back standing inside my room, I bolted from my hiding spot and started running toward the stairs.

Keeping quiet wasn't important anymore. I had to get out of the house and get help.

But where? There were no houses next to ours, and I knew that running away wasn't an option anymore. Instead, that same anger that took a hold of me before I attacked Lilly reappeared, igniting the blood in my veins, leading me where I needed to go.

His footsteps thundered behind me as I rounded the corner and started running down the stairs, but stopping wasn't an option, even though my heart threatened to jump out of my chest. Even though the tears continued streaming down my cheeks, I didn't stop when I jumped from the second stair to the ground and headed toward the kitchen.

I didn't stop when I heard him coming closer, closer, so close that if he just took a few more steps, he would be able to catch me.

But I had to survive. I wanted to survive. All that talk about wanting to die, wanting to disappear, and now when I was faced with the situation that would give me an easy way out, I couldn't bear the thought of dying. At least, not like this.

If my death was inevitable, I wanted to be the one to decide how and when, not some deranged monster cutting girls left and right, fixating on me.

My foot slipped on the tiles in the kitchen, but I managed to straighten myself up, reaching toward the knives placed on the counter. But before I could grasp one of them, a strong set of hands lifted me from the ground and pulled me backward, slamming me into the opposite wall.

"No!" I screamed, scrambling to get away from him. Before I could run outside of the kitchen, he managed to get a hold of me again, pressing his chest to my back, caging me in his embrace.

"Please," I cried. "Please don't hurt me."

I couldn't see his face, but I could hear his labored breathing as he lowered his head to my neck, scenting me, sending shock waves through my body as fear gripped my insides.

"Please," I begged, whimpering in his arms, but he

didn't budge even when I started thrashing in his arms. If anything, his grip tightened, and one of his hands sneaked toward my throat, pressing soft touches, caressing me.

"I'll do anything," I pleaded, but he didn't answer. Instead, he turned me around, pulling another scream from me at the sight in front of my eyes.

A mask covered his face, hiding his eyes, hiding his entire identity. Its golden hue shone underneath the moonlight peeking in through the windows. I didn't dare move. I almost didn't dare to breathe as this stranger perused my face, his hand still wrapped around my throat, the hidden warning cloaked by the soft caresses he kept inflicting on my skin.

I pressed my hands on his chest, feeling the strong muscles beneath my fingers, but he stopped me from going any further when I tried sneaking my hands around his neck, trying to pull off the hood hiding his hair. Tilting his head to the side, he started walking forward, pushing me out of the kitchen, all the way to the foyer area where a chair stood right in front of the door.

My whimpers, my pleading, it all fell on deaf ears as he sat me down, pressing harder against my throat. As a warning, as foreplay, I didn't know anymore. He didn't kill me — yet — but that didn't mean he wouldn't hurt me.

"Are you going to kill me?" I asked as he pulled out the rope from a pocket in his cloak and bound my wrists to the arms of the chair. I wanted to hear him talk. I wanted to learn anything that could give me an advantage over this person. "Why aren't you talking?" I tried softening my voice, because if he was truly obsessed with me, then maybe he didn't want to harm me more than he thought was necessary.

But there was no answer. Nothing but the rustling

of his clothes and our breathing.

"Did you kill those girls?" I braved to ask—the wrong thing to ask—because in a second, he gripped the back of my neck and pulled my hair, exposing my throat to him. Trailing a path with his gloved finger over my skin, he went over my chin all the way to my lips, stopping just below my lower lip. "Did you?" I croaked, because dying and not knowing who he was, was unbearable.

I could've missed it, almost did, when he nodded slowly, before he pressed his thumb into my lower lip, moving his finger from one side of my mouth to the other. He leaned down, his face inches away from mine, and I closed my eyes, knowing that this night wasn't going to end up well for me.

"Why can't you let me go?" I cried. "Why are you doing this?" I asked as I opened my eyes, realizing that he'd moved back. But my momentary relief was short-lived when I saw the knife in his hand.

"No, please!" I started pushing against the chair, but it was futile fighting against the ropes he tightened around my arms. "I'm begging you," I pleaded as he took a step closer, turning the knife to the side, looking first at it then at me.

"You don't have to do this. Please don't do this."

But the faceless man continued to be quiet, staring at me, and when he took the final step, standing right next to me, he lifted his other hand, pressing his finger against his lips.

"I'm not gonna keep quiet, damn you!" I screamed. "They're gonna find you. My brother is going to find you!"

But even I knew that these were empty threats, my last attempt to stall him, to stop him. No one would hear me. Nobody was coming to save me.

I was alone.

All fucking alone, and I was going to die tonight.

I flinched as his hand shot out, but instead of hitting me, he gently moved the hair from my face, putting it behind my ear.

My stomach lurched, because how could somebody behave like this? Both a killer and a gentle man? I thought that he would've killed me by now. I kept staring at his face when he pressed the tip of his knife to my arm, pulling another shriek from me.

"Noooo!"

But he kept going, carving and carving and carving, while pain kept ricocheting through my arm, through my body.

"Stop!" I thrashed and thrashed, but he didn't stop even when my head started getting woozy and his masked face started getting blurry. "Please," I wept, feeling the blood dripping from my arm.

My head started falling, and unable to keep it standing, to keep fighting, I closed my eyes when he began cutting me again, drawing line after line over my arm.

As the edges of my vision darkened, I just prayed that he wouldn't drop my body somewhere in the woods. I didn't want to be found like Megan.

EIGHTEEN

ASH

I couldn't get last night out of my head. No, I couldn't get the entire day out of my head.

Skylar's frightened face, her holding that girl against the lockers, Skylar touching me in the woods, and then leaving the car without a second glance. And another body was found. Yet another victim of this sick game they were playing, and no one would ever know why she died.

And that fucking note I saw yesterday, with their symbol embedded on top of it, glaring at me, mocking me even from the paper. But the text, those clues left for Skylar, those weren't written by people from The Order. No, it was glaringly obvious to me that she didn't know what her family was involved in. Then who would leave such things to her?

If she was being initiated, she wouldn't look so spooked when I saw it.

I spent the entire night going over the words I saw, thinking about all the people that could've left it for her, but no matter how much I tried to uncover the person that could've given it to her, I came up blank. A sleepless night, and no clues on how to fix this shit.

Not to mention that I wasn't even close to uncovering the way to enter the catacombs, or that the lines between what I had to do and what I wanted to do were on opposite sides. The battle raged inside my body, both sides fighting for dominance. I had to avenge the death of my parents and what they did to us, but I wanted to take Skylar, my brother, and get us all out of here.

Indigo's words were on repeat as well—his warnings, his advice, but my brain was too fried from the lack of sleep to even try to make sense of anything that was happening around me. I avoided my uncle as soon as I got home last night. Sebastian was out of the house, so I didn't have to deal with the full Spanish Inquisition.

Then why couldn't I look my uncle in the eyes? Why couldn't I tell him the truth? I lied to his face when he asked me about Skylar and our plan. I lied because she wasn't just a pawn anymore. She wasn't a girl I hated, or somebody I just wanted to use.

She wasn't just some face in the photo, the privileged spoiled princess. She was so much more.

Everything I did lately, I did it with her in mind. The sky, the river, the silvery blue color of my shirt, it all held pieces of her because I couldn't stop thinking about her. Even now as I puffed out the smoke from my cigarette, staring at the sunrise on the horizon, I only thought about her.

I thought about her soft skin, that small smile she so rarely gave... I thought about everything, and I shouldn't have. Maybe I needed to be reminded about our mission here. Maybe I wasn't the right person for this job.

Maybe getting involved with her was the wrong way to approach this, but if I told this to my uncle, he would question me. And how could I tell him that Skylar Blackwood managed to sneak inside, hiding next to my heart, because she wasn't who I thought she would be?

This war we waged was meant to have casualties, but I never thought that one of them was going to be the one I couldn't bear to see hurt. I couldn't bear the thought of her hating me, and she would. After all of this was done, she was going to hate me.

She would never want to see me again. She would never let me touch her, and I would have to learn to live with it. Or I could stop right now.

I could go downstairs and tell my uncle that the plan we had was wrong. But how could I have her without betraying the memory of my parents?

I couldn't, that was the problem. I couldn't have one without betraying the other one, and I just had to figure out which one was worthy of betraying.

Was I going to let the ghosts of my past control my life, or was I going to take the reins and decide what I wanted to do without this revenge hanging above my head?

Think, Ash, fucking think, I thought to myself. *Which one was a lesser evil?*

"Ash?" I almost jumped up from the chair when my brother's voice tore through my thoughts.

"Jesus, fuck, Sebastian," I groaned. "I almost jumped over the fence." I turned around looking at his tired face.

"Dude, I was woken up, thanks to your phone." He yawned. "So, trust me, I'm tempted to push you over the fence myself."

"What do you mean by my phone?" I looked around, noticing for the first time that my phone wasn't anywhere near me.

"This phone." He lifted the device with a black cover and threw it toward me. "It's been ringing nonstop for the last hour. You left it in the hallway, right in front of my room."

Shit.

"And if you don't mind, some of us are not psychopaths like you, waking up at an ungodly hour."

I didn't bother telling him that I didn't sleep last night, and the only reason I was outside on the balcony was to clear my thoughts. Before I could utter another word, he turned around and walked out of my room, leaving me alone again, with my phone lying in my lap.

I picked it up, and as soon as the screen lit up, my heart started beating faster at the sight of the missed calls showing on it.

"What the fuck?" I mumbled, unlocking it with the press of my finger.

I clicked on the green icon with the telephone on it and saw fifteen missed calls from Lauren, and half a dozen messages as well.

Ash, for fuck's sake, pick up your damn phone.

That first message was sent three hours ago.

Fine, don't pick up your phone, but I need your help. Skylar needs you.

Shit, shit, shit. I stood up, going over the rest of the messages, my blood turning into ice when I came to the last one.

I hope you're having a very nice sleep, you dipshit. We are at Winworth Memorial Clinic, in case you would like to know. Skylar was attacked.

Skylar was attacked?

The air whooshed out from my lungs, my legs feeling weak as I reread the message she sent an hour ago.

Skylar was fucking attacked, and Lauren's been trying to reach me for hours. Motherfuck—

I jumped up and went into my room, walking toward the wardrobe. I pulled off the shirt I had on and took another one, pulling it on. I tried calling Lauren, but the calls were going to her voicemail. I had a feeling that she was either ignoring me, or her phone died.

Without waiting another minute, I took the leather jacket from my bed and walked downstairs, grabbing my keys from the stand next to the door.

"You're up early." My uncle's voice stopped me in my tracks, just before I exited the house.

"I have somewhere to be," I answered through gritted teeth, praying that he wouldn't ask for more than I was willing to answer. "I'll catch you later."

I turned the doorknob and stepped out when he started talking again.

"Ash." I turned around, waiting for him to continue. "We need to talk later. I have news."

Of course, he had news. He always had some kind of news, but for the first time in my life, I couldn't give a shit about the plan, his news, or the revenge we came here to enact. All I cared about was the girl who was getting caught in the crossfire, who was now lying somewhere in that hospital, probably scared.

"Yeah, sure," I mumbled. "I'll talk to you later."

I almost sprinted from the doorway toward my car when he called out again.

"Ash!" *Dammit.* I turned around, holding my keys, ready to get out of here. "Remember why we're here."

God-fucking-dammit. He knew. He knew my head wasn't where it was supposed to be, and I could bet that the "talk" he wanted to have later on, would turn into a full-blown lecture, trying to remind me who the enemy was.

As if I didn't know. As if I didn't have scars to remind me. As if I didn't have nightmares for years, tormenting me every single day, keeping me awake at night.

But I couldn't deny that being with Skylar made me

think twice about the plans we created before coming to Winworth. My resolve was wavering, and it had nothing to do with me being scared. No, it had everything to do with a pair of angelic eyes, feathery touches, and sweet nothings whispered in my ear. I thought I was playing the game, making her fall for me, but I had a feeling that I became a pawn, letting my emotions lead.

Instead of answering him, instead of reassuring him that I knew what the stakes were, I simply nodded and unlocked my car, sliding in without a second glance at my uncle. We disagreed on many things but bringing The Order to its knees wasn't one of them.

If I wasn't mistaken, that was one of the rare things we agreed on — exacting revenge on those that killed my parents, his friends. People should be thankful that there was somebody out here, brave enough to stand up to them.

Then why did I have a sour taste in my mouth every single time I thought about the Blackwood family now? Where was the anger, the viciousness I used to have? Maybe my uncle was right. Maybe I needed to be reminded of everything we lost, in order to continue this ordeal.

Seeing Skylar, being with her, it all made me rethink about what I was supposed to do, and I could see now how it affected my resolve to get things done. Perhaps going to the hospital like a lovesick fool wasn't the best idea, I decided.

Even if my heart protested against me, I knew I had to put some distance between us. Because if I didn't, I would destroy us both.

I had to erase the memories of her from my head and remember who she really was to me — an enemy, a foe. This wasn't the great love story of my life, where I could get the girl even though she belonged to the opposing family.

We were more like Layla and Majnun, and I planned not to go mad from grief because I couldn't have her. I could pretend. I could lie. I could make her believe in this sweet little lie where she was mine, and I was hers, but that's all it was and all it would ever be—a lie.

A fantasy I allowed to happen, forgetting what was important.

And Skylar couldn't become someone too important to me. She couldn't become more than she already was. So what if the colors around me looked brighter since she came into my life? I was okay with my gray world before she came, and I will learn to be okay with it again.

I could do this. I could make her fall for me without falling for her. And if I gripped the steering wheel tighter now, it wasn't because I ached to touch her, to see her, to make sure she was okay.

It wasn't because I was worried about her and pissed off at myself.

The fog I was still getting used to still coated the streets, lingering over the bridge as I passed into the West Side of Winworth, wallowing in my misery, refusing to turn on the radio. I always sought music when my mind couldn't come up with an explanation on its own.

When I couldn't put my emotions into words, when my chest became too heavy, burdened by the ghosts from my past and things I had to do, music was always there as a solution, to show people what I really wanted to say.

The first time I expressed what I wanted was when Uncle Neal bought me a CD player and the greatest hits from Iron Maiden. Maybe not the best choice for a seven-year-old, but neither one of us knew how to deal with the situation we found ourselves in.

He saved us, Sebastian and me, and I didn't want to disappoint him, no matter how much we disagreed on mundane things. And going to see Skylar, that would disappoint him. That would break his heart, because he was the one who had to change the gauze on my burned skin. He was the one who had to listen to my screams, to my cries when nightmares couldn't be contained in the realm of dreams.

So when I came to the crossing, where the sign on the right glared at me with the name of the hospital and the directions to get to it, I turned left and headed toward the school, ignoring the nagging voice in the back of my head, telling me I'd made a mistake.

Perhaps I did, but Skylar didn't need me. She had other people who could tend to everything she wanted, everything she needed. She was just a body I liked to fuck, and nothing else.

She was nothing to me.

NINETEEN

Skylar

Time passes differently when your entire life gets turned upside down. Seconds feel like minutes, minutes like hours, and hours like days, all to the point where I wasn't sure if it was one, two or three days since they admitted me to the hospital.

Since I woke up screaming in an ambulance. Since that maniac carved something on my arm, leaving me tied to the chair, until our gardener found me in the morning, when he saw an open door and my blood on the floor.

But after they gave me a sedative, after I closed my eyes, my mind became blank, and it was as if somebody flipped a switch in my body, turning off all the bad things swirling in the back of my head. There was no pain, no happiness, no love nor sadness.

There was nothing.

Pure emptiness.

I knew Dylan was here. Lauren, Kane, my mom and dad, but there was one person I wanted to see, and he never came.

Ash.

I knew I should be feeling happy that I was still alive, but it was as if my heart refused to cooperate with my mind. I knew what I was supposed to be feeling, but no matter how hard I tried, nothing came up.

Dylan talked to me, begging me to reply. Begging me to say anything. To cry, to scream, to be angry, but I couldn't be bothered. Not anymore. I was done pleading for my life because I shouldn't have to. I shouldn't have to beg for happiness, for a little piece of paradise.

I didn't even flinch when my father placed his hand on my forehead, pretending to be concerned about me. I didn't move when my mother faked her tears, holding my hand, and letting Dylan comfort her. I didn't utter a single word when Kane got angry, all but yelling at me.

I simply didn't have the strength to answer any of their questions. I didn't have it in me to pretend anymore. I just couldn't. You know how people say that your life flashes before your eyes in your last moments?

Nothing flashed in front of mine.

No memories. No happiness. Just an eternal darkness as I slipped into an unconscious state, while he mutilated my body. And I wanted to be angry because yet another person touched me without my permission. Yet another person hurt me when I wanted nothing more but to be held.

Just for a moment, one fleeting moment, I wanted to feel protected without the fear gripping my insides.

But I was too tired to feel anything. I was too tired of constantly fighting, constantly thinking ten steps ahead, dreaming of a brighter future, because the reality I was in right now was not what I wanted to have.

I could hear the voices now right outside the open door. Dylan and Lauren. I wanted to call them, to invite them in, to share what was bothering me. I wanted to tell them that I couldn't do this anymore. I couldn't live my life like this.

But as soon as I opened my mouth, the words died,

swallowed by my shallow breathing. They choked me, wanting to spill out, but they couldn't.

Even after, I didn't even know how many days, my throat was still sore from screaming that night. I wanted to tell them that I was okay. I was alive, and that's all that mattered.

But that would be a lie, wouldn't it?

Just another lie on a long list I made over the past two years. Just another omission of truth because I didn't want to see the pity in their eyes. Self-destruction was a fucked-up thing.

You wanted to get better, you knew that you needed to get better if you wanted to live, but at the same time you couldn't get yourself up from the bed. You couldn't stop yourself from taking just another pill, just another drag of the cigarette, just another sip of alcohol, just to make yourself feel better.

We were all either chasing the lack of feeling, or we wanted to feel something, anything. Some days, I wanted to drown myself with my sorrow and to forget the nightmares haunting me. Other days, I wanted to feel something, just to remember that I was still alive.

I was still here.

On other days, those dark, dark, dark days, I had to remind myself how to breathe, how to smile, how to act as if I was there. How to behave, because more and more I felt like I was just watching a movie while my life passed right in front of my eyes.

And everything I did, every single word I spoke, it was my muscle memory keeping me afloat.

Get up in the morning.

Stare at the wall until I remembered that I had to move.

Brush my teeth, take a shower, put on my clothes… One, two, three, four breaths before I go outside of my room, especially if Dylan was home. Remember how to smile. Remember how to respond to questions.

Remember not to doze off.

Remember.

Remember.

Remember.

But I couldn't remember anymore. Since they brought me to the hospital, I couldn't remember. I couldn't remember who I wanted to be. I couldn't remember my plans, my dreams, or how to act... I couldn't remember any of it.

I could only remember the golden mask, empty sockets where the eyes were supposed to be, and his tilted head as he started carving on my arm. For a moment there, I thought he would want to make it seem like I killed myself — not that it would come as a surprise to most people — but he didn't.

I lifted my arm, staring at the white bandages hiding whatever it was he left beneath, hiding the wounds for now. I wished I was strong enough to tear them off, to see what was so important to knock my life upside down. I wanted to see what he did to me.

I was familiar with scars. I carried them hidden in the dark parts of my soul, masking them from the rest of the world. Those were the scars that never truly healed, but at least no one could see them.

This one... This one was going to be visible to every single person. This one was going to be one I would never be able to hide, and I would still have to carry it.

I could already hear the whispers in school and on the street.

A survivor.

Such a brave girl.

Poor thing.

But I wasn't a survivor. I wasn't brave. I was a liar.

I lied to myself, to my friends, to my family. I lied every single day, because facing the truth was much harder than any of us knew. Facing the truth meant that I would truly have to think about things cutting me every single day, and I wasn't ready for that.

"Sky?" Dylan's voice echoed around the room, muffled by the buzzing sound of the air conditioner. I really wanted to turn around, to cry, to let him hold me, soothe me, but I couldn't. His deep sigh was the only indication of how frustrated he was, but instead of telling me how my indifference to everything was killing him, he just continued talking. "Lauren brought some clothes for you. They're releasing you today."

Releasing me. To go home. To go back to the place where I was hurt, where I faced my worst nightmare.

"Do you want me to help you get dressed?" he asked, but we both knew the answer to that question. Yesterday, he tried holding my hand, but I tore it out of his grasp faster than he could blink, teetering on the edge of a panic attack, because even thinking about anybody's hands on my body these days sent fear rolling over my skin.

"Right." He exhaled as I turned around, taking in the dark circles around his eyes and the disheveled blond hair.

"You need a haircut," I croaked for the first time in days, taking him by surprise. His eyes widened, lips parted, as if he was witnessing a miracle right in front of him. Truthfully, it should've pissed me off, but it didn't.

"Yeah, well," he shrugged, "I had more important things to do."

A small smile played at the edges of his lips, softening his eyes, and as I sat up from the bed, letting my legs dangle from the end, I tried remembering again. I tried to remember how to be normal again.

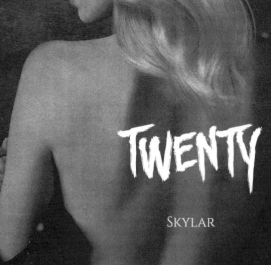

TWENTY

Skylar

I t was weird how everything looked the same when we pulled in front of our house, yet I knew that nothing was as it used to be. Or maybe I wasn't who I used to be.

Dylan turned the ignition off, staring at the house just like I did, as if it was some entity that could hurt me. Truth be told, I wasn't afraid of the house. I wasn't afraid of anything right now, and that was bad.

Fear, anger, love, happiness, all those were part of us so that they could guide us, show us the way, steer us in the right direction, and without them, we wouldn't be able to function like normal human beings. Without them, we wouldn't be able to run away from people that were dangerous, because our senses wouldn't be functioning properly.

Well, my senses were obviously fucked up.

"We don't have to go inside if you don't want to," he mumbled.

I knew I didn't have to. Dylan would never make me do anything I didn't want to do, but if I didn't overcome this, I would let the monster win. I would give the nameless, faceless person power over my life, and I

I didn't want to live a life filled with regrets, with fear, and thinking about that night. I didn't want to let fear rule my life. There were already things I couldn't control. Things I couldn't escape, and I wouldn't let this be another.

The problem was, I didn't feel anything. I should've been afraid, terrified even, because that bastard carved me up in the foyer of my own house.

Instead, I was… I was calm.

Since we left the hospital, I kept expecting the nausea to hit. I kept pressing my palms together, thinking they would be sweaty, that my hands were going to shake, or that my eyes would sting from the unshed tears, caused by fear.

But none of that happened.

Apathy took a hold of my body, and I couldn't escape its vise-like grip. Not that I wanted to.

Being apathetic was better than being terrified, and right now, I would take any win possible. If I could continue feeling like this, empty and cold, I wouldn't have to deal with the mess I was now keeping locked away in the back of my mind.

If I could continue being empty, I wouldn't have to think about other things. The things that, up until three days ago, haunted my days and my nights. The things a seventeen-year-old girl shouldn't have to worry about.

I shouldn't have to worry about my phone ringing in the middle of the night, because I always knew it was my father calling for me to play out his sick fantasies. I shouldn't have to worry about a killer on the loose, who was obviously fixated on me.

"Sky?" Dylan started again, agitation obvious in his voice.

I moved my eyes from the house in front of us — the house that should've been my personal nightmare, but it

258

wasn't — and took his hand in mine, squeezing it tight.

"I'm fine, Dylan," I muttered as I looked him in the eyes.

Pain. So much pain was reflected in those blue orbs, and for a moment, my breath caught in my throat, hating the vision in front of me. Hating the worry etched in the corners of his eyes, or the dark circles marring his perfect face.

I both hated and loved that he cared about me, because I was a train wreck, a disaster waiting to happen. And Dylan... Dylan was heaven in hiding. He was the pure light, and I was the pure dark.

Some people might say it was poetic, seeing the two of us as opposite sides of the same coin, but in reality, it was nothing but tragic. Life had a fucked-up way of throwing yin and yang references at us, and Dylan and I were the best example of it.

I didn't hate it because I envied him, no. I hated it because caring for me would only destroy him. Loving me would devastate him because I was a bomb waiting to explode.

As he gripped my hand tighter and placed his other one on my cheek, words weren't needed for me to know how much he cared about me. He didn't have to give me a speech. He didn't have to tell me that everything was going to be okay, considering that we both knew none of this was okay.

But I knew he was there for me. He was the shoulder I could lean on. He was the person I could count on when everything else went up in flames.

"Are you ready then?" he asked, while his thumb slowly worked over my cheek. I leaned into his touch, relishing in the warmth of his hand, of this safe cocoon he was providing me with.

I closed my eyes and slowly exhaled, letting myself

feel. Letting myself remember how to be me again, how to live and love and be afraid. And maybe it was a process now. Maybe I would never be who I used to be prior to the entire ordeal, but I could try.

And I would have Dylan, even if I didn't have anyone else.

"Let's go inside," I whispered, opening my eyes. "Let's go home."

A smile played on the edges of his lips, braving me to open my door, to go out. He exited first and went around the car from the front, all the way to the passenger side, and opened my door, holding his hand out for me. It was these small things, small deeds that made me feel better.

I placed my hand in his, letting him lead me out of the car. I was still feeling dizzy from the three days of doing nothing but lying in the bed and the medication they gave me, but as the brisk air caressed my cheeks, and the wind started playing with my hair, I knew I was going to be okay.

I looked around our front yard, while Dylan took my bags out of the trunk, and I smiled for the first time in three days.

I was stronger than this. I was stronger than I gave myself credit for.

The air smelled like rain—cold and damp, yet somehow freeing and almost nostalgic. I could see the white clouds gathered on the darkened sky, and I hoped we would get rain tonight. Everything always seemed fresher, newer, better after the rain.

As if it somehow managed to wash away everything bad that has happened in the past. Or maybe it was my wishful thinking, but whatever it was, I wanted it tonight.

I wanted to be freed of this darkness in my bones. I

wanted to feel like a new person.

"Ready?" Dylan came from behind, placing a hand on my upper back.

Was I ready? Not really.

I looked toward the front door, and I feared that once we entered inside, this wall I somehow built up would come down, shattering, and my broken mind would attack me. But I lied to him.

"Of course, I am." I lied when I talked. I lied as I smiled, trying to reassure him that everything was fine. I lied to myself as we started walking toward the front door, up the three stairs and two steps over the porch.

I lied to myself as I kept that smile on my face, even though my heart started thundering in my chest. I lied when Dylan looked at me again, unlocking the front door, that line of worry back on his face.

But when he stepped in, when he left me outside to gather my thoughts, I realized something.

I still wasn't afraid.

Even when I took the first tentative step inside, seeing the marks on the floor where he let my blood fall, I wasn't afraid.

I was angry, so fucking angry.

But I didn't know if I was angry at that man, or at myself for not being able to outrun him.

"Little One." Dylan was suddenly in front of me, blocking the view of where that chair *he* had tied me to used to be. "Hey." He took my hand, and only then did I realize how hard I was pressing my nails into my palm. "It's okay. Everything is going to be okay."

But it wasn't going to be okay.

Nothing would ever be okay unless I found out who the golden mask was, and what the fuck that letter I found in my locker meant. Nothing would ever be okay if I turned a blind eye to this, just like I did to a million other things.

I always thought it was better to pretend that you didn't see anything, but I was wrong. I had to do something, seeing that nobody else was going to do anything.

"Skylar." His voice trembled, but I couldn't move my eyes from the spot behind his back.

Somebody dared to violate me in such a way. To enter my house, to enter my life, and make all these demands, and they had no right.

"I think I'm gonna go to bed." My voice sounded robotic even to me, and I knew that he wouldn't let me go that easily. "I'm fine, Dylan." I looked at him. "Trust me, if I start breaking apart, you'll be the first one to know."

Probably the only one to know. I could see he didn't believe me, yet instead of questioning me, and having a full-blown discussion about what happened here, he let me go. He took a step back and nodded before disappearing into the kitchen.

Maybe I should've stayed. Maybe I should've talked to him about these things, but how could I talk to him when even I couldn't understand what was going on in my head? Normally, I would've been terrified of being back here, but the only emotion I could feel right now was anger.

So much fucking anger, and I knew what I was going to do with it.

I was going to unravel all the secrets of Winworth.

◯

It was the sound of rain that pulled me out from a deep slumber.

As soon as Dylan disappeared around the corner, going to the kitchen, I took my bag upstairs and took a shower, careful with the bandages on my left arm. Dylan didn't come up before I went to sleep, and I had a feeling it was better that way.

He wanted to talk, and I wasn't ready to relive that night all over again. He wanted me to tell him all my worries, all my issues, as if that would help any one of us. If I burdened him with my secrets, he would end up with the same scars I had, and that was the last thing I wanted.

This pain was mine to carry. These scars were mine to deal with, and brother or no brother, he didn't deserve to feel like I did.

Helpless.

Scared.

Angry.

I didn't want him to lose the good in him, and if he knew what our father was doing to me, the picture he had of him would shatter into a million tiny pieces, and I didn't want that.

No matter what, our father was there for Dylan. He was teaching him about the family business, about other things he needed to know, and I didn't want to destroy the idyllic picture Dylan had of him.

I shivered and pulled the covers higher up, covering my neck, only to realize that this wasn't the usual temperature of the room. As my eyes adjusted to the dark, I turned to the side, seeing the open balcony door and hearing the downpour of rain outside.

I definitely didn't open my balcony before I went to sleep.

Maybe I should've learned from my past mistakes. As soon as I saw that door open, I should've run away from the room, but that anger was still coating my insides. Instead of calling for Dylan, calling for help, I threw off the covers from my body and stood up, going straight for the balcony.

"You seem okay," a voice boomed through the night, mixing with the sound of the rain.

I all but jumped around, ready to face the intruder, and froze in my tracks when I realized who it was.

"What the fuck are you doing here?" That anger I talked about? That suffocating feeling, the one keeping me afloat right now, wasn't just directed at the faceless man who destroyed my body and soul.

No. It was also directed at him—at Ash.

Sitting on the floor, in the corner of my room, his back pressed against the door, was a boy, a man—whatever you wanna call him—who wasn't there when I needed him the most. Day and night, I waited for him to show up in the hospital.

I waited for him to bring his moody ass inside, to tell me that everything was going to be okay. I just wanted to see him, to feel him, to have that smell of pine trees, cigarettes, and rain infiltrate the entire room, to replace that horrible, horrible hospital smell of antiseptic and coldness.

But he never came.

Every time Lauren came to me, I expected him to be right behind her. Every night, when everybody else cleared out, when I was left alone with my thoughts, I expected him to sneak in, to do anything, really.

To fucking call me if nothing else.

But nothing. One big, fat nothing, that's what I got from him.

I assumed he cared about me, at least enough to see if I was still fucking alive, but I guess that I wasn't that important. Just another wrong assumption, another disappointment in my life.

He slowly stood up and walked to the bed, staring at the spot where I slept.

"I asked you a fucking question, Ash." I slammed the balcony door shut and took a step toward him. "What are you doing here?"

But just as usual, I didn't get an answer. Talking to him was like pulling teeth — painful and exhausting. I had enough time while in the hospital to really think about this shit that was going on between us.

I tried telling myself that what we had was nothing more but meaningless sex that one night, but I lied to myself. Nothing new there, except that I didn't want to keep lying.

I cared about him. I cared if he was happy or sad.

I wanted to hear his thoughts on random subjects. I wanted to talk to him about his past, his parents, where he grew up, because I didn't know anything about him.

I knew the color of his eyes, and that dark, dark hair. I knew how he made me feel, but I didn't know anything else, and it fucking sucked.

I knew that he made me feel like I was floating on air, that every second I spent in his company felt like an eternity because he made me forget about other things in my life. I knew he loved nature and the wilderness and that he carried violent things inside his heart, but I didn't know why.

I knew that his lips tasted like sin, but it was the kind of sin I didn't mind committing.

He knew everything about me, which made me feel like I had a disadvantage from the very start.

"Ash," I started again, approaching him slowly. Sometimes it felt like he was a wild animal, just waiting to attack. One wrong move, a wrong word, and he could destroy me in a second. "Can you, for the love of everything, just answer one simple question?"

Thunder sliced through the air, angry and devastating, just how I felt right now.

"Ash!" I whisper-yelled, pushing his shoulder, but he wouldn't move.

His head was hanging down, his forearms firmly placed on his knees, and that dark hair I loved so much was dripping wet. I knew that if I touched it, even as wet as it was, it would feel like silk beneath my fingers. I also knew if I allowed him to stay like this, we would never get out of this vicious circle, and I would allow myself to get sucked into yet another toxic situation.

I couldn't.

I had to choose myself this time.

"You know," I took a step back, "the first time I saw you, I felt like I knew you from somewhere. Maybe it was just my mind playing tricks on me, which wouldn't be the first time, but in the eternity of sorrow, I saw you. And I thought you saw me, the real me."

"Sky—" He lifted his head and looked at me, but I wasn't finished.

"And you looked beautiful, even with all that pain swirling in your eyes. You felt like mine, and God knows that I kept looking for something or someone that would feel like mine. But I was wrong, wasn't I?"

"I don't—"

"You made me forget, Ash. You made me think about something else—about you—but I can see now that what I started to feel for you wasn't the same as what you felt for me. I can see now that you won't be my salvation. You will be my destruction. I was looking for paradise, but I found hell instead."

"Hey, that's not—" He stood up, and I took another step back, putting much-needed distance between us.

"When I woke up in the hospital, the first person I thought about was you," I whispered, my voice breaking. My chest hurt, tearing me apart as all the things I kept locked up for the last three days started tumbling out. "I was terrified, and you weren't there." I placed a hand to my chest, as if I could keep myself from falling apart right in front of his eyes. "Why weren't you there, Ash? Do I mean nothing to you?"

"Skylar, please," he choked out, reaching for me, but I couldn't handle his touch on me until I was finished, until I knew the whole truth.

"Don't touch me," I gritted out. "You don't get to disappear from my life when I needed you the most and then show up here as if nothing happened. As if I wasn't attacked by a maniac in my own house, thinking I was going to die. You don't get to fucking touch me! Not now, not ever."

"No, baby —"

"Where were you, Ash?" I broke down. "I-I know…" I hiccupped. "I know we aren't together, but I thought that you at least cared about me."

"I do." He grasped one of my hands, his touch burning my skin.

"Then fucking show it!" I pushed him away. "I don't care about words, Ash. I don't care about any of these things, but I do care about deeds, about things you would do to show me you care."

I thought he would argue with me. I thought he would try to make me believe in another lie, but he said nothing. He kept standing in front of me, tilting his head to the side, hiding his truths behind those eyes.

"I think you should leave," I mumbled, taking a step to the side, and showed him the balcony door. "Now!"

"No!" he roared.

"What do you mean, no?" I asked. "Get out of my house."

"Goddammit, Skylar."

One minute he was aggravated, and in the next one, I was airborne over his shoulder as he started walking to my bed.

"Let me go!" I hit his back. "This is fucking idiotic."

"No," he fired back and dropped me to the bed. Towering over me, he started removing his shoes and then climbed onto the bed, hovering over me. "I'm not going anywhere, and you're just gonna have to deal with it."

"The fuck I will." I pushed at his shoulders. "If you don't leave—"

"You'll what?" he bit back. "You'll call the cops? Or what, you're gonna yell for your brother to save you."

"No, you fucking asshole. I don't need my brother to punch you in that pretty face."

"You think I have a pretty face?" He smirked.

"That's not the point!" I started getting up, but he pushed my hands above my head, holding them down.

"I fucked up!" he bellowed. "I fucked up badly because I was scared. When I saw the message from Lauren, I headed toward the hospital."

"Don't f—"

"I was! But I couldn't come and see you, Skylar. I couldn't because I tried telling myself that this thing between us means nothing, and I was wrong." He breathed heavily. "I drank myself to oblivion because I tried to forget you. I tried to forget how you made me feel. I tried to erase you from here." He pulled my hand and pressed it against his head. "But you're not only in my head, you're here as well." He then pressed my hand against his chest. "You're in my veins, in my mind, in my heart, and I didn't want this. I didn't want to feel this way, but I don't wanna fight it anymore. I don't want to lose you."

Did he just… Did he just admit that he… "Ash—"

"No, I don't wanna put a label on these feelings, because I don't know what they are. I don't know what to call them or what to call us, but I know I want to be with you in every way possible." He dropped his forehead to mine, making me close my eyes. He let go of my hands and placed both of his against my cheeks, holding me steady. I wrapped my free hand around his head, entwining my fingers with the strands of his hair. "I. Want. You."

And that was when the dam broke. When everything I tried suppressing, everything I didn't want to think about, started coming out. My throat constricted as the first sob tore out of my chest.

"I'm terrified," I cried out. "H-he… He broke into the house, and… and—"

"Shhh." He pressed his lips against my forehead and moved to the side, hugging me. I pressed my face against his pectoral muscles, letting myself cry over everything that had happened. "It's going to be okay, Sky."

"How?" I cried out. "How is everything going to be okay?"

"I don't know," he mumbled, brushing the hair from my face. "But it has to be. I want to believe that we will be able to catch this guy, whoever he is."

"I just… I'm so angry. And I'm scared, and sad, and it's like I'm going to explode from all these things I'm feeling inside."

"Then let it all out. Let them all out and tell me how you feel. I'm here now and I'm not going anywhere. Not tonight, not tomorrow. I'll be here for as long as you want me to be."

And I somehow knew that he would be here with me no matter what. Maybe I knew because what he felt for me was very similar to what I felt for him.

Maybe it was because my soul finally recognized its equal.

Or perhaps it was because he made me feel things I didn't think I was capable of feeling. Whatever it was, I trusted him almost as much as I trusted Dylan.

TWENTY-ONE

SKYLAR

When I was ten years old, I asked my parents to buy me a hamster for my birthday. I couldn't recall why I asked for a hamster, but since my parents didn't want me to have a cat or a dog at that time, I guess that in my young mind a hamster seemed like a reasonable solution.

I really wanted to have a pet.

Most of my friends had a dog, a cat, a parrot, and I wanted to have a pet I could call my own.

I still remembered the day, as if it just happened yesterday, when my dad brought two small boxes home with tiny holes punctured on the top. His lips were pulled into a wide smile, and as he crouched in front of me, he placed both of those boxes in my hands.

"Happy birthday, Lar," he said.

I believe that that was one of the last good memories of my dad. I liked to believe that there were many more, but I read somewhere that our minds tend to lock down all those good times when something traumatic happens. Maybe because it was ea___r forgetting how we used to perceive a person versus who they really were.

But in that moment, when he handed me those two boxes, he was the best dad in the entire world. He didn't have to tell me what was inside because I knew. I just fucking knew.

My heart pounded so hard that I had a feeling I was going to pass out. I all but ran toward the living room, leaving my dad behind in the foyer, anxious to see my new friends. I asked for one hamster, but he bought me two.

"A male and a female," he said. "They need to have a companion."

He must have said something else, but at that moment, my whole attention was on the two boxes and two tiny creatures waiting for me inside.

I placed them carefully on the table, afraid that if I shook it, they would get afraid, and I didn't want them to be afraid of me. I'd been dreaming of that moment for so long, that once it started becoming true, I didn't know what to do.

"Why don't you open the boxes?" Dylan's voice broke the tension in my body, but I kept staring at the boxes, unable to move.

"What if they hate me?" I asked him as I turned around. He was already starting high school, and I couldn't wait to go to his football games since he just made the team. "What if they don't want to play with me?"

"Hey, hey, hey." He crossed the small distance between us and sat next to me. I didn't realize he was holding a small cage in his left hand, and it warmed my heart that he did this for me. "I chose them for you, and I just know that they're going to love you."

"Promise?"

"I promise, Little One. Now," he leaned forward

and pulled the two boxes closer to the edge of the table, "open them. Don't make them wait for too long."

And I did.

The first box revealed a scared little guy, coated in brown fur with one white line running over his back. He sat on his back legs and stared at me, his dark eyes full of wonder and a small amount of fear. I gently pushed the box on its side, and after a minute or so, with tentative steps, he came out, sniffing over the table, trying to understand his new surroundings.

"He looks beautiful, Dy," I mumbled. "And he has a white stomach," I pointed out, my voice high-pitched and filled with excitement.

Dylan slid down from the couch and sat on the floor, extending his hand toward the hamster. "This is the male one," he murmured as he dragged his finger over the hamster's back. "And that other one," he looked at the second box, "is the female. I really think you're going to love her."

I slid down to the floor and started opening the second box. The moment I opened the lid, a lithe, white body jumped out, and stood on all fours, staring at me.

She was the most magnificent creature I had ever seen.

Dark red eyes stared back at me, and her entire body was pure white, just like the first snow. She didn't move, didn't sniff around like her male companion did. She just sat there, observing us just how we were observing her.

I was in love.

As soon as I showed my hand to her, she approached me and sniffed my fingers before climbing onto my palm.

"Hi, Nala," I murmured, feeling Dylan's eyes on me.

"Is that her name?"

"Yep." I smiled. "And he is Donny."

273

"Those are amazing names, Sky."

I extended my palm and placed my hands next to each other, letting Nala climb from one side to the other. The sound of the cage door opening made me turn to Dylan, who was already taking Donny and placing him inside. I slowly did the same with Nala.

The only problem was, as soon as the doors closed behind her, she attacked him, chasing him through the cage.

"What is she doing?" I asked, with panic lacing every word. I wanted them to be friends, to be good to each other, but Nala had other plans.

"I don't know, Little One, but I'm sure they'll be fine. They're just getting to know each other."

And I believed in that.

I was happy when she finally calmed down after three weeks of relentless chasing, of wounds on Donny's body, and one morning we found out why.

Nala had babies, but she didn't want them. She refused to tend to them, while my poor Donny behaved like a mother hen. I again thought everything was going to be fine, that it was just an animal phase, but when I came home from school, only two days after they were born, the grim look on Dylan's face told me that something was wrong.

He took me to my room, where their cage was located, and the sight in front of me was one I would never forget.

"S-She," I stammered. "She ate them all."

Nala was sitting inside the cage, chewing on the body of one of the pups — unapologetic, satisfied, and beyond monstrous. But I couldn't see Donny.

"Where is — "

"I'm sorry, Sky. She, uh… she killed him."

My perfect albino hamster with red eyes and the

missing piece on her ear, ate her pups and killed the male she shared a cage with. My ten-year-old mind couldn't understand, but I tried.

And the older I got, the more I understood her actions.

Nala died two years after that, but her defensive behavior and the need to always be alone somehow stayed with me.

Just because somebody is biologically your father or a mother, or even a sibling, that doesn't make them your family. Blood is just that—blood—but actions are what matter.

I've been going over the things my family did for me, the actions and reactions they had, and even excluding how my father behaved, none of them were behaving how a real family should.

None of them except Dylan.

He would be disappointed if he knew that every single night since I came back from the hospital, a dark-haired boy he didn't like all that much sneaked into my room just to hold me. Just to talk to me. Just to tell me that everything was going to be okay.

Ash was fast asleep, his head on my chest, his arms wrapped around my torso as if he didn't want me to leave. That first night we didn't talk. He held me while I cried, while I wept for the little girl in me that wasn't alive anymore.

On the second one, he told me about his brother, Sebastian, and how smart he was. On the third one, he kissed me for the first time since the forest, and I felt as if thousands of butterflies invaded my stomach. As if it was my first kiss.

And perhaps it was. It was the first light kiss I ever got.

The gentle touch of his lips on mine, no rush, no

panic, no dark thoughts invading my mind, just him and I, holding each other.

I just wanted to stay here forever, with Ash wrapped around me, far away from the outside world. Far away from the things that could hurt me. Far away from my family who didn't even call to see how I was doing.

I spent my days with Dylan, who refused to go back to Seattle until the culprit was caught. But my nights… my nights were reserved for Ash.

Ash who held me while my whole body shook, when the fear I was hiding away from finally managed to find me. Ash who wiped the tears from my cheeks and played with the strands of my hair, humming songs I had never heard of.

Ash who made me watch the entire *Lord of the Rings* trilogy when I couldn't sleep, too afraid I would see the golden mask instead of the usual darkness.

But Ash still hid parts of himself from me. Even though he talked about himself, about his childhood, about his brother and his uncle, I still had a feeling that he didn't share the most important parts, and that sucked.

It sucked because with each passing day, he went deeper and deeper, burying himself in my soul. It also sucked because I didn't know what reality would bring to us once we got out of this warm cocoon we created.

Would he still hold me like he was holding me now, clinging to me like I was important to him, or would he go back to the painful game of indifference?

I was too afraid to ask what was happening between us. I was terrified because he became the air I needed to breathe, and I didn't want to lose him.

In the endless darkness I was surrounded with, he felt like the light I was desperately looking for. But I wondered if this was real, or if my fucked-up mind just found another thing to be addicted to. I wondered if maybe Ash was just the replacement for all the drugs I used to take, for the alcohol I used to drink.

Maybe he was just another form of self-destruction. But no matter how unhealthy this was, I couldn't let him go.

He stirred in his sleep as I dragged my thumb over his eyebrow, wanting more than ever to know how he got the scar slicing it in half. I wanted to know his deepest, darkest secrets, but as much as I wanted to know, I also wanted to keep him in this idolized box I created.

I learned that sometimes the truth wasn't what we actually needed, and right now I needed to believe that not everything was dark. I had to believe that there were people in this fucking town who didn't want to see me fail.

I had to believe that the guy I was falling for was also falling for me, for all the good and bad things I had inside me. I had to believe he was okay with the mess swirling through my head, because if I didn't, this endless hole I was falling through would swallow me whole.

"Your thoughts are loud," he murmured, halting the movement of my hand immediately.

"Excuse me?"

"I said," he pushed himself up, and leaned closer to me, "your." *Kiss*. "Thoughts." *Kiss*. "Are." *Kiss*. "Loud."

I wrapped my arms around his neck as he pulled me closer to him and then flipped us, so that I was on top of him. What would life be like if I could do this every day? Wrapped up in the cocoon of warmth, consumed by him, consumed by these feelings he was evoking in me.

I swiveled my hips, earning a grunt from him,

feeling the rising of his dick. He gripped my hands as I started dragging them down his chest, toward the edge of his jeans. There was a warning in his midnight eyes, but I wasn't one to shy away from danger. If I was, maybe I wouldn't be in all these fucked-up situations lately.

"You're playing with fire, baby," he grunted, earning a smile from me.

"I know," I whispered, swiveling my hips again. "But I like fire." I leaned down and pressed my lips against his, torturing both of us with excruciatingly slow movements. He wound one of his hands around my neck, holding me at the nape, while his other one slowly dragged over my lower back, all the way to my sleep shorts.

I moaned as he slipped his hand inside my shorts and my panties, and started kneading my ass, moving me on top of him.

God, if this was just a fantasy, I didn't want it to end.

He started lifting his hips, now fully controlling my movements on top of him, letting me know that he was in charge. And I didn't mind it. I didn't mind it at all.

Sometimes I had a feeling that he knew what I really needed. Whether it was for him to give me space, or to take control, but he knew.

As he pulled my head back, holding my hair, I realized that I wouldn't be able to accept his cruelty after all these nights together. The world was a cruel place already, where the strong fed on the weaker ones, and sometimes you had to become a villain to survive. But that I could live with.

What I wouldn't be able to live with would be the world in which he and I ended up being simple strangers. Just two people who used to know each other but weren't talking anymore. I wouldn't be able to survive this entire year if he started behaving like this didn't mean anything to him, because it meant everything to me.

Even though I was too afraid to voice all this out loud, I prayed to God that he would hear the cry of my heart, and that he would know not to let me go. If he did, I didn't want to think what would become of me.

If he was just another addiction, just another toxic thing I accepted in my veins, I still didn't want to stop, even if it killed me.

"Stop thinking so much," he growled and bit into my lower lip.

"I'm not."

"Yes, you are." He moved the hair that fell between us as he let me go, placing it behind my ear. "Here." He tenderly pressed his thumb between my eyebrows. "You have lines here, and I don't like seeing them, Moonshine."

"And why is that?" I asked, my voice barely audible. I was scared he would hear the tremble. That he would know how much he affected me, how much I didn't want to get back to the real world where he and I could never be together in the open. Where monsters like my father would never let me live my life how I wanted to live it.

Where my life was planned for me before I was nothing more than a little blip in my mother's stomach, just because I was a legacy and I had to do something with my life. They wanted to control me. They wanted to tell me who I needed to be, just like they did with Dylan.

Every time I saw him since he finished high school, it was as if the brother I once had was slowly disappearing in front of my own eyes. I couldn't remember the last time that he smiled, a real, genuine smile.

Before he started college, he used to smile all the

time. People used to joke that the two of us were like the sun and moon—completely different on how we dealt with people, yet so similar.

Now that sunshine was gone from him, and I feared what would become of me if I allowed them to control me later. That's why I had to leave.

That's why I had to run as far away as possible, because there was no way in hell that my father would stop looking for me. Dylan might, if I told him I was safe and happy, but my father... No, that monster would never stop haunting me.

"There it is again," Ash protested. "What are you thinking about?"

His eyes were a molten lava, burning into my own, waiting to hear answers I couldn't give him. It wasn't that I didn't want to, I did. I just didn't know how to form the words, how to explain what was passing through my head. Or maybe I was still unable to come to terms with everything that has happened in the past two years.

He suddenly pulled himself up and leaned against the headboard, taking me with him. My legs were on his sides, my center pressed against his hardness, but I knew that he wouldn't let this go, even if I started stripping right now.

He had that determined gleam in his eye, and the way he looked at me told me everything I needed to know.

He cared.

Ash cared about me—a thought that both scared and excited me.

It scared me because I didn't know if he liked it or not. Did he despise it? Did he wish I was somebody else? Did he like me for me or just because I was a Blackwood?

Was he suddenly nice to me because he had something to gain?

But no matter how much my brain pushed me into overthinking, the fact that he seemed to care about me excited me. I couldn't remember the last time that someone besides Dylan cared about me.

I couldn't count my friends because it wasn't the same level of caring. I loved Lauren, I loved the rest of our crew of misfits, but I couldn't help but wonder if we would ever hang out if it wasn't for our families.

"Moonshine," he murmured, pulling my head closer to his. He pressed his forehead against mine, exhaling softly. "You need to talk to me. I don't like seeing you worried."

"I'm just…" I shrugged. "I don't know. I guess I just don't want to go back to reality." I played with the soft hair at the nape of his neck, while he held me in a tight embrace. His chest pressed against my chest, his heart beating in the same rhythm as mine. "I don't want to lose this," I whispered, admitting my biggest fear.

I wasn't afraid of a faceless man that was still out there. I wasn't scared of pitiful looks or judgmental ones, but I was terrified of losing this, whatever this was.

"I'm scared that once the light comes up in the morning, you'll go back to ignoring me—"

"Hey." He moved back, looking straight at me.

"No, wait. Just let me get this off my chest and then you can say whatever you want to say."

I thought he would protest, that he would try to convince me without listening to me, but I should've known that Ash wouldn't do things I would expect other people to do.

I moved further away and sat at the edge of the bed, avoiding looking at him. If I looked at him, I would lose all the courage I gathered, and I needed to get this off my chest.

"The last two years have been filled with sorrow

and cruelty you could never imagine," I started, looking at my hands folded in my lap. "Some days, it felt like I was stuck in an endless loop of bad dreams, and I could never wake up. At first, I thought I was imagining things, that my mind started creating scenarios that weren't real, but they were. They were so real that I sometimes woke up in the middle of the night with screams waiting on the tip of my tongue. Sometimes I remembered those things in the middle of the day, and it was like a flashback slamming into me. And no matter how many drugs I swallowed, how much alcohol I drank, how many faceless guys I slept with, I could never forget."

"Moonshine," he choked out, reaching out for me, but I moved further away.

"Wait, you need to hear this. Just… Let me say these things, okay?"

"Okay," he agreed.

"But then you came, and I still don't know what pulled me to you, what called to me, but something did. Ever since that day in that first class, you were living in my head, and you didn't even know. And then, well, things happened between us, and you started ignoring me. Which was fine, because I made myself believe that it didn't mean anything, because it couldn't. How could I care about somebody else when there was nothing left inside of me to accommodate another person?" When he didn't say anything, I continued talking, playing with the bracelet Dylan gave me when we were just kids. "But as usual, as with everything else, I was wrong. And now you're here. You're everywhere, Ash, and I don't know what to do once you go back to your usual cold demeanor." I looked up, only to see him listening carefully. "I don't know what to do once you decide that you don't want to have anything with me and my fucked-up head, because I care. I care about you more

282

than I would like to, and it sucks, because I don't know if you care about me. I can't take one more disappointment after everything I went through."

My hands started shaking, and I pushed them underneath my thighs, hiding how nervous I was. I was baring my soul to him, and I hoped that he would accept it. I hoped he wouldn't reject me, that he wouldn't run from what we could have.

"And I'll understand if you can't do this, whatever this is, in front of everybody else, but I think you should know that I can't do it only behind closed doors. I refuse to be a secret. If that's all you're looking for, I think it would be best if we just end it all here."

One second... two... three... four... and then a whole minute passed before he reacted. Of all the reactions I would've expected him to have, this one was the last one on my list.

Ash smiled.

Not one of those wicked, little smiles I liked so much. Not the egoistical one that Kane so often had, but the relaxed, satisfied smile that took over his entire face, lighting up his eyes, warming the entire room. I never saw him smile like this, and I cherished the moment, because it was only mine.

His smile was only mine.

I didn't care that he was forbidden fruit, and my father would've killed me if he knew I was sleeping with a guy he didn't know about. He would make my life a living hell, more so than now, if he knew that I wasn't collecting his precious information from Kane and his family.

I thought Ash would be angry, that he would get up and leave, but when he moved from the spot where he was sitting and closed the distance between the two of us on the bed, I knew I made the right choice by telling him how I really felt.

"Are you trying to get rid of me, Moonshine?" The bastard smirked as he pressed his palms against my cheeks, pulling my head higher so that the only thing in sight was him. "Did you really think I could let you go after all this? Do you know what I do the entire day that I'm not here with you?" he asked, as his thumb started making circles over my cheek.

"What?" I croaked, burning with the need to know.

"I think about you. I think about the taste of your lips, or how you lift your eyebrow when somebody is pissing you off. I think about this body of yours," he said as he placed one hand on my hip. "This body that was made for me." He lowered his head and pressed his lips behind my ear, eliciting shivers all over my body. "I started putting vanilla syrup in my coffee because it tasted like you. I want to be with you every single moment of every single day. I want to hold you. I want to tell the world that you belong to me. You know why?"

I shook my head, unable to utter the words. He was destroying me and building me up with his words. He was taking the broken pieces of me and starting to glue them back together.

"Because I belong to you, Moonshine."

It wasn't a declaration of love. It wasn't a promise of forever, but it was a promise of something better. He was giving me everything I never even knew I wanted, and he was doing it so delicately, so carefully, as if I was made of porcelain.

As if he knew that one sudden movement, one more surprise, would shatter me.

"Y-you... You drink your coffee with vanilla syrup?" I frowned as I asked because vanilla syrup in coffee tasted like pure shit.

"Of all the things I just said," he started laughing,

"you only heard that?"

"Vanilla syrup sucks," I protested. "You can't blame me for —"

I didn't manage to say anything more, and before you could say sex, he had me pinned down, hovering over me, holding my hands above my head.

"But it tasted like you." He bit into the crook of my neck. "Sweet, delicate, and forbidden to be in coffee, but I still want it. You don't scare me, Skylar. You and whatever is going on in that pretty little head of yours, it doesn't scare me. What scares me is that you will never look at me like you're looking at me now when I tell you my story."

"Ash —"

"No, don't tell me that you won't. I promise I would never lie to you, but please don't ever lie to me either."

The way he looked at me, the way his eyebrows pulled together, I knew that whatever it was that he wanted to tell me wouldn't sit well with me. But I didn't want to think about the future and what it would bring.

For the first time in my life, I wanted to live in the moment. I wanted to enjoy the things I had right now, instead of daydreaming about things that could come.

He moved to the side, and pulled me to him, my back to his front, his hands around my middle and his mouth pressed against my neck.

"Tell me something I don't know about you," I murmured as his lips skimmed over the soft spot behind my ear, fighting the goosebumps threatening over my skin.

"What do you want to know?" One of his hands traveled beneath my shirt, and he spread his fingers over my stomach.

"Anything," I said, but my mind screamed, *Everything*. I didn't just want to know trivial things, like his favorite colors, or his favorite band. I wanted to know who gave him his first kiss, what made him smile, what made him angry. I wanted to know more about his brother, about his family. I wanted to know every single thing that made him who he was today.

He paused for a second, his hot breath caressing my skin, as if he contemplated where he would start. As much as I wanted to push him, I knew I had to be careful not to scare him away. Even after everything he said, I had a feeling that we were still on very thin ice, and the last thing I wanted to accomplish was to push him away.

"My last name," he started, "isn't really Weber." His voice was laced with pain, and my gut told me there was more to this story.

I turned around and faced him, seeking his eyes in the dark. So much pain, so much sorrow, guilt, and anger, hid there, swirling in the midnight blue. Lifting my hand, I placed it on his cheek, earning a deep exhale and the closing of his eyes. He placed his other hand over mine and turned his face, kissing my palm.

"You don't have to tell me that," I whispered, as if I was talking to a frightened child. "If it hurts you, you don't have to tell me."

He pinned me with his eyes, a thousand stories told in that one look. He moved the hair away from my face before he started talking again. "I know I don't have to tell you, but I want to."

God, I wanted him to tell me every single thing as well, but not if it made him feel uncomfortable.

"But this… this thing you want to tell me, it hurts you?"

He nodded and moved away from me, the grim expression on his face now directed at the ceiling.

"There is not one single part of this story that doesn't hurt, Moonshine." He exhaled and took a deep breath again. "But I want to tell you. I want to share this with you."

Tears threatened to spill over my cheeks, my heart piercing with the pain lacing his every word, and I grasped his hand in mine and kept quiet, waiting for him to continue.

"My parents were killed when I was six years old." Oh God. "Truth be told, I can't even remember what they looked like anymore."

"Oh, Ash."

"And I was there, you know?" He turned his head to the side and looked at me. "I was there that night when they were killed. And even though I can't remember their faces anymore, sometimes when the wind blows too strong, I can still hear my mother's screams."

"Did they—" I choked. "Did they catch the murderers?"

A sorrowful smile played on the seams of his lips. "No, Moonshine. They never caught them."

"I'm so sorry, Ash," I murmured as I placed my head on his chest. "I am so damn sorry."

"You have nothing to be sorry about." He started playing with my hair. "You weren't the one holding the knife."

Jesus Christ.

I tightened my hands against his shirt, as if me being here could erase the pain and anger he lived with.

"What happened to you guys after that?"

"Uncle Neal adopted us. He's not really our uncle, at least not by blood, but he took care of us. He took us away from Winworth and gave us his last name."

And I thought I had a fucked-up life. I couldn't even imagine the pain, the suffering he went through. He was just a child.

287

"You're too quiet now," he said, and I could hear the worry in his voice. "I didn't want to scare you, I just—"

"You didn't scare me." I lifted myself up and looked at him. "I'm just sad, Ash. Sad that you and your brother had to go through something like that. Sad that you were dealt such a shitty hand in life."

"I'm okay, Sky." He pressed his lips against the pulse on the inner part of my wrist. "You don't have to be sad. Hell, I don't want you to be sad. I'm okay. I'm alive, Sebastian as well, and that's all that matters."

"I know." I sighed. "I just… I don't know. I'm just pissed, that's all."

"I like you when you're pissed." He grinned and pulled me on top of him. "But trust me, we are okay now."

"But you shouldn't be only okay." I frowned. "You should feel amazing, full of life, wonderful—"

"And I do. I feel all those things when I'm here with you." His lips found mine, and I let myself fall deeper and deeper, wrapping my arms around his neck. "You make me feel alive, Moonshine. You make me feel, and I cherish every single moment spent with you."

All the worry, all the pain, they just melted from my heart, like ice on a sunny day. It felt as if a swarm of butterflies flew through my stomach, lifting me higher and higher, all the way to him and his perfect smile.

"Wait." I stopped and smiled down at him. "What was your family name?"

His hands on my hips tightened, and his eyes glistened in the dark. "Crowell." He swallowed hard. "I used to be Asher Crowell."

Crowell.

Why did that sound somewhat familiar?

"So, you were a little crow then?" I smiled and leaned down, stealing another kiss. "I like it. I think it suits you."

"Yeah?" A smile slowly returned to his face. "You think so?"

"Mmhmm." I nodded. "It suits you better than Weber."

"I think so too." He lifted his arms and wrapped them around my lower back, holding me tight on top of him. "Maybe one day I'll go back to being a Crowell."

"Maybe." I grinned. "And maybe I'll be there to see that."

And maybe, just maybe, we would be able to protect each other from the wicked past.

TWENTY-TWO

I fucked up.

I fucked up majorly, and now I didn't know what to do.

My entire life has been wrapped in all these plans, all these things I needed to do—train, move back to Winworth, get our revenge, and get the fuck out.

But now things have changed.

God, I didn't expect to mess up the entire thing by falling for the one girl I could never have. Out of all the girls in Winworth, hell, in all the places we've been to, she was the one I was only ever supposed to use. But I couldn't even fathom hurting her, even though she was an enemy.

She belonged to them, and I would always be on the other side. I knew she was going to choose them when the time came, but I wanted her to choose me. I wanted her to keep looking at me how she looked at me one week ago, when it was only the two of us in her room, when she told me the things she kept hidden.

I wanted her to tell me more, but whatever was haunting her didn't want to be revealed yet.

After she was admitted to the hospital, I had a chat

with my uncle, who insisted on me getting closer to her because he thought Skylar was the key. I was trying to do the right thing, dammit. I tried ignoring the fact that my chest hurt every single second while she was in the hospital.

Updates from Lauren stopped on the second day, and I knew that if I wanted to know how she was, I had to be there. I had to see her, but I couldn't fathom seeing her and not breaking apart.

Because that's what she did to me. She broke me.

She took all those pieces I was hiding and ripped them away from me, making me see only her. A month ago, I would've been furious. I would've been angry at myself, but right now I didn't give a fuck.

The problem was, I lied to her. I lied when I told her that she would always get the truth from me. I lied while I held her, while I told her that everything was going to be okay, because it wouldn't be okay.

Not until she gets out of this town. Not until she forgets about me and everything that happened here.

And even though she was sitting next to me, talking to Lauren, it already felt as if we were a million miles apart from each other. Because the truth I was hiding was going to destroy what we had.

My arm was loosely hanging around her shoulders, while she kept her hand on my thigh, as if she too didn't want to stop touching me.

We were in Danny and Rowan's house, celebrating their birthday, and instead of going through their house, trying to find more clues, trying to find out more about their family, I was wrapped up in Skylar. I didn't want to be anywhere else.

I just had to figure out how to avenge my parents without burning her in the process.

A good man would let her go. A better man would

tell her all the secrets this town was hiding, giving her a much-needed advantage, but I never said I was one of the good ones. I lied, cheated, played the people around me, and I would do it all again if it would bring me back to her.

I would burn everything in my path, if I knew that she would be waiting for me at the end of the road.

"Now you're the one thinking too loud." Her voice penetrated through my thoughts, and I turned to the side, seeing her smiling face. Her eyes were already bright from all the alcohol she consumed since we came, and it was only a matter of time until her pupils would dilate. There was no way that she wouldn't take the drugs Lauren brought.

The rest of the group was hanging somewhere around the house, but I didn't give a fuck about any of them. If it were up to me, the two of us would be back in her room, getting lost in each other.

We didn't have enough time. With October creeping up on us and Samhain just around the corner, I feared I wouldn't have enough time to do what I needed to do and to save her from this world.

If she hated me after that, at least I would know that she was safe. That she was as far away from here as possible. I couldn't save my parents because I was too young, but I could save her. I could make it better for her, even if it killed me letting her go.

I hated being here, surrounded by all these people I didn't know. I didn't have control and any one of them could be the killer. Any one of them could be the masked monster who attacked her the other night.

We've been in Winworth for four months, and I still knew as much as I did when we came to the town. They kept their secrets well-hidden, and every single attempt to sneak into City Hall failed, filling me with more and more anxiety.

They had the upper hand here, and I hated that even after all the preparations, after all those stories, all those sacrifices we made, we were nowhere near close to the truth. I had no idea who was killing those girls or why. It was obvious it had something to do with the Black Dahlia.

The runes carved into their skin, the way they were dismembered, Skylar's name on them, somebody went through a great trouble to prepare for Samhain.

I just couldn't understand why Skylar was involved. That was one piece of information that never fit in. One puzzle piece neither my uncle nor I could understand. If the documents were right, the last time they did ritual killings like these, was when they had just arrived in Winworth. So why now?

I was getting frustrated by the lack of information from Lars, our only source as to what The Order was planning. After that meeting with Indigo, all I got was radio silence.

It was getting harder to hide the truth from her, especially when she looked at me how she was looking at me now—innocently, with stars in her eyes, as if I could make the world a better place just by being here with her.

I stood up, letting her hand fall away from my thigh. "I'm gonna get another drink." I shook my plastic cup. "Do you want anything?"

She knew something was up, of course she did. Skylar wasn't as clueless as she wanted people to think, but instead of pressing me and asking about my behavior, she just shook her head, and turned back to Lauren, who was talking with Danny.

Right. Drinks then.

Truth be told, I just had to get out of here for a

minute. The room was filled with more unfamiliar than familiar faces, and I slowly started feeling like I was suffocating. As if I carried all the weight of the world on my shoulders, and I didn't know how to shake it off.

Getting lost in her was one way, but once the high wore off, when she wasn't there to hold my hand, I was left alone with my thoughts and the things that were weighing me down.

Was I going to fail?

Was I doing the right thing?

How could I hold her, sleep with her, and still lie to her?

I passed a couple kissing in the hallway and entered the spacious kitchen, heading straight toward the counters in the middle where bottles of alcohol, known and unknown to me, laid scattered. I didn't want to think anymore, and instead of reaching for another bottle of beer, like I should've, I took a bottle of Jack Daniels and started pouring it into my empty cup, not even bothering to mix it up with some Coke.

Lifting the cup up to my lips, I took a hefty amount inside, relishing in the burning sensation spreading from my throat, all the way to my stomach as the liquid started spreading through my system. I poured another one when I finished the first, wishing for all these things to get the fuck away from me, just for one night.

I just wanted to be an eighteen-year-old who liked a girl and had the usual teenage problems. I didn't want to be fighting in a war where I was a commander without an army.

I leaned against the counter as I downed the second drink, my knuckles turning white from the force with which I held on to the marble top. Music suddenly increased in volume, and I focused on that instead of the thundering of my own heart. I hated parties, but Danny and Rowan had amazing taste in music. As the first beats of "Temptation" by Imminence spread through the house, I straightened up and closed my eyes, letting the familiar lyrics wash over me.

My teeth tingled, and I knew I was close to getting drunk, but I didn't care. None of us were heading home tonight, and I wasn't driving. Maybe I should've stopped. Maybe I should've drunk some water instead of pouring another glass filled to the brim with the amber liquid, but everything was slowly catching up with me, and I didn't know how much longer I would be able to hold on.

Every time I thought I was closer to finding out the truth, I ran into a wall, and I had to start all over again. I couldn't even remember what my parents looked like. All our pictures were burned with the house we had, and with every new day, I wondered if what I was doing was correct.

People came and went, neither one of them talking to me or asking me if everything was okay. The liquid in the glass bottle of Jack Daniels went down and down and down, and when I took a step back from the counter, when the room started spinning around me, I knew I drank too much and way too fast.

"Ash," a voice from my dreams and my nightmares whispered, barely audible over the sound of music, while her hands plastered against my back. "Are you okay?"

"Moonshine," I said, or at least that's what I think I said. She really did remind me of moonshine—so bright and yet so dark. She kept illuminating my life just by existing, but she was going to hate me.

She was never going to want to see me again.

I turned around, and almost fell on her as my right foot slipped on the marble floor. The laughter erupted from my chest while she kept me upright, but she didn't laugh with me.

"Oops." I smiled down at her, placing my hands on her shoulders. She was so tiny, so much shorter than me, and I wanted to hide her in the pockets of my soul where no one would be able to take her away from me. "I think I'm a little bit drunk."

"You think?" Uh-oh, she didn't sound happy, and I wanted her to be happy.

I placed my hands on her cheeks and my thumbs at the edges of her mouth, pulling them to the side.

"Smile, Moonshine. I love it when you smile."

"Ash—"

"Shhh." I pressed a finger against her mouth. "No talky-talky. You need to smile first."

But she didn't. She wasn't angry. She didn't seem worried like all those other times when she allowed me to see what she was feeling, but she didn't look happy either.

"How the fuck did you manage to get drunk in the last half hour?"

I simply shrugged, because pronouncing Jack's full name felt like too much hassle right now, and all I wanted to do was to take her to one of the rooms upstairs to show her how much I loved her.

Oh.

Oh.

I loved her.

There. I finally admitted it to myself. I was in love with Skylar Blackwood, and that wasn't supposed to happen. How could I fall in love with the enemy? My parents would be so disappointed in me if they knew what I was doing.

"He's drunk because he knows you will never belong to him," somebody slurred from behind me.

When I turned, I saw it was Kane, leaning against the door leading to the backside porch. He looked like hell, and that was saying something, especially coming from me, because I almost always looked like hell.

I would rather go through the Spanish Inquisition than deal with him right now. Ever since Skylar came out of the hospital, Kane was evasive. He never spent time with the group anymore, and even Lauren started noticing his absence.

"Shut the fuck up, Kane," Skylar sneered as she stood next to me. The only thing that was keeping me standing now was her. I wanted to erase the smirk from his face, but wanting and being able to were two very different things. If it wasn't for her holding me up, I would probably be on the floor.

"Why?" He took a step closer and threw the beer bottle he was holding to the floor. The sound of glass shattering overpowered the sound of music, and I had a feeling that it wouldn't be too long until we had company. "It's true. You will never be his, not really. Not how he wants you to be."

"And I guess she belongs to you?" I bit back. "Jealousy looks bad on you."

"You stupid, stupid, fool!" he yelled and came closer to us. I pushed Skylar behind me, afraid of what he might do, and stumbled before she grabbed me by the shirt, balancing me.

I was on the receiving end of his wrath once and I'd be damned if I let him harm her in any way. The guy I met that first day of school was nowhere to be seen. He used to look calm, collected, a true Golden Boy of Winworth High, but the person in front of me was everything but calm.

The crazed look in his eyes froze the blood in my veins, and I worried what he might do to Skylar. I didn't have to be a genius to know that he had an unhealthy obsession with her. Whatever the story was between the two of them obviously left scars.

Scars that would forever be there.

"She will never be yours, but she will also never be mine," he cried out. What the fuck was he talking about? "Can't you see? Can't you see what they're doing to us, what they're doing to her?"

Skylar gripped my elbow, hiding behind me, but I wanted her gone. I wanted her out of here because I knew where he was going with this. I knew that he didn't have control anymore over what he did or what he said, and what he could say in this state could shatter Skylar forever.

"What are you talking about?" she asked, her voice small, almost shaky, because she also understood that Kane knew more than he was voicing. "Kane?"

He gripped his hair and started walking backward, murmuring, shaking his head.

"Kane?" She stepped around me and attempted to go to him. When I pulled her back, shaking my head, she sliced me with those stormy eyes. It wasn't safe.

"They're coming. They're coming. They're... He will get her, and she will be gone, forever." Kane continued crying, his voice bouncing against the walls of the kitchen, mixing with the painful lyrics Amy Lee was singing through the song. He suddenly looked up and came in front of me, grabbing me by the shirt.

"You have to save her. You have to," he begged. "He will take her from us, Ash. He will—"

"Who is he?" Skylar asked,

Whatever was going through Kane's head was too strong, and instead of answering her, he bypassed me and stopped in front of her, as still as a statue. He lifted one hand and placed it against her cheek, while his shoulders shook.

"I'm so sorry, Sky. I didn't know," he sobbed. "I didn't know that this was going to happen."

"What, Kane?" She placed her hand on top of his, and if that burning sensation in my gut was jealousy, I would never say it out loud. He needed her now more than I did, and whatever was going on with him, obviously messed him up enough to act like this. "You didn't know what?"

For a moment, the only sounds in the kitchen were the sharp inhales of breath from him, and Skylar's soothing voice, trying to calm him down.

Not once did she look at me, and I couldn't blame her. He was fucked up, and I didn't mean only about alcohol and God knew what else he poisoned his body with.

"You have to run, Sky," he murmured, barely enough for me to hear. "You need to get out of here now, because if you don't—" He stopped and turned around, facing me now. "You need to get her out of here, Ash. Just get her out of here, before he comes back for her. Please. I'm begging you, man. Save her."

He swayed on his feet as he tried coming closer to me, and if it wasn't for Skylar who rushed after him and held him up, I was pretty sure he would have ended up on his knees.

"Kane, calm down," Skylar said. "No one is going to take me."

But as Kane lifted his head and looked up at me, pleading with his eyes, I recognized the fear coursing through him. He knew and he hated it.

He knew about The Order, and it was eating him alive.

He was asking for help.

"Please," he begged. "You don't have much time."

Samhain.

Something big was happening. Something I had no idea about, but he did. I just had to get him to talk.

"Kane, please. What are you talking about? Who's coming? What's coming?"

"The man that gave you that." He looked at her bandaged arm. "He's coming, Sky. And this time, he won't be leaving without you."

TWENTY-THREE

Skylar

Some nights I could sleep like a little baby, and my brother often joked how even a Third World War wouldn't be able to wake me up.

Last night wasn't one of those nights.

While Ash slept next to me in one of the guest rooms Danny sent us to after the scene with Kane, I couldn't stop thinking about everything he'd said.

The Kane I knew never looked so disheveled, so scared. Not even when Zane went missing. He hated looking anything less but perfect, and to see him so distraught made me think twice about everything he said.

Yeah, he was definitely drunk, but that didn't diminish the fact that he knew something but was too scared to voice it out loud. I got the feeling he would've never said what he had if he was sober.

What bothered me even more was the fact that Ash seemed to be unmoved by Kane's words, because I was fucking terrified. It bothered me to the point where my overactive imagination started coming up with all these different scenarios, and the more I thought about it, the more I realized that I didn't know anything about our town.

I didn't know anything about our families, so I did what I should've done a long time ago.

I followed the letter I received the other day, and instead of going to school, I headed straight to the library. I wasn't missing much, if I was being entirely honest. I hated Fridays at school and skipping today was probably one of the best decisions I had made in a while.

I couldn't shake this weird feeling in my stomach that had nothing to do with the deranged maniac running on our streets, but had everything to do with Ash. What did I really know about him? Yes, he was allegedly born here, and he told me what happened to his parents. But why did they come back? And why was he so calm when Kane went crazy last night?

I had a million questions and no answers. I knew that even if I talked to him, he wouldn't tell me the truth. I also knew he cared about me, but I understood better than most people that every single one of us carried secrets we didn't want others to know about.

But what was he hiding? And the most important question that came to my mind as I glanced at the gauze on my arm, hiding whatever that monster carved on me — did he know who did this? I couldn't bring myself to fully look at the scars *he* left behind, changing the bandages as fast as possible whenever I needed to.

I didn't want to think this way. I didn't want to think that Ash had anything to do with the disappearances at night and all the deaths putting yet another stain on our town, but I was paranoid.

Every single person that passed next to me as I walked down the street toward the library could be a suspect, so why not Ash?

Wouldn't it be ironic that the one person I started

caring about turned out to be a deranged killer? I could already imagine more pitiful looks, and the whispers behind my back. I could already imagine the look on Dylan's face, and the disapproval on my father's.

Little Skylar Blackwood, in love with the murderer.

I shook my head, trying to rid myself of these thoughts. Ash wasn't a killer. Yeah, he was an enigma, but he wasn't a killer. Or at least that's what I told myself as I started climbing up the stairs, toward the library entrance.

As much as I hated Winworth, I loved the architecture. Our ancestors came from Europe, and if you paid close attention to the older buildings, you would recognize Gothic and renaissance styles mixed with the modern.

The town library was a clear example of it, with its high, arched ceilings and stained-glass windows. Sometimes I imagined I was somewhere in Europe, exploring the books hidden in the old libraries, containing knowledge I could never even dream of.

Two gargoyles stood perched up high on the wall, on either side of the tall, wooden entrance door, as if they were guarding the building with all their might.

I never asked who designed these buildings, but whoever it was really knew what they were doing.

Maybe they were guarding what I came here to look for. Maybe I would finally have the answers I desperately needed. As I entered through the already open door, I turned right, heading toward the wide staircase leading to the first floor.

The library was split into three floors, where the first one housed more modern books, mostly fiction. The second one was mixed, where you could find some of the greatest books ever written and non-fiction ones. The third one was the one I needed to go to.

I was there once, back when I was finishing elementary school, when I needed to write a paper on Mother Teresa and our teacher wanted us to actually use books rather than the internet to do so. The smell of old books was the first thing that hit me when I came here for the first time, and up until two years ago, I used to spend most of my time here, borrowing more books than I could read.

I just loved the smell of them, and the hidden worlds they all contained.

"Eleara?" A feminine voice pulled me back from my daydreaming, and as I turned around, I saw a very familiar face. A face I haven't seen in a very long time.

What did she just call me?

"Mrs. Montgomery?" I smiled at the old librarian. I couldn't remember the exact day when I met her, but Marissa Montgomery was always a part of our library.

She must have been in her late sixties by now, but the graceful way with which she held herself made her look at least ten years younger. Her long, gray hair was pulled into some kind of chignon on top of her head, and the glasses I always used to see her with were perched high on her nose, their dark rim highlighting steel-blue eyes.

Mrs. Montgomery was in her usual outfit—black suit pants and beige shoes with white tips, and a red blouse buttoned all the way up, with the sleeves rolled at her elbows.

"My God," she gasped when I came closer to her, pressing one hand to her mouth. With widening eyes, she scanned me from head to toe. What had me worried was the sudden paleness of her face.

"Mrs. Montgomery?" I looked around but none of the other workers were anywhere nearby. I didn't want her to collapse in front of me.

"You look just like —" She cut herself off and took a step back, still looking at me with a shocked expression on her face. "I'm sorry, Skylar."

"I look like who?" Confusion laced every single word, because I knew I didn't look like my mother, nor did I look like my father. Even my hair wasn't as light as theirs was, but I always thought that Dylan and I had similar color eyes. "Mrs. Montgomery?"

I started sounding like a parrot, repeating her name, trying to figure out what was wrong.

But whatever she wanted to say and whatever spooked her seemed to go away as fast as it came, and in the next moment she straightened up, and smiled at me.

"No one, my child. You just reminded me of someone I lost a long time ago."

But I knew who I reminded her of.

Her daughter.

There wasn't a single occupant of Winworth that didn't know the story of Eleara Montgomery. I wasn't really sure what was the truth and what was a lie, but she went missing long before I was born, and she was never found.

Some said she ran away, that she couldn't handle being in the small town filled with secrets. Others said that she was murdered, but her remains were never found.

She was just a few years older than I am now when it happened, barely twenty-two. I knew that her mother, Mrs. Montgomery, never stopped looking for her.

I couldn't imagine the kind of pain Mrs. Montgomery went through, and I hoped I would never have to find out how it felt to lose someone you loved so much. I knew why she almost told me that I looked like her daughter.

From everything I heard, Eleara had long, blonde

hair, just like I did, and the brightest pair of blue eyes. So I could understand why Mrs. Montgomery looked like she saw a ghost.

"H-how…" she cleared her throat before continuing. "How can I help you today? You haven't been here for a very long time."

And I hadn't. So long in fact, that I didn't even know if the sections were still the same.

"I know, and I feel terrible about it. But life got in the way, and I just…" I trailed off. "I don't know. I guess I lost track of the things I loved doing."

She blinked slowly, and her eyes shuddered for a split second, one moment before she smiled, and I had a feeling she was all too familiar with the feeling I was trying to describe.

"Well, whatever it was, I'm glad you're back."

"Me too."

She started walking toward the desk on the other end of the hallway, and I followed, while our steps echoed in the hallway. The right side was lined with the high, arched windows, and I could see City Hall from here, as well as the fog hiding the tops of the mountains separating Winworth from Emercroft Lake.

Nature here was truly mesmerizing, but the people were a stain, and I hoped that one day in the future, this town wouldn't be plagued by the monsters hiding in the dark, wearing their perfect little masks in the daylight.

Monsters like my father.

Monsters like the man that attacked me.

"What happened to your arm?" she asked out of nowhere as we reached her desk. We both knew what happened, the entire town knew, but she still asked, and I couldn't be angry at an old lady for being curious.

I knew that people spewed their versions of the story, and I also knew that they somehow knew that it was my name carved on the bodies of all those dead girls, but I didn't have it in me to care anymore. They could talk as much as they wanted to, but I wouldn't entertain their crazy stories.

I decided not to react anymore, because that was what was feeding into their twisted stories.

"I had an accident," I replied, begging her with my eyes not to ask me anything else. I didn't want to think about that night, let alone talk.

The crazy messages had stopped since he carved me like a pumpkin for Halloween, and no other girls had disappeared so far. But that didn't mean that it was over. No, I had a feeling it was just starting, but this time I wasn't going to run and hide.

I had no idea if I would find anything that could help me to solve this, but I had to try. Whoever left that letter in my locker, they left it for a reason, and I would be stupid not to follow up. Besides, I was in a public library, and it's been, what, two weeks since I got the letter.

If they wanted to harm me, they would find other ways. They wouldn't leave me with clues.

"But you're okay now?" She looked at me above the rim of her glasses, and I felt as if she could see inside my soul.

"I'm all good now." I sounded too perky for someone that went through something so traumatic, but if I wanted to get over this incident, I had to at least pretend as if everything was okay.

Even if my hands still shook from fear every time I was left alone inside the house, I imagined it was because of low sugar levels and not the absolute terror I was still experiencing.

"I wanted to go up to the third floor, to read more about the history of Winworth. We have this assignment at school, and I couldn't find anything on the internet." I changed the topic before she could ask me anything else.

It would be a long time from now that I would be able to talk about that night without reliving everything as if it was happening right now. Maybe one day, but not today.

"O-kay." She nodded and started typing on the computer. She didn't comment on the sudden change of topic, and I was thankful for small miracles today. "I have your membership here." She looked up at me. "Do you have your old card, or should I issue you a new one?"

"Could I get a new one, please? I searched the entire house for my old card, but—"

"Skylar," she cut me off with a smile. "It's okay." The computer beeped, and she pulled out a white plastic card from the drawer and scanned it on the flat, square machine positioned next to the computer. "Here you go."

The card hung in the air between the two of us for a second too long. A second for me to think if I really wanted to know the truth and what that poem meant, or if I wanted to continue living in this oblivious state of mind.

But I was tired of all the lies, secrets, and the history no one wanted me to know about.

I grabbed the card from her and with one final thank-you, I ran toward the elevator and pressed the button.

I just hoped I would find what I was looking for, even though I still didn't know what exactly it was.

Two hours.

It'd been two hours since I arrived at the library, and all I was able to find were facts I already knew. The year when Winworth was established, the names of our founding fathers, and well-known facts I could find with a simple click of my mouse.

But there was nothing deeper.

I was getting frustrated with the lack of information here, and when I glanced at my phone showing that it was already five in the afternoon, I knew I either had to leave or make a plan.

There was still one part of the third floor I hadn't checked. In the far corner, right next to the statue of a weeping angel that was actually creeping me out, stood a cupboard probably older than me, with several books on its shelves.

I stood up and closed the book I was currently reading, and started walking toward the cupboard with glass doors, ignoring the eyes of an angel that once probably looked beautiful. But time got to him, and the once white marble now looked dark, creating a sinister feeling to it.

And who the fuck put statues of angels in libraries these days anyway?

People of Winworth, that's who.

You know how every town had that one person that was allegedly crazy? Well, our town was filled with crazies. I looked back at the angel and remembered Molly Stallen. An old lady who lived on Crosshaven Street, near our school, who spent her life walking on the streets alone and talking about those that were hiding in the shadows and angels that would save us.

Somebody should've told her that there was no such thing as salvation in a town like Winworth.

I scanned the dusty shelves, looking for something, anything, any kind of title that could tell me more about the history of Winworth. When I saw a familiar sign, my entire body froze.

While I hadn't recognized the symbol on the mysterious letter, I knew this one. I'd seen it before, heard about it through the stories told by my father and grandfather. Hell, it was in my house, carved on the door leading to the attic.

Ouroboros.

The original symbol of infinity. A snake eating its own tail, living, dying, and over and over again, for all of eternity. Dylan had this same symbol tattooed on his chest, and when I asked him about it, he just said it was a family legacy.

A legacy I had no idea about.

But the circling snake wasn't the problem and what had me stopped in my tracks. The problem was the symbol resting within. The same symbol that was on that letter, only that one didn't have a snake circling the triangle with upturned ends.

The sound the door produced once I opened it made the hair at the back of my neck raise up, sending goosebumps all over my skin. I had a feeling I was about to find out a lot more than I wanted to, but the truth was at the tips of my fingers and I'd be damned if I ran away now.

The dust rose up and blew in my face, infiltrating through my nose, going all the way to my lungs. My throat seized, and an involuntary cough escaped from my chest, making me take a step back.

Why the fuck was nobody cleaning these shelves?

I could feel the tears gathering in my eyes, and as my vision blurred, I just hoped that there wasn't anything else mixed with the dust. The last thing I wanted to have was some weird bacteria to start spreading through my system.

And that fucking angel was still staring at me, as if it was daring me to take a new step, to see what was inside the book.

So I did. I took a step back, fighting the foul taste in my mouth from all the dust I inhaled, and took a book from the shelf, turning its front side to me. *Secrets of Winworth* was engraved into the leather cover, cracked and dusted, kissed by time. There was no author listed, just the title and the dark broken leather.

"What in the—"

I walked backward and sat down at one of the tables closer to the cupboard, right next to the high window casting the last rays of sun for the day. The golden lettering was beautiful, without a doubt, but as I touched the front side, a tremor ran through my body, coiling in my gut with fear.

I willed myself to open it up, and the smell of old, of forbidden, of secrets and stories I could never imagine, slammed into me as I placed my palm on the first page, gliding over the text written in cursive, right in the middle of the page.

Sanguinem Sacrificium
Sanctum Sacrificium
Vita Tua
Vita Meae
Tuo Amore
Sanguinem Meum

Did it really have to be Latin? Though I might not have been fluent in it, I did know what *Sanguinem* meant.

Blood.

I pulled my phone out, just in case the need for a translator arose, but when I moved from that opening yellow page, I saw that the rest of the text was in English.

"*The Beginning*", the chapter title read, and I looked down, going over the text.

"*Winworth was founded by five, to represent the five sides of His Unholy Majesty.*" My eyes almost popped out. "*Five supremes, five to rule, and five to bring His rule to the new soil.*"

Was this... Was this book saying what I thought it was saying?

"*Forsaken by the Old Countries, they sought shelter in the New World, fleeing away from those that wished them harm. From those who couldn't understand their mission.*"

No, no, I would know. I would know if our ancestors came from something sinister.

"Five commanders and ten Red Maidens," I read out loud. "They were brought here to strengthen the bonds and to unite the blood. Blackwood, St. Clare, Lacroix, Maddox and Crowell—"

Wait.

No, it couldn't be. It couldn't be what I was looking at.

Crowell. The fifth family. Crowell, just like Ash.

Asher Crowell.

TWENTY-FOUR

SKYLAR

Four weeks later

It was funny how fast things could change.

Four weeks ago, I thought I'd finally found the one person that could understand me, that could maybe even help me overcome the demons I was battling on a daily basis, but it turned out that I truly didn't know him at all.

After finding out about Ash's family, I started realizing that I wasn't the only one hiding the truth. But why would he?

I sneaked away from the library and took that book home with me, trying to decipher the Latin text woven throughout, and the stories about our families, but nothing really made sense. Okay, I basically stole the book, but I couldn't exactly tell Mrs. Montgomery that I needed it with me because I thought my family was involved in something sinister. The articles I discovered about the Crowell family were scarce, and the only thing I could find was a newspaper article from the Seattle Daily, mentioning the death of the Crowell family—a mother and a father and their two sons.

But they weren't dead.

Maybe Ash's mother and father were gone, but he and his brother were very much alive. I wouldn't be thinking this way, if he actually told me this himself.

The name of the fifth family was always kept from us—not that we asked—and I didn't know why. The more I read about the history of Winworth, the more I started realizing that there were things I never wanted to discover.

Things that made my blood run cold, while my brain battled with the horrible picture all those stories painted. And the worst thing was that I couldn't talk to any of my friends about what I had found.

Kane was already behaving like he was close to a nervous breakdown. Lauren pretended everything was okay, and every single time I tried to bring up us finding Megan's body, she shut me down.

Danny and Rowan were on a mission to drink themselves to death, and Beatrice and Hailey were doing God knows what.

The only person I was spending time with was Ash, and I hated these suspicious thoughts filling my head every single time I even thought about him. My own heart was torturing me because it didn't want to believe that he had some nefarious plan. But with everything that was happening around us, with the cloak of darkness that fell over Winworth, I started suspecting everyone and everything.

We agreed to study in the school library today, and even though he was sitting right across from me, I had a feeling he was a million miles away. It was as if after I found out that he belonged to one of the founding families, everything changed.

He behaved the same, but I knew things now. Things no one else knew, and I feared that the deeper I went, the darker it would get. I wasn't sure if I wanted to see everything that book was hiding.

I was hoping that I would be able to find out who the hooded figure was, who the attacker was, or at least who left me that note in the locker, but I found a lot more than I was looking for. I found an intricate world woven with lies, secrets, and betrayals.

Only a couple of pages of the book were innocent enough, talking about the area, and where our families came from, but the more I read, the more I realized that there were borderline insane things happening in Winworth.

Words like *sacrifice*, *Samhain*, and *rituals* kept being repeated over and over and over again. On the fifteenth page of the book, a black-and-white photograph fell out from between the pages — three kids, all standing in front of the altar I saw in that photo I received. Their faces were robbed of smiles, while three hooded figures stood behind them, with their hands on their shoulders.

I didn't have to be a genius to know that those kids weren't there of their own volition.

What bothered me the most was the fact that the book wasn't simply written and left alone. No, different handwritings were etched on its pages, and when I turned it to one of the last pages, the date written was October 31st, 2007.

It was the date of my fifth birthday.

"Is everything okay, Skylar?" Erin Dagonn, the girl sitting on my left side, asked, pulling me back to reality and away from the thoughts of a certain malicious book. We had a couple of classes together, and we studied together from time to time.

I wanted to tell her that nothing was okay. Nothing would ever be okay. But I could feel Ash's burning gaze on the side of my face, and instead of voicing what was really wrong, I smiled at her, and closed the biology book I was holding.

"I'm okay."

We had a test next week, but no matter how much I tried studying about genomes and all the other things we were going to have on the test, I just couldn't. Every time I looked at the pages of the book, trying to study, different text appeared in front of my eyes, and I gave up.

I was here today only because I promised Erin, and because I agreed to spend some time with Ash after we were done.

I'd been avoiding him as much as possible, and he knew something was up, but I couldn't bring myself to talk to him about the things I'd found. Maybe it was from fear. What if I looked him in the eye, telling him all these things I'd found—about his family, all our families, actually—and he wasn't looking back at me?

What if he started hiding his midnight eyes from me, afraid I would see the truth there? Afraid that I would see the secrets he'd been hiding.

I kept my eyes on Erin while she talked about her sister studying in Toronto and how much she missed her, but if she asked me to repeat everything she said, I wouldn't be able to.

My body was in tune with Ash—my Ash—silently staring at me, while Erin talked my ear off. I could already imagine the storm swirling over his face because I was ignoring him. I've been doing this for days whenever somebody else was with us, and I was avoiding staying alone with him.

I dreaded the moment when we would be left alone, because then I would have no choice but to look at him, to talk to him, to really miss him.

Because I did, miss him, that is. I missed him when

he was gone, and I missed him when he was with me. And now my father knew about Ash.

He knew I wasn't working on gathering information about Kane's parents, and he was livid.

"All righty." Erin suddenly stood up and started collecting her things. "I have to head out. My mom wants me to come home before dark today. They're all spooked about—" She bit her lip as she looked at my scarred arm. "Well, you know what they're spooked about."

Yeah, I did know.

I had a list of things I was terrified of right now, and at the top of that list was a monster they still couldn't catch. There were no prints inside the house, no further evidence that could point to one person, and the police were as clueless as the rest of us.

I was glad for October and the colder weather it brought to us. At least now I could wear long-sleeved shirts without looking like a lunatic, while everybody else wore short-sleeved shirts and basked in the rare bouts of sunshine in Winworth.

When the doctor removed the bandages from my arm, I wanted to cry, scream, shout, fucking break something, because he didn't just slice me up like a turkey for Thanksgiving. No, he left a mark.

A mark I knew.

A mark I had seen two times already.

Once on that paper in my locker, and the second time on the spine of the book I found in the library.

The only thing it was missing was a circle or *ouroboros* around the symbol, but it was exactly the same mark—the triangle with upturned ends.

Dylan held my other hand while the doctor removed the stitches and applied ointment. I was furious, but I held it inside. At least I tried to hold it inside, until we reached home, when I broke down, letting the tears stream freely down my cheeks, uncaring who was going to see me. And Dylan… Dylan broke a vase that always stood in the foyer of our house, smashing it against the wall as soon as we stepped inside, not once looking at me.

That was the last time I saw him before he went back to Seattle.

"Call me?" she asked as she started heading toward the exit, leaving me alone with Ash.

I should've turned around and looked at him instead of staring at the space now vacated by Erin, but I couldn't.

My stomach churned as worry spread through my body, settling at the pit of my gut. When he finally spoke, his voice ricocheting against the shelves, falling over me like a blanket, that churning sensation increased tenfold, but I still refused to look at him.

"I'm not sure if I should spank you," he started in a low vibrato, my core clenching and unclenching, my body begging for his touch. "Or if I should just walk out."

I turned at that.

"What?" I asked breathlessly. He would leave? The nerves from earlier were suddenly replaced by fear, and as I dropped the book on the table, he leaned over, placing his elbows on the dark mahogany wood, his eyes never leaving mine.

"What is going on, Skylar?"

He never called me by my name anymore, at least not my full name. After those nights at my house, something changed in him, and true to his word, he never went back to ignoring me or to pretending that what was happening between us wasn't real. So hearing him use my full name felt like lead settling in my body, rendering me speechless.

Unmoving, I blinked, and then blinked again as he dragged his hand over his face. He was furious with me, I knew that. But I didn't know that he would be furious enough to walk away.

"You would leave me?" I murmured, dreading the answer.

Panic gripped me, my heart protesting against my rib cage, afraid it would lose its anchor. But I already lost him. I wasn't sure if I ever really had him.

Not because he didn't tell me about his family.

Not because he never tells me anything about him.

But because I was never supposed to be his. My father, my monster, already wrote every sequence of my life, and no matter what I did, I would never have my freedom. At least not while I'm in Winworth.

Ash was mine to love and mine to lose, but I couldn't bring myself to tell him. I was going to break my own heart, and if I could, I would rid myself of my last name, so that the only thing standing between the two of us was only this table in front of me, and nothing else.

He suddenly stood up and rounded the table, crowding me, cutting off my oxygen supply, because he was everywhere. The sky was not just the sky anymore. It held colors hidden in Ash's eyes, and every night when I looked up from my balcony, I saw him.

The forest didn't smell only like wet soil and pine trees. It held Ash in its arms, making me think of him even when I didn't want to think of anything.

The sound of the chair scraping over the floor sounded around us as he pulled me around. He was on his knees, his hands on my bare legs, inching higher and higher, going underneath the black skirt I wore today.

"I don't know, Moonshine," he murmured, looking at me. "I don't know what's wrong with you lately, and it's driving me insane. You won't let me touch you, you won't let me kiss you... You're here, but you're not here."

If only he knew how much I wanted to be here, to be present. Not just physically, but mentally as well.

He gripped my bare thighs, his thumbs dangerously close to my core.

"So, you tell me." He pressed his lips against my knee, his dark lashes fluttering as his eyes closed. "Do you want me to leave?"

My chest rose and fell, and I closed my hands into fists, battling the need to touch his dark silky hair. I didn't want him to leave, but I had to let him go.

"I-I..." I stammered.

"What do you want, Moonshine?" he asked again, pressing his lips to my other knee.

"I want—"

He licked his way from my kneecaps to my inner thigh, lifting my skirt higher and higher, until it was hunched around my hips, barely covering my drenched panties. If somebody walked inside, there would be no doubt in their mind about what we were doing.

"Do you want me?" His grip on my thighs became painful. "Because if you don't, I'm not sure if I would be able to let you go."

Thump.

Thump.

Thump.

My heartbeat echoed in my ears until I bit my lip, tasting blood.

"You've ruined me for everybody else, Moonshine," he whispered, dragging his finger over my soaked panties, sending small rivulets of pleasure through my body. "And I don't give a shit if you think that this couldn't work, it has to." He pushed my legs apart, planting his face between my thighs, inhaling me, tasting my skin, devouring me until I couldn't remember why I had to stop us.

"You can't decide that you don't want us anymore. You simply can't. And you know why?" He looked up, a small smile dancing on his lips. I shook my head, my ability to form words stripped away from me. "Because I belong to you, Moonshine. I belong to you today, tomorrow, a hundred years from now. I will always belong to you."

I wanted to tell him I would always belong to him as well. I wanted to tell him how much it hurt not having his hands on me, loving me, teasing me, caressing me as if I was the most precious thing. But I couldn't tell him any of those things.

I couldn't tell him that my soul cried every time I thought about leaving him, protesting against me.

But I had to leave him, even if I didn't want to.

I had to, because if I didn't, the next dead body would be his, and I wouldn't be able to live with myself if that happened.

So this, this here… This was our goodbye.

"Ash," I murmured, making him lift his head as he started peppering my skin with kisses. "I want you."

Something blazed in his eyes. Something dangerous, sinfully delicious, a vicious desire that was coursing through me as well, and it was like flipping the switch—in one moment, he was soft, and in the next, it was as if everything he was holding in came out.

His pupils dilated, punishing touches pushing at my shoulders until my back was plastered to the chair.

"I hope you're not too fond of these."

"Wha—"

The sound of my panties ripping in two filled the air, and before I could comprehend what was happening, he lowered his head, spreading my legs wider and wider. My skirt went higher up, and I lifted my butt to let it go all the way over my hips.

He inhaled, his breath caressing my clit. "You smell like heaven." He pressed a kiss on the hood of my pussy and then licked all the way from my opening to my clit. A moan escaped me, and I threw my head backward, pushing my hips toward him. "You taste even better."

"Please," I begged, willing him to play with my fire. He licked me again, running his tongue over my clit, over my lower lips, while his fingers spread me wider, baring me to him. "Ash!"

"Is this what you want?" He smirked as he entered me with one finger, lazily dragging it up and down.

"Ash!" I protested again, bucking my hips, begging him to go faster.

"Or this?" He pushed inside with a second finger, then the third, mixing pain with pleasure as he dove and bit on my clit.

"Fuck!"

He increased the pace, then slowed down, then again increased, driving me insane with need, with lust. I started forgetting about everything that worried me.

His tongue danced through my folds while his fingers brought me higher and higher until he pressed against the spot inside my core that made me see stars. The pressure that was building at the bottom of my stomach started slipping from my grasp, and as my entire body started convulsing, he murmured against me, the vibrations elevating me to a new level.

"Let go, Moonshine."

I screamed in an empty library, trying to hold on to him, hold on to his head, gripping the silky strands as my body finally gave in. He continued stroking me, licking and biting, prolonging my orgasm while I kept shaking, unable to stop my body from giving in.

"Good girl," he purred against my heated skin and removed his fingers from my body. I felt high, drunk on him. When he stood up, taking me with him, he gripped the back of my neck with one hand, while the other one played with the hem of my shirt, lifting it higher, until his hand reached the silky material of my bra.

"Hmmm." He smiled and bent his head down to my neck, grazing my skin with his teeth, while his fingers circled around my nipple, over my bra. I pushed my chest at him, letting him take full control of my body.

He played me like an instrument — one hand on my chest, the second one in my hair, his lips on my neck, leaving a blazing trail all the way to my mouth. He nibbled on my bottom lip, then kissed me as if his entire life depended on it.

Our teeth clashed, the fight for dominance coursing through both of us, but I knew that it was a fight I would never win.

I already belonged to him — body, mind, and soul.

"You're mine, Moonshine," he murmured between kisses. "I don't give a fuck what anybody else says... You. Are. Mine."

For the first time since I met him, his emotions were written all over his face. Lust, anger, passion, love, and the one I hated seeing — fear.

Midnight blue stared back at me with uncertainty, as if he thought I would disappear. I knew if I asked him about it, he would deny it, but I didn't need words to see everything he felt reflected back at me.

"Ash," I murmured, going up to my tiptoes and pressing my lips to his. "I will always belong to you, baby. Always and forever."

He abruptly turned from me and knocked over all the books from the table.

"What—"

I didn't manage to finish asking before I was airborne, held tightly in his arms. In the next second, my butt was firmly placed on top of the table with him between my legs.

He lifted my shirt all the way above my chest and pulled me to him, lining my core with the bulge in his pants.

Possessive lips descended on mine, branding me forever. Skillful hands owned my body, and without a word, he started unbuttoning his pants, letting them fall to the floor.

"You're not wearing underwear?" I smiled, breaking the tension in the room.

Instead of answering me, he bent down and took out a condom wrapped in a silver packet, then ripped it open. His dick was pointed right at me, and my mouth salivated at what was coming. Unable to help myself, I got off the table and stood right in front of him, placing a soft kiss in between his pecs.

Then another one lower, right against his stomach, until I started going down, dragging my nails over his skin, over his abs, until I reached the delicious V pointing to his dick. I could feel his eyes on me, his burning gaze. When he didn't stop me, I slid down, all the way to my knees, licking my lips when the angry red head appeared in front of my face.

"Moonshine," he rasped, empowering me by letting me have this control over him. He wrapped one hand in my hair, pulling it away from my face. I dragged my nails over his thighs, inching closer to his balls, and then pulling back, earning a groan from him. "Sky, please."

It was music to my ears, his pleading, and his sharp intakes of breath. Without waiting any longer, I wrapped one hand at the base of his member, and licked the vein straining against the soft skin, all the way to the bulbous head.

"Fuck!" His hips bucked forward, and I grinned, knowing that all this was for me. Only me. "Open your mouth, Moonshine."

But I didn't. I wanted to play more, to explore every inch of him, to savor his moans, his groans, his begging.

"Please," he begged when I placed a soft kiss on top of his cock, dragging my hand up and down. I looked up only to see him already looking at me. We were playing with fire, but I didn't mind burning if it was with him. "You're a very bad girl today," he murmured. "And you know what happens to bad girls?"

I did. I closed my eyes as my other hand traveled to my pussy, collecting the juices dripping over my thighs, to the floor, and lifted it up, massaging his balls then his dick with it.

"Fuck, fuck, fu—" he started chanting, and before he could say anything more, I wrapped my lips around him, swirling my tongue over the head, while I pumped him with my other one. "Fuuuuck!" erupted from him as I started bobbing my head up and down, feeling the pressure build up at the base of my stomach.

I bit into the skin of his butt cheek with my nails, pulling him closer, holding myself up. He suddenly tore away from me, breathing as if he ran a marathon.

His hand wrapped around my ass cheeks, lifting me up until his lips mashed with mine, fighting for dominance, fighting for something I couldn't explain.

"You taste like me," he muttered against my lips. "I need to fuck you, Moonshine. I need to be inside you."

He didn't have to say anything else. I moved backward and sat on the table, moving myself further away from the edge, waiting for him to come to me.

Ash rolled the condom over his member, fisting

himself at the base of his dick, and took a step toward me, like a predator with its prey.

Words weren't needed as he unclasped my bra from the front, letting it fall to the sides, devouring me with his eyes. His greedy hands ran over my stomach, his thumbs digging into my ribs, as if he was holding himself still, trying to control the animalistic urges rushing through his veins.

"Ash," I panted.

I arched my back, pushing my chest higher, as his fingers started circling my erect nipples, driving me out of my mind.

"You are the most perfect thing I have ever owned," he murmured, peppering my chest with kisses, going lower and lower, until his face was above the hem of the skirt he lifted earlier. "I'm going to ruin you for every other man out there."

"I don't want other men," I gasped. "I want you. Only you."

"Then you'll have me, Moonshine."

In a move too fast for the human eye to catch, he pulled me to the edge of the table and lined his dick with my opening. He dragged his member over my slick folds until he found the welcoming heat of my body.

I pushed myself up, holding my weight on my hands, as he pushed inside in one swift thrust, knocking the breath from me.

"Fuck!" he roared, stilling inside me, letting me adjust to his size. "You feel so good, Moonshine." He stared at where the two of us connected. "This is my favorite place on earth."

"Ash, please," I whimpered. "I need you to move."

And he did. Painfully slow at first, wearing that self-satisfied little smirk on his face while I begged him to increase his pace, to give me what I wanted, and then something snapped, taking over him.

More animal than man, he pushed me down, my back pressing against the cold wooden desk, and wrapped one hand around my neck. He pressed on my clit with the thumb on his other hand, the maddening inability to move, to see what was happening, driving me insane.

Something unfolded in my stomach, the fire rushing from my body to that one spot, threatening to erupt.

"Hold it," he growled against my ear, bending down, and increasing the pace.

The table groaned beneath us, its legs scraping against the floor, creating a cacophony of noises. I turned my head to the side and looked at the ceiling-high window, trying to think of anything else, just to hold off a little bit longer.

"Ash!" I cried out, losing the grip on my body. "I can't—"

His hand tightened around my throat, cutting me off. "Yes, you can!"

Pistoning his hips, he moved his hand from my clit, and held onto my hip, keeping me in one place. My entire body was one big bundle of nerves, like a guitar string too tightly wrapped around the tuning keys, ready to snap.

I was close, so fucking close, when the motherfucker slowed down and suddenly stopped, letting go of my throat.

"What the fuc—"

His hand wound around my neck, lifting my head up, pulling me to him. "This is for all these weeks I spent without you, Moonshine." He thrust his hips upward, knocking the breath out of me. "This is how you made me feel when you didn't talk to me like you usually do." Another thrust. "Now I'm gonna show you the insanity

I went through when you kept these lips from me." He smiled and bit my lower lip. "When you shied away from my touch." He started strumming over my clit, bringing me back to the fire.

"Oh. My. God." My eyes rolled to the back of my head when he suddenly stopped again, depriving me from the sweet release I needed. "Ash!"

"No!" The grip on my neck increased, but he didn't move. "I own this body, Skylar." He started moving his hips again, but it wasn't enough. "I own all your orgasms."

"Yes, yes, yes," I started chanting. "Just… Please, let me—"

He pushed me back to the table and slapped my clit, all the while slowly moving in and out.

"Shhhh." He pressed a finger to my lips. Gritting my teeth, I closed my eyes, trying to focus on anything else but the pleasure ricocheting through my body. "No, not yet!" he roared as I clenched around him, wailing, tears streaming down my cheeks.

"I'm… I-I…"

He gripped my hips with both his hands, and I knew I would have purple marks to remind me of this night. "Fuck, fuck, fuck." I placed one hand over his, and with the other one, I started rubbing at my clit.

"Now!" he yelled. "Now, now, no—"

The orgasm shattered through me, muting out any sounds around me. My back arched, my mouth open, but no sound came, my walls holding him in a tight grip. Our eyes connected, and I could see everything I felt reflected in him. The shirt he wore was soaked with sweat, and as he collapsed on top of me, my legs wrapped around his waist, I lifted his shirt and started drawing circles on his skin, reveling in this feeling.

But it couldn't last.

"I love you, Sky," he whispered against my ear, making my whole body lock down.

Those words... Those were the words I wanted to hear. Words I wanted to say, but we couldn't.

I couldn't.

I couldn't be the end of him. I couldn't be the reason behind his demise, so I did what I should've done earlier.

I pushed him away, wincing when he finally detached from me. The furrow of his eyebrow told me that he knew something was wrong.

"What's wrong?" he asked carefully, slicing with the standoffish way he stood in front of me.

He removed the condom and wrapped it up, throwing it in the bin next to the table.

I pulled my shirt down, and jumped from the table, barely holding myself straight. My knees shook, muscles trembling, but I had to do this now.

Fixing my skirt, I turned around and faced him.

"We need to talk."

TWENTY-FIVE

ASH

This isn't working for me anymore."

This isn't working for me anymore.

Her words echoed in my head on repeat, even after she left the library.

I couldn't chase after her. I couldn't hold her to me, like I wanted to, because she managed to escape before I could pull up my pants.

This isn't working for me anymore.

No.

NO.

This isn't working for me anymore.

Right after I told her I loved her.

This isn't working for me anymore.

Right after I showed her what she meant to me.

This isn't working for me anymore.

Right after I thought that everything was okay.

Fuck.

"Fuck!" I roared out loud, throwing the book she left behind to the other side of the library.

I had no idea how long I stood here, holding onto the table where she was mine. Those six words just shattered this fantasy I had created in my head, but I'd be damned if I let her get away with this so easily.

I asked her why. I begged her to talk to me as I tried to pull on my pants, but the only response I got was the tear-stained face, and the sobs I could still hear as if she were right next to me.

Dragging a hand over my face, I took a deep breath, willing myself to calm down, so that I wouldn't do anything stupid. Like march over to her house and demand that she talk to me, to explain what the fuck just happened.

But knowing her, she would just close down even more, and I would be nowhere near solving this shit she threw at me.

I thought we were okay. I went insane over the last four weeks when she completely shut me down, allowing me to hold her hand when we were in public, but that was it. If we were alone, she wouldn't utter a word, and it was driving me mad.

But I gave her space because I thought that's what she wanted. I thought she wanted to deal with the aftermath of that attack on her own, and instead of suffocating her, I just wanted to be there for her.

Apparently, she didn't want me at all.

I rubbed the spot on my chest, as if the visceral pain she left me with was physical, rather than emotional. In one split second, she destroyed everything I loved about my life right now.

I defied my uncle when he told me to just fuck her and leave her. I defied what I promised my parents a long time ago, because she meant more than revenge.

She was my present and my future, and I tried leaving the ghosts of the past where they belonged—in the past. But she literally shat on everything I tried to do for her.

I sat on the chair she was previously sitting on and

grabbed my head with both my hands, placing my elbows on my knees, and for the first time since I was a child, I wanted to cry.

To weep, to shout, to scream at the top of my lungs, because this was tearing me apart. Her birthday was coming up tomorrow, and I had plans, dammit. I didn't give a shit about fucking Halloween and the bonfire at the riverbank.

I just wanted to spend it with her.

And now she was gone, leaving me behind as if what we had meant nothing. I knew she was lying. Her tears and her eyes told me everything she didn't want me to know.

She was terrified, but not of me. Something happened in the last four weeks. Something she didn't want to say, and I was going to find out what it was.

The other problem I had was the fact that The Order seemed to be quiet. Too quiet for my liking.

The last time I saw any of them going toward City Hall was three weeks ago, and since then, most of the founding families were either out of the town, or were generally nowhere to be seen. Lars, the only person that seemed to know things about the Black Dahlia, was completely silent.

To make matters worse, Sebastian was on my case lately to stay in Winworth after our mission was done, and that was one thing I promised myself I would never do. We got into a fight yesterday, and I had a feeling life decided to just fuck with all my relationships lately.

The lights in the library suddenly turned on, making me almost jump from the chair I was sitting in.

I knew I had to move. I knew I should probably go home, but my body wasn't listening to my mind. Instead of getting up and leaving this place, I placed my hands on the spot where Skylar lay earlier and closed my eyes, imagining we were still in the same spot, at the same time.

"I wondered if you would still be here, or if you left already." A deep, gravelly voice broke the silence of the library, and when I turned around to see who it was, the blood running through my veins turned cold.

Judah Blackwood.

The devil himself.

Clad in a black designer suit that probably cost more than the house we were currently living in, he stood between the two shelves leading to the door with his hands in his pockets, smiling, as if seeing me was the best thing that has ever happened to him.

I often dreamed about the first time I would see him, thinking about all the things I would say to him, the things I would do to him. But now that he stood in front of me, I realized he held more power over me than I initially thought.

He started walking toward me, looking around the library as if he owned the place. Hell, maybe he did, I wouldn't know. Nothing would surprise me at this point.

"Ah, this place brings back old memories." He laughed and took a seat across from me, placing his hands in his lap. I pulled my phone out of my pocket, but I knew that if he wanted to do something to me, he would've done so already.

Judah Blackwood isn't the type of man who would wait around or try to meet me just so that he could kill me, like he killed my parents.

"You look just like your father," he said, as if it was the most normal thing to say in this situation. My body froze, the muscle in my cheek ticking with each passing second. I knew I wore a murderous expression on my face. I was bigger than him, probably stronger as well, and I could take him, but as he sat there, a self-satisfied look on his face, looking at me with something more than anger, I realized that this might be my way in.

"You mean the father you killed?" I gritted through my teeth, the flashbacks of that night slowly leering from the darkest parts of my mind.

"Oh, come on, Asher, don't be hasty. That was, what, twelve years ago?"

"To me it feels like it happened just yesterday, old man."

Instead of getting pissed off at the nickname, he laughed, the lines around his eyes crinkling as he stared at me.

"I think I'll like you, kid." He opened his suit jacket and pulled out a packet of cigarettes from the inner pocket. He took one out and dropped it on the table, right in front of me. "You smoke, don't you?"

I said nothing, and I hated myself for just sitting here like a little schoolboy, letting him lead this conversation. My parents would be disappointed in me if they could see me now.

Asher Crowell rendered speechless from fear in front of the man he vowed to destroy.

His eyes, a lighter shade than Skylar's, roamed over my body, going from my head, all over my chest, and back up again, as if he was trying to read me, to see who I really was.

"Take one," he said as he lit up his own cigarette. "And don't worry about school rules." He snickered. "You'll find out soon that people in this town do what we tell them to do, not the other way around."

And there it was, the entire truth of Winworth. No secrets, no lies, just fucked-up families behaving as if they owned everybody's lives.

I lifted the packet of cigarettes from the table, and

took one out, lighting it up with my own lighter, letting the smoke coat my insides. Letting it calm me down enough so that I wouldn't jump over the table at the monster sitting across from me.

"You know," he started as the smoke circled around him. "When I was told my daughter was dating some new guy, I had to see who you were. Of course, I told her to stop this nonsense, considering that she was a Blackwood and couldn't date some outsider, but then I got some really interesting information."

"You mean, you found out my brother and I are both alive and here in town."

"Oh yes. Imagine my surprise, well, imagine everyone's surprise when they found out."

I moved the chair backward and placed my foot on the table. "So, what now? You're planning to kill us both?"

He dropped the ash from the cigarette to the floor and grinned at me.

"If I wanted to kill you, boy, you would already be dead." That fear intensified. "But no, that's not why I'm here."

"Then why are you here?" I scowled. "Forgive me for the lack of faith, but the last time I saw any of you was the night that changed my life forever."

"I hear you, but you are still a Crowell. You are still a founding family, and you still deserve to have a spot within The Order."

An involuntary laugh broke free from my chest, and as he started frowning, I realized that this wasn't the reaction he expected to get.

"Sorry," I wheezed. "But… It's just…" I coughed. "Are you telling me that you want me to join your little order?"

The expression on his face changed so fast, that if I

hadn't been looking at him, I would've missed it. He stood up and dropped the cigarette to the floor, extinguishing it with his foot.

"You may laugh now but being a part of The Order gives you opportunities and opens doors you could never even imagine. What happened to your parents was tragic, I agree. But that was in the past, and this is now." This motherfucking son of a bitch. "You should join us tomorrow. It's Samhain, one of the holiest nights for us." I almost shuddered. "And there is a place for you there."

Tomorrow? Tomorrow was Skylar's birthday.

"I don't kn—"

"I'll wait for you in front of City Hall at eleven tomorrow night. We have something special going on tomorrow, and trust me," the bastard smirked, "you won't want to miss this."

And just like his daughter earlier today, he walked out, leaving me alone with my thoughts.

I should be happy. This was exactly what we were working on, what we were hoping to achieve. Then why didn't I feel happy? Why instead of the happiness I was expecting to feel, did dread settle in my gut?

Maybe because I knew that Judah Blackwood never did anything out of the goodness of his heart. Maybe because I knew that whatever they offered, whatever fairy tale they were trying to sell, would always come with a great cost.

I just had no idea what the purpose of this visit was, but I would be a fool to pass up this opportunity. Being inside The Order was exactly what I needed to take them down once and for all.

TWENTY-SIX

Skylar

Eighteen years old.

Eighteen years old and not a day wiser. If I were, maybe I wouldn't have fallen for a guy when my life was a mess.

Six thousand five hundred and seventy days, and I wished I wasn't here anymore. I wished I lived a different life, with a different family, in a different town, with different circumstances.

But wishes were one thing and reality was completely different, and no matter how much I wished that things were different, I couldn't change who I was.

But I could still run from what was happening, if even just for a minute, for a second, for a teeny-tiny moment, I could run from my reality.

It was my birthday, and the only thing I wanted to do was to drown in my despair. But I couldn't disappoint Lauren or the rest of our friends. The Halloween bonfire was an annual thing, sometimes happening at Infernum, sometimes deeper in the forest, and this year it was on the riverbank, close to Lauren's parents' cottage.

I honestly didn't want to be surrounded by people

tonight, but I knew it was better than getting high on my own.

Dylan also wasn't here. He promised he would be home for my birthday, but all I got was a text message this morning, telling me that he wouldn't be able to make it.

No birthday wishes, no apologies because I actually needed him here, nothing.

I wanted to be angry at him, but since I broke my own heart and ran away from Ash, I couldn't bring myself to care about anything at all. Not the major party Lauren was throwing, not the deranged killer who was still out there, not Kane who was behaving like a lunatic, nothing. I couldn't care about anything.

It felt as if somebody punched me in my chest. I couldn't breathe. I couldn't sleep last night, and I looked more like a zombie than a girl who was celebrating her birthday.

Fortunately, or unfortunately, Lauren didn't comment on my appearance or lack of makeup when she picked me up. Instead, she hugged me and led me to her car, and I was thankful for that. Putting makeup on was the least of my concerns right now.

"Tonight is going to be epic." Lauren grinned, her voice mixing with the song.

"What is the name of this song?" I asked, instead of commenting about the bonfire and my lack of enthusiasm.

She looked at me, then at the console and picked up her phone, giving it to me. "I have no idea. Danny added it the other day, and I kinda like the voice of the singer."

"There are two of them," I murmured.

"What?"

"There are two singers."

I felt her eyes on me as I scrolled through her phone

until I found the full playlist Danny made for her.

"Enemies with Benefits" by Blind Channel. I scowled at the name.

"What's wrong with you lately?" Lauren asked and when I looked at her, she was already looking toward the road.

"You mean, except getting attacked and all this weird shit happening around town?" I scoffed. "Nothing really, everything is just peachy."

"See. That there. You would never respond like that before."

"Oh, I don't know, Lauren. Maybe having a near-death experience made me realize that I shouldn't be keeping my mouth shut when people say something I don't like."

"That wasn't a near-death experience." She frowned.

"And how the fuck would you know?"

Ever since we found Megan's body, Lauren had turned into someone I didn't know. Or maybe that's how it worked in life. People you once called your friends would always start turning into acquaintances. Or maybe I was just too tired, too angry, too much of everything to care about trivial shit like parties, school, and other things she obviously wanted to talk about.

"You know what," I started. "Forget I said anything. In a few months, none of this will matter either way."

"What do you mean?" she asked as she turned toward the old gravelly road leading to the cottage.

I placed her phone in the holder and turned toward the window. "There's only a few months left of school, and after that…" I trailed off.

"After that, what?" Her voice had a tone I didn't like.

"You know what." I turned toward her. "We'll be

leaving."

Something passed over her face—something close to sorrow, close to pain. Something I didn't notice before. But before I could ask her about it, she schooled her features and smiled.

"Yeah, we will be leaving."

If it was disbelief lacing her voice, I didn't ask, because I didn't want to know right now. The only thing keeping me sane at the moment was the prospect of me leaving and never seeing this town ever again.

We rode in silence after that, the music filling the empty space and the miles separating Lauren and me. I had no idea how we got here, but something had changed between the two of us. We were friends since kindergarten. Our parents were friends, but somewhere after the start of this semester, we became distant, and while it bothered me in the beginning, I was starting to get used to it now.

The lights from the cottage started getting visible in the distance, but what pulled my attention was the bonfire not too far away from it.

"Holy shit," I exclaimed as we came closer.

They really outdid themselves this year. The bonfire must have been at least nine feet high, and the silhouettes of people gathered around it were noticeable as Lauren parked closer to the fire than the house.

"That's fucking huge."

"Right?" She smiled her first real smile of the entire evening, and I hoped that tonight would go without unnecessary drama.

Mostly, I hoped he wasn't here.

She shut down the ignition of the car, and I slowly exited, shuddering from the icy evening air surrounding us. Winworth was already cold at the end of October, but going further into the mountains or near the river during this time of the year felt like you were walking down the streets of the town in the middle of February.

"It's so fucking cold," I cried, wrapping my arms around me. "Why are we doing this again?" I asked as Lauren opened the trunk of the car, pulling out the two plastic bags I haven't seen before. "What's that?"

"More booze, of course." She smiled. "And to answer your question," she placed the plastic bags on the floor, "it's your birthday, and it's Halloween."

No shit, Sherlock.

"Besides, we already had bonfires at every other place in town, but we never thought about having it next to the river."

And I wondered fucking why. The lights on the cottage and the blazing fire should've been enough to illuminate the night, but it was as if the shadows hiding in these woods were defying light, clawing, crawling, coming closer and closer, whispering through the icy wind playing with my hair, luring me into their nest.

I was with Lauren, but I felt all alone, reliving the day we found Megan. Reliving that night the monster marred my skin, leaving his permanent mark on me. And their cold hands touched my shoulders, their claws piercing through the thick coat I wore. The crows sang, the forest watched, and the air I was inhaling became painful in my chest, my lungs seizing with each new breath I took.

I knew my mind was playing tricks on me, but there were eyes in this forest, watching my every move. Maybe it was *him*, waiting to snatch me away from my friends, to take me into his depraved world.

"Skylar!" I jumped as hands landed on my shoulders, swallowing the scream threatening to erupt from my chest. "What are you looking at?"

I turned around, calming myself down when

Danny's blue eyes connected with mine. I soon realized that Lauren wasn't anywhere to be seen, while I stood at the edge of the forest. If I took another step, I would've been completely engulfed into the darkness surrounding the area.

Thankful for the distraction, I wrapped my arms around Danny's middle, soaking in the warmth he emanated.

"I've missed you too, dude." He laughed and wrapped his hands around me. "But what are you doing here? Lauren said you were still at the car, but I went there and, well—"

"I was thinking, I guess. I don't know." I moved away from him. "So much has happened in the last couple of months, and to think that I'm turning eighteen…" I trailed off. "I don't know, Danny." I shrugged and looked at him. "I just feel kinda lost, I guess."

And this was why I loved Danny more than Rowan. Instead of bullshitting me and trying to tell me that everything was going to be okay, he just hugged me tighter, as if he could truly understand what I meant.

As if he could understand that all my choices were taken away from me, and this suffocating feeling wouldn't go away. I was drowning in my own misery, and nobody said a thing. No one even noticed.

It was so easy slipping into a dark abyss, but once you were there, you suddenly realized that this wasn't what you wanted. That you didn't want your heart to die. That you wanted to fight. You wanted to live.

You didn't want life to pass next to you while you stood in the same place, unable to move, because you locked yourself up.

I constantly spoke about leaving Winworth after graduation, but if I was being entirely too honest with myself, I could've left months ago. I could've found a place to call my own, without leviathans flying over my head.

I could've left Winworth, but something held me here. Something couldn't let me go, and maybe it was destiny, or maybe it was a fucked-up game life was playing with me, but whatever it was it had to let me go.

"You're going to be okay, Sky. You'll see." He pulled away from me and hugged me around the shoulders, slowly pulling me with him as he started walking toward the bonfire, toward the voices and the music in the night. "I promise. This darkness can't last forever."

This darkness can't last forever, echoed in my head as we approached the rest of the guys. And even when we stopped next to Lauren who already had a drink in her hand, Danny didn't remove his hand from around my shoulders.

"Happy fucking birthday, Sky!" Rowan shouted, bringing the attention of the rest of the people gathered around the bonfire to us. He hurriedly closed the distance between us, and the next thing I knew, I was airborne, held tight in his arms as he started turning me around, singing the "*Happy Birthday*" song to me.

Others joined, the clapping of their hands echoing around us, even while the scenery became blurry and my mind fuzzy.

I heard Lauren's shouts and Beatrice's melodic laughter, and for the first time in weeks, I felt happy.

But then as if the shadows felt my happiness, they brought it down, bringing back the memories of the one person I didn't want to talk about tonight.

He wasn't here.

Even though all my friends sang and laughed, cheered and celebrated, my mind kept going back to

Ash. To the stricken look on his face when I told him that our relationship wasn't working for me anymore.

My mind went back to just minutes before that, when he told me he loved me, when everything seemed perfect and the world around us didn't matter.

It went back to those nights spent in my room, when he held me in silence, drowning out the noise in my head. And those dark, filthy shadows, they gripped my chest, clawing at my heart, until the tears gathered in my eyes.

I placed my hands on Rowan's shoulders, willing him to stop, but he couldn't hear my cries.

None of them could.

"Ro!" Danny shouted. As Rowan slowed down, the world around me started spinning. "Put her down."

Wetness coated my cheeks, while my stomach churned from all the turning and the lack of food.

"Shit," Rowan exclaimed as he finally put me to my feet. "Are you okay?"

I stumbled away from him and placed one hand on my face, hiding myself from them. And then it came all at once.

When we found Zane.

Megan's lifeless eyes.

The first time my father tarnished my soul.

The midnight blue of Ash's eyes.

The golden mask in the night.

The pain ricocheting through my body as he carved that symbol on my arm.

It all rushed in, like an avalanche, a volcanic eruption, all colors and feelings. My tears and the poisonous Winworth rain. My pain and their ugly words. My heart shattered in a million tiny pieces while the entire town watched.

The picture of a perfect family that was anything but

perfect.

Our mom's constant absence and the vicious words my father spewed at me.

I started shaking my head, taking a step backward, while they all threatened to erupt, to escape from my body. All these things I was keeping inside. All these depraved little secrets I couldn't say out loud.

The poetry of my life, the fucking misery. The unholy invisible hands wrapping around my throat, choking me, suffocating me, forbidding me from saying all these things I wanted to say.

And I just wanted to forget.

The music, the voices, and the laughter, all woven into one; they all echoed around me until I realized—I was the one laughing. My body shook from the force, and I finally opened my eyes, seeing the worried faces— first of Rowan and Danny, then Lauren, and finally Beatrice and Hailey.

A glass shattered somewhere on my right side, and I walked to them, placing one hand on Danny's shoulder.

"I'm good." But the expression on his face was one of disbelief, as if he expected me to break right in front of his eyes.

Maybe I was breaking. Maybe the shadows came to me at last. Maybe the sanity I was holding on to was slipping through my fingers.

Maybe I didn't care anymore.

I walked around the two brothers and bent down, retrieving the glass bottle of vodka from the ground. I uncapped it and lifted it in the air, smiling at all my friends.

"Happy fucking birthday to me!"

*A*live.

I finally fucking felt alive.

It must have been hours since we arrived, and after that first bottle of vodka, the second one came, then the third one, and somewhere along the way Lauren told me to open my mouth.

"Wider, Sky." She snickered as she placed a pill on my tongue.

We danced, and we laughed while the fire flickered around us, enveloping us in its warmth.

I couldn't feel the shadows anymore. Their eyes didn't bother me anymore. Their claws couldn't touch me.

I was here, but I wasn't here.

As I looked at my friends huddled together, my cheeks hurt from the wide grin I sported, happy that we were finally together. Lauren was leaning against Danny, her cheeks flushed from all the dancing and the warmth, from the alcohol and drugs as well, but she looked happy.

Happier than ever.

Hailey was perched on top of Rowan's lap, his hands on her hips, his face hidden behind her hair, while she talked to Beatrice, the only one standing.

Kane wasn't here, but in my fuzzy brain I figured that it was better this way. He'd been getting distant, almost as if he was both angry and sad, and I didn't know why. Perhaps I could've been a better friend, but somewhere between growing up with him, then sleeping with him, then trying to get rid of him, we grew apart, and I had a feeling that no matter what I did now, we would never go back to being what we once were.

Best friends.

Ridding myself from thoughts about Kane, I stood up and shook the debris from my pants. My knees felt wobbly, like Jell-O after sitting down for so long, but my bladder's protests were louder than the little bit of discomfort I felt in the moment.

"Where are you going?" It was Lauren that asked, moving away from Danny and slowly sitting up.

"Toilet," I mumbled. Or at least that's what I hoped I'd said.

My teeth felt numb from all the alcohol we consumed, the tingling sensation in my fingers slowly spreading throughout my body, reaching the center.

I turned around and started walking toward the forest. I didn't feel cold anymore. I didn't feel anything anymore.

No pain.

No pressure.

The trees seemed darker tonight, the full moon shining bright above us, but the light couldn't reach the ground of the thick forest.

Leaves and dirt groaned underneath my boots, mixing with the noises from the bonfire following me all the way inside.

"Wait for me!" Lauren's voice traveled to me, making me turn around.

Her ginger hair bounced around her shoulders as she stepped around the large rock in between the two trees. I couldn't see her eyes, but I could feel her energy matching mine. As soon as she reached where I stood, we started walking together, going deeper into the woods, further away from the crowd.

"I missed this." I was the first one to break the silence between us. "I missed us." I looked at her.

She looked down at the ground, as if contemplating her next words. "I did too. It's been too long, and it feels as if all of us just... drifted apart."

"Yeah," I agreed. "I didn't think it would happen

this fast."

"Mmhmm," Lauren mumbled. "I think this is okay." She suddenly stopped. "I'll just go around the tree and you can go there." She pointed toward the larger tree not too far away from us.

Without waiting for my confirmation, she took a step back and started walking toward the tree behind us, while I started heading to the one further away. An owl hooted as soon as I stopped beneath the tree, announcing its presence.

"Shush." I snickered, unbuttoning my pants, and crouching down to pee.

I could still hear the faint sound of music, and the rustling of leaves as the wind whooshed between the trees. I pulled my pants up and walked back to where we separated. The feeling I never wanted to feel again crawled all over my neck, and even in my drunken state, I knew it wasn't because fucking unicorns were observing me.

"Lauren!" I called out, but no answer came.

"Lauren?" I walked toward the tree where she went, but when I looked around, she wasn't there.

I jumped as the owl hooted again, my heart racing a thousand miles per second.

"*Skylar…*" My name all of a sudden came to me on the wings of the wind howling through the forest. The hair at the nape of my neck stood up, my eyes widening, my hands shaking. "Skylar," echoed again around me. A cacophony of sounds, of female laughter, and a shriek breaking through the night made me sprint in the opposite direction.

Fuck, fuck, fuck, I chanted in my head, running through the forest, evading the trees in my path. I had no idea if I was on the right path. I had no idea if anyone would hear me if I called out for them.

But most of all, I had no idea if I was imagining it.

Laughter came from behind me, a sinister feminine laughter, and I ran faster and faster, sweat beading on my upper lip even under the cold October night.

"Skylar!" a singsong voice called out again, cackling, taunting, coming closer.

And that was when I saw them.

Three figures standing next to each other, cloaked in red robes, their faces hidden behind white masks. Expressionless, cold, eerie, otherworldly.

I turned left, but three more were there, already waiting for me.

"No, no, no."

I swiveled around, coming face-to-face with one of the masks.

They were surrounding me and whichever side I turned, they were there. Red robes and white masks. The two in front of me tilted their heads, coming closer and closer, creating a circle around me with the other hooded figures.

"Let me go!" I tried pushing through the wall they created, but their hands stopped me, pushing me back to the ground. "Please," I cried.

"*Sanguinem Sacrificium.*" They started chanting in unison. "*Sanctum Sacrificium.*"

"Just… Please!" I pushed myself backward until my back hit the legs of one of them. I tilted my head and looked up, twelve white masks looking down at me.

"*Sanguinem Sacrificium. Sanctum Sacrificium,*" they continued, uncaring of my cries, disregarding my pleading. "Two will become one. One will become many."

"Get the fuck away from me!" I started pushing myself up, but the one standing behind me pushed me back to the ground.

"The Union is about to start."

"What Unio—" I tried asking, when something pierced my neck from the right side. "Ouch." I shook them off of me and pressed against the place where they pierced me. I looked to the side, only to see the needle held by one of them, lifeless eyes staring back at me.

"W-what did you do?" I slurred. "What is this-s?"

I moved my hand back, checking for blood, but there was none.

As my eyes started closing, my mind slowly shutting down, I realized they had drugged me.

The darkness welcomed me into its warm embrace, and the last thing I saw before closing my eyes was Lauren's face in front of me, holding the mask in front of her chest.

TWENTY-SEVEN

SKYLAR

D*rip-drop.*
      Drip-drop.
      Drip-drop.
Water kept sprinkling to the floor as I slowly opened my eyes, fighting the throbbing pain in my head.

The first thing I saw was the ceiling, illuminated by lights carefully placed in each corner on four sides. Shadows played over the painting high above me, touching faces of angels holding swords, fighting against the men in black cloaks emerging from darkness.

Where the fuck am I?

I first moved my toes, quickly realizing that I wasn't wearing my boots anymore, then my fingers, slowly drawing my arms around my body and lifting myself up. The pain sliced through my temples again, and I winced as I tried to take in my surroundings.

There were no windows, no other furniture except for the bed I was lying on. I dragged my hand over the soft blanket placed beneath my body, but when I looked down, I was no longer wearing the clothes I had on earlier. A white, silky dress hugged my body,

What the fuck happened to me?

The memories were just there, at the edge of my mind, but I couldn't reach them. Slippery, hiding away from me, they didn't want to be touched. I closed my eyes and tried harder, until I grabbed one of them, pulling it back to me.

"Oh my God," I gasped, opening my eyes, when it all started coming back.

The forest.

The hooded figures.

Lauren.

Lauren was one of them.

I turned to the side and dropped my legs to the ground, my toes curling from the cold surface.

They drugged me. That was the only possible explanation. I couldn't recall anything that happened after I saw Lauren's face, but I didn't have to.

She betrayed me. A girl I knew my entire life betrayed me. A girl that used to be my best friend.

Those women, or whatever they were, wore the same cloak like he did during that night. The color was different, but the design was almost the same.

I stood up abruptly, only to fall back down on the bed, my legs giving up on me, shaking, weak.

What did they give me?

I ran my hand over the silky dress they dressed me in and shuddered from the thoughts running through my mind.

What if they were going to kill me now?

What if the stories I read about Winworth were true?

What if, what if, what...

A door I hadn't seen before suddenly opened, and a woman in a red cloak entered, her face fully visible to me now. The mask was gone, but I had no idea who she was.

"Where am I?" I asked before she could fully enter

the room. I pushed myself all the way to the headboard. "Why am I here?"

My blood ran cold when she lifted her head, revealing the same scar I had on my arm, engraved on her forehead.

"Oh my God." What the fuck was this place? "Please, let me go. I didn't do anything."

But she said nothing while she stood at the entrance observing me. Her dark brown eyes held no trace of life in them. The paleness of her skin only told me that she didn't go out all that much, but I couldn't see anything else.

There were no emotions playing on her face. I wasn't hurt, that much I knew, but that wasn't a guarantee that they wouldn't hurt me now that they had me here.

I wondered if the rest of our friends looked for us. I wondered if they thought that Lauren was in danger just how I was.

I wondered where I went wrong for her to be a part of this—whatever the fuck this was.

"What's your name?" I tried a different tactic, keeping my voice steady, while she walked toward me slowly, as if she was afraid to approach me.

"Can you tell m—"

"Leah!" somebody roared from the doorway. A voice I knew too well. A voice that belonged to my friend.

I moved myself to the side, having a clear sight of the doorway, the pain from Lauren's betrayal intensifying with every passing second.

"Kane?" Disbelief laced my words, barely above a whisper, barely audible. "What are you doing here?"

Tall and regal, this was the Kane I used to know. His dark hair was slicked back, his eyes brighter than ever, and as he walked inside the room, he took one look at the girl, Leah, and pointed toward the door as if she was a dog.

"Leave us."

She complied almost immediately, but she didn't run. No. In the same way she entered the room, she also silently moved backward, bending her head down.

"Kane? What the fuck is going on?"

I wanted him to tell me that this was just a joke they were playing on me. I wanted him to tell me that the rest of our friends waited outside this room, ready to continue the party. But when he finally looked at me, I knew that all my wishes wouldn't be fulfilled.

"I wanted to tell you about all this, but I couldn't. They told me I couldn't tell you, at least not yet."

"Who?" I moved closer to the bottom part of the bed, closer to him. "Please, tell me. What did you want to tell me?"

He exhaled softly and looked up at the ceiling. "For centuries, our families held this town in their iron fists, ruling from the shadows, dictating who did what and who married who."

I frowned. "I don't understand."

"You found a book, Sky. I think you understand more than you think you do."

The book?

Oh God.

"It was you," I exhaled. "You left that note in my locker."

He nodded rapidly and took a seat close to me. "I wanted you to know, but I couldn't tell you everything by myself. So, I planted a book that could give you some answers."

"I-is this…"

"The cult they mention in the book?" A sorrowful

smile grazed his beautiful face. "Yes, this is the Black Dahlia. And you are the bride, Sky."

My right eyebrow lifted, and I still waited for him to start laughing, to start joking around. But his face grew serious instead. "You are the one he wants," he whispered. "But before the ceremony starts, I need you to know something."

"You mean, besides the fact that you guys kidnapped me, or that you're mentioning something about brides and ceremonies. There's something else I need to know?"

He winced at the tone of my voice and dragged one hand over his face. "You're gonna hate me, but you need to know before you get out of this room."

"I need to know what?" I yelled.

"You are not a Blackwood."

What?

What did he just say?

"That's ridiculous." I scoffed. "Of course, I am."

"No, you're not, darling. Your mother was a Red Maiden, just like those girls in the forest that got you here."

"A Red Maiden?"

The sound of something breaking on the floor came from outside of the room, and his head turned toward the source, immediately tensing.

"We don't have enough time now." He suddenly turned to me. "But I'll tell you everything you need to know later."

"But—" I protested as he stood up.

"Just remember, you are not really a Blackwood. Not that it matters now, but still. It might make this night a little bit easier for you."

"What the fuck are you talking about, Kane?" I asked and stood up after him, slowly regaining my strength.

"Who am I if I'm not a Blackwood?"

"I don't know, Sky. I know that your mother was killed when you were barely four years old, but that's all I know so far." He moved away from me and started heading toward the door. "Just remember." He stopped. "Don't fight him."

"Who?" I asked, but he was already moving away from the room. "Kane!" I ran toward him, only to be intercepted by four ladies in red cloaks. "Get out of my fucking way." I tried sidestepping them but there was no use. Four of them together were much stronger than me, and in less than a minute, they held my arms on each side, and started leading me through the narrow hallways, illuminated only by the candlelight, flickering over the walls.

We took a swift turn to the left side, entering a completely different hallway.

A hallway whose walls were lined with thousands of skulls, spanning from the ground all the way to the ceiling.

I knew where we were, or at least I knew the stories.

Winworth's catacombs.

I tried pushing against them, but whoever they were, they weren't budging. Unlike the girl that entered my room, these four still wore their masks, their hair hidden beneath the hoods of red cloaks.

"Where are you taking me?" I asked, hoping I would get an answer, but it never came.

Their fingers dug into the skin of my bare arms, and I was certain that bruises would appear sooner rather than later.

Unless you end up dead, my consciousness reared its ugly head. *Maybe they'll kill you like all those girls before you.*

Oh, fuck off.

We soon entered a wide chamber shaped in a circle, where candles lined the floor, showing the path toward the door leading into another room. I heard them then, the voices chanting inside.

Latin I couldn't understand. Voices I didn't recognize.

"No, no, no, no." I thrashed against them, pulling them from one side to the other. I saw stairs on the right side, and if I could just reach them... If I could just run to them... But my body locked down, preventing me from moving any further, when he came into view.

Sinister, unmoving, the golden mask that haunted my dreams and my days. With that black cloak hiding his body, he stood at the entrance, staring at me.

All four of them went down on their knees as soon as they noticed him, while I stood there paralyzed, looking back at him.

Just like before, just like in my house, he didn't say a word, but instead turned around and walked inside, leaving me behind with the four unknown women.

As soon as he disappeared inside, they stood up and started pushing me forward.

I didn't fight them anymore. I didn't try to run toward the stairs even though they were close, so fucking close as we approached the tall door, with swirls decorating the wall around it.

I didn't try to scream as we entered the room, as I came face-to-face with a dozen others, all of them wearing black masks and dark gray cloaks. They all stared back at me, dissecting me, swallowing me from head to toe.

On the right side, the ones with black masks and gray cloaks stood, while on the left side, twelve figures in red cloaks kneeled, their faces turned to the ground.

As I took my first tentative step, then another one, the gray ones went down on their knees, and the chorus of voices echoed in the room.

"*Sanguinem Sacrificium. Sanctum Sacrificium.*"

My eyes strayed to the middle of the room, to the wide set of shoulders and the altar behind him with the chalice on top of it.

"*Sanguinem Sacrificium. Sanctum Sacrificium.*"

He took the chalice and moved it in front of him, hiding it from my sight.

"*Vita Tua. Vita Meae.*"

He lifted his hands and looked up, but I didn't know if he chanted with them. My captors pushed me forward when I stopped in my tracks.

"*Tuo Amore. Sanguinem Meum.*"

He lifted the chalice as the last person finished the incantation.

"*The Union,*" they all stood up as one, "*is about to start.*"

One more step, then two, and finally three, and I was just inches away from the monster haunting me. From the monster who turned my life upside down.

He turned around, and for the first time, I could see his eyes.

Blue as an ocean.

Blue as the clear skies above Winworth on those rare sunny days.

Blue.

Blue.

Blue.

No!

It can't be.

The four holding me stepped back, blending in with the rest of the crowd, but I couldn't move my eyes away from him.

He came closer, his hand wrapping around my cheek, softly, carefully, as if he was worried I was going to disappear.

"Who are you?" I asked, my voice raspy. If this was the night I was going to die, I wanted to know who killed me. I wanted to know if my assumptions were correct, and I prayed they weren't.

"Please," I begged when he didn't move. "I have the right to know."

His hand dropped from my face, and he took a step back.

The mask was the first thing that fell, followed by the hood, revealing the hair I knew all too well.

Those steel-blue eyes looked at me. No remorse, no apologies; there was nothing there I used to love. And I loved him, at least I used to.

My heart broke at the same time as my tears fell over my cheeks, and his eyebrows furrowed seeing me like this.

He was my savior. My everything. And now... He was the monster.

"Oh God," I exclaimed, shock and pain mixing in my body. His usual calm and kind face was nowhere to be seen, replaced by sinister lines and the poison hiding behind those eyes.

He came closer and took my hands in his, as if it was just another day. As if I didn't just realize that the real monster was never too far away. He was closer than I could ever possibly imagine.

"Happy birthday, Little One." He pressed his lips to my forehead. "Welcome to our Union."

An involuntary sob escaped from me, and I closed my eyes as he trapped my hands between the two of us. With one hand, he dragged the hair away from my face, while the other one lifted my head, holding my chin.

"Give me those pretty eyes." He smiled while I wanted to die.

"Dylan?"

TO BE CONTINUED

ALSO BY L.K. REID

Sign up for the Newsletter to get exclusive news, giveaways and teasers!

THE RAPTURE SERIES
Ricochet
Equilibrium
Oblivion

SECRETS OF WINWORTH
Apathy

TWISTED TALES COLLECTION
Elysium: Hades and Persephone Dark Romance Retelling
(January 21st, 2022)

ACKNOWLEDGMENTS

A re we okay? Breathing? Can I come out from my hiding spot?

I would say that I'm sorry for that cliffy, but I'd be lying. After my alphas and betas finished reading *Apathy*, sending me *"WTF"* messages, I kid you not, I sat down, petting my cat and snickering at the same time. Honestly, this is the first time where I truly felt comfortable writing a book, even though I knew that it wouldn't be everyone's cup of tea. But I am truly happy how it turned out and I hope you guys truly like it.

We all know that I'm terrible with this entire acknowledgments part, but this book definitely wouldn't be here without my tiny army.

My Momager, my beacon of light, and the first person that believed in me, outside of my family— Stephanie. Thank you for being you, for the late-night talks, and the love you have for these characters. I still have those screenshots of you screaming at me when Ash appeared for the first time.

To my friends—thank you for understanding my need to disappear from the real world when characters talk a bit too loud.

To my mom and my brother, thank you so much for all the love and endless support.

To one very important person, Zoe. Thank you for loving the story and for being such an amazing friend.

To Meredith and Brianna, and their shouty messages.

To all of my author friends, and you know who you are, I cannot express how thankful I am to have you in my life. Thank you for all the advice, for words of encouragement, and just for being you.

My absolutely fabulous editor, Maggie. I am so glad to have you in my life. Thank you for prettying up my words and helping me deliver this book in the best way possible.

My amazing Street Team, my Queens of Carnage. You guys keep surprising me with your support, and I wouldn't be here if it weren't for you.

Needless to say, my ARC readers, you guys are absolutely amazing. Thank you!

To every blogger, bookstagramer, thank you for taking a chance on me and reading my books. Never in a million years would I have expected this level of support.

To all of the readers, thank you so, so, so much for reading.

And last but not least, to music. For always being there, keeping me afloat and helping me shape this book, this whole world into what it is today.

ABOUT THE AUTHOR

L.K. Reid is a dark romance author, who hates slow walkers and mean people. She's still figuring out this whole "adult" thing, and in her opinion, Halloween should be a Public Holiday. She has a small obsession with Greek Mythology and all things supernatural. Music has to be turned on from the moment she wakes up, all the way throughout the day and night.

If she isn't writing, she can be found reading, plotting upcoming books and watching horror movies.

Stay in Touch

.instagram.com/authorlkreid
pinterest.com/authorlkreid
facebook.com/authorlkreid
.goodreads.com/authorlkreid
The Reid Cult

Printed in Great Britain
by Amazon